CU00656505

Back Stronger

Alec Munday series book 2

Phil Savage

Published by SBC Media 2022

PHIL SAVAGE

In memory of Kevin Roberts, founding editor of SportBusiness Magazine, for your welcome to the business of sport.

Published by SBC Media

Back Stronger is a work of fiction. Names, characters, businesses, places, events, locales, and

incidents are either the products of the author's imagination or used in a fictitious manner.

Any resemblance to actual persons, living or dead, or actual events is purely coincidental.

Readers' Club Download Offer

Free bonus book. **Give Back** is the next episode in the Alec Munday series and is available to you now as a free download. Get your copy of **Give Back** by Phil Savage absolutely FREE

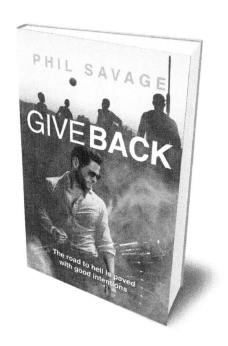

Get your free no-obligation download today. Visit www.philsavage.org

Part 1

Chapter 1 February 2021

'I'm as broadminded as they come, Alec, and don't let anyone tell you different. But I feel like I'm being ambushed. I've had our Player Liaison in here, then the lad's agent and now you. And I'll tell you what I told them: I've got nothing against Scott being gay, obviously. It's the 21st Century. I get that. I think we all accept we should, you know… celebrate love wherever we find it.'

The implied bunny ears around this last sentence hung in the air, but there was no stopping him having his say.

'So, don't take it the wrong way, but this is football. It's tribal. It's brutal. If he comes out, he'll learn just what an ugly place the terraces can be. I don't worry about our supporters: Scott's one of their own and they'll accept him whatever. But imagine we're playing somewhere like Burnley or Newcastle or any derby game or, or just about bloody anywhere, frankly. The opposition fans would destroy him and not just him, the entire team. If they scent blood, they'll be all over it. And once the gay boy chants are ringing out round the grounds, it'll be like we're starting every game a man down. And I'm telling you, it won't stop there. This ends with us dropping out of the Premier League and that's everything we've worked for down the khazi. I'm not having that. I will not have this club brought down by a poof with a taste for publicity.'

Alec felt himself grimace at the word, but the man across the table from him was only getting started.

'You saw what they did to poor old Jack Cardle last year. He goes a bit doolally, the press dubs him Whacko Jacko, chuck in the word Schizophrenia, and the fans are all singing *'There's only two Jacky Cardles.* That's after all the work we've done on mental health, so you can only imagine the abuse a gay player would get. And another thing. He'd kiss goodbye to his England career, wouldn't he? It's one thing getting a fair hearing at Brighton, but can you just imagine what an away fixture in Belarus would be like? Gareth's a nice guy, but with the squad he's got, there's a decent chance of winning something. Taking the knee is one thing, but there are limits. There'll be out and proud campanologists on the pitch one day for sure, Alec, but not yet. Some of our European neighbours can't even watch a black player without chucking bananas. Can you only imagine what they'd make of a gay lad? We'd be praying for the return of the monkey chants.'

Alec let him sound off, uninterrupted. As Chairman of a Premier League club, Bill Kenilworth had earned the privilege. He was a dinosaur, but he knew he was a dinosaur and Alec liked him. He also knew he had a point. However genuinely they wished it was different, any individual player coming out would face the full force of toxic masculinity every time he ran onto the pitch no matter how many rainbow laces his teammates wore. But Alec was coming under pressure from Scott who was finding it tough. On the face of it, he had it all: beautiful wife, two gorgeous children, lovely family home. But living a double life was taking its toll. Something was going to give, and Alec had to find a way to release the pressure which worked for all sides. It wasn't proving easy.

'Bill, you know me. We've worked together for years, and I completely get where you're coming from. That's why you're talking to me and not the agent or anyone else. We're both football men and I think we know instinctively when something needs to be kept quiet. But you have to look at it from the player's perspective. He's an honest lad, he wants to be true to himself and to the game. I'm worried he'll quit football completely if we can't bring everyone together and move forward.'

'Move forward,' the Chairman repeated, his eyes narrowing. 'I can already tell I'm not going to like this. What have you got in mind?'

'There's no perfect solution, but I think we can afford to be a bit... pragmatic.'

'You've lost me, Alec. You're going to have to spell things out a bit more clearly if you're expecting me to sign up.'

'Hear me out, Bill. I'm just thinking, his wife's sticking by him, at least until the kids are older, so she's not going to do anything to force things out into the open and, realistically, he's only got so many close contacts outside the game. If we can build a circle of trust around him, then he can be *out* to the people that really matter to him without having to go public. Then, at the end of his career, he can say he was out all the time, and no one ever suspected; that he didn't think it was relevant when his club and his teammates all knew, and no one cared; that he got one over on the media and opposition fans and had the last laugh all along.'

Kenilworth stood up and walked to the window of the first-floor boardroom. He parked his belly on the sill and let his gaze wander over the training ground. He was an old-school football boss; he knew each of those players personally, even the foreign imports. Especially the foreign imports. He knew their families, their backgrounds, knew what made them tick and what they needed from him to give their best on the pitch. He, more than anyone, knew how much it had cost to get the club to where they were; the money and energy and time he'd invested, and what it meant to the fans.

'Do you think it would work?' he asked, with a resigned sigh.

'I think there's a chance, Bill. And you know Scott wouldn't be the first either. The circle would have to be wide enough for him not to feel he was hiding his true identity all the time, but he'd also have to accept that he'd be kept out of the limelight, for his own protection. He'd need to keep a low profile, stay out of the media and think carefully about his personal endorsements. But, yes, I think it could work.'

Kenilworth came around, as Alec knew he would. The footballer in question was a key part of the squad's attacking line and had the goals and assists to prove it. The Chairman knew that the club's finances, as well as the goodwill of its loyal supporters, depended on him keeping a winning team together. The reality was, he had very few alternative options.

Whether the circle of trust would stay complete was a different question. As a battle-scarred media fixer for some of the Premier League's top stars, Alec knew that money talked. He'd already had to kill a story about the player cruising gay nightclubs on the flimsy premise that he'd wandered into *Queer* by accident. The way he'd spun it, Scott had no idea that, despite the beard, the 'girl' he was chatting up was actually a bloke. If only he'd stick to Grindr.

Kenilworth still had half a smile on his face when his secretary knocked and told him the car was waiting to take him to lunch. He shook Alec's hand leaving him in the boardroom as he headed off downstairs, still chuntering. Alec stayed behind for a few minutes looking at the familiar drills and routines going on below him. He always reckoned he could tell if a club was well managed or not just by looking at the team, and this one deserved its shot at European football. It was always hard to pin down, but he knew it when he saw it. Something about the relentless work rate, the commitment even in training, but also the selfless camaraderie on display. God, he missed the team. Even now, five years after his injury, he felt a stab of regret that the close bond of the dressing room would forever be behind a closed door.

It was only a few minutes into his reverie that Alec realised he couldn't see his player. When he enquired, he was told Scott had picked up a knock earlier and the club masseur was working on him. Alec decided to brave the physio room for a quick chat with his client. As he walked through the players' gym, he saw another familiar face holding an awkward pose.

'You look like a game of Twister gone wrong, Ryan. You trying to pull a goal out your arse?'

The player collapsed. 'Fuckin' yoga, innit? The gaffer swears by it.'

'Well cheer up, mate. Right now, you're looking more down in the dumps than downward dog. Don't let the boss see you like that.'

He moved on to the inner sanctum, his sharp suit and leather shoes looking out of place among the discarded kit and damp towels. Things might have moved on from the days of horse liniment, but the massage room still stank like mentholated Manchego. He laid out the bones of the arrangement to his client but received only a grunt for his trouble. Two minutes later he was on his way to the car park and enjoying the cleaner air of a February lunchtime.

Alec Munday had always driven a BMW. It was a status symbol when he was starting out as a footballer, and he always smiled when he thought back to that battered 1 Series with the sound system bigger than its engine. He graduated to an M5 in Dakar-yellow when he signed his first Premier League contract. Driving that car, he felt like a dog with two dicks. He sold it to help keep him afloat after his injury but stuck with the marque, and he was still driving a 12-year-old 5 Series until a few weeks ago. The first thing, almost the only thing he did after his change of fortunes was to upgrade to a top-of-the-range 850. It would have been obvious as the boss's car outside most workplaces but here it nestled modestly alongside a Bentley Bentayga, a Maserati Grancabrio, two Mercedes G-Wagons, a Ferrari Spider and no fewer than four pimped out Range Rovers.

Pulling out of his parking space, his phone had just connected to the in-car audio when a call came through. The number was vaguely familiar, but he regretted picking up as soon as he heard the voice.

'Alec? It's Simon Cauldwell. You may remember we spoke a couple of weeks ago. The interests I represent really are quite insistent on a meeting at your earliest convenience. Shall we say tomorrow morning? I'm looking at your calendar now and you appear to have a slot for us. We'll arrange for a car to pick you up from your house. Shall we say 8.30?'

'Who the hell are you, and how come you're hacking into my calendar?'

'You'll be able to ask all the questions you want when we meet. See you tomorrow, Alec.'

In his former life, training started promptly at 10am so he'd be up soon after seven to get some food inside him. It had become a habit, so he was already suited and booted when a dark Vauxhall Insignia pulled up outside his modest semi in Enfield, North London. Inside it smelt of cigarettes and stale food. The driver was large, ex forces and monosyllabic. He barely spoke as he ferried Alec the ten or so miles to an office building just off the Finchley Road.

'Bell six, sir,' was his parting message. 'Take the lift to the third floor.'

A blond man in a blue suit and open-necked shirt was waiting as the lift doors opened. He was in his thirties and Mr. Average in every way, as if engineered not to stand out. His stance was relaxed and unthreatening, but his blank, grey eyes clearly hadn't got the memo.

'Alec. Thanks for coming,' he said, ignoring the new arrival's complaint that he hadn't had much of a choice. The empty open-plan office looked like it had been cleared in a hurry. The detritus of a workplace – a broken chair, an open file, coffee stains on carpet tiles, untethered cables – gave no hint as to its former or current business. Alec was led into a glass-panelled meeting room where an older man, also in a dark suit, sat to one side talking urgently into his mobile.

'Mr. Munday. May I call you Alec?' He said smoothly, hanging up and gesturing towards a chair. 'Sorry about the cloak and dagger stuff. One final indignity, I'm afraid. Could you let Simon have your phone, please.'

Alec shrugged and handed his mobile over. The man he assumed to be Cauldwell pocketed it and left the room taking up a position outside the closed door.

'Sorry again and thank you for cooperating. My name is Nigel Rushbourne and, as I think Simon explained, I represent certain key interests in the British establishment. I'll come straight to the point: your track record as someone well-connected in the world of football has come to our attention. I wanted the chance to meet and perhaps persuade you there was some mutual benefit in keeping in touch.'

Alec sized up the figure across the desk. Unlike the man outside the door, he was round shouldered and creased as if a squarer, bigger-boned version of himself had developed a slow puncture. His eyes were expectant, though, looking to Alec for some acknowledgement, perhaps.

'Go on,' was all he got.

'Yes, well, as you know, one of the ways our political masters are encouraging everyone to put Covid behind us is to stage some of the key matches in the European Championship finals this summer. You'll be aware, of course, that the tournament was delayed from last year due to the pandemic. Our advice, along with the public health boffins, was to ditch the thing completely on the basis that we don't want thousands of the great unwashed spilling beer on our socially distanced streets. However, it seems the bosses of European football twisted arms rather more effectively than we did. So we're opening our doors alongside the likes of Baku, Bucharest and St Petersburg. You'll be all over the fixtures, I'm sure, but we've got four games in Glasgow, then three more regular games, a knockout round, then both semi-finals and the finals at London's Wembley Stadium.

'The last time we put on anything of this scale was the Rugby World Cup in 2015 and, before that of course, London 2012. So, I think you'd have to say we have a fair idea of what we're letting ourselves in for, and that includes all the stuff the public never gets to hear about. In fact, our objections were not pandemic related at all: we're more concerned with all the things that go on on the periphery of these mega sporting events. Putting our heads above the parapet makes us a target for any publicity-seeking lunatic ready to sacrifice themselves on the altar of whichever deity they're peddling. But it also provides cover for international crime at a time when their regular supply lines have been cut off by Covid lockdowns.

Rushbourne opened up a dossier in front of him before continuing.

'Aside from the fans, it's the sheer numbers of people officially involved in an event like this that's the challenge. Between the teams, the coaches, the officials, the media, the sponsors and their VIP guests, there are literally tens of thousands of them. What makes it worse is the rightsholder, UEFA in this case, but FIFA and the Olympic crowd are no different. They insist that we suspend some of our natural distaste for certain individuals and practices. So, for example, if in normal circumstances we know that you're a convicted criminal and you fancy a visit to the UK, then we have the choice to turn you away at the border. However, this summer, if you can show that you're part of an official football delegation, then we have to roll out the welcome mat. Same goes for the media, sponsors' guests and all manner of hangers on. If they're accredited, they're in and nothing we can do about it.'

Rushbourne paused, the look of expectancy still alive in his eyes.

'Mr. Rushbourne,' Alec offered, in response. 'I can see the Euros are going to be a policing headache, but I'm struggling to see what you think it has to do with me.'

'I'm about to explain,' Rushbourne twinkled, 'and here, Alec, is where I must ask for your absolute discretion.'

He wafted a hand in the general direction of the centre of London. 'You are entirely correct that the policing headache, as you put it, is our responsibility and in a general sense, we're confident. Now that Covid restrictions have been lifted, we're back to having dozens of football matches every week in this country, and the lads and lasses in the border force process upwards of ten million international visitors a month. On the security front, we have become depressingly familiar with the need to keep a large group of would-be terrorists under surveillance. But an international sporting event on this scale opens the door to a world of potential problems.

'Let me give you an example. When the Scottish FA bought Hampden Park a few years ago they were bankrolled by the Saudi Sovereign Wealth Fund. Now, let's imagine that Hampden is picked to stage a game involving the Israeli national team and that happens to coincide with some new incursion or intifada. The Arabs have a long-standing disagreement with the Israelis, as I'm sure I don't need to tell you, but what we cannot have are the bone cutters who did for Jamal Khashoggi running around the streets of Glasgow chasing Israeli diplomats. And that just one possibility out of hundreds. Do you get my drift?'

Alec tried to look interested. 'It's a fascinating story and good luck with keeping everyone apart, but it's really not anything I would have the first clue about.'

Rushbourne looked across the desk as if his point should have been clear by now. 'I really think you're being too modest, Alec. Anyone involved in the kind of caper you pulled off against one of the smartest international criminal gangs around feels, if anything, somewhat overqualified for an assignment like this. The issue is a simple one: we've had no need to try and infiltrate international football and, between ourselves, we've been a bit busy elsewhere. As your Serbian adventure showed, there are some deeply unsavoury characters operating around the sport and we're feeling rather… on the back foot. Isn't that what you'd say? What we need is somebody who can operate on the inside and tell us what we're missing. We're looking for a football man with the instincts of a criminal and I'm rather hoping you'll re-form your partnership with Michaela Dagg and make yourselves useful.'

Rushbourne sat back in his chair, watching Alec intently as he absorbed what he'd just been told. Michaela Dagg was a former high-flying police officer and would not take kindly to suggestions she had been conniving with a criminal. Alec felt he ought as least to act offended if only on her behalf. He opened his mouth then thought better of it.

He was quiet for a good twenty seconds. 'So, are you offering us a job?' he asked, finally.

The spook's eyes lit up. 'That, Alec, is a great question and the answer is nothing so conventional. You wouldn't be employees or consultants and no money would flow in your direction. If it came to it, we might be able to support you with certain specialist skills but otherwise you'd be operating on your own. Not that it should be an issue. We've asked you because we need someone who's already part of the footballing world, someone who can keep their eyes and ears a bit wider open than usual guided by the multi-talented Miss Dagg. Just carry on doing your thing, the pair of you, and pass anything unusual our way.'

'So, off the books and thrown under a bus if it goes tits up.'

Rushbourne looked pained. 'We prefer to call it plausible deniability, but you're not too wide of the mark, Alec. You would have no responsibility for following up any irregularities you uncover but if your links to the security service became in any way public, our standard approach would be to deny all knowledge.'

Alec was quiet again then said: 'I'm sure you already know that some of the things we did in Serbia wouldn't be considered strictly legal.'

Rushbourne nodded, eagerly, as if to confirm that Alec was starting to understand the brief. 'It's not at all uncommon for the people we work with to find themselves crossing the line into the moral or legal twilight zone. If you were caught *in flagrante*, as it were, there would be a limit to what we could do but, within reason, we would shut down any active police enquiry into your activities. You'd have a licence to snoop, but not a licence to kill, if that helps clear things up.'

'And when you say 'no money would flow in our direction', assuming we would even be interested, are you saying that there's no budget of any kind to work with?'

'Correct.'

'What makes you think we would be in a position to operate like that even if we wanted to. I mean, I'm flattered, but those are not terms anyone's going to sign up to.'

Rushbourne put his hands behind his head, a triumphant look in his eye, as he played his trump card. 'Alec, we know that the operation in Serbia netted you a little over one hundred million pounds on which Her Majesty's Revenue and Customs has yet to levy anything by way of tax. We're just hoping you'll see the wisdom of spending some of that windfall to serve your country in a slightly different way.'

Alec was beginning to realise what they were up against. 'And if we don't agree?'

'No threats, Alec. It's your decision, although it would be a shame for the taxman to get his teeth into your fortune.'

Rushbourne pushed back his chair, decisively and stood up. 'Look, I have somewhere else I need to be,' he said, walking towards the door. 'Talk it over with Miss Dagg, by all means, then contact Simon. We have a busy four months ahead of us and need you to get cracking. I shall expect to hear from you within two days.'

Chapter 2

Alec found his phone on the floor outside the meeting room as the two spooks disappeared into the lift. When he emerged onto the street, neither they nor his chauffeur were anywhere to be seen. He shrugged and set off on foot towards Finchley Road wondering what Michaela would make of his conversation. The pair had been a lot more than casual acquaintances although he wasn't sure at the moment quite how she'd describe their relationship status. It was two weeks since he'd last seen her and, though they'd parted on friendly terms, it was an awkwardly long time not to have been in touch. He made the call.

'I thought you'd forgotten me,' she said, answering on the second ring.

'How could I? I've just been busy, that's all. Can I see you tonight?'

'I'm not sure. I've been staying at my parents place in Kent and hadn't planned to come back to London for a while.'

'I could come to you, I suppose.'

'I don't think that'd be a great idea. You're not exactly flavour of the month in our house.'

'I got that impression when I dropped you off. What's their problem?'

'Do you even need to ask? Before I met you, I had a career, albeit one which had hit a speed bump. Now I'm out of a job, facing multiple disciplinaries and with the death of two policemen on my conscience. Maybe we all just need to move on.'

'Well, I might have something to help us do that. Meet me tonight and I'll tell you about it.'

She agreed reluctantly to his suggestion of a restaurant in Covent Garden then hung up without ceremony. It took Alec over an hour to get home, but the tube was quiet and it game him time to think. The threat to inform the UK tax authorities wasn't one that worried him. He hadn't expected the windfall from his run-in with Serbian match fixers and apart from the new car, his life had barely changed. He wasn't sure he'd even notice if the authorities took a chunk. He had to admit he was flattered at being approached by the Security Services but genuinely at a loss to know how Rushbourne thought he could help. It was a view he knew Michaela would share.

Back home, he pulled on running gear and hit the streets. The pins in his ankle meant he would never again go ninety minutes on the football pitch but he could still run. Staying in shape was a mantra and he found his brain worked best when the rest of him was distracted. When he stepped into the shower two hours later, his decision was made.

They had arranged to meet outside Charing Cross Station, and he stood there with a bunch of flowers in his hand feeling foolish. After half an hour despite the chilly evening, the flowers had started to wilt in the heat of his grip. Another quarter of an hour later that he dumped them in a nearby bin. When he finally caught sight of Michaela among the crowds in the station entrance, she was over an hour late, but it was worth the wait.

'It's great to see you,' he said, kissing her hungrily on the lips and hugging her close. 'You look fantastic.'

'This is the first time I've worn anything except pyjamas for over a week, so you should feel honoured.'

'I do,' he said, holding her at arm's length and admiring the view. She had pushed her dark hair into a loose up do; her makeup was minimal but applied to great effect.

He kissed her again. 'Let's go and eat. You look like you could do with a meal.'

'If that's your way of saying I've lost weight, I know. I also know I didn't need to. I haven't been that great, to be honest.'

'Well, let's try and help you escape your troubles and have a good evening.'

Alec had booked a table at Clos Maggiore a couple of streets away, and they walked hand in hand, happy to be in each other's company. The maître d' helped Michaela out of her coat revealing a scarlet knit dress cut low at the back and front.

'Wow, you really do look amazing,' he said, 'although I love you in pyjamas too.'

'Don't get any ideas, not here at least.'

She hadn't been sure she would come at all this evening and the effort to get ready had been as much an excuse to put off leaving the house as it was to impress Alec. His reaction and the warming effect of a gin and tonic were making her feel she'd made the right choice.

He gave her the gist of his morning meeting over the starters, skating over Rushbourne's insinuation that they had been partners in crime. As anticipated, Michaela was slow to warm to the prospect of working for the security services, although the fact that anyone thought she could still be useful as a law enforcement professional was a boost.

'What do they expect we're going to be able to do?' she asked when he'd finished.

'Don't know, but they made it clear I need to do something for them, or they'll shop me and my Serbian bonus to the tax man.'

He could feel he was losing her and tried to turn it around. 'There are a couple of England friendlies in a week or so's time. I thought we could offer to go along and see how things pan out. The first one's against Spain in Madrid at the end of next week if you fancy the trip. We could make a weekend of it.'

'Why would I go? I hate football.'

'That's what I thought. So you won't be distracted by anything as trivial as the game and you can give your full attention to seeing how criminals might try and exploit an international fixture. I'm sure my new friends will get you a ticket. I'll sort myself out with media accreditation and run with the pack to look at things from a different perspective. Then we can regroup afterwards to compare notes. A couple of days later, there's a home game against Poland at Wembley. I'm interested in that one as that's where the sharp end of the Euros is taking place.'

Whether it was the food, the wine or just the prospect of having something useful to do, Michaela was surprisingly amenable.

'I can't see either of us making very convincing spies, but if you're offering to take me away for the weekend, then I accept.'

Alec knew better than to overthink her reasons, so when dinner was done, he crossed his fingers under the table and suggested they get an Uber back to his place.

Cauldwell was predictably nonplussed when Alec called the following morning. 'Nigel does a very good impression of the bumbling spook,' he said, 'but don't be fooled by the old-school act: he's a tough bastard, and he's going to expect you to sing for your supper. It'll take a lot more than the odd foreign jaunt and a football match to satisfy him.'

'What supper would that be, exactly?'

'He's someone used to getting his own way, that's all, so don't think his threat of going to HMRC is an idle one.'

'Listen, I've agreed to give up my weekend and fly to Spain at my own expense and cover our costs while we're there. All I need you to do is get me press accreditation and Michaela a ticket to the game. Can you do that?'

'I'll have them delivered to your house,' said Cauldwell, flatly. 'Just make sure that what you come back with is worth the price of the courier.'

The friendly between England and Spain was one of the first international fixtures to take place with crowds since the end of the Covid-19 lockdowns. Alec signed up for the media charter flight the day before game expecting a festival atmosphere among the journalists who had been functioning via Zoom for months. The letter accompanying his accreditation promised an 'exclusive' with a senior member of the England camp. That probably didn't mean any more than the chance to ask a question no one else had thought of, but that wasn't his motivation for going, so he arrived at Luton Airport just after 5.40am on Friday morning in expectant mood. He grabbed a coffee and stood in line along with forty-five other journalists representing various print, broadcast and online outlets. Despite the auspicious occasion, the early start meant the group was scratchy and the mood did not improve when the senior member of the England camp turned out to be a PR girl.

'Morning everyone. For those that don't know me, I'm Samantha Carew and I'll be answering any questions you've got on the way to Madrid. I know it's an early one but, if it's any consolation, I was out until two with sponsors, so I'm sure I know how we're all feeling.'

Any one of the increasingly cantankerous press pack could have shot her down, but it was Andy Grubber of the Mail who got in first.

'You fuckin what?' he shouted. 'You have no idea how I'm feeling. I've got the hangover from hell, and I should be in my pit until lunchtime. And if you think your ponytail-swinging, spray-on t-shirt routine is going to make up for not having anyone we can actually talk to, then you're going to be seriously disappointed.'

She was unphased. 'Meeting you in person, Andy, I can imagine you're used to being a disappointment to women. I'll just have to try and get over it.'

Smart move. The laughter in the queue indicated she now had the pack's attention, if not their sympathy. Grubber as he was universally known, was momentarily stunned into silence giving her the chance to breeze on cheerily.

'Now, before I was interrupted, I was about to say that at great expense and no inconsiderable inconvenience to himself, we will have FA Ambassador and former England defender Tyrone Pelforth on board with us. He'll be moving among you during the flight and taking questions in groups of four or five so you should all get something you can work with. For now, though, I'm sure we could all do with some coffee, so let's get the other side of security and I'll see you all in Wetherspoons.'

Alec shuffled forward finding himself uncomfortably close to Grubber who licked his lips salaciously, a leer on his mottled and flaking face. 'Well, she's game, don't you think?' he said, to no one in particular. 'Disappointed my arse; I'll have her moaning on the end of my dick before the tour's over. By the time I've finished with her, she'll have a face like a plasterer's radio.'

Alec couldn't leave the comment unchallenged. 'I could have sworn that look said she wouldn't hop in the sack with you if you were the last man standing between her and twenty years of celibacy, but I'm sure you read the signs better than the rest of us, mate.'

Grubber turned his head and struggled to focus his jaundiced eyes on who was speaking. 'Alec Munday? Fuck! Life as football's turd polisher in chief must be bloody dull if you've deigned to hang around with the rest of us mortals.'

'Oh, you know, Grubber. I'm all about keeping it real. Good to see you've not lost your touch though. Turning the pack against you before the first coffee in the morning? That must be a record even for a man with your talent to offend.'

Grubber thought for a moment then a grim spark of recognition lit up in his red-rimmed eyes. 'Oh, I get it. Tyrone's a fuckin' client of yours, isn't he? So, while the rest of us are picking up the cliché-laden crumbs that spray from the royal gob, you're being paid a king's fuckin'ransom to make sure we don't write down what he actually says and print something off message when he… mis-speaks.'

'Jealousy's not a good look, Grubber. As far as I see it, we've all had to get up at the sparrows and I could definitely use another coffee. See you around.'

He walked through security with Grubber's West Midlands whine trailing after him. 'Ta-ra Alec. I won't hold my breath for you to file any copy. You leave the words to us real journos.'

He emerged airside at the same time as Tyrone Pelforth came through fast-track with Samantha already in his ear.

'They're all on fine form, Tyrone and looking forward to hearing what you've got to say. But if I could just go through this crib sheet with the key messages we'd like you to push. It's all quite self-explanatory, you know: young squad, result isn't really important, there are no expectations, just asking them to play with freedom and express themselves.'

Tyrone looked wearily towards Alec. 'Hello mate,' he said, holding out a large hand. 'Sam, could you grab me a coffee. Strong and black please. It's all going to go in a bit easier once I get some caffeine on board.'

'You're getting used to this ambassador life,' Alec said, as the PR gave a tight smile and headed for the coffee queue. He and Tyrone had been friends for as long as either of them could remember and it was good to see the former footballer making his way. 'Tell you what, though,' he warned, 'she just gave Grubber a roasting, so I wouldn't push her too far.'

'Shit, man. What does she expect? The game isn't until nine o'clock tomorrow evening and we're all up in the middle of the bloody night.'

'I'd lay bets that the hotel rooms aren't going to be ready until after four this afternoon. I suspect some of my colleagues are using the coffee to summon up enough energy to go ballistic when she tells them.'

'That I'd like to see, but not so much that I'm going to ditch the limo picking me up for the hotel.'

'Are you staying at the Eurostars Madrid Tower? Tyrone nodded. 'You might run into a friend of mine there. You've met Michaela, haven't you?'

'Of course, but why aren't you two staying together? What are you up to, Alec?'

'Nothing, it's just been a while, and I thought I ought to hang out with my colleagues. I'll tell you what, though, I'm going to need a large one in the Eurostars bar after the game.'

Tyrone dutifully did the rounds on the short flight, but he made a quick exit on arrival in Madrid. The mood in the press pack was mutinous when Samantha announced the programme of events for the rest of the day.

'The coach will be here shortly to ferry us direct to the…' She checked her crib sheet. '…the Santiago Bernabéu where you're all signed up for a complimentary stadium tour. There's a buffet lunch laid on, then the rest of the day's your own until the presser at five pm local time. You're welcome to use the press centre at the stadium if you prefer, as access to your hotel rooms will be from four.'

This time it wasn't Grubber who protested but the normally charming Chief Football Correspondent for the BBC. 'I suspect I speak for most of us when I say that, impressive as the Bernabéu is, there isn't a cat in hell's chance of us going on that tour. Lads, if any of you would like to join me at Paddy McGinty's Goat, I'll buy the first round. And Samantha, if you've got any sense after dragging us here at this ungodly hour, you'll be there to buy the second.'

The press conference seven hours later was a predictably raucous affair with Samantha struggling to keep things polite on both sides. The lack of sleep was starting to catch up with her and she had the hassled look of a woman who knew accounts were going to take some persuading to approve her drinks bill.

Despite spending the day in the nearest Irish bar to the stadium, the journos filed some impressively lucid copy, and listeners to the BBC man's contribution to the build-up on 5Live would never have suspected he was on the wrong side of ten pints of Guinness. Energised by the press conference, the pack got a second wind, and it was back to McGinty's where it was Alec's round. He was sober enough to work out that anything he learned would be forgotten by the morning, but he knew better than to duck his obligation. He left the bar before midnight marvelling at his colleagues' stamina. It had been an instructive nineteen hours, but he hadn't got wind of anything that would remotely impress Cauldwell or his boss.

Matchday meant everyone took the opportunity of a late start. Alec appeared at breakfast in time to grab a tostada and some coffee before it was cleared away, then stationed himself strategically in the lobby. Half hidden behind an English language version of El Pais he was free to observe the comings and goings undisturbed. The print and online journalists only emerged from their billets after lunch, although, to be fair, most had spent the morning pulling together their pieces for the next day's papers. The bookies and pundits had the game down as a draw and the England manager had talked about experimenting with players and formations. That allowed them plenty of scope to get at least the bones of an article together before a ball was kicked.

Early that afternoon, Alec took the press shuttle to the stadium along with members of the broadcast media. With the enforced interval since the last international game, there was no shortage of human interest, and they were planning to fill the time recording vox pops. The anchors and TV commentators swanned by at 3.30. They glided through their prerecorded packages for the early evening shows before retiring to the press area to mug up on the players likely to perform that evening. This was the birthing suite for their apparently spontaneous quips and one-liners and Alec knew it was not a process to be interrupted. He saw nothing of interest inside of the stadium so took himself off in search of a café to while away the time until kick-off.

Michaela's time in Spain was very civilised by comparison to life in the press pack. She arrived in Madrid early on Friday afternoon, after a decent Business Class lunch, and stepped into a waiting car. It was not a place she had visited before so, after checking into her luxury hotel room, she spent a few happy hours as a tourist. Traveling supporters were a breed apart as far as she was concerned, but a slow coffee in a sunny Plaza Mayor was a great way to observe them in their natural habitat. Spring fever had gripped the city which was a mecca for football fans worldwide. The English contingent had travelled to Spain in their droves, and they jostled good naturedly with their Spanish counterparts at the many bars around the Centro. The Policia Municipal were out in force, but officers looked typically insouciant. Having seen enough for now, Michaela folded five euros under her coffee cup and took herself on a sightseeing tour before returning to her hotel and taking advantage of its spar and restaurant. She didn't do it often, but she could feel her mind clearing amid the luxury and anonymity of her surroundings.

The crowds were more clamorous the next day and starting to move with greater purpose towards the Santiago Bernabéu. Preferring to be driven rather than join them, Michaela asked the taxi driver to go round the stadium a couple of times. For an investment of five minutes and a few extra euros, Michaela got a good view of the perimeter within five minutes of arriving. Council workers were in the process of erecting barricades and laying a temporary walkway from the nearby metro station. For a ground that accommodates over

80,000 spectators, the space around it is limited. That alone suggested there would be very few people near the Bernabéu on matchday without a ticket or other good reason to be there.

Cauldwell had helpfully provided an 'access all areas' stadium pass and she made the most of the freedom to wander unchallenged through its historic interior. Real Madrid's legendary president of the 1940s, after whom the stadium is named, was renowned for bringing a business-like approach to a game that was largely amateur at the time. Today, Michaela saw a well-practised operation with lots of moving parts working professionally and efficiently. The broadcast media were already in place with OB trucks lined up on the venue's eastern side. The security presence increased steadily to screen the hospitality, catering and bar staff as they arrived for their shifts. Marshals were in place two hours before the game and the first ordinary fans took their seats soon afterwards. The photographers and written media were in their tribunes an hour before kick-off, leaving officials, sponsors and their guests and other dignitaries to be spirited in moments before the referee's starting whistle.

Michaela learned little about matchday security that she couldn't have guessed in advance. Stewards were positioned on every level, but there was little for them to worry about. She heard some racist chanting during the game, but even that seemed to lack conviction. It was as if the bigots and xenophobes were struggling to hawk up the usual amount of bile after such a long time away from international football.

Whether viewed from the stand or the media tribune, the match did its best to live down to expectations. If the England manager really was working towards his first-choice World Cup squad, there were few clues in his team selection. For the first sixty minutes it was a story of England's under 21s being narrowly outplayed by the Spanish youth team. Only when both managers started to ring the changes did the fans get anything like the spectacle they had paid for. When the coaches shook hands after the final whistle, they seemed as pleased no key players had picked up an injury as they were with the result itself.

The players clapped the fans self-consciously, knowing they hadn't had anything like their money's worth. As the cameras followed them down the tunnel, the attention of those in the stands was diverted by a scuffle in the VIP seating area immediately above the entrance. Security staff were quickly on the scene forming a cordon around the area, and medics scurried up the steps moments later carrying their green kitbags. From his position in the press box Alec had only a limited view of what was going on. Michaela was better placed and saw the worried faces among the uniformed staff. There was a lot of yelling into radios but not much else, so she allowed herself to be swept along by the crowd down the access steps and out into the street.

She had arranged to meet Alec and Tyrone in the hotel bar, but it was nearly two hours before they joined her.

'Why the serious faces you two?' she said, when they finally appeared. 'I'm just glad it's over. Why fans pay to travel halfway across Europe to watch football is one of life's mysteries.'

'Yeh, not the greatest game, but the FIFA Press Secretary getting shot will probably make the big headlines in the morning.'

Chapter 3

Michaela was up first the next day and made coffee from the in-room Nespresso machine.

'I can only imagine what Cauldwell's reaction's going to be,' she said, as Alec stirred. 'I mean, I was actually in the stadium when a senior FIFA official was murdered, and I didn't even know anything had happened until you guys got back.'

'He'll get over it, but what it does show is watching on from the stands or even the press pack isn't going to get us very far.'

'Maybe we can redeem ourselves a bit before we have to report back tomorrow.'

'I suppose we should show willing and ask some questions while we're here. There was a story going round last night that the Spanish had been tipped off so maybe you could work that angle. I think I'll wander down to breakfast to see if the team heard anything.'

As he anticipated, Alec was soon sharing a table with Tyrone Pelforth and some of the more experienced England players. Some of them were clients, the others he knew from the regular track days and other jollies he organised on their behalf.

He waited until an opportunity presented itself then asked: 'Have you heard anything about who might have been responsible for the shooting last night?'

'Whoever it was, he definitely missed the target,' said Danny Duckham. 'He had his pick of some of the biggest cunts in world football and who does he chose? The bloody Press Secretary. Talk about shooting the fucking messenger.'

'Did anyone know it was going to happen?' he followed up, naively.

'We never heard anything around the England camp, did we, or we wouldn't have been playing,' Duckham confirmed. 'It's always touch and go in Spain, what with the monkey chants and stuff, so any excuse and the PFA would have been all over it.'

Tyrone agreed. 'The suits from FIFA and UEFA all seemed to have a proper wedgie at the reception last night,' he said. 'The Spanish tried to make the best of it, but there was none of the usual speeches: they were just in a huddle the whole time. I reckon they'll be too shit scared to turn up at Wembley on Tuesday.'

'I think some of the Spanish guys knew it was going to happen,' said a quiet voice in the corner. It was Shayne Jordan, first choice England goalkeeper. 'We've got a couple of their players in our squad and there were a few comments flying around at our last session before the international break. They were saying things like, "keep your heads down" and "watch your backs". We assumed they meant there was going to crowd trouble, but I think maybe they'd got wind of something.'

Alec was about to ask whether Shayne had mobile numbers for any of the Spanish players when Helen Bell, the England team director of operations appeared at the side of the table. She looked suspicious.

'Alec Munday. I'm never sure whether you're media or what you are, but I do know the boys shouldn't be talking to you.'

'Morning Hells. Don't worry on account of me. I'm here with Tyrone, so strictly professional.'

'Very reassuring, I'm sure. Anyway, time's up, lads. The coach'll be out front in fifteen minutes, so let's hustle please.'

'That's me too I'm afraid, mate,' Tyrone said to Alec. 'I'll see you Tuesday, yeh?'

Alec watched them troop out and googled the Spanish players in Shayne's team. He left it twenty minutes before messaging.

Hi mate. I'm guessing it was Sergio De Léon who gave you the heads up about events last night. Could you give me his mobile – I think there could be an opportunity for him. You know I'd do the same for you.

He was rewarded with a number but not before a promise had been extracted to include him in the next lads outing. Alec calculated that De Léon would be taking advantage of a home game to spend Sunday morning in bed. He went back to his hotel room hopeful that he and Michaela might do the same. His plan hit the buffers as soon as he opened the door and heard her on the phone.

'Gracias Señor. Por correo electrónico por favor. Adiós.'

She looked up, saw Alec and said, 'Ok, let's give that a couple minutes and we should have the preliminary police report from last night. Cauldwell did say we had licence to snoop so I'm pretty sure claiming to be MI5 South European desk is covered. What have you found out?'

'One of the lads gave me the number for one of the Spanish players he reckons knew in advance. I'll call him in an hour or so once he's had chance to start his day.'

She was distracted by the ping of an email arriving on her laptop.

'Ok, this is what the police are saying. It's in Spanish obviously, so not sure there's a lot of point you looking at it.'

She stared at her screen for five minutes then gave him the headlines.

'They've been busy,' she said. 'The victim is named as Pascal Deschamps, FIFA Press Secretary, a thirty-four-year-old Swiss citizen. He was seated in the third tier of the VIP seats just above the players entrance and died from a single gunshot wound to the upper torso. A 9mm slug was found embedded almost immediately behind his seat placing the shooter at a very similar point on the opposite side of the stadium. A sweep of that area produced a Russian VSS Vintorez sniper rifle left beneath a camera gantry. The distance from the gantry to the victim is 114 metres and the angle of fire suggests this as the most likely shooting position. The Spanish are working on an apparently well-substantiated theory that the killer posed as a photographer.'

'How would someone get a sniper rifle past security?' asked Alec.

'I don't know the Vintorez, but some of these weapons break down into sections. Dismantled, it would fit comfortably into the kind of hard camera cases most pros carry. From what I saw earlier, security don't do any more than glance inside the camera bags and boxes. All it would take is an accreditation and he could pretty much walk straight in.'

'Have they got any footage showing that's what happened?'

'Yes, they've done quite a good job on that. There's a range of stills in the report taken from a trawl of match footage and stadium CCTV. I'd guess they've put the squeeze on the head of security who is trying to make up for the fact that he let everyone, including the shooter, out of the stadium. We have our man on the side of the pitch during the first half wearing his fluorescent official photographer's bib and apparently taking pictures. He's wearing a baseball cap so we can't see his face, but we do have the photo that he submitted for ID. There's a chance it could be him or someone who looks enough like him to pass a security check. During half time we see him casually pack away his gear and enter the stadium interior. He emerges three levels up but now without his vest. While the crowd is moving around, he crawls under the skirt of the camera and is completely hidden. Then, forty-five minutes later, the skirt is pulled back and he take his shot. Unless they knew it was coming, not even a security expert would ever spot it on the video. He waits for the crowd to start moving then reveals himself again, this time empty handed. He joins the tide and that's almost the last we see of him. A man in a similar baseball cap shows up briefly walking to the metro station and then he's gone.'

Alec thought for a minute, then said. 'The victim seems odd to me. I mean, it's possible that Deschamps had some dark personal secret but, if they wanted to execute him, there's got to be an easier place to do it than in a stadium full of people. Could it have been a mistake?'

'It could be an identity mixup, but when the killer took his shot, I think he was as sure as he could be that the man in his sights would end up dead. This guy is a professional who gets himself past security, into the stadium and into position carrying a large and obvious weapon. He coolly fires off his shot, leaves his calling card behind and gets out again without being picked up. His shooting position was less than 120 metres away and everything else suggests he is a pro. No one who's any good is going to miss from that range.'

'So, if Deschamps wasn't the intended victim, what are the possibilities?'

'Only two, really. Either the killer or whoever sent him is flexing their muscles: showing they can do whatever they want to whoever they want even in the most public setting. Or the actual target was someone who they couldn't get to anywhere else. Either way, I'd be looking at FIFA.'

'Guillermo Salz, FIFA Secretary General was at the game last night. He's staying in the hotel so maybe we should try and talk to him.'

He looked at Michaela, expectantly.

'What?' she said. 'I don't have any magic way of finding out which room he's in. You'll have to try the switchboard or wait in the lobby.'

Alec called the switchboard but was told Salz was screening his calls. He left his name, saying he was with British Security Services and was surprised when Salz rang back a few moments later. The voice on the line sounded cautious but scrupulously polite.

'Mr. Munday, I'm intrigued. Perhaps you could tell me how it is that a member of the British secret service is staying in the hotel the night after someone murders one of my staff.'

Alec put on his best spook's voice. 'I assure you, Mr. Salz, my being here has nothing to do with what happened in the stadium, however, it may prove useful to us both if we have chance to speak.'

'So, your presence is unconnected with the events of last night?'

'That is correct.'

'And why is it that you think we should speak?'

'As you know, sir, the UK is hosting the Euros in a few weeks' time. I am here with a colleague to get some first-hand experience of the various security risks that go along with an international football tournament. I think we'd both have to say that last night definitely counts. From our side, we have the initial police report of the incident, if that's of interest.'

Reluctantly, the FIFA man agreed to meet in a discreet corner of the hotel lobby one hour later. Alec hung up then pulled out a piece of paper and dialled another number, this time a Spanish mobile. The call was answered after a couple of rings and he went into a well-practised spiel.

'Morning Sergio. My name's Alec Munday. I do media for Shayne Jordan and some of the other boys. Listen, sorry to call you on a Sunday morning but I just had breakfast with Shayne, and he mentioned you might have something the papers would be interested in, you know, about the shooting at last night's game? If you do know anything about it, I'd be happy to try and sort you out a deal. It's got to be worth a few quid.'

With the player on the hook, Alec was able to extract what he knew, which wasn't much.

'It was around ten days ago,' De Léon confided.' I just got a call from our S&C coach. He said it's possible something will happen in the stands during the game and not to worry because they knew about it already.'

'This is a Spanish coach, right? Did he say what was going to happen?'

'No, just that they knew there was something.'

'Ok, there's plenty of newspaper stories that have been built on a less, so I'll do what I can. What's the name of this coach?'

'We just call him Raúl. I can give you his number if you want, but I don't think he speaks English.'

'That'd be great, Sergio. I'll get onto him and let you know when I've got the papers lined up.'

He hung up and turned to Michaela. 'That confirms it,' he said. 'The Spanish were tipped off that something was planned for last night, and all their players knew. Now we just need to find out where they got the information from. This is the number for Raúl, the strength and conditioning coach of the Spanish national team and the guy in the know. I suspect he got it from someone else within their setup. He doesn't speak English, so can you speak to him and see where he leads us.'

'What's my cover story?'

'Erm, let's see. You're a junior comms person with Wembley Stadium but the only Spanish speaker on the team. You've been asked to find out whether there is any risk the attackers will have another go on Tuesday.'

A few minutes and several calls later, Michaela had confirmation direct from the head of operations at the Bernabéu that it was he who had taken the message and passed it on to the team. The call had come through to his direct line from MARCA, the local sports newspaper, ten days before the game. The journalist he spoke to said they'd received an anonymous tipoff that there was going to be a minor incident in the stadium. There were no details, and he didn't think too much of it, assuming it would be some sort of stunt. He stepped up security a bit, but not knowing what was being planned, all they could do was check everyone more thoroughly.

'Sounds like whoever organised the job must have been confident their man was going to be able to get in and out easily enough,' Alec said. 'Do you think you could get any more out of the journo?'

'You tell me. Even assuming he knows who it is, do you think a journalist is going to betray a source?

He shook his head, glumly. 'Fair enough. Anyway, I've just googled Vintorez. It's a rifle used by Russian special forces. So, are we thinking Russia set this up?'

'I've no idea how available they are on the black market, but it's going to be a lot easier for one of them to get hold of a Vintorez than anyone else. I'd say it's either Russian or someone has gone to a lot of effort to make the world to think it is.'

'Sounds like we've got quite a bit of information for Mr. Salz. How much do you think we should tell him?'

'Standard rule, as little as possible, but we've got plenty to trade if he's not keen to talk.'

They found Guillermo Salz huddled over a cup of coffee behind a pillar in the lobby bar. He was unshaven and, if he had slept at all, it looked like it was in the suit he was still wearing. Like most in his organisation, Salz had once been a footballer, but today his swagger was gone and the greying temples and lines around his eyes made him look a lot older than his reported forty-three years. Most striking was a fine spray of dark red on his shirt collar. Alec had to remind himself that the man had been sat next to someone who had taken a bullet through the neck a few hours earlier. He introduced Michaela then handed over a hastily produced paper copy of the report giving the headlines as she had presented them earlier.

'I'm sure you'll want to study it more closely,' he said, 'but that's a reasonable summary and matches up with our assessment that Deschamps was executed in a carefully planned and carried out assassination.'

Salz took a moment's thinking time, then shook his head vigorously. 'Impossible. You must be mistaken. Deschamps was a nobody. No, sorry. Don't mistake what I'm saying. He was good enough at his job, but he had no status or influence. He was only sitting there because the President decided not to make the trip.'

Michaela took her cue, leading Salz towards the obvious conclusion. 'Did he have any enemies that you know of? Is there anyone, particularly anyone in Russia, who could have a reason to wish him harm?'

At the mention of Russia Salz sat up. He blinked hard and shuffled uncomfortably in his seat while Alec and Michaela viewed him impassively.

Salz continued, slower and more hesitant. 'I didn't know him personally very well, but I find it completely unthinkable that someone would want to kill him.'

'And he was sitting in the President's seat?'

'No, I was. When the President decided not to travel, I moved up to deputise for him and Pascal filled in behind me.'

'Do the two of you… look alike?'

The FIFA functionary went grey and slumped back in his chair. Shock and a lack of sleep had clearly dulled his brain, but he finally seemed to get the point.

'You think I was the target?'

Michaela paused, then said: 'Let me ask you the same question. Is there anyone, particularly anyone in Russia, who could have a reason to wish you harm?'

Salz started babbling. 'As you know, Russia hosted the FIFA World Cup in 2018. In the awarding of that event, in the build-up and during the tournament itself, we all of us came into contact with any number of groups. Some were connected to football, some to local organisers, some to the government and some whose affiliation was never clear.'

He stopped, trying to collect himself.

'It may be that there are some loose ends that remain to be tied up.'

'Loose ends,' repeated Alec, watching the man opposite him squirm.

'Yes. As I say, loose ends. I will report back to the President with your conclusions and advise that perhaps we should make every effort to tie them up sooner rather than later.'

'I assume that you and the President will be attending the finals of the Euros in June and July at which you will be our guests and protected by British security. It would be reassuring to know that these, err… loose ends will be tied up well before that. Do you think that will be possible?'

Salz seemed to recover some of his confidence and stood up to leave, extending a hand first to Michaela then to Alec.

'Being on the ruling council of FIFA is a lonely and often difficult job,' he declared, loftily. 'I would not want to give you the impression that your security can in any way be relaxed this summer, but I think you can assume that this particular situation will be resolved by then. It was good to meet you and thank you again for the report. Now, you must excuse me. Enjoy the rest of your weekend.'

Alec and Michaela watched as he walked away and entered the lift.

'When he signed up, I'm not sure our friend Guillermo read the *taking a bullet for the boss* line in his job description,' he mused. 'You can only imagine what their next conversation's going to be like.'

Had they been standing outside Salz's room a few moments later they would have heard exactly how that conversation went. While Alec and Michaela were planning how they would spend the rest of the day in Madrid, a row was blazing over the phone lines between Spain and Switzerland.

Chapter 4

Alec felt bullish as he picked up the phone to Simon Cauldwell, but his bubble burst a few seconds into the call.

'We try and use intelligence to stop attacks rather than mopping up afterwards. The fact that two agents were in the stadium when an assassin successfully gained access, completed his mission and left unchallenged has to be chalked up as a failure. However, your conclusions are broadly in line with ours so let's hope that the message has been sufficiently well received that a repeat won't be staged on Tuesday. We'll go through the security protocols: reissuing lanyards on the morning of the game and circulating the shooter's photo. Obviously, the photographers are going to have a tougher time getting into Wembley, but none of that should affect you.'

'The point for me is that the Spanish knew something was planned even if they didn't know exactly what,' said Alec, pushing back against any suggestion that he and Michaela were in some way to blame. 'We need to be much closer to the footballers themselves, the backroom staff and everyone around the game if we're to have any chance of getting advance warning of events like this.'

'That is why you were brought in,' came Cauldwell's caustic reply.

Undaunted, Alec continued. 'And it's not just the England players. If anything, they're going to have the least to tell us. We need to target players from Europe who also play for their national teams. I know a few, of course, but I'm not going to have a player from every country on my books. To be anything like comprehensive we're going to have to do some recruiting.'

'Again, I'm struggling to know why you're still talking.'

'Because, while you've been about as much use as a marzipan dildo, I've thought of something you might actually be able to do to help.'

Alec pushed on without waiting for a response.

'Normally I let my network expand of its own accord with players bringing their mates along to events that I organise. I was going to get a group together for Cheltenham Festival next month, but I think we need a bigger push. So, I was thinking, how about a day's training with the SAS? Everyone I know was watching *Who Dares Wins* when Wayne Bridge won a couple of years back. I think the lads would bite our arms off if we could set up a taster for them. You know the sort of thing: one of those courses where the targets spin round and you're only supposed to kill the bad guys, then maybe some hand-to-hand combat training and then finish off the day with a zipwire parachute jump.'

Cauldwell was quiet a beat then asked. 'And how do you think I might be able to help?'

'Oh, come on, Simon. You're all part of the same team. If you weren't in the Regiment yourself, you'll know someone who is. Anyway, I'd bet they'd all like to meet a bunch of Premier League footballers, so I'm going to leave that one with you. It'll take me a while to go through the players and get a comprehensive list together, so it doesn't need to be for a week or so. Meanwhile, I'm in the press pack again tomorrow at the Poland game and I've pulled a couple of strings to get Michaela in as a guest of one of the sponsors. I don't anticipate we'll learn much, but that's the plan.'

He hung up with a flourish then looked at Michaela who shook her head, taking the wind out of his sails for the second time in as many minutes. 'It's been a nice weekend Alec,' she said, 'but now I'm going home.'

He was taken by surprise but saw the pain in her eyes, perhaps for the first time since they'd been together almost a week ago.

'What's the matter?' he asked, genuinely at a loss. 'I thought the old team was back together. You know? You and me against the world.'

'Yes, I know. You're in your element again, mixing it with football, spooks and international crime. But all I can think about is what happened to me and my guys last time. Sitting with Salz, realising someone had lost their life just hours earlier, it brought it all back.'

The experiences they had been through, putting their lives on the line to try and rescue a footballer's wife, had affected both of them, but Michaela's wounds cut deepest. She'd had two friends brutally murdered and been drummed out of the police as a result. Alec's face flushed at his own insensitivity. He put his arms out and held her for a long time, not speaking.

'You know I really care about you, don't you?' he said, in the end. She nodded into his shoulder. 'And I want to do this with you.'

'I know you do, Alec, she said, pulling away from him. 'I just need to think of what's best for me and I'm not sure being with you is the best right now. I'm not saying it never will be, just not right now.'

Her words stung. He tried to cover up his disappointment as she got her stuff together and stowed it in the BMW for the drive back to Kent.

'What do I tell Cauldwell? They wanted us as a team, and you're the only one who can do the background, digging into any names that come up and finding out where the money's moving around.'

'I'm not saying I'm out of the loop completely. I'll do all that stuff and let you know what I find.'

'So, it's me, not the job,' he said, his hurt feelings rising to the surface despite his efforts to control them.

'Alec, it's neither. I can just feel myself being sucked into something that I'm not ready for.'

'That's how life is,' was all he could say in response. 'We stumble around, stuff happens, we meet people and all of that combines to make a life. Yes, we might all look back and wonder how things could have been different, but we can't let fear stop us moving forward.'

It was a big speech, and she didn't reply, just looked out of the car window as he drove through the faceless suburbs towards London's orbital motorway. When they did speak again it was transactional: how long before she could make a start? what help could she expect from Cauldwell? He pulled up by the side of the road outside at her parent's house, she grabbed her bag from the back seat and stepped out of the passenger door.

'I care about you too,' she said, then walked away. 'I promise I'll be in touch soon.'

Two weeks later a lot had changed. England's friendly against Poland had ended in a decisive win for the home side and the media were talking up the hosts' chances of lifting the Henri Delaunay trophy for the first time. 1996 was the last time the Euros had been staged on home soil and Gareth Southgate's penalty miss against the Germans had cost his team a place in the final. The symbolism of the man who was now England manager having the chance to right a historic wrong was not lost on the tabloid press who were ramping up the jingoism and the wild predictions. Their infectious enthusiasm was starting to weave hope if not expectation through the nations' heartstrings and Alec was not immune.

He had spent hours going through each Premier League squad identifying European players who were likely to be in training with their national teams over the coming weeks. The playoffs had thrown up a few surprises of which Israel and Kosovo were perhaps the most eye-catching, but most of the usual suspects were represented. By the time his initial research was complete, there were still a few qualifying teams without a player on his list plus another twenty UEFA members with no Premier League player. Despite failing to qualify for the Euros, they would still have a ticket allocation although none of them would be considered a threat to national security. The biggest and most worrying unfilled gap that Alec could see was Russia.

He decided to invite all the footballers on his list and at least one additional English player from each of their clubs. It would make for a large party on his SAS survival day, but the British Army could cope. He needed as many eyes and ears as he could recruit.

Hereford was equally inconvenient for everyone, but that didn't stop a succession of upmarket motors roaring into the park and ride on a bright Monday morning in March. Some of the group were regularly late on parade, but there were surprisingly few stragglers for the 08.00 rendezvous. When Alec arrived, most were already shuffling around beside their cars apparently determined to outdo each other in the fashion stakes. There were jeans with more rips than seams, enough suits and designer knitwear to open a concession in Harrods and more Gucci man bags than Milan fashion week. To the startled early-morning shoppers they looked like visitors from another planet, but Alec greeted them cheerfully as he handed out the coffees.

'Morning lads,' he said. 'Welcome to the most glamourous carpark since Grand Theft Auto. Well done on making it here so early and particular congratulations to Kieran. Looking at him, he's definitely the bookies' early favourite for player most likely to score with a soldier.

'By the way, Jermaine,' he said to a lad in a long frock coat. 'The 1870s just called: they want their clothes back.'

'You should know,' said the player standing by his lime green Lamborghini, 'You have to go back in time to visit your hair.'

'Ooh, you're spiky for this time of the morning and I'll have you know this barnet is all original. But I see a lot of you have dressed up for the occasion so it's a good thing our hosts are going to be supplying something a bit more practical for us all to change into. Before we go any further, can I ask, are there are any homicidal maniacs here this morning? Just let the rest of us know so we can keep our heads down when you've got a gun in your hand. Of course, I'm joking. We're assuming you're all homicidal maniacs which is why today, for one day only, we'll all be firing blanks.'

'Some of this lot are used to it,' said a voice in the crowd. It belonged to a tall young lad who Alec recognised as Connor Flynn, midfielder at a South Coast club and team member of one of the Belgian players.

'Nice to see you too, Connor,' said Alec. 'There'll be plenty of time for the pissing contest over the course of the day. Meanwhile, well done on rocking the Megan Rapinoe look. Before our hosts arrive, I just want a quick word about why we're here, other than to have a good time, obviously. Most of you know that I take care of business for a select bunch of clients in the Premier League, but that's enough about me and Connor's missus. What you won't know is that I'm also involved with the Euros, and I need your help. There are people out there who see the tournament as their number one terror target, and we've been asked to stop them. Obviously, the police and security are all over it, but they think we can also play our part. All of us come across things where we think, "that's a bit dodgy," So what I'm asking you to do is keep your eyes and ears open and report back if there's anything you think it would be good to know.

The sight of half a dozen army green transport lorries caught Alec's eye, so he wrapped up.

'That's all I'll say for now, but I'll have a chat with each of you later. It looks like our chauffeurs are here so let's have a great day and I'll see you on the firing range.'

Simon Cauldwell emerged from the lead vehicle and surveyed the situation. He looked at the players, then at Alec, then back at the players. His expression left no one in any doubt just what he thought of the day's nursemaid duties. Fortunately, the drivers were more welcoming and there was a lot of hand shaking and mutual admiration as they loaded their increasingly excited payload onto the trucks. Fifteen minutes later, they pulled off the main road, through a security barrier and parked up. The low rise 1970s-style buildings looked drab and disappointing, but Alec needn't have worried. Once the guys were suitably kitted out, Cauldwell stepped up to deliver on the *Who Dares Wins* promise.

'Good morning gentlemen,' he started, then paused. 'Right, that's as polite as it's gonna to get today. Once you've heard from me, the instructions are going to come thick and fast, so listen up. You're going to be dealing with genuine weapons and tangling with some real fighting men so, for your own safety, you need to focus and pay attention. If you do, you're going to have a day you won't forget. But if you step out of line, you'll be out with my Sergeant's boot up your arse. Do I make myself clear?'

'Yes sir,' came a muted response.

'Do I Make Myself Clear?'

'YES SIR!'

'That's better. Now, I'm going to hand you over to that Sergeant. This is Sergeant Geddes and he holds the keys to how today is going to go for you. Cross him at your peril.'

Geddes stepped forward without any stamping or saluting and looked along the line. A hard as nails man of around forty with a deep tan and watchful eyes, he was clearly unimpressed and muttered as much to Cauldwell.

'What d'ye expect me to do wi' this shower o' shite?'

Geddes sounded like a man who thought grindr was something found in a Govan shipyard. He turned to address the group.

'If this was the army, you'd be spending a few months in basic training where, among other things, you'd learn some Self-Re-Spect. As we only have a day, we're going to have deal with you looking like the bunch o' bastards that you are.'

He sniffed the air, ominously. 'But one thing my men will absolutely not tolerate is scent. So, if any of you are wearing aftershave, cologne or eau de fucking toilette, you have thirty seconds to get to your pampered pussies to the latrine and come back smelling like men.'

There was awkward shuffling among the players. Then, after a moment's hesitation, three of them broke cover and dashed for the proverbial brick shithouse. The others fell about laughing until Geddes brought them up short.

'Shut Up. And you, pretty boy at the end, count yourself lucky that we don't have two minutes to spare, or that fucking man bun would be down the khazi too.'

Alec looked along the line at the lads, all wetting themselves with excitement. There were plenty of managers out there, he thought, who could learn a thing or two from Sergeant Geddes approach to man management.

Having established himself as king of the hill, the Sergeant divided the party into four sixteen-man troops creatively named Alpha, Bravo, Charlie and Delta. These he instructed to further divide themselves into patrols of four before giving each their instructions. They spent the first part of the morning working in their troops with a designated SAS trooper. First it was weapons handling where they learned to break down and re-assemble the Glock 17 pistol and Diemaco C8 assault rifle favoured by the Regiment. Then it was time for close-quarters combat training with Sergeant Geddes in command.

'If the SAS ever gets into hand-to-hand combat,' he said, 'it means something has gone wrong either with the plan or with our weapons. However, if things do get up close and personal, we are not going down without a fight. With all due respect, if any one of you boys comes up against a determined and capable attacker, you're going to lose. But you're fit and you're fast, so your best option is always going to be to run away. And don't think that makes you a dickless wimp; you're just making sure you live to fight another day. So, run for the exits. Clear?'

The players stood around nodding, but Alec was doubtful. He had seen several of them in compromising situations where they should have run away, but none ever had.

Fortunately, Sergeant Geddes carried on. 'We should probably end the session right there but that's not what you came here for, is it? So, we're going to give you some strategies that you can use for when you can't run away or when you're too pissed to remember that's what you're supposed to do. What you're going to learn now could save your lives: just don't expect it to look like Queensberry Rules. These techniques can be used by anyone, even girls.'

The ripples of laughter were subsiding and by now there were a few disappointed faces. This wasn't what they'd come for either.

Geddes pressed on. 'In fact, they work especially well for girls, so when you ladies have learned them, feel free to pass them on to your wives and girlfriends. The reason they work well for the fairer sex is that girls don't do any of that macho pushing and shoving bollocks. They just get stuck in quick and get out.'

The SAS troopers went to work with each patrol and what followed was a lesson in some of the dirtiest street fighting any of them had seen. By the time the session ended, the players could gouge eyes, kick shins, grab balls and punch throats with the worst of them. And no one had any doubt how effective they would be in real life. Alec was impressed. the guys had survived without any injuries, and they'd all learned some useful life skills.

As lunchtime beckoned, Bergens containing food, water, navigation and other equipment were distributed to each troop and Sergeant Geddes introduced the next challenge.

'Next up, you're going to do an exercise which is the closest insight we can give you into some of the real work of the SAS without you getting your arses blown off.'

He gestured to the countryside around them which was a mix of woodland, scrubby grass, bare hilltops and lakes. 'Out there, in hostile territory, there is a hostage being held under armed guard in a complex of farm buildings. Your mission is to mount a rescue operation and bring them home. Looking at you, it's clear our hostage's situation is hopeless, but we'd like you to see how far you get. Your time will start when you leave here. The clock will stop when you reach the first rendezvous point then start again when each troop mounts its assault and continue running until you get back here. Any of you who reaches the farmhouse unscathed will earn fifty points for his troop. You'll be wearing a sensor vest which will register a clean body shot so if you feel a buzz, it's game over and you just have to make your way back as quickly as possible to this location. There are bonus points for every minute you come in under two hours, but you start losing points if you take any longer. I will also be awarding style points for those of you who do something my guys consider to be particularly mpressive. As you can imagine, they're a hard bunch to impress but I've asked them to be generous. There are also penalty points for anyone who makes a dick of themselves, and the winners are the troop with the most points at the end.'

Geddes ordered them to get their weapons together and tab over to separate rendezvous points between four and five miles away. The players were fit, and their packs were light. Most were hardly out of breath as they met up with instructors who handed round mugs of steaming tea boiled over a portable stove. As they drank and chowed down on a range of dried and processed calories, they were given detailed instructions and a grid reference indicating the target. Each troop had a time when the clock would restart and they were in a race against time to complete the assault and return to base.

Alpha Troop approached from the West. They kept out of sight by approaching through a wood but were then faced with the apparently insuperable barriers of open ground on three sides and a lake on the other. They fanned out as best they could, but each of them was picked off as they emerged from the cover of the trees. Within twenty minutes of starting, they were on the long run back to base. Bravo Troop seemed to judge that 'death' was inevitable so they should just get it over with as quickly as possible and make up points with a quick return time. They soon felt the tell-tale buzz of their sensor vests despite approaching from all corners and were last seen haring off through the woods and back to the start. Charlie Troop were more circumspect, crawling along on their stomachs to minimise the chances of a clear body shot. They got a few yards closer to the target but were quickly neutralised as soon as they tried to get up off the ground for the final assault.

Connor Flynn was the leader of Delta Troop and dead set on getting further than his rivals. Despite being one of the youngest, he had taken charge throughout the day and his unit had performed well in the challenges they'd faced so far. Alec and the other lads under Connor's command sat around drinking tea while the first three troops made their attempts. Their leader was much more attentive. He noted where the enemy shots were coming from and picked up on any obvious errors to avoid. By his reckoning, fifty points for reaching the farmhouse would far outweigh a time bonus and he was determined they would succeed. He called the troop together and shared his tactics.

'Ok, boys we are absolutely going to win this thing. We're going to go through everything now so we can deal with any questions. Then, once we set off there's no talking. You're all going to stick in your patrols and each one is going to take a different route. Alec, you've done alright today for an old man so you can lead patrol one, I'll take two and Toby and Thibaut, you can head up three and four.'

Alec was flattered, but he was about to find out why he'd been chosen as patrol leader as Flynn continued his briefing.

'There are no prizes for speed, only for getting the closest, so while we're in the woods, we're going to take our time and make ourselves useful. My lot and patrols three and four, pick up some forest camouflage like plants and twigs and stuff to stick in your helmets, and rub dirt over those persil-white faces. When we're through the woods we're going to position ourselves in line with the corners of the building to make the sightlines awkward. Then we'll leave on our bellies and take it really slow. Alec, patrol one, you're going through the lake.'

'What? You are joking. It's fucking Baltic in there.'

'Nope. Next time perhaps you'll think twice before making comments about my girlfriend. Anyway, from what I've seen, they're not patrolling in that direction, so you've got the chance to be the heroes of the day. And even if we all get shot, you'll get loads of style points, so we win either way.'

'That's if we don't die of hyperthermia first.'

Connor ignored Alec's protests and pushed on. 'If we make it that far we'll need to stay flat to the farmhouse walls then we'll do the classic assault. We'll signal each other, then on three, one person per patrol throws a pretend flashbang through the window and the rest of us kick the bloody doors down. Obviously, that's as far as we'll get, but that would count as a 'W' in my book.'

In the event, the land patrols lost most of their members within ten metres of the woods, but the remaining few pushed on slowly and relentlessly whilst Alec's group passed undetected through the lake. As they reached the building, the sightlines narrowed enough for two of Connor's patrol to risk lifting their heads for the final assault. The buzz of their vests was proof that it had been error, but it allowed their leader to push on towards the grey stone wall of the farmhouse. From this vantage point he could see guys on the other corners about to do the same as Alec's quartet dragged themselves from the water relying on adrenalin to keep them warm. Connor picked up a handful of stones then gestured to the others before hurling them through the open window yelling "Bang! Bang! Bang!" as he did so. The others launched themselves at the doors only to bounce off and fall helplessly onto their backs. When they opened their eyes, they were face to face with the wrong end of a rifle and the cold eyes of a special forces soldier behind them.

'Fair play,' said Connor. 'We'll call it a draw, hey lads?'

The players laughed, but the soldiers kept up their guard until their targets were safely out of the game. Then they stripped Alec's patrol to their underwear and wrapped them in thermal blankets before shoving them off in the direction of the base.

Despite not completely evading capture, Connor was buzzing when they got back to the debrief hut.

'Wayne Bridge, eat your fucking heart out,' he said, triumphantly, as they poured through the door.

'Sadly, you lost points on account of being thrity minutes late,' said Jermaine, who had led Bravo Troop.

'I think you'll find you're still a LOOSER,' shot back Connor, making the familiar 'L' sign on his forehead.

'Only time will tell,' said Cauldwell, taking control of the situation. 'Now that our late arrivals are finally here, I can tell you that I have had chance to confer with my men and we have the following awards to make. First up is the award for quickest strip down and reassembly of the Glock 17. To put this into context, one of my guys would complete the task in around ten seconds but for a first attempt you didn't do badly. So, with a time of seventy-three seconds, the prize goes to Bastien. Please, step up to receive your award.'

He pulled out a small plastic water pistol which the Belgian midfielder accepted with a smile. He sprayed it around the room to cheers from footballers and soldiers alike.

'The next award is the girliest-girl award for close combat. Remember what we said: get in quickly, hit them somewhere painful and then run away. And the winner, the girliest girl with some down and dirty street fighting, is Marcel. Please, step up to receive your award.'

The room erupted into wolf whistles as the embarrassed player was forced to put on a bright pink sash.

'He'd make someone a very pretty WAG,' said Cauldwell. 'Now, there is one more award before we get to the serious business of selecting the winning troop and handing out a Distinguished Service medal. In football, you have the man-of-the-match. Well, we do things a bit differently in the army. So, I give you dick-of-the-day, an award which I'm sure needs no explanation.'

He held up a small plastic trophy in the shape of a tiny gold-coloured penis with a red ribbon tied round it. At the sight of the offending object the cheers in the room were muted.

'The winner of dick of the day had to beat off some strong competition,' Cauldwell continued, 'and I do mean "beat off". First there was Ashley. Not only was he an aftershave bellend, but he was also seen picking up his Diemaco by the barrel. So, definitely *a* dick, just not *the* dick. Next up we had Alec who led his patrol through a lake. Fed by mountain streams. In March. I mean, fair play just for getting in the water, but all I'll say is you were lucky your "enemy" was ready with a thermal blanket otherwise you'd have all died of exposure. Definitely *a* dick, but again, not *the* dick.

'No, against that sort of competition, our dick of the day had to pull off a total worldie not just once, but right through the day. Everyone can be a dick, but this dick turned being a dick into an art form. The dick I'm talking about was always going to be one of the aftershave bellends, but he was also the only one who failed to reassemble his pistol. Not only that but he managed to insert the recoil-spring assembly round the wrong way which is about the only way to actually break a Glock. I make that four hundred quid you owe the British Army. If that wasn't enough, he managed to kick himself in his own shins in the hand-to-hand combat and he got lost returning to base after a mission so ill-fated that he was neutralised before he even left the woods. So, let's hear a mighty cry of "fuckwit" for our dick-of-the-day, Mr. Frank Siddle. Please, step up to receive your award.'

The boys duly obliged and Siddle walked the walk of shame to the front of the room where he was presented with the plastic penis. To add to his embarrassment, he was forced to hold the trophy aloft surrounded by SAS troopers while the rest of the room took photos.

When the noise died down, Cauldwell continued. 'Now we come to the day's honours and my guys were unanimous that the award goes to Delta Troop for a very impressive mission even if you would all have been killed, captured or died of hypothermia.'

Sixteen guys came up to collect SAS pin badges to the groans and cheers of their mates.

'One word of warning,' Cauldwell said. 'Don't think about wearing those badges when you're out on the town or you'll definitely be writing cheques your fists can't cash.

That leaves just one final award, the Distinguished Service medal which goes to the leader of Delta Troop. So put your hands together for Honorary Trooper Flynn.'

Billy tried to stay cool but couldn't help punching the air and grinning broadly as Simon Cauldwell handed him a mounted SAS winged dagger badge. Cauldwell nodded to Alec who had finally stopped shivering and took over smoothly.

'Time to show our appreciation lads,' he said. 'It's not every day these guys take time out from saving the world so, gentlemen, it's been a real privilege.'

There was loud applause and handshakes all round before Alec started to speak again. When the players next turned around, the soldiers had gone.

Chapter 5

It was mid-morning and Michaela sat in pyjamas. She was in her old bedroom staring at the pink ballerina spinning on top of a sparkly plastic jewellery box. The toy was an appalling relic of her eighth birthday. It looked like something left behind at a car boot sale. It was still here, though, and something stopped her throwing it out. She tried to tell herself that it had been a present from someone now long gone. But was it that she saw a mirror of her own life in the fixed grin and pointless pirouettes? She wasn't prepared to draw a conclusion.

She hadn't been entirely honest with Alec about her reasons for walking away. Now his words kept repeating themselves over and over in her mind. *We stumble around, stuff happens, we meet people and all of that combines to make a life. We might look back and wonder how things could have been different, but we can't let fear stop us moving forward.* Was that what she was doing? Was she like that ballerina, rooted to the spot for fear of crashing off into emptiness? She'd been fine when they met, and she had genuinely enjoyed Madrid, but on that Sunday morning she'd felt haunted and needed to get away. Since then, she'd tried half-heartedly to chase down the information Alec was after, but progress had been glacial.

She closed the lid of the jewellery box with a snap, using the action to jolt herself into life and a standing position. She tried to inject some energy into her movements as she pulled on a t-shirt and leggings. If her body could do a decent impression of being alive, she felt, then her brain would pick up the signal and get with the programme. She'd put off going downstairs to face a disappointed, or worse pitying, look from her mother, so she was relieved when she made it to the kitchen and there was no one there. Instead, a brief note.

I made an appointment for you with Doctor Jupp but I didn't know how to tell you. It's today so try to be there for 11.30.

Michaela could have used the fact that 11.30 was only twenty-five minutes away as an excuse not to go. Instead, she surprised herself by grabbing her trainers and heading out the door to run the two miles to the surgery.

Maybe the appointment was a turning point, maybe it just came at the right time, but she left the GP consulting room in a rage; it was the best she'd felt for weeks. The doctor, a grey middle-aged man, had not endeared himself to her with his opening gambit.

'A lot of single women your age find themselves depressed from time to time,' he wheezed. 'Have you tried looking for a boyfriend? I hear online dating is quite the thing nowadays.'

She dismissed as patronising his suggestion that she be kinder to herself and embrace her mental health as part of who she was. And the prescription for anti-depressants had been mentally screwed up and hurled in the bin before he had even signed the scrip. She rejected the easy excuses and what she considered to be the *woke shit* that surrounds mental illness. There was no way she was going to be dependent on happy pills. What she did come out convinced of, however, was that she had a problem and needed help. By the time she left the surgery she had made up her mind and called Alec.

'Hello stranger,' he said, breezily. 'How are you?'

'I've just come out of the doctor's surgery.'

'Shit, you're not pregnant, are you?'

'No of course I'm not bloody pregnant. I'm ill, sick in fact, and I need your help.'

'Whatever I can do, you know that. What's wrong with you?'

'I've got some sort of mental health issue. I don't know whether it's depression or PTSD or anxiety disorder or what, but I can't get up in the morning, I've got zero energy, I can't focus and I keep crying.'

'And you're sure you're not pregnant?'

'You're not making this any easier, you know?'

'Sorry. What did the doctor say?'

'He listened to my symptoms for about five minutes then basically said I should accept who I am, take a load of pills and go and dribble myself into a jelly mould.'

'And you're not prepared to accept his diagnosis.'

'The diagnosis is ok, as far as it goes. It's the prescription I can't stomach and that's where you come in. I don't need pills, I need therapy, the kind of treatment soldiers get when they come back from warzones. Theoretically it's available on the NHS, but the waiting time is years, and I can't afford to pay for it, so I'm asking you.'

'How much is it going to be?'

'I don't know, I'll need to look into it, but I'd guess at somewhere around £200 an hour.'

With the amount he had in his offshore bank account, Alec knew he could pay for therapy twenty-four hours a day for a year if he had to, but he was hesitant. 'I'll do it on one condition.'

'No strings, Alec.'

'I just want you to give us a chance when you're better.'

'No strings.'

The next few weeks were a waiting game. Alec had put all his hooks out there; now he had to wait and see if any fish took the bait. He had put together a shopping list of information he needed and, true to her word, Michaela had come up with the goods. She had researched each of the UEFA member associations from countries who had qualified for the Euros, their staff, financials and a list of representatives who had travelled to the last World Cup. Alec's thinking was that the Russian event had been a success, which suggested that the delegations were clean so any changes could be significant. The argument had the benefit of being just about logical, but he knew it wasn't much of a start.

As far as his players were concerned, Alec called them all once a week, but it was not until six weeks out from the start of the tournament that he got his first hint of any intel. Paradoxically, after going to the effort of recruiting a new group of contacts, it was one of his oldest clients who called first. Alec was sat at his desk early on a Wednesday morning when his phone buzzed, and Kevin Mooney's name flashed up on the screen.

'Hello Kev. I haven't heard from you for a while. How's tricks?'

'I'm grand, Alec lad,' came the broad accent of the Ulsterman. 'How about yourself?'

'Yeh, all good, mate. What can I do for you?'

'I heard a wee whisper that you were looking for information on dodgy stuff going on around the Euros. I think I might have something for you.'

'That's interesting,' said Alec, thinking quickly. He hadn't involved the Northern Ireland international as his country hadn't qualified. When they met in the playoffs, the Republic of Ireland had put paid to any slim hopes their Northern neighbours had of becoming European champions, and Alec assumed it would still be a sore point. As ever with Mooney, though, it was cash not country that talked loudest.

'We're not going, as you know, but that doesn't stop the odd rumour from circulating and I wondered whether it would be worth anything to you.'

Alec winced. 'I'm doing this for Queen and country, mate, so not really in the market to be paying for information.'

'I'm sure whoever you're passing stuff on to would be though, am I right? And if it goes well, who knows what else I might stumble across. We've got a lot of European players at the club, so we have. They could be a mine of information.'

Kevin had been a client for long enough that Alec knew he had a price for everything, but he normally delivered value for money.

'Tell you what,' he said, 'you give me what you've got, and I'll ask the question.'

'I'll lay out the bones of it, right enough, then you see what you can get me for the details. Sound ok?'

Alec agreed, albeit reluctantly, knowing what Cauldwell's reaction would be. He changed his attitude slightly when, over the next five minutes, Mooney outlined a Europe-wide ticketing scam involving the football federations of Turkey and Croatia. His sources were impeccable: players from the national sides of each of the countries. Separately, they confirmed that both national football authorities had put a large chunk of their ticket allocation onto the black market through a fly-by-night touting operation. The result was hundreds of illegal tickets and a sizeable windfall for someone at the federations.

'Doesn't that happen at every major tournament, Kev?' Alec said when he was finished.

'Aye, it does and normally it's the same fuckers that do it. But I've been thinking and I'm asking myself 'why are you suddenly part of the event security for the Euros?' I mean, no offence mate, but there are professionals at that game. Someone's put you up to this, someone maybe in the police or more likely a bit more shadowy. The regular security guys are doing their regular stuff, but as a wee bit of extra insurance, they've drafted you in to sniff around the football world. Am I on the money so far?'

Alec didn't reply.

'I'll take that as a yes. So, I'm thinking there's a reason, like they've got wind of the fact that there's something being planned; something big. Something too big to fuck up. And I think someone ought to be very interested in just who's bought those illegal tickets. They were allocated to the federations which means they're unnamed, so there's no way to find out who's got them. It could be anybody and they can just walk into the opening ceremony, the finals and practically every other game. And no one's going to stop them.'

Alec was impressed and slightly cross with himself at the same time. There was no doubting Kevin's intelligence, and it made sense that the threat level must be higher than normal around the Euros. Otherwise why would he be involved?

'You really have been thinking, haven't you?' he said. 'But what I don't understand is how you can help identify who's got those tickets. Don't take this as a confirmation, but let's say my contact is someone in the security services. They're going to need to be dead sure they're targeting the right people otherwise they'd risk triggering a diplomatic incident.'

'Aye, so they would. But if I could give you the agency who's selling the tickets, that'd be a wee bit of a head start, wouldn't it?'

Alec could see the information might be valuable, although whether Cauldwell would be prepared to a put a price on it, who knew. He decided to try a little fishing himself to see what else Mooney might have been thinking about.

'You said you might stumble across other useful bits of information. Did you have anything specific in mind? It might help as a convincer if I could say what else you've got up your sleeve.'

'Oh, you know me, Alec. I've always got a few different irons in the fire. The security firm at the club has won the contract to do stadium security for the Euros, and I'm sure someone would like to have a look over their staff list and vetting processes. And I've got a good few contacts in the betting world, as you know, so quite a few possibilities.'

Alec was sure the security angle would have been covered already but betting scams were a possibility. On instinct alone, he knew Kevin Mooney could be helpful. He had much more of the instincts of a criminal than Alec and the kind of rodent brain that would be very useful working on the inside of football. He'd go beyond the obvious, but he'd be expensive, more expensive than his spymasters would be likely to swallow. His suspicions were confirmed when he next spoke to Cauldwell.

'Ticket scams by the national football federations have been going on since tickets were invented,' he said. 'In fact, taking advantage of opportunities to cream off cash is probably one of the main reasons for lots of federation presidents to take the job. Knowing the agency involved in the resale of tickets would be a first for us but, in terms of the value we might put on that information, it's extremely limited. We already know the serial numbers of tickets allocated to each federation even if we don't know exactly who's holding them. And there's no guarantee that someone who buys a ticket from a reseller isn't going to sell it on again.'

'Kevin had various ideas as to angles we might pursue. I just thought he might be useful, but he won't work for free.'

'You're welcome to pay him if you think he's worth it, Alec, but we're not in a position to compensate you. Budget aside, it would create a paper trail and the nature of our relationship means we can't allow that.'

'Ok, I'll give it some thought. He did say one thing which rang true for me, though. He reckons there must be a concrete threat, something that you're worried about; that you wouldn't even be talking to me if you were just covering all the angles.'

'That's not entirely true. To be honest, it was serendipity as much as anything. You know? Right place, right time. You're well connected in football so who knows what you'll turn up that we might otherwise miss.'

'Not *entirely* true, or just not true? Because I'm telling you is he's putting two and two together, and if he can work out there's something going down, then so can everyone else. As it stands, what I'm doing is sending a message to all the teams competing in the Euros that we're worried about a major terrorist incident. Maybe, if I knew what that something is, then I could stop spreading negative rumours and start being a bit more useful.'

Cauldwell said nothing for a moment, then seemed to concede the point. 'I can't go into details, but your friend is correct in the sense that we have received intelligence that a group is planning to use the Euros to promote their cause.'

He stopped, reluctant to continue, until Alec pushed him. 'Go on.'

'It may just be straws in the wind, but GCHQ have picked up various communications where the Euros are linked with the word "spectacular", and we don't think they mean there'll just be lots of goals. As you probably know, that word has been used in connection with terrorist incidents in high-profile public places. 9/11 was the most audacious *spectacular* but not the first or the last. Our relentless war on terror has reduced our enemy's operating room, and as a result, the attacks have become less sophisticated and more opportunist. However devastating for those directly involved, the threat of a knife attack in Westminster is of a completely different order to flying planes into buildings. But, while there are still individuals prepared to sacrifice themselves and drive lorries into crowds of people, there is still a risk.'

'But why are you more concerned with this threat than any others?'

'According to what we tell MPs, the security services monitor around three thousand persons of interest at any one time. Whether that's true or not, I couldn't say, but it's certainly a large number and takes up a lot of manpower. And those are just the individuals in this country. We share information with various different intelligence agencies, but since Brexit, that collaboration is slower and less reliable. Also, the focus has shifted among our

European neighbours; most are looking to tackle migration or trying to find ways to get their economies back on track after the Pandemic. A football tournament is just not very high on their list of priorities. The whispers picked up by Cheltenham suggest a larger, well-funded operation which is going to use the cover of a major event to move people and equipment around. Unfortunately, there's very little we can do about it because of the way the hosting agreement is framed. Unless we have knowledge of a credible threat, we can't prevent individuals with a connection to one of the teams from coming here. We can't search team trucks or broadcast lorries and the same goes for sponsors and their guests and equipment. So, the threat is more sophisticated than we've seen for a while. At the same time we're struggling for support in Europe and we've got one arm tied behind our backs at home.'

'I can see your problem. Any sense of where the whispers are coming from? Can we narrow it down a bit?'

'The names on the list won't be any surprise to you: Saudi, Syria, Lebanon. The immediate concern is that we haven't intercepted any electronic chatter over the past three weeks despite doubling the effort and spreading the net as widely as possible. That could mean it was nothing, but the messages were pretty conclusive. The only working assumption we can make is that whoever's involved knows that we monitor the airwaves and has decided that the time for communicating is over. They have the funding, equipment and expertise in place, they've been given the green light by whoever they answer to, and they've gone operational.'

Chapter 6

Over the next few weeks, Alec had plenty of opportunity to mull over his conversation with Simon Cauldwell and two words kept going through his mind: spectacular and operational. He wasn't a worrier by nature. Years of being told not to look beyond the next game had been coaching for life, not just for football. But he felt that amorphous threat taking on an almost physical form as the clock ticked down to the Euros Opening Ceremony. His concern was non-specific; it had no focus or foundation in reality, but the feeling of it was ever present. He wondered whether Cauldwell and those like him could ever really sleep undisturbed in their beds.

While his night terrors were metaphysical, the challenge of his days was much more concrete: none of his players had come through with anything. He contacted everyone personally each week and the message was consistent: they'd neither seen nor heard anything unusual about the Euros. He kept asking the English boys to push their European teammates but the result was still the same. He kept the conversation going with Kevin Mooney if only to feel like he was doing something. He even tried to slip the player some money when it looked like *The Guardian* wanted to run the ticketing scam story as an exposé. Mooney turned him down flat.

'I don't think we're quite on the same page here, Alec,' the player said, during one particularly awkward phone conversation. 'I can't be giving up my time for the odd few quid tossed my way when you feel like it. I've got my career after football to think about and that's just not going to cut it.'

'I didn't mean to insult you, mate, but I think you're barking up the wrong tree if you reckon there's money to be made from this kind of work. That's not to say there won't be information that's worth paying for but, well, you know how it is...'

He trailed off, hoping he'd said enough to encourage Mooney to keep his eyes open without actually putting him on a football-style retainer. Alec knew the player's mindset and the challenge all footballers face as the curtain starts to come down on their careers. Sums of money that would have most people thanking their lucky stars seem so insignificant they are hardly worth picking up the phone for. It's a lot easier to be grateful for the occasional five-hundred quid when you haven't had any money coming in for a few months.

Michaela was causing Alec no such problems and insisted on itemising to the penny what her therapist was costing even though he always rounded up his regular transfers to the nearest hundred pounds. The pair had not seen each other since he dropped her off after Madrid, but they talked regularly, and he pushed her just as hard to keep digging for information. She had done a first-rate job of analysing the finances of each national federation and come across some interesting anomalies. But there was nothing so far out of the ordinary that either of were inclined to dig deeper. With three weeks to go, they were given access to the list of each country's UEFA delegation. This gave Michaela another entry point and she started with the larger federations reporting to Alec after three days with her progress.

'I think I can confidently say that football is one of the dodgiest industries I've come across,' she said. 'I've only looked at Germany, France and Holland and already I've got seven petty criminals, four used car salesmen – which probably amounts to the same thing – a murderer, a pair that are obviously money launderers and a banker. And before you say it, yes, the banker is the worst of the lot.'

'Everyone needs a hobby,' Alec replied, 'and football's fit and proper person test hardly set the bar very high. Any of them got an Islamist connection?'

'Not even a hint. The only time any of this lot get on their knees is when they've dropped some change. Like the money trail, there's so much going on it's hard to find a reason to single out any individuals.'

'Ok, then I suppose we keep looking. What I'm after are some names with enough suspicion around them to bring up with a player in the national squad. Right now, none of them are hearing anything. If my guys had something or someone they could ask questions about, then they might make some progress.'

'I'll do what I can, but so far they're pretty much all as bad as each other. What amazes me is the girlfriends. I mean, what does a thirty-year-old model see in an overweight balding, septuagenarian? At least Harvey Weinstein could get you into a movie.'

Alec thought he'd chance his arm and ask the question that had been on his mind for several weeks. 'Glad to hear you're sounding a bit more like your old self. How's the therapy going?'

'None of your business,' she snapped back, suddenly defensive, and he could have kicked himself.

'Sorry, that's not fair,' she said, more gently. 'I'm not ready to talk about it but I'll say one thing: it's helping.'

'Great, that's all I need to know. Anyway, I've got another call coming through, so I'll speak to you again later.'

He recognised the name on his phone as he picked up the call.

'Hello Connor. How's it going?'

'Good thanks, Alec. Look I just had a conversation and I thought you ought to hear about it.'

'Go on, mate. I'm all ears.'

'You know how the physio knows everything about what goes on at the club: all the secrets and everyone's business?'

'Yeh, like a confessional with deep heat instead of incense,' said Alec, slapping his forehead in a mental 'D'oh!' for not thinking of targeting physios before.

'Anyway, I was having my usual massage yesterday when our guy, Alan, said the lad before me had a lot on his mind. Apparently, he was going on about the Euros, said something about his team are going to be amazing. But he was really stressed about it, like he was trying to say something without actually coming out with it. I know it's weird, but you said we should pass on anything we heard.'

'That is weird. Who does he play for?'

'One of those new countries. Kosovo, I think?'

'Ok, tell me again what he said,' Alec said, Googling while he listened.

'He was going on about the Euros and saying Kosovo were going to be amazing or really special or spectacular or something.'

'Spectacular? Are you sure that was the word he used?

'Yeh, that was it. They're going to be spectacular. I know, right? That's the strangest bit 'cos Kosovo haven't got a chance.'

Alec called Michaela as soon as he got off the phone to Connor.

'Change of plan,' he said. 'I've just had the tiniest sniff of something, so I need you to switch over to the Kosovo FA, their money, their leadership and who they're planning to bring in as part of their delegation.'

'That shouldn't take long; they're the smallest country still in the tournament. But what's the lead?'

'Connor Flynn, you know, the one who won the SAS dagger? That was him on the phone and he reckons one of their squad, a lad from Kosovo, is all stressed about the Euros, saying they're going to be spectacular. It reminded me of something Cauldwell said a few weeks back. It may be nothing at all, but it's at least a reason to look a bit harder at one of the teams.'

'Sounds flimsy, but I'll let you know what I come up with. By the way, what's the player's name?'

'His name's Kushtrim Larmar. I've barely heard of him but I'm due to give him a call. I should know more in a while.'

Despite Connor's introduction, or maybe because of it, Larmar was brief to the point of rudeness on the phone.

'Kushtrim? It's Alec Munday here. Connor Flynn said were expecting my call. Is now a good time to talk?'

'It's ok,' came the response, in a deep gravelly voice.

'I don't know what Connor's told you about me, but I used to be a footballer, I went into the media and now I'm helping the organisers of the Euros. My job is to keep an ear to the ground and pick up on any chatter about security, you know, after that business in Madrid a few weeks ago. Connor thought maybe you'd heard something. Is that right?'

The line went quiet then as if the words were being dragged out of him. 'I don't tell Connor nothing. I talk to Alan, he talk to Connor and now you call.'

'Don't be too hard on the guys. From what I was told, Alan felt you had a problem. How about you tell me about it, and I'll see if I can help.'

'Not on the phone.'

'Ok, no problem. It's good to meet in person, I always think. I could come over to your place later if that works.'

Another pause before Larmar said, 'I'll text you the address,' and the line went dead.

The advantage of visiting footballers after training was that mid-afternoon traffic was generally light. Even so, it took well over two hours to reach Larmar's house on the western edge of the South Downs. The player lived in the middle of nowhere in an ancient low stone cottage which was about as far away from a typical footballer's mansion as it was possible to imagine. As he rapped the black iron knocker Alec could picture the door being opened by an apple-cheeked farmer's wife. Instead, it swung back to reveal a large, bearded man with intense dark eyes.

'Kushtrim? I'm Alec.'

The player stared unblinking at his visitor for a moment then accepted Alec's outstretched hand.

'The guys call me Kendrick,' he said, in a voice as big as the frame it came from.

'Kendrick?' he said, feigning surprise. 'Oh, Kendrick Lamar. Very clever. Do you mind?'

'Only my mother calls me Kushtrim.'

The player showed him through the house and into the garden where Alec got his first glimpse of the cottage's appeal. The sun was low in the sky and it cast a gentle orange glow over hundreds of acres of vines.

'My parents had a vineyard,' Larmar said, then went quiet, staring out over the idyllic sunset.

Hating an awkward silence, Alec said, 'I'm more of a city boy, myself. I don't really understand the countryside. It's all a bit quiet. Do you live here on your own?'

'My wife is out.'

Alec prided himself on getting people to confide in him. Listening as someone opened up about their lives within minutes of first meeting was when he felt most like a real journalist. But Larmar was a challenge. Not unfriendly but apparently unconcerned with social niceties. The pause was becoming excruciating, and Alec could tell this was as much of an insight into the player's life as he was likely to get. He came from a place where conversations have consequences and was innately wary as a result. And yet he had wanted to share what he knew with someone. Alec decided he would have to make the running.

'Look, you don't know me from Adam, but I'm a football man and you can trust me. I can't say if it'll help or not, but I can promise you that no one else will know unless that's what we decide between us is for the best.'

The player looked uncertain, but Alec's charms were working. Reluctantly at first, then all in a rush Larmar told him what he was worried about.

'So, let me get this right,' Alec said, when the big man went quiet again. 'There are some unfamiliar faces around the national team, people from the old days who left the country when the war ended in Kosovo in 1999. You think they were trying to avoid being tried for war crimes. They've spent the last twenty years fighting for various Muslim causes in the Middle East and now they're back and they're planning something *spectacular*. Does that word mean something particular?'

'The word is *spektakularno,*' Larmar confirmed, 'and it means the same as in many other languages but in the mouth of a terrorist I think the meaning is clear. We are a young team, and we play football without complications. We don't think about the past or about politics or religion, but these old faces were talking about the war, about enemies and about getting back our pride. They said the Euros would be a spectacular chance to show the world who we are.'

'But it's quite a leap from that to blowing up a football stadium or something. What is it specifically that makes you think there's a plan to launch some sort of attack?'

'They weren't talking about pride in Kosovo; they were talking about Muslim pride. They know that as a football team, we can travel without being searched, we can go to places behind the security screens and get access to all the special occasions of the Euros. I don't know what they've got in mind, but…' He stopped and Alec gave him space to complete the sentence. '…I think they are planning to use the only team from a Muslim country as a suicide squad.'

The player was quiet again and Alec nodded slowly, giving himself time to think. He was about to respond when the sound of a small car approaching broke the silence.

'This is my wife,' said Larmar, his attention snapping quickly back to the present. 'I know what she's going to say. Drinks.'

'Hello, I'm home, so make sure you're indecent,' came a voice.

He stood up blushing behind his beard as a small blonde woman bustled through the back door carrying a large handbag.

'Oh, Kush, you didn't tell me we'd got company, and you haven't even served any drinks.'

'You see, what did I tell you? This is Meg. Meg, this is Alec. He is helping me with some media work.' He glanced at their guest to make sure he got the message.

'Nice to meet you,' said Alec, smoothly. 'I was just admiring your place. It's a lovely spot.'

A quick Google search before he left meant Alec was familiar with the basics of the Larmar's domestic arrangements. Meg was Mary-Ellen Grundy, an estate agent who had sorted out the player's accommodation when he arrived at the club and then moved in. They married soon afterwards, and she was now his agent. If he was being honest, Alec was expecting a girl on the make, but seeing the pair together, he had to revise his opinion. For a start, she didn't look like your average gold-digging bimbo. Her eyes were huge to the point of bulging, her nose was slightly hooked and her small mouth was full of teeth. But in combination there was an elfin beauty about her and a tinkling laugh in her voice. It was obvious that the big man adored her, and Alec could see why.

Larmar took a drinks order and disappeared into the house leaving Meg with a question on her lips.

'Media work?' she asked, doubtfully. 'Good luck with that one. I can't even get him on the club TV channel.'

'Yes, well maybe it's just about the right timing. I'm thinking with the Euros and Kosovo qualifying for the first time there might be some interest. Anyway, tell me how you guys ended up here. I know you're an estate agent, but I can't imagine it's the kind of place you take most footballers.'

'We're both country people. I was born in the next village to here and Kush's family had a vineyard in Kosovo. He was only quite young when the war destroyed everything, but he still remembers the feeling of being able to run freely through the vines. So, here we are. From a practical point of view, it works well. Everyone knows I'm a local girl and they tend to look after us a bit. You had directions, but if another journalist was snooping around, there's no way the neighbours would let them have our address.'

The drinks came and the three sat for a few minutes admiring the view before Meg made her excuses, going inside to make dinner. Although the evening was warm, a chill came up from the damp ground once the sun went down and the time for sitting outside was over. Sensing he wasn't going to make any more progress, Alec thanked the couple for their hospitality and pointed his car in the direction of home. He couldn't help but envy their domestic bliss as he turned out of their drive.

He turned the music up and settled back into the BMW's leather-bound luxury. He had always coveted expensive cars and taken dozens of footballers on track days, but the joke was that he was actually a terrible driver. The evening gloom made the narrow country lanes narrower and even harder to negotiate and he found himself unsure where the road stopped and the verges started. Seconds later, he was momentarily blinded by an oncoming car and then the world went black.

Chapter 7

Alec woke up with his face full of airbag, feeling like he had been punched with a brick, albeit one tied round with bubble wrap. His car had left the road and carved out the start of a new bypass in the undergrowth. A grassy ditch had slowed his progress and stopped him hitting any trees, but he felt dazed and disorientated. He couldn't feel any broken bones so got out to inspect the damage. He watched the lights of the car he assumed was responsible as it wound its way at high speed across the valley and parked in front of Kush and Meg's cottage. After a few failed attempts to reverse out of the ditch he resigned himself to calling out a tow truck and settled back to see what happened at the footballer's house while he waited. While he did, he put in a call to Michaela.

'Anything to report?' he asked.

'It's pretty much as we thought, although the Football Federation of Kosovo seems to have more money in its bank account than others from much larger countries. Their staff is the usual mix of former players, coaches and wannabe politicians but that's nothing out of the ordinary.'

'Anyone with gaps in their history? I'm looking for people who may have had to disappear for a few years and now they're back.'

'Don't think so. They all look reasonably legit.'

'Maybe they're just hangers on. What about any former war criminals who have sneaked back onto the business or political scene, or is that like looking for a needle in a haystack?'

'No, that's like looking for hay in a haystack. The only people who are completely clean were either too young or too old to matter during the war, but I can't see any reason to connect the federation with any sort of plot. I think we just have to move on.'

'So why am I sitting in a ditch waiting for my car to be towed having been forced off the road by someone who's now sitting in Larmar's house?'

'Coincidence?'

'I don't think so and the player seemed convinced that something was going on. If I was a proper spy, I'd have a trusty pair of field glasses and I'd have bugged his house. As it stands, all I'll come back with is a raging face ache from the airbag.'

'Anyway, if you're ok, I'm going back to my list. Before my detour to the Balkans, I was about to start on Belgium.'

'As ever, your concern for my safety and wellbeing is touching. I'll call you tomorrow.'

It was an hour later and fully dark when an ancient breakdown van trundled into view with a driver who smelled like his evening pub session had been disturbed. He seemed to find Alec's predicament highly amusing and took great delight in telling him that he pulled some city dweller or other out of this ditch a couple of times a week. Five minutes later, the BMW was back on the tarmac and, after a brief inspection, the tow truck driver disappeared into the night £150 better off.

Rather than drive away immediately, Alec decided to wait around for a few minutes to see if the inconsiderate visitor would make the return journey. Sure enough, half an hour later, he was tucked into a dark layby when the car sped past again. He followed at a discreet distance dropping back further as they joined the lights of the A3. As they approached the junction with the M25 Alec decided he wasn't going to learn anything by continuing the tail. He closed up the gap, made a mental note of the make, model and registration plate of the car and pulled off to take the motorway home. He made a call to a typically taciturn Larmar as he went.

'Your dinner guest nearly killed me,' he said. 'Anything I should know about?'

'No.'

'So, just a coincidence that they arrived just minutes after I left.'

'I guess.'

'You're going to have to start learning how to talk if Meg is going to be convinced by your media work cover.'

'Yeh, ok. I gotta go.'

Simon Cauldwell listened carefully as Alec reported in the following day.

'Straws in the wind,' he concluded,' but at least we're starting to see which direction it's blowing from. Stick with it, Alec, but keep across the other countries as well. It's a bit early to be putting too many of our eggs into a Kosovan basket at this stage.'

'It would be handy though,' Alec continued. 'Kosovo are up against Belgium and Netherlands in their group so they're very unlikely to progress. None of their preliminary games are in Britain so their only chance to mount an attack here would be at the Opening Ceremony. If we knew that was the plan it would cut down the possibilities, wouldn't it?'

Cauldwell was noncommittal. 'As I say, stick with it and keep me posted.'

'That's going to be tricky in the next couple of weeks. My media work for the England squad is ramping up from here on, so I'm going to pulled in all directions. The players are all hoping to use the Euros as a career platform and some of them have got a lot of ground to make up.'

'I thought they were supposed to do their talking on the pitch.'

'That's part of the problem. The England camp have got themselves tied up in knots over this Black Lives Matter taking the knee thing the players are insisting on. Had we been in normal times, the fans would have had their say from the stands and it would have been quietly dropped. As it is, the only thing the FA can do is double down and try to persuade as many other teams as possible to join in. So, that's my first job. Then I've got to deal with the fallout from two players who sneaked out of England training to meet some girlsin the local pub and it's only going to get busier from here on.'

'Alec, do you ever wonder whether you're making a meaningful contribution to society?'

'Not really. I guess I'm lucky not to be troubled by existential doubts. Speak to you soon.'

Despite his claims to the contrary, the day's media rounds seemed more than usually contrived and, for the first time he could remember, Alec struggled to play the game. He knew that, given half a chance, the journalists would have been in the pub themselves, the journalists knew their faux outrage wasn't fooling anyone but pissed players sold papers. And at the end of the day, the England manager knew results were the only thing anyone would remember so he was going to choose the players he wanted whatever they might have done. It was all Alec could do to stop himself going full open kimono and saving everyone a lot of time. In the event, he used the time to think about Cauldwell and the threat they were trying to neutralise. At a suitable break in proceedings, he got alongside the FA's head of media, Chris Pendle, and asked whether he could have an impromptu tour of Wembley the next day.

'Why not, Alec? I hadn't got you down as a stadium fan though.'

'I'm not but I'm in the area and I've got an hour or so to fill. Thanks for helping me out.'

'No worries. Just make sure you bring your own hot beverage or be prepared for a coffee enema. The stuff in the office is filthy.'

Alec hadn't seen Kevin Mooney for a while so, to keep the player sweet, he called him with an invite.

'I guess I could come along if you think my eye for security would be helpful,' he said.

'Yes, well that and the fact that all my other clients are training or on sponsor duties ahead of the Euros and I thought you could use the company.'

'I can't deny I've got time on my hands,' Mooney admitted, 'but don't feel you have to be filling it up for me. I'm perfectly happy with a quiet game of golf, you know?'

'If I'm honest, I just need someone to bounce ideas off and we've always been quite good at that. We could get a couple of the others and make up a four ball at The Grove afterwards. How would that be? I'll pick you up around ten-thirty.'

Alec thought about calling Tyrone Pelforth but in the end settled for his oldest friend Mikey Reid and roped in Stevie Mac to make up the quartet. Both of them were Premier League footballers and Stevie, at least, had made Wembley almost his second home. In the car the following morning, he briefed them on his reasons for the tour and the four of them descended on a rather startled FA media staffer just before midday.

'I thought it was only going to be you, Alec,' said Chris Pendle, the organisation's head of media,' but you're all very welcome. It's always good to have some real footballers around the place even if you're unlikely to be playing here anytime soon, eh Kevin.'

'Very funny, yer wee gobshite, although I'd remind you that, with FA cup and Ireland friendlies, I've played here more than most, with the exception of Stevie here.'

'Where do we start, Chris?' Alec asked, keen to move the conversation on. 'I'm interested in the bits behind the scenes that regular punters don't even notice.'

'The official Stadium Tour takes in the dressing rooms, the players' tunnel, the royal box and the press room. Any interest?'

'What about the VIP areas and the hospitality? Could we start there?' Alec asked.

Pendle shrugged. 'Sure, that's just near our offices so you can put your head around the door. We're all fans, obviously, so the guys will be pleased to see you.'

The small party wandered through the offices shaking a few hands as they went, before emerging into the main banqueting hall and surrounding hospitality boxes.

'This is where all the VIPs and sponsors' guests will come during the Euros. It'll be a mini trade show with exhibition stands and a lot of networking going on. As part of our commitment to the local area we're also offering local businesses the chance to get in here and meet potential clients, for a premium on top of the price of a ticket of course.'

'Generous as ever,' Alec muttered, his journalistic cynicism coming to the surface.

'Is it the same security for fans and VIPs?' Kevin wanted to know.

'Same company, different team,' said Pendle. 'Different skillset. All the same, I wouldn't mind giving some of those promotional girls a pat down.'

Alec and his friends' attention was elsewhere and the joke fell flat. It wasn't until they came out into the stands that the tour really got into its stride.

'This view never fails to get to me, you know?' said Mikey. 'I've only played here once but it stays with you for ever. That pitch is like playing on carpet. What's the secret there?'

'That's down to the ground staff. Normally over the summer, we'd literally be letting the grass grow under our feet, but at the moment it's cut and rolled every day and watered on a volume-controlled system that keeps the level of moisture constant. The boys are walking around twenty miles a day, so they'll be glad you noticed.'

'Who's behind all the overlay,' asked Mooney, pointing to the screens, banners and wraps that turned the normal blank Wembley canvas into a recognisably UEFA venue.

'That's organised by a UEFA partner agency who have done all the Euro venues. Naturally, we're paying, but we have to use their contractors. Something to do with consistency, I think.'

And those big screens are new, aren't they?' Mooney pressed.

'Yes, they were only installed last week specially for the Euros,' said Pendle, proudly. 'They're twice the size of the old ones with a super-sharp display and yet they use a fraction of the energy. Just shows how much technology has moved on in a few years.'

'Who did the work?' asked Alec.

Pendle switched into PR mode. 'There are only a couple of manufacturers in the world capable of producing screens of this size and quality: one in South Dakota, USA and the other in China. The lead contractors were SE Consulting based in Moscow. Our procurement guys did the usual and persuaded them that the showcase of Wembley and the European Cup Finals would be a great platform to become the leading player in Europe. I guess their cold-war relationships with the Chinese also helped as they got us a killer deal on the cost of the project. I'll dig out the press release if you'd like more details.'

'That could be useful,' Alec confirmed. Where are the screens controlled from?'

Pendle was getting increasingly baffled by the turn the conversation was taking. 'Ermm, everything runs off the network which is powered by two RAID array industrial servers. They are mirrored by secure remote offsite backup providing complete redundancy and the whole thing is driven from our control room behind the media centre.'

'Very good, mate,' said Mikey. 'You know your stuff.'

'As I said, it was only last week, but thanks anyway. Look guys, I'm happy to keep answering your questions but what's your interest in all the hardware? We all know sport's about the sizzle.'

Alec had his answer ready. 'Sorry, I should have said. It's a bit hush, hush, but we've been asked my MI5 to assess the security of the venues staging the Euros.'

'Really?' said Pendle, astonished. 'They're trusting footballers with major event security now?'

'Nah,' you're right. Mikey's got a mate who's trying to drum up some business doing stadium fitouts, but it sounds like you're already well covered.'

They made their excuses and grabbed some lunch at the Grove before their 2.15 tee time.

'Nicely played, Alec,' said Kevin. 'But do you think we learned anything?'

'Hard to say. What did you think?'

'I was looking around and thinking to myself, a stadium would be the last place I'd be looking to plant a bomb.'

'I don't know, Kevin,' said Mikey. 'Lots of people in one place, TV cameras everywhere. It would make for a lot of publicity.'

'I know, but beyond that, they're a bastard, so they are. The ceilings are really high, and you've got nothing much that's going to burn or do any damage so you're really just looking at a bloody great bang unless you can pack a load of shrapnel or some other material around your explosives. I mean, you remember that Ariana Grande attack. The guy could barely walk with all the nails and what have you that he was carrying, and he only killed twenty-two people.'

Stevie Mac hadn't spoken throughout the tour, but he flinched visibly at the casual way Mooney talked about the Manchester bombing.

'That was twenty-two lives and young lives at that, so watch your mouth,' he said, his fiery temper at risk of boiling over. 'My niece was in the arena that night and she was traumatised for months, so it's not even just about who died.'

'Don't get me wrong, mate,' Kevin backpedalled, rapidly. 'It was horrific, but my point is, he just wandered in. At Wembley your bomber would have to get his big bag of nails past a secure perimeter. That's just not going to happen.'

The group was quiet, chewing over their lunch before Alec said, 'Mikey, you were the criminal mastermind when we were kids. How would you do it?'

'Obviously I wouldn't do it, would I? But I do think Kev's got a point. To get a bomb or even a weapon into Wembley you've got to be able to get past security and that's not easy. I know they look like rent a crowd in hi-vis jackets, but they do a job.'

'It didn't stop someone pulling it off at the Bernabéu, did it?'

'Yeh, but a lone-wolf gunman, Alec,' said the Irishman. 'That's always the worst security nightmare. The main thing they depend on is that the gunman wants to get out alive at the end, but this latest bunch are fucking crazy, so they are.'

'So, you all think there's no danger?'

'I'm not saying that, Alec. Just that it's not as easy as they make it look in the movies. Seems to me you've got to think about the stuff coming in and out of the stadium immediately before the game. I'd be starting with the catering deliveries, the bar, the merch, even the sponsors and what they're bringing in. Chris said it's like a mini exhibition so that's a lot of gear to bring in right there, and there's some pretty dodgy names on UEFA's official partners list.'

'What about…'

'Alec, enough,' said Stevie, who had calmed down but was now restless. 'Let's play golf.'

'Well said, mate,' said Mikey. 'Al, I hear you're missing a lot closer these days. Are you going to make a game of it or are you going to get your ass kicked as usual?'

They were lining up to tee off on the eighth, a 340-yard par four, when Mikey stopped and said: 'Remember when we used to bunk into Highbury?'

'Blimey, that takes me back. How old were we, around nine?'

'It was just before they moved to the Emirates so we must've been. It was always a toss-up between getting there early and spotting an unmanned turnstile or ducking in under the barrier with the surge of fans just before the game.'

'Yeh, the fans would shuffle along with us between their legs. Happy days, man and we saw some great games.'

Kevin had heard enough. 'I hate to break into your little dream world, but I promised the wife I'd be back by Tuesday, so can we just get on with the game.'

Mikey, though, was not to be put off. He might not have had much to offer at the stadium, but something had clicked in his head.

'It wasn't that hard to get into the ground and once we was inside nobody ever checked for tickets and stuff. The big games were the toughest 'cos it was hard to find a spare seat, but if it was like an early round of the FA cup we was basically like any other fan in the ground. We could've done what we liked.'

Alec was beginning to see where his friend was going.

'What are you thinking, Mikey?'

'I'm just thinking, what if we're looking at this the wrong way? I mean, how many seats are there at Wembley?'

'Dunno, what is it, eighty-eight, ninety thousand?

'Yeh, and they're playing at sixty percent capacity for the finals, right, so that's like thirty-five thousand spare seats.'

Kevin was catching on, quickly. 'So, you're thinking if some bastard did want to launch an attack on Wembley, all they've gotta do is jig into the ground before the security really gets going and lie low for a while.'

'Not even. There's loads of ways in if there's empty seats. You just find out what the tickets look like then get some printed up or you bribe a steward, or even just rush the stewards on the disabled entrances. There's no way they'll stop you and, when you're inside, you can basically do what you want. I mean how many people with weapons would it take to cause panic in a crowd that's already on the edge?'

Alec went quiet. It felt like their job of preventing a terrorist attack just got a whole lot harder.

Chapter 8

Alec couldn't help himself. He reacted instinctively as the two young footballers came through the door.

'Fuck me,' he said, facepalming in despair. 'Added together you two wouldn't make an idiot. I said dress smart and sober, not like you're going to the school fucking disco. We need the public to like you, not look at you like something they've picked off their shoe.'

'It's me only suit,' said one of the players, the one with the acne scars.

'Yeh, me too,' said the other, the braces on his teeth complimenting his wispy attempt at a hipster beard.

It was three weeks after the stadium tour, and Alec was reminded of Peter Crouch's two-word answer to the question of what he'd have been if he hadn't been a footballer. He asked himself in what other universe would these two have four Icelandic glamour models climbing through their hotel window. They were in a conference room in The Ned, an upmarket members club in heart of the City of London where the FA had booked a suite to entertain visiting football dignitaries for the duration of the Euros. Normally it would radiate old-school British charm but today it looked like a work experience day trip. Alec decided to take charge.

'Right, we've got forty minutes. Where's the nearest Marks and Sparks?'

'M&S?' said the adolescent with braces. 'That's where me nan gets her knickers.'

'Yeh,' said acne face, insightfully.

'That's official tailor to the England football team, Marks and Spencer.'

The players looked chastened. If there was one thing they'd had drummed into them it was never to diss the sponsors.

'Anyway, your nan's knickers are going to generate more sympathy than that shirt you're wearing, so let's go.'

Fortunately, it was only a short hop from Finsbury Square where the everyman retailer regularly helped debagged City boys drop £300 to persuade their employers they were sober enough to be at work. Alec steered his young charges away from racks where the trousers came with a belt, and they were back thirty minutes later doing a passable impression of apprentice accountants. They walked quickly into the lobby and through the expectant press pack who were still hoovering up coffee and croissants, and Alec gave them their final briefing.

'One thing to remember, this is just to clear the air ahead of the Euros. We're only doing it because we suspect some of the papers are holding back for a splash during the competition itself. You know your lines, right? You've learned your lesson and you're sorry for the mistake. You are now fully focused on your football, and if you're lucky enough to be selected you'll give the manager 110%.'

The lads stuck to the script so, from that perspective, the presser was a success, although Alec had his doubts. Gareth had insisted the only way he'd pick them was if they apologised in a public, so this was a tick in the box for him and his England leadership. What Alec didn't like was raking stuff up two days before the Championships when the story had moved on to something and someone else. Most of the media outlets had sent along their most junior journos but even they knew the score and avoided him as he tried to work the room. If he thought he might extract a few promises of support from this lot he was going to be disappointed. Fortunately, he was saved the bother by his phone. It was Simon Cauldwell.

'Can you talk privately?'

'Just give me a minute,' he said, waving the players off and finding an empty side room. 'Ok, what have we got?'

'We've got nothing, Alec, and that's making us all nervous. It's thirty hours and counting until the Opening Ceremony of an international event that's going to be televised around the world, and it's completely quiet. London is a cesspit of the mad, bad and sad and something like this would normally have them crawling out of the swamp. I should be looking at a range of threats, triaging them by risk and seriousness and getting teams deployed ready to act if required. If I told you that top of my list of hostiles was a possible unnamed and unidentified assassin for which there is absolutely zero evidence, then you can see what I mean.'

'Not even the militant wing of the Salvation Army?'

'Not even. So, either everyone suddenly lost interest in football, which seems unlikely, or someone's cleared the usual suspects out of the way, so they get an uninterrupted view.'

'Could anyone actually do that?'

'At this stage I don't know. What I do know is that it's too quiet, so I need you to go back round the houses. Contact everyone, call every player in every squad. If anyone in football knows anything, I don't want to hear about it after the event.'

'I'll do it, of course,' Alec agreed, 'but I wouldn't worry too much. My feeling is that tomorrow night just doesn't matter. There hasn't been a decent Opening Ceremony at any sporting event since London 2012. At the last Euros in France, the producer pulled off the impossible and made the Can-Can look like Riverdance. I mean, talk about putting the less into burlesque. The only reason they had an audience at all was because stadium security insisted fans took their seats an hour before the game and then wouldn't let them out. And there's not even a game on at Wembley tomorrow. The actual tournament opener is in Italy.'

Alec sounded relaxed but, in truth, he was nervous too. None of his players had come up with anything. Kush Larmar had gone completely off the radar, despite several attempts to contact him, and was now with the Kosovo team at their training camp in Prague. And with the way the group stage was looking, they almost certainly wouldn't even make it to England. Michaela had turned up plenty of dirt on the delegation members, but it was all greed not creed and nothing remotely likely to end in a terrorist attack. The lack of news meant the days were free for Alec to concentrate on getting his clients ready for the glare of international publicity, but the nights were a different matter. He wasn't sleeping well and found himself waking up with his heart racing and a deep sense of foreboding. He was beginning to think he wasn't cut out to be a spy.

He thought about going to the opening ceremony at Wembley Stadium but couldn't bear to put himself through another game of PC bingo: diversity – check, disability – check, sexuality – check, gender – check, youth – check, awkward post-colonial angst – house! What ever happened to Cool Britannia? He decided instead to call Michaela and suggest she came round to his to watch the event on TV.

'I thought you might like to cook,' he said, knowing she was unlikely to accept his standard offer of a Just Eat meal deal.

'Anything to avoid takeaway curry. I'll text you a shopping list.'

'Sounds good. I'll get the supplies before I pick you up. What sort of wine do you want?'

'Wine? I thought we were working.'

'You know me, always mixing it up. Anyway, if we have to do anything that looks remotely like work tonight it means someone's fucked up big style, so let's just hope for a very quiet evening.'

A glance through Michaela's shopping list told him everything he needed to know about the kind of evening they were going to spend. Best chicken in the shop, wild mushrooms, double cream. He was salivating just thinking about what she was going to turn them in to and the mundane process of navigating his local Waitrose took his mind off the reason they were getting together. Finding the 'best red burgundy in the shop (spend at least £25)' and a half bottle of sauternes took longer than anticipated, so he was a few minutes late to the station. As he approached, he saw her standing beside a small suitcase, looking like a wartime evacuee.

'I hope this means you're planning to stay a while,' he said, as he opened the boot for her luggage.

'It's great to see you, Alec. Let's leave it at that for now.'

Back at his house, Michaela was completely uninterested in watching the ceremony unfold, preferring to cook and leave him to it. The programme was a predictably tired buffet of overweight youngsters in garish costumes dancing flatfooted routines to Coldplay and Morrissey in front of a bored-looking audience. The camera crews had had plenty of practice filming in empty stadiums during the pandemic and kept their lenses trained tightly on the action, such as it was. But when the producer momentarily allowed them to pan back, it just confirmed Alec's theory that the Opening Ceremony didn't matter. Wembley was less than ten percent full and any attack would just tell the world that the terrorist masterminds behind it were as poor at choosing their targets as they were their ideology. Nevertheless, Alec was surprised how relieved he was when it was over and the release of tension together with a great smell from the kitchen meant he was more than ready to eat when the meal came.

'Do you remember the first time I brought you back here?' he asked, clearing away the empty plates and pouring another glass of wine.

'How could I forget? I made a judgement about you that evening and I'm sticking by it.'

'Thanks for telling me. Sometimes I'm not sure you still feel that way.'

'Well sometimes you don't make it easy, but I thought you were ok then and I still like you now.'

'I had no idea how that evening was going to go, you know?'

'And you think you know what's going to happen this evening, do you?'

He said nothing, just picked up the wine glasses and led her upstairs.

In the end, she stayed for a long and lazy week. The start of the Euros meant very little work for Alec although he did a daily scan of the newspapers for any coverage of dumb and dumber, his dynamic footballing duo. Mostly they used the time to rediscover the chemistry they'd felt on that first evening over a year before. Mornings were late, there were day trips and meals out, but the thing they both loved most were the evenings spent enjoying Michaela's cooking, a glass of wine and making love wherever and however the mood took them. Cauldwell couldn't have known, but it was during one of these intimate moments that he chose to make his call. The phone caused Alec to drop the bottle of massage oil he had just opened, and the loved-up pair were helpless with laughter as he tried to speak.

'Sounds like I'm interrupting something,' said the spook.

'You are,' said Alec, wiping tears from his eyes and massage oil from Michaela's lower back.

'Well, err, sorry I guess, but you need to hear this. We've just had more information about an attack on British soil, and this time it's a clear and credible threat.'

Alec sobered up rapidly, putting the phone on speaker so that Michaela could get the information first-hand. 'What do we know?' he asked.

'Not a great deal except that our contact in the French D.R.S.D. says that a terrorist group from Chechnya has just appeared in Brussels. They are planning an attack and London is the target.'

'Chechnya? That's bloody miles, isn't it?'

'About 2,500 miles which might explain why we've heard nothing for the past few weeks. They came through Ukraine where they switched to fake European passports, probably Greek, to get into Poland. From there they would have entered Germany then on to Belgium. They made contact with an Islamist cell in Molenbeek, Brussels. The Belgians missed them, of course, but the French had infiltrated the cell and were tipped off. Apparently, they're now in France and planning to cross the channel imminently.'

'So, we're assuming Islamist terrorism?' Michaela confirmed. 'I thought Chechens were only fighting to get the Russians out of their country.'

'It's not certain they're Chechens but you're right to say it's probably an Islamist group. After the Chechen wars of the 90s and early 2000s the main groups of fighters joined up to form the Caucasus Emirate. Their intention was to create a northern outpost of ISIS's Muslim Caliphate but the religious project soon followed the same descent into corruption and chaos that we saw in Syria and Iraq. The difference is that whereas other Muslim countries have limitless supplies of hydrocarbons to prop up their economies, Chechnya is a basket case and relies on the support of wealthy backers in the Middle East.'

'So, we're looking at a cash-strapped regime supplying rent-a-rebel mercenaries to please their crazy paymasters.' Alec summarised.

'Either that or they train foreign revolutionaries, and you can add that they are also very well equipped with ready access to Soviet era weapons and explosives. Assuming these are Chechens, their favourite tactic is to pass themselves off as Russians putting the blame on Putin's regime and giving their sponsors complete deniability, which might explain the Russian sniper rifle recovered in Madrid.'

'Any idea who the sponsors could be?' Michaela asked.

'The biggest backers of Islamist terror are Iran, Saudi and Qatar. Take your pick.'

'Why Greek passports?' Alec asked, not really interested in the answer but giving himself time to think.

'It's just supply and demand. Greece is the most common European landing point for migrants and there's a huge demand for documents so they're the easiest to buy on the black market.'

'How many groups of men drive through the channel ports on Greek passports? You could surely stop them all and check.'

'We're checking, of course, but there are too many assumptions to be sure we've closed things off safely,' said Cauldwell. 'They've probably switched documents by now anyway. The Molenbeek cell supplied them with five blank German passports which they're likely to be using, and that's about all we know. They have gone to great lengths not to be identified, travelling completely off grid for almost two weeks. In Brussels, the two groups never actually met; the passports order was made earlier by phone from Chechnya which is our main reason for thinking that's where they're from. No news for weeks, then another call two nights ago. The caller spoke English and said they'd find payment in a plastic carrier bag by a litterbin on a quiet side street where they had to leave the passports in exchange. Our French source says they were told they would be killed if the passports were not delivered or there was any attempt to double cross or follow their customer. They just picked up the money, checked it, dropped the passports and didn't look back. That was two nights ago, and now they've dropped out of sight again.

'So, we're back to chasing shadows,' Alec said. 'No contacts, no credit cards, no phones. What about the vehicles?'

'The Poles are going through CCTV from the border crossing with Ukraine and we're trying to see if there is a match with anything picked up in Brussels this week, but they're being so cautious I'd be amazed if they hadn't changed plates at least once since then.'

'Remind me why we think they're targeting the Euros,' said Michaela.

'That came from the original intercepts mentioning a group mobilised and preparing for a spectacular attack on the Euros in London. Since the initial chatter we picked up several weeks ago, the airwaves have been quiet. There's the usual background stuff but nothing more until this week when we eavesdropped on several more exchanges mentioning the same thing. They were discreet but clear, nonetheless. The Americans also picked up the messages and were sufficiently concerned to warn us themselves.'

Alec took a moment to think. 'You said this group was about to cross the Channel so the attack could be any day. I mean, we've already got games going on in Wembley Stadium. Any one of them could be the target.'

'I'd be interested in your thoughts,' said Cauldwell, the first time he'd ever acknowledged Alec and Michaela might have something to offer. 'We think we might have some time. So far, all the evidence points to a highly trained and well-disciplined group. They are more likely to be motivated by money, and a lot of it, than by martyrdom. That means the target has to be highly visible. Alec, you'll know better than me the difference in profile between, say, a last-16 game and the final itself, but I'm sure it's significant.'

'Depending on which teams are fighting it out for the top honours, the TV audience for the final could be around five hundred million across Europe. The knockout games will all generate a huge audience but it would be a quarter of that or less, so I'd agree we're likely to be looking at the finals.' He thought for a moment, then said, 'Hold on, they're not for over three weeks and yet the attackers are already as good as here. Why?'

'That's what we've been asking ourselves, and this is where we get to good news and bad news. Paradoxically, a long and well-planned operation makes the final attack easier to prevent. Unlike say, a random suicide bomber operating alone, this is an attack planned for a specific date and time, so all we have to do is find out where and when.'

'If that's your definition of good news the bad news must be horrendous.'

'The bad news is that there is a plan and, so far, it seems to be working. Whatever setbacks the terrorists may have experienced, they are here in Western Europe, and we must assume they are confident they will make it to England. If we are correct, they are going to attack a venue that, on the night, is going to be the most watched in Europe if not the world. The security net will be complete and there will be cameras everywhere. And yet, on paper, their plan stands a good enough chance of success that someone was persuaded to pay over a large amount of money to back it.'

'If they are so confident in their plan, why the paranoia over being identified?' Michaela asked.

Alec agreed. 'They've gone to all that trouble, and we still know they're coming so that's got to be a big setback, right?'

'Maybe, although it could just be to make sure they got safely through the border checkpoints and across the Channel. But rewind a step, Alec, to your first question, "why are they already as good as here?" We think that's the key to the kind of operation they're planning.

'Maybe they allowed for their schedule to be blown off course,' said Alec, feeling under pressure to answer his own question. 'After all, no one's going to rerun the finals if they're late.'

'Certainly, building in extra time to cover delays would make sense, but no one gets themselves into position three weeks ahead of time without a good reason. The longer they're here, the more likely it is that they will be discovered. No, my guess is that they are either keeping their heads down in the Calais Jungle refugee camp, or the operation, or at least their part in it, will be carried out in the next few days leaving them free to leave the country or whatever the exit route is.'

'Ok, so what do we do now?'

'We've increased the alert level at the ports checking for Greek and German passports although you can imagine how many of those come across the Channel every day. We're upping the security around Wembley Stadium and at the training camps and team hotels including in the air. UEFA has a clause in its contracts which obliges hosts to stop planes or drones flying over games. It's supposed to prevent unauthorised video footage and ordinarily, we wouldn't give a toss, but at the moment it's a useful smokescreen for the police helicopters that you'll see on permanent patrol. That and the two RAF Typhoons on combat alert when games are on. We're relooking at the in-stadium personnel and redoing the vetting of all casual security staff, bar and catering staff and volunteers. We've asked all registered media and sponsorship agencies to reapply with biometric IDs and those will be built into newly designed lanyard accreditation for the finals. They won't be anything like what's been used before, so anyone trying to get past security without authorisation will stick out a mile. Lastly, we're investigating conduits of Iranian, Qatari and Saudi cash to see if we can get a fix on the money trail. I know that feels like locking the stable door, but there may be a tiny window of opportunity if our terrorists contact their backers to confirm final orders.

'So that's what *we* are doing. You, on the other hand, need to get back out there and start pulling in favours from your football contacts. We know this is happening, we know where and we have a pretty good idea when. My one worry is the black swan: the event we haven't thought about which seems obvious afterwards but beats our security cordon. We need everything, no matter how odd or implausible it sounds and, much as I hate to say it, we're relying on you.'

Chapter 9

The mood had changed completely as Alec ended the call, and he felt more under pressure than ever. Much as he genuinely wanted to respond, Cauldwell's call to arms left him with a problem. This was mid-June during one of the biggest football tournaments in the world and that meant one thing; there were no footballers within a hundred miles of their clubs. Those European players not locked down with their national teams had removed themselves as far as possible away from the ignominy of being left out. They were on well-earned holidays in five-star destinations around the world. Although he didn't want to admit it, there was no one left around that Alec could think of who would be remotely useful.

'It's not for want of trying,' he complained to Michaela, 'but Cauldwell's just not listening.'

'Try and look at it a different way; maybe it removes the distraction of the players. I mean, they haven't been too helpful so far. You looked at the stadium with a bunch of footballers too and what did they come up with?'

'Our main thought was that a stadium would be low down on our list of targets if we were looking to get the world's attention. They're hard to get into unless you've got authorisation, they are searched thoroughly before every game, and even if you could smuggle in some explosives, we couldn't see how anyone could do much more than make a lot of noise and smoke. We've looked at the possibility a group could rush the gates on the day but that doesn't' fit at all with what we know about the terrorists. The only way to bring in a package of any size would be to pose as a sponsor, a caterer, official supplier, maintenance or security.'

'Ok, there you go. That gives us a good few leads to follow up. And I wouldn't be so quick to dismiss the damage that even a small amount of explosive could do either. Imagine something going off in the changing rooms or the media area and there's got to be a VIP hospitality area that's going to be full of high-profile guests for the final.'

'You said 'us'.'

She groaned. 'I knew you'd pick up on that. Let's just say I'm happy to stick around, if you still want me.'

'I always want you,' he said, reminded of what they had been about to do when his phone went off. 'Now, where were we?'

There were four matches to be staged at Wembley before the final and as each one came and went, the tournament felt like an increasingly high stakes game of Russian roulette. Having got this far, Alec felt certain the finals would be the ultimate target but, with the passing of each game came, it felt like an extra round had been loaded into the chamber and he knew their luck was quickly running out.

He started with Chris Pendle at the FA but hadn't got halfway into the conversation before Pendle asked the obvious question.

'Alec, you'll understand us being a bit busy at the moment, so if this is a fishing trip for your mate's new business, than it's going to need to wait until after the Euros are over.'

'I wish it was, mate, but this is deadly serious.' Alec kept the details simple if not strictly accurate. 'What I told you before was actually the truth; I have been hired by MI5 to bring a footballer's perspective to Euro security. We have intelligence of a credible threat to the finals and evidence that a terror cell is preparing as we speak to launch an attack on

Wembley on that evening or before. There is a large team of professionals covering all the obvious angles. My job is to use my knowledge of the game to identify any gaps or things we might have missed.'

He didn't give Pendle the chance to ask any questions but pressed his advantage. 'Can you give me a list of all suppliers working for you, for the media, for the sponsors and any catering concessions?'

'Err, not sure how I'd do that, even assuming you're entitled to ask. What sort of attack are we talking about?'

'We don't know exactly, but we do know who, where and when so the net is closing. We just need enough information to be able to stop them before it goes any further.'

'I suppose I can get our suppliers from accounts, and we should have had accreditation requests in from most of the others on your list. I can't guarantee it's complete though.'

'You're a star, mate. That would be a great head start. I'll ping my email to your phone, and it goes without saying, if you see or hear anything suspicious, just call.'

Despite Pendle's assurances, Alec was still surprised when the information he'd asked for appeared. He split the list of possibilities with Michaela to get through the desk research more quickly. He took sponsors and caterers while she worked through security, maintenance and official suppliers. The list of sponsors looked daunting but proved relatively easy. UEFA has eight top-tier partners but that represents the tip of a moderately-sized iceberg of tournament-specific sponsors, official partners and suppliers. Add in the hosts' local partners and those of each participating team and the list looks enormous. However, most hadn't made the extra investment to buy any real presence at the finals, and those that had were limited to logo boards, perimeter advertising and the all-important hospitality tickets. Their staff and guests would all have a bag check and go through a body scanner, so Alec felt reasonably happy to dismiss any concerns on that score. For sponsors with the option to bring in an exhibition stand they had to go through the official stand builders, SpExS, who were also responsible for delivering marketing materials. Alec assumed the top-tier sponsors were all intending to run experiential promotions and spent a couple of hours persuading their activation agencies to reveal their plans. He found they were much more cooperative if he said he was a journalist than if he claimed to be calling from MI5, but either way, he had a comprehensive list by the time he had finished.

Alipay, a Chinese digital wallet, was promising to load up a free drinks voucher for fans who downloaded its app; Booking.com was branding all the hospitality areas; and Volkswagen was using an on-ticket code to generate enquiries and test drives for its dealerships. Hisense, another Chinese tech company, had planned to install TVs carrying exclusive content in the VIP area and, for reasons only known to them, the toilets, but had opted in the end for branding around the existing screens. The only partner that presented any kind of challenge was Fedex. The international courier was going to drive one of their vans onto the pitch at the top of the show to deliver the Henri Delaunay trophy to the podium, presumably only if there was someone in to sign for it. Socar, the State Oil Company of Azerbaijan was the only sponsor which didn't have an agency. No one he spoke to had any idea what they were planning or, indeed, why they were sponsoring at all. Alec wanted more but contented himself with the thought that tankers full of gasoline or crude oil would be easy to spot. He sent a quick note to Simon Cauldwell recommending they put in place a routine inspection of SpExS and give the Fedex van a thorough going over. Then he moved on.

Catering was even easier than sponsorship since just one company, an American food service giant, held an exclusive contract for all the Stadium's hospitality, restaurants, kiosks and bars. The firm's UK operations were based within Wembley itself and Alec made a note to pay a visit to the unit's MD next time he was there. He got up from his desk feeling like he'd made progress, but one glance at Michaela's face told him she didn't share his confidence.

'What's the problem? I thought you'd be finished before me,' he said, helpfully.

'My list was about 1200 entries long, and even ignoring all those who haven't done any work for the past year, it's still over 700 companies. Half of them never come on site so I feel like I'm wasting my time. There's got to be a better way.'

'You're right. Only the ones who have stadium access are relevant and that includes couriers who won't even be on the list of suppliers because someone else has sent them.'

'Maybe they've got a visitor log showing who has entered the stadium in the last few weeks. If we could get access to that then we can start to build up a picture of the firms regularly on site.'

'Great idea. I'll call Chris Pendle again.'

The conversation was short and awkward.

'I've been told in no uncertain terms that I shouldn't have given you that supplier list, Alec. Apparently, I've breached data protection and GDPR and God knows what, so don't ask me for anything else. You'll have to get the visitor log from our head of security, Rutger Palme. If he'll give you it.'

Alec hung up and called back through the switchboard asking to be put through to security. When the call found its way to the right desk, Palme was polite but firm. No, they couldn't have a copy of the visitor log; no, they couldn't come to the stadium and expect to see it; but if Alec could leave his name and credentials, Palme would have someone call him back if they could be more helpful. Alec ended the call certain that he would never hear any more but Palme was the model of cooperation when he called half an hour later.

'I have been told I should give you every assistance,' came German-accented voice. 'Perhaps you would like to visit us?'

'That would be very helpful Mr. Palme. We could be with you in a little over an hour if that's ok with you.'

'This will not be possible. We have entered our highest security protocol ahead of the game on Tuesday, so no one goes in or out unless they are pre-cleared. I understand you have quite a unique clearance, Mr. Munday, but my responsibility is to the teams, our fans and guests. After the game it will take us all day on Wednesday to stand our systems down so I will be ready to welcome you next Thursday.'

Alec was reasonably sanguine at the prospect of not gaining immediate access. The final was where the action would be taking place, so anything before that would be an information trip at the most.

'It's your decision, but please take all possible precautions for the game. The threat we are facing is not an idle one.'

With their access to Wembley blocked and no other leads to chase up, Alec and Michaela were back on holiday although the carefree spirit of a few days ago was gone. Their frustration at not being able to do anything was compounded by the knowledge that the clock was ticking. Alec was grateful for the distraction when his phone buzzed and a message came through which was about to take their mission in a very different direction.

Chapter 10

'Hey, Mikey wants us to join him in La Manga. Do you fancy a few days in Spain?'

A week with Chenille, Mikey's wife, was not Michaela's idea of a holiday, but neither was the alternative. 'Ok, I guess,' she said. 'What's there for us to do?'

Alec suspected Mikey's main motivation was to have someone to split the bills with, but he didn't fancy kicking around a half-empty London either. 'Good food, a few rounds of golf, a bit of r'n'r and wall-to-wall sunshine. What's not to like?'

La Manga, a British enclave on Spain's south-eastern coast, was once a bit of a cliché in the football world. It was built as a golf resort in the 70s but gained notoriety as a warm-weather training camp as the money poured into football twenty years later. It was the colourful backdrop to many an extramarital scandal and an accident waiting to happen for a certain type of player for whom money and celebrity weren't quite enough. The rollcall of shame includes many a household name from the back in the day, but now the footballers tended to be long past their prime. Visitors attracted to the resort's tennis courts and pools are more likely to encounter a Match of the Day pundit walking his dog than any of the Premier League's current cohort. Nevertheless, there were a few old faces, like ghosts at their own wake, as Alec and Michaela strolled into the Piano Bar at La Manga Club a few hours later. Mikey was at the centre of the action with his brother and agent Billy. It seemed like they'd been there for a while.

'Here he is lads, the international man of mystery,' he yelled across the room.

Alec waited until they had reached the table before replying. 'Evening, Mikey. Had a few sherbets, have we?'

He took a drinks order and strolled to the bar to set up a tab. Mikey's voice rang out again.

'No, I'm serious,' he slurred. 'This is the man with the golden knob. He is literally the spy who shagged her,' he said, gesticulating crudely at Michaela.

Alec observed the awkward laughter and judged that the party was fizzling out rather than just getting started.

'Alright, Mikey,' said one of the old timers. 'You're starting to embarrass yourself.'

'Is that right, Yawn Connery? Who are you, Doctor fuckin' No?

'That's us done, Mikey,' said another one of the group, getting up to leave. 'We're away to our beds.'

Mikey protested as the numbers dwindled but soon it was just family. Chenille turned to Michaela and asked, 'Have you guys eaten? The club sandwiches here are legend but we'll have to ask Mateo if he'll go in the kitchen and make some.'

She grabbed Michaela's arm and dragged her off to reception leaving the lads on their own.

'How's the golf going to be tomorrow?' Alec asked.

'Don't you worry about me; I'm fine. So, grab yourself another pint of whipass 'cos I've got something to tell you.'

Alec gestured to the barman and his friend lowered his voice to a conspiratorial holler.

'Right, you're gonna love this and, I'm telling you, it's going to help your career on Her Majesty's Secret Service no end.'

Alec had grown up on the same London council estate as Mikey and the two of them had run as a pack with Tyrone Pelforth. The likelihood of all three of them making it into the professional game was vanishingly small, but that's what had happened. Despite the bond between them, there were times when the footballer could really try his patience.

'Come on, Mikey. Does this story have a point?'

'That it does, my thunder balling friend; a point that will scare the living daylights out of you. Fuck, I am on fire tonight.'

He paused, but Alec wasn't laughing.

'Listen,' he said, theatrically, keen to keep up his banter. 'I know the identity of the criminal mastermind you're chasing: your Le Chiffre, your Lex Luthor.'

'Wasn't he in Superman?'

'Yeh, whatever. Are you even listening? I know the person behind the plot.'

'Are you serious, Mikey?'

'Yeh. Why d'you think I brought you out here?'

'Go on,' Alec said, bracing himself for the inevitable punchline. It didn't come. Instead, Mikey launched into his tale.

'You know I was in Doha last week, yeh? Billy reckoned he could get me two hundred thousand a week playing in the Qatar Stars League so, you know, I'm interested. I said, *'just set it up and tell me where to sign'* but he said, *'it doesn't work like that'*. So, it turns out we have to go down there and look into the whites of their eyes. Anyway, a couple of days later we're sitting outside an office on the 41st floor of this fuckoff skyscraper which is like football city in Qatar. We're waiting to see the President of Al-Gharafa, their number two club, when who should come out of the office but Ashley Cole. I know! Now me and Cashly go way back, as you know, so we're like giving dap and catching up and stuff and there's this little fellow in a dish-dash just standing there. I'm ignoring him and, in the end, he just turns around and stomps off into his office. I look at Cash who's pissing himself laughing and it turns out this is only Walid Al Kubaisi, the President of the Club. Right now I'm waving goodbye to my gig, so I send Billy in to go and patch things up while I see Cash on his way. Billy comes out of the office and says I've got to be all apologetic and I'm like, *'I'll suck his fuckin' dick for two hundred g's a week'*. So, we go in and I start to apologise, saying I didn't recognise him. But he just launches into this big rant about how the British never show Qatar any respect, we're just taking their money and we think they're idiots. I'm thinking, *'you've got a point mate, to be fair.'* I stand there letting him get it out of his system, but he just gets more and more chapped, you know?'

At this point Mikey slowed down, as if he was quoting. 'In the end he says, we will be sorry, we will reap the holy shamal, we will pay with the blood of our footballers and that our downfall will be spectacular.'

'Fucking hell. You're sure that's what he said?'

'Exact words, mate. Billy wrote it down as soon as we got out. Apparently, the shamal is like a like a local wind that makes a violent sandstorm. See, I knew you'd be interested, man.'

'Who is this guy? I thought all the top Qataris were members of the Al Thani royal family.'

It was Billy's turn to take over the story. 'Walid Al Kubaisi; Squalid Walid we called him. Anyway, I did a bit of digging when I was trying to set the deal up for Mikey. He's Club President but the chairman is an Al Thani, Sheikh Abdullah Bin Saud. There's hundreds of them, but from what I could work out this guy is the main rival to the Emir. They're all loaded, but he's supposed to be richer than all of them apart from the Emir, obviously. But get this; he's the black sheep of the family. Seems he's also got an appetite for getting people done over. I asked a local football reporter who said he's never mentioned in the press and any journalists that go sniffing around tend to disappear. I found a few references to Walid online but no business connections or anything to link him to money. So, I'm guessing he's the front man bankrolled by the Sheikh.'

Alec took a gulp of his beer and said, 'This is gold, man. It's exactly the kind of connection we've been looking for. Can you just run me through the names again? I need to take some notes.'

Back in their apartment, Alec relayed the conversation to Michaela and between them they called Simon Cauldwell, excited to be sharing some live intelligence at last. Cauldwell took down all the details they had, asked a couple of supplementary questions that they couldn't answer, and ended the call promising a response by the following morning. Alec and Michaela were too pumped to sleep so poured themselves a large drink and spent a noisy and enthusiastic hour making love before fatigue finally got the better of them.

The following morning was Sunday, a long lazy day in Spain, but the first day of the working week in the Middle East. Michaela was up early so had chance to see Cauldwell's email, cc'd to Nigel Rushbourne, before Alec woke up. She brewed some coffee and sat in the sun on their balcony to consider its contents on her own. According to the message, Sheikh Abdullah (SA), half-brother of the ruling Emir, was indeed a fierce rival but, in typical Emirati style, also a useful ally. They were both sons of the previous Emir, but by different mothers. Abdullah could trace his lineage jointly to the Qatari Royal Family and the House of Saud giving him access at the highest level in both countries. This has proved extremely useful at a time when official diplomatic relations between Qatar and Saudi Arabia are buried deep under several layers of permafrost. Cauldwell went on:

SA has carved out a role as unofficial go-between, able to oil the wheels without either side losing face. He always makes sure he is richly rewarded taking a cut of up to 15%

of value when trade blockades needed circumventing and, with a looming World Cup, that is an increasingly frequent occurrence. Thus, despite having only a modest (by Qatari standards) royal stipend, he is believed to have amassed a fortune that puts Jeff Bezos in the shade.

Michaela scrolled through the briefing looking for something to capture her interest. She soon found it as Cauldwell went on:

SA is as close to a ghost as it is possible for a member of the Royal Family to be. He is never seen in public and seems to have no time for the haunts and trappings normally associated with the super-rich. He travels in Qatar surrounded by a convoy of armed guards and when he goes abroad it's by private jet accompanied by his own handpicked militia. Despite there being no effective tax in Qatar, he has gone to great lengths to make his wealth invisible, hiding all evidence behind a carefully constructed firewall of anonymous funds, offshore bank accounts and shell companies. Such is the labyrinthine nature of the protection, that no international agency has got close to discovering either the source or amount of the money involved. One recent coordinated attempt to crack open his finances reported that "the structure involved is deliberately and calculatedly opaque" which, in the experience of the service that carried out the surveillance, was an indication that funds have likely been obtained through illegitimate means. Numerous attempts have been made by security services around the world to get closer to SA. All unsuccessful.

A few years ago, in her former life as Detective Inspector with the City of London Police Michaela would have been only too pleased to investigate an opaque financial structure. Now she would struggle to call in any favours with her ex-colleagues. Surely, Cauldwell would be able to open up a portal into this shadowy world, assuming he was interested in the finances of the shady Sheikh. She read on, half wondering why, on a Saturday night/Sunday morning he had spent a good hour researching the information and composing the note. As she scrolled down to the next paragraph on her phone, the answer was crystal clear.

SA is tolerated by the regime in Doha because they value him as a deniable asset. There is also a strong suspicion that they use him as the conduit through which to support violent extremism in their proxy battle with the Saudis. As with all his dealings, almost no hard evidence has ever been found to confirm the suspicions, but rumours persist. This lead, the connection through Al Kubaisi and the link to a terror attack on the Euros may feel like a leap of faith, but they are the most substantive and up-to-date connections to be made. If SA is behind the attack, as this intelligence suggests is possible, it will be well funded and those carrying it out will know that the price of failure will be paid with their lives. He needs to be stopped and this is a rare chance to do it.

SA's one weakness is a love of football, although this would not show up in the ownership registry of any clubs around the world. As well as the Al-Gharafa club, he is linked with a number of second-tier sides: Saint Etienne in France, Eintracht Frankfurt in Germany, Udinese in Italy and Sevilla in Spain. He invests through a Panamanian shell company, Peninsula Pearl Holdings and Al Kubaisi has a seat on the board of each one (a condition of any investment). SA himself is never seen. The obvious gap in his portfolio is a Premier League club and it is here we think you may be useful.

We have identified Southampton FC as a possible target club and would like you to use the pretext of brokering a deal for a stake to lure SA to a meeting. They will do basic due diligence in advance, so you'll need to be well briefed on the background. I will send that separately but, to summarise, the club is currently 80% Chinese owned, although the family concerned have made it known that they want to sell. The other shareholder is Anastasia Schlaffenhoff, daughter of a Swiss magnate. She inherited the club from her father. There was a valuation in 2020 of £260m but the fallout from Covid-19 means it's effectively a distressed asset, so you can hint that there's a deal to be done.

We have intelligence that SA is in Doha and you can make contact through Al Kubaisi. The Swiss miss (as fans call her) is practically a recluse so Dagg, you'll be posing as her. Alec will go in as himself, but bear in mind it's only a cover to get as far as a meeting. Will brief you further when there's confirmation that they'll agree to meet. Get weaving.

Maybe it was Cauldwell's casual assumption that they would drop everything and run for the next plane, but Michaela didn't react well. She clicked delete on the message then thought better of it and restored it from her junk. She read it again and was left with more questions than answers. Assuming they could even get a meeting with the Sheikh, what would they do then? Appeal to his better nature and ask him to call off the attack? Confronting him was a sure-fire way to make sure they never saw the light of day again and, as deniable agents, no one would even come looking.

Alec could see the look on her face as he came through the sliding doors onto the balcony.

'Let me guess,' he said. 'Cauldwell wants us in Qatar.'

'What does he think we're going to be able to do? This guy is seriously bad news.'

'Worth thinking about, though, isn't it? And it beats going through suppliers to Wembley Stadium.'

She sighed and shook her head. 'Alec, I know you've managed to talk your way out of a couple of scrapes in the past, but you can't just assume to stay lucky. Sheikh Abdullah won't think twice about having you killed and there's no cavalry going to ride to the rescue either. The last time I went into enemy territory, I left two men behind and I don't want the same to happen to you.'

'Let's try and get hold of Al Kubaisi anyway and see if there's any chance of a meeting.'

'You're not listening to me, Alec. I have a really bad feeling about this.'

'I told you that we can't let fear stop us moving forward and I think this is one of those moments. Beneath all the military-style bravado, Cauldwell sounded genuinely desperate on the phone the other day. I think they're out of options, otherwise they wouldn't be asking us to do it.'

'Do what, though? Is there any sort of plan for what's going to happen once we're in that room?'

Alec poured some coffee and thought for a few seconds. 'There'll be some techie thing he'll want us to do,' he said, 'like plant a bug in the room or hack into his computer. If we can get in there and keep the meeting going long enough, I'm sure we'll get a chance. I'm due on the first tee with Mikey in half an hour. Can you use your best schoolgirl Arabic and see if you can't get a meeting set up while I'm gone?'

'I don't know what the schoolgirls were doing in your day, but I had an Arabic lover.'

'Ah, yes. I'd forgotten your favourite way of learning a language. Maybe the call will bring back happy memories.'

She still looked dubious but said she'd do what she could. Mikey looked very second hand, but was ten strokes ahead before they started the back nine.

'I don't know how you do it,' Alec said. 'I thought I'd be in with a chance of beating you today.'

'I'd have to be feeling a lot worse than this to lose to you, Al. I don't know about *Moonraker*, you're more like ball slicer.'

'Don't start with the James Bond cracks again. Anyway, it's more like *To Qatar with Love*. They want us to go out and follow up that lead of yours. Do you fancy tagging along? You can show us around.'

'No chance, mate. After last time I'm right off the idea of seeing out my days in the desert. Squalid Walid was a real piece of work though, and his boss sounds worse. You guys sure you're gonna be ok? You do know you're not an actual spy, don't you?'

Chapter 11

The happiest part of the trip turned out to be the time spent buying appropriate business wear from the boutique shops at Madrid airport. After that and seven hours overnight in the luxury of the upper deck of a Qatar Airways flight, things went markedly downhill. For locals, June in Doha counts as winter, one of the seven months of the year when they venture outside only briefly, if at all. Looking through the smoked glass of the airport, there was no way to tell the outside temperature, but the sun was already high in the sky despite it still being early morning. Their limousine met them in the airconditioned carpark and eased into the line of traffic streaming towards the city's thrusting skyline. Apart from the occasional construction worker, they saw no one on the streets as they inched along the Corniche, Doha's shoreline boulevard. Despite the rush hour congestion of a Tuesday morning, there was still over an hour to go until their meeting when the driver pulled up at the base of the tallest building in the downtown business district. Alec squinted against the sunlight as he gazed up at the twisted architecture of the Al Bidda Tower. Three hundred feet up one side, window cleaners suspended in a cradle toiled in an endless quest to keep the glass sparkling. Opening the car door and stepping onto the street was like entering a furnace and they were both breathless and sweating by the time they had crossed the thirty metres to the entrance. The gleaming glass and steel structure looked like the ultimate corporate headquarters, but inside the lobby and reception were dingy and tired looking. The building was home to the Supreme Committee, the vast administration tasked with the organisation and oversight of Qatar's World Cup.

Alec and Michaela's arrival coincided with the start of the day for dozens of expat workers of all nationalities. They filled the lobby as they queued for the elevator which would haul them up to their respective berths inside the giant organisation. Rather than join them, the visitors took installed themselves in a mezzanine coffee bar to watch and wait. The queue moved slowly but no one seemed in a tearing hurry to start work. Occasionally, a local in white robes would approach a separate lift where there was no queue and no waiting time. This was dedicated to serving the top five floors of the tower where the executive offices were. By the time they finished their second coffee the queue had all but disappeared. From their vantage point they watched as a white Escalade pulled up outside. Two passengers emerged, large men in dark suits and sunglasses, their wrists chained to mid-sized suitcases. They walked across the lobby and disappeared into the executive elevators. Ten minutes later they reappeared, now without their luggage and the Escalade drove them away. Fifteen minutes elapsed then another car pulled up, this time a white Mercedes. Another two passengers emerged: one large and dark suited, the other small and furtive. Alec sat up as he recognised one of the most famous faces in football: the President of FIFA known to all as the Old Man. They too walked across the lobby and into the executive lifts and ten minutes later they reappeared, this time with the large man carrying identical suitcases to those delivered earlier. Seconds later they were loaded into the Mercedes which pulled away.

'What just happened?' asked Alec.

'Without knowing what's in the cases it's hard to tell. But I'd say someone just picked up his dowry.'

'Wow, this place.' Alec breathed, shaking his head.

After waiting the full hour, and another thirty minutes for good measure, Alec and Michaela were directed to the executive lift themselves. With no stops, it took just twenty seconds to reach the 41st floor, but there was no welcoming committee waiting for them when the doors opened. Their ears popped as they stepped out into a completely empty lobby and walked down a corridor lined on both sides by glass-walled offices, all unoccupied. The corridor turned sharply left past more vacant cubicles until it reached a reception desk which stood unmanned under the unblinking gaze of a security camera. They approached and waited, looking at each other with raised eyebrows. After five minutes a young man, traditionally dressed, appeared from an inner office and asked for their business cards. He slowly scrutinised each one in turn, holding it between the index finger and thumb of both hands. Whether they passed the test or not was unclear as he asked them to wait and took the cards with him back through into the office. It was ten minutes before he reappeared.

'Mr. Al Kubaisi will not be coming to the office today. He asks you to return tomorrow.'

'That's it?' said Alec, incredulous. 'We fly from Europe for a meeting, and he just doesn't turn up.'

The minion looked sheepish, although there was no apology. 'He is a very busy man, but I'm sure he will be ready to welcome you tomorrow.'

Michaela stepped in and asked in Arabic whether it was possible to meet him later in the day or somewhere else in Doha. The response was longer and appeared more friendly, but the answer was still the same: a polite but firm request to return the following day. Alec put down the new £400 Mont Blanc document wallet inside which nestled the sales presentation the two of them had been working on throughout the previous day. He clenched his fists, dragged a breath in through his teeth and turned on the receptionist. Michaela grabbed his accusing finger before he had the chance to raise it and calmly pulled him to one side.

'Leave it,' she hissed. 'Suck it up and save it for the boss.'

He held his breath until they were in the lift and then exploded.

'Have I fucking missed something? So much for Arabic hospitality. What is it about this tin pot little shithole of a country that gives them the right to treat visitors like that?'

'It's cultural, not personal. Their society is rooted in a time when they lived in tents in the desert and the summer months were spent doing as little as possible. They have simply no concept that being out when a visitor calls is remotely rude or insulting, so if you react as if it is, they just don't understand your frustration. That, and the fact they're lazy, spoiled, arrogant bastards.'

'You got that right. I'm going to drop the best part of 10k on this trip and they can't even be arsed to turn up for the fucking meeting.'

'Yeh, well, money and how much it's worth isn't something they've got much of a concept of either.'

The pair stood in reception wondering what to do next. They were booked into the Sheraton which was only a short distance away but stepping outside was like straying into the path of a giant blowtorch. The light was dazzling and the mercilessly hot wind meant walking wasn't an option. Alec called the hotel and asked reception to send a driver for them and their luggage. They had brought mainly holiday clothes with them from Spain which meant they were at least geared up for a day on one of the shady kabanas on the hotel terrace. However, they were melting within ten minutes and not even the chilled swimming pool was enough to cool the blood.

'No wonder the locals look forward to October,' said Michaela. 'It's just too hot to be outside.'

'Yeh, I got the impression that Mikey was quite pleased he wouldn't have to run around out here. Even for two hundred grand a week.'

'I don't know anything about football, obviously, but I thought the thing about Qatar holding the World Cup was that they were building airconditioned stadiums.'

'They are cooler, but they've still had to move the event out of its normal slot in the calendar. If you're interested, maybe we could get someone to show us around one.'

'You are joking, right?'

In the end they settled for the indoor pool and gym where jetlag and being parachuted into a completely new culture left them both with a feeling of unreality. After the gym and some lunch, he slept on a sun lounger leaving Michaela alone with her thoughts. When he woke her mood had darkened.

'I told you I didn't have a good feeling about coming here and it's not going away. Something feels really wrong.'

'Are you sure it's not just your brain reacting in the way that it learned in Serbia?'

'Oh, so now you're the therapist, are you?'

'No, of course not, but it's the classic thing isn't it? We're in a foreign country trying to get a meeting with a powerful and possibly dangerous man. The last time you did that, people ended up dead so it's not the biggest leap to imagine that your brain is telling you that you're in danger again.'

The look she gave him would have stopped most men in their tracks. 'When I was a police officer, I had a pretty good instinct for danger. It kept me alive on more than one occasion, so I learned to trust those feelings, not dismiss them with psychobabble.'

Their argument was interrupted by a member of the hotel staff dressed in a dark suit.

'Mr. Munday?' he asked. 'I have a message for you from Mr. Al Kubaisi. He would be grateful if you would join him this evening. He is sending a car for you which will be here in one hour. He was very insistent that only you and not your friend should join him.'

There was no one to argue with and no way to discuss the request. He had to choose whether to go or not to go. Which was no choice at all. He was back in his suit and standing in the hotel reception sixty minutes later when a spotless white Yukon SUV pulled up. They drove past low-rise buildings on wide streets for close to an hour before the driver pulled off the main road and stopped nose on in front of a blank wall. The light was fading rapidly but Alec could still see security cameras placed every few yards stretching away into the distance. The driver waited patiently for several minutes then two sections of the wall moved apart to reveal a large campus which was otherwise completely hidden from view. They moved forward slowly past a huge water feature, on a par with Barcelona's Magic Fountain, which formed the centrepiece to some formal gardens. Submerged lighting illuminated a complex display of arcing water beyond which was a building the size of a hotel. It spread over two wings, each four floors high, on either side of a central quadrangle. More lights mounted at ground level were directed up each of the walls picking out ornate pillars and geometric inlays in the cream sandstone. The overall impression was an artful and expensive marriage between Medici Italy and Las Vegas bling.

The car carried on past the main entrance following the intricately paved road and pulled up outside a second building. The driver opened Alec's door indicating that he should enter. As he stood in the entrance, Alec heard the hiss of tyres as the car pulled away. He suddenly felt very exposed as he walked through a set of sliding glass doors and into a large wide hallway beyond.

He had been inside enough footballers' houses to think he had seen most of what money could buy, but this was beyond anything he had experienced. The floor and walls were inlayed marble with more of the geometric patterns he'd seen on the outside. Subtle recessed lighting highlighted oversized marble and glass ornaments. The walls curved gradually inwards turning darker as they did so before converging into a midnight blue ceiling set with a thousand pinpricks of light. He was still trying to decide whether he was looking at the night sky or an optical illusion when a white-suited butler appeared. Alec was relieved of his jacket, shoes and mobile phone and offered the chance to freshen up. He was given a pair of slippers to put on before being led through a set of double doors and into a different world.

In place of the echoing marble were woollen rugs and walls inlayed with fragrant agar wood. Low-slung sofas strewn with ochre-coloured fabrics were arranged into a quadrant in the centre of the room and surrounded by ruched floor to ceiling curtains gathered into a tented roof several metres above. It was dark outside the tent making it impossible to judge its extremities, but in the middle, all was light with a traditional brass dallah coffee pot surrounded by matching cups set on a large round brass tray. The smell of burning bakhoor filled the air.

Alec was invited to sit, and coffee was poured into two cups. As the butler withdrew his place was taken by a diminutive Arabic man in his thirties, a neat beard framed by a traditional white Arab headdress.

'Good evening Mr. Munday,' he said, in a high reedy voice. 'My name is Walid Al Kubaisi. Welcome to our Majlis. Here we can sit together and talk perhaps more freely than in the office. It is not our custom for men and women to mix on these occasions, so I hope your colleague was not offended at being left behind.'

'She was only confused. As she is the one selling the club, why a meeting would be arranged without her?'

There was a flicker of irritation on the host's face, and he waved a small hand as if to dismiss the interruption. The butler returned carrying trays of nuts, dates and Arab sweetmeats. He glanced towards a dark corner as he set down the food and Alec became aware for the first time of someone else in the room with them. There was something unsettling about the presence and he began to wonder whether Michaela hadn't been right after all.

'All in good time, Mr. Munday. We have plenty of time for business, but first let us take the opportunity to get to know a little more about each other. Tell me, you were a footballer, and you are now a journalist, is that correct?'

'I provide a number of services for clients in football,' Alec replied, smoothly. 'When my playing career came to an end, I worked for a newspaper as a football writer, but I soon found I was of more use advising people in the game how to work with the media. I think I have built a reputation as someone with discretion who can be trusted to undertake various delicate assignments. Sport is an industry where who you are and who you know is at least as important as what you are trained to do.'

'That is certainly true. I myself trained as a military engineer before entering the world of football. And yet it is most unusual for someone with no business experience to be asked to secure a buyer for a Premier League football club, wouldn't you agree?'

'We have both been around the game for a while, Mr. Al Kubaisi. I'm sure there is not much that we don't know about what it takes to run a football club. You will no doubt employ a team of lawyers and accountants who will scrutinise the minutiae of the deal, if we get to that stage. For now, my job it to make the introductions and tell you a little more about the club. If you feel it is of interest and that we can do business together then we can both inform our bosses that there is more to discuss.'

There was a sigh from the corner and Al Kubaisi's eyes flicked sharply to one side. The undefined feeling of evil was starting to take on solid form and Alec sensed that time was rapidly running out. He reached inside his document folder and retrieved a USB stick.

'I have here a presentation which I would like to share with you. Is there perhaps a computer I could use?'

'Enough of this charade,' came a powerful voice from the gloom. 'What is it about your tin pot little shithole of a country that you think you can come in here and treat us like fools?'

Alec heard his own words repeated back to him and knew the game was up. His heart thumped as he shielded his eyes and peered into the darkness trying to make out who was speaking.

'You can leave the memory stick for us to analyse,' the gravelly voice continued, Arabic inflections with transatlantic overtones in his accent. 'When we do, I'm sure we will indeed find a presentation about Southampton Football Club but also a phishing programme designed to harvest data from my computer network. You Brits are all the same; you think you still rule the world when the reality is you are irrelevant amateurs dabbling in things which no longer concern you. Your story was exposed as a lie as soon you booked a double room at the Sheraton. Even if you had kept up the façade of the woman you are traveling with being a client, the office junior would have known you were lying from the moment you approached his desk. They told you Anastasia Schlaffenhoff was reclusive, didn't they? What they should have known is that it takes constant vigilance not to be photographed by the swarm of cameras in every airport, train station or city street. In Ms. Schlaffenhoff's case it was even easier; she has been pictured at the club several times. A quick search by a child would have shown that she is around one metre fifty, 45 years old, blonde and very overweight. Your lover, Miss Dagg, isn't it? She is a disgraced police officer and bears absolutely no resemblance to the Swiss woman. You are here on the instructions of someone you think is MI5 investigating an unfortunate and momentary loss of control by Mr. Al Kubaisi in conversation with another footballer last week. Have I missed anything out?'

Alec shook his head, resignedly.

'Your mission will fail,' the voice continued, 'and you can go back and tell the people who sent you that I am insulted they ever thought the plan could succeed.'

Alec thought quickly, looking for a way the situation might be salvaged and not finding one. He decided to cut his losses.

'You know,' he said, trying to keep the tremble out of his voice, 'the funny thing is, I could actually have sold you Southampton Football Club.'

'That is why you are here talking and not at this moment being buried in an unmarked grave in the Empty Quarter of the desert. Mr. Al Kubaisi has drawn up some heads of terms that you can take back with you. They are non-negotiable and please do not insult my intelligence any further by asking for a finder's fee. I'm sure that if you have any influence at all with the club, they will be very happy to cover your expenses. Walk away Mr. Munday, and count yourself lucky you still have the legs on which to do it.'

Al Kubaisi slid a single sheet of paper across the table towards Alec. He picked it up and placed it into his document folder without reading it then decided to make one last direct approach.

'Your Excellency, you know that if there is an attack on a football match, thousands could die. I appeal to you as a football lover to help us prevent it.'

'Like every football lover, we are doomed by hope, Mr. Munday, and, come what may, today cannot be the end of history.'

'I feel like I should write that down.'

'You should. It is a quotation from one of the Arab world's most famous modern writers, Saadallah Wannous. He mourns the decline of Arabic societies and sees our fractious politics as part of the cause. I share his view that we are, indeed, doomed by hope. His answer was theatre; I have come to different conclusions and, inshallah, we will have the chance to see who is right. Now, your driver is waiting.'

Cauldwell didn't hide his disappointment on the phone an hour later.

'So, you were actually in the room with one of the world's most wanted men and you came out with nothing except a deal to buy a football club and some dodgy Islamic poetry.'

'Hey, that was the only thing that kept me alive, plus it means we'll be in contact again.'

The spook sounded as if Alec living to see another day was a long way down his list of priorities. 'You're hazy on the location and you can't even give us a description of him. What was the point?'

'You know what? You tell me. You sent us stumbling in so deep over our heads it was embarrassing. They'd made us before we even stepped off the plane, and before you say it's basic tradecraft, I have to remind you that we've had no training and no support. We're out here under some misguided impression we were helping our country now I'm not even sure I know who we're working for.'

'There'll be a time and a place for that conversation. For now, you two are stood down. We'll just have to save the world the old-fashioned way.'

The phone went dead, and it was all Alec could do to stop himself hurling it at the wall. He raged around the hotel room while Michaela watched him blow himself out.

'Are you all done now?' she asked, in the end. 'Look at it this way, we knew we were just being used and now we're off the case so let's just get out of here.'

'That's not the point, is it? There's still a plot to destroy Wembley and Cauldwell still hasn't got a fucking clue how to stop it. We can't just walk away.'

'That's exactly what we're going to do. There's a plane out of here in just under three hours and we're going to be on it. So, you can hang up your cape for tonight, at least.'

He conceded that there was nothing to be gained from staying and called down to the concierge to arrange a transfer. As they were arriving at the airport the next Euro match at

Wembley had just kicked off. They made their way to the enormous business lounge where the game, a quarter final between the Netherlands and Spain, was being televised. It was a lively encounter on the pitch and mercifully uneventful off it. They helped themselves to the ample buffet and a couple of glasses of wine and were able to see the fans leaving the stadium peacefully as their flight was called.

Chapter 12

Michaela bailed on him at Heathrow. He hadn't intended to bring up their previous disagreement, but when she said that her mood was lightening the further they got from Qatar, he couldn't help himself. His parting shot had been to suggest she pick up the idea with the therapist that he was paying for. That was the point at which she climbed into a taxi, slammed the door behind her and took off in the opposite direction. On reflection, it wasn't his proudest moment in the stormy history of their relationship.

He took Cauldwell's instructions to stand down as purely advisory and was waiting outside the Wembley staff entrance at ten o'clock on Thursday morning ready for his meeting with head of security Rutger Palme. The German former soldier walked him through the same areas as he'd seen a couple of weeks before but was able to throw some reassuring light on the details of the security arrangements.

For the ground staff, the pitch was the main focus of activity with repairs, watering, mowing, rolling and marking out done by an in-house team.

Palme could see Alec's interest. 'The surface is a weave of grass and twenty percent durable plastic fibres on a sand, soil and rubber bed. Non-flammable of course.'

'Wayne Rooney would be proud,' Alec joked, but couldn't find any reason to change his conclusion. Hi-tech though it may be, it was essentially just grass and highly unlikely to be combustible.

He had looked at them before, but this was Alec's chance to explore behind the signs, banners and wraps that make up the stadium overlay. The acres of foamex board and acrylic gave the appearance of a uniform interior, but they covered numerous hollows which could, in theory, be used to hide explosives.

'Could someone plant something casually behind the signage where it wouldn't be discovered?' he asked, suspecting Palme would have a ready answer.

'The stadium design means there are actually very few voids behind the signs,' he explained. 'Those that do exist are subject to visual inspections before every game and sniffer dogs cover all the public areas. You have already seen our screening system at the entrances. No one carrying anything bigger than a cigarette packet can get in without it being searched. And even if they could bring in a larger package, the area is patrolled 24/7 so there really is no prospect of anything like a bomb being planted.'

Alec took a moment to think through the various physical barriers and safety checks and had to agree with the security man: the overlay could be dismissed as a serious security risk. He looked around aimlessly, hoping for inspiration but was privately beginning to wonder whether the whole thing might be a red herring. As he looked up, he saw a small team at either end of the stadium working high above them on the giant screens. He thought back to his previous tour with Chris Pendle.

'Those screens are new, aren't they? Why would there be a maintenance team working on them?'

Again, the German had all the answers. 'We conduct reliability tests before each major game. It would be embarrassing to suffer a failure in front of the world's sports fans. The installation consultants put meters on each panel and replace any that are not operating within an acceptable range. I'll be pleased to take you up for a closer look.

'Each panel is only a few millimetres thick,' he explained, when they had climbed up to the stadium's top tier. 'There is a small space behind but again the same physical checks are conducted here as with every other area.'

An hour later and the pair had seen every corner of the stadium and Alec had not found a single weakness.

Palme seemed pleased to have thought of everything. 'Never say never, Mr. Munday, but I think you have to agree that it would be hard for anyone to smuggle a quantity of explosives into the Stadium undetected. It would be harder again to hide explosives somewhere and even less likely that they would remain in place to cause damage during a game.'

Alec didn't know whether to be pleased or disappointed as the pair sat eating lunch in the staff canteen. 'You've been very helpful and reassuring Mr. Palme, but the problem I have I this: we still have a credible threat of an attack and no intelligence to suggest the perpetrators are any less confident of pulling it off. Let me ask you, if you were trying to blow up Wembley Stadium, how would you do it?'

'Please don't get the impression that we are complacent. I ask myself that exact question at least every week and this morning has been a good opportunity to have someone else ask testing questions too. My team and I look at every successful attack on a major building or installation anywhere in the world and many others that are unsuccessful that the public never hears about. I try to put myself into the mind of the terrorist and I think the darkest thoughts you can imagine. But I have to tell you, if Germany gets through to the final, I will be happy for members of my family to attend the match.'

The tour had taken four hours and they were back at the starting point when an urgent call came in for Palme. Alec sat and waited still looking around in the loading bay behind the main gates. The area was covered by CCTV and one final thought struck him.

As Palme re-emerged, he asked. 'Could I get access to the CCTV from around the entrances for the last two weeks and going forward, and also the visitors' manifest for the same period?'

Palme sighed but nodded with a smile. 'Mr. Munday, I don't envy you your job. You are in for a very boring few days, but you are welcome to the information. I will have my assistant make copies of the visitor manifests for the past two weeks and we will also send you a daily report from now on. As for the CCTV, it's all online in the Cloud and we will set you up with password access. I have also anticipated your next request and ordered you access-all-areas lanyards for all the upcoming matches. I'm sure we will see each other soon.'

Chapter 13

By the day of the final Alec was sleep deprived and nervous. He had spent every waking moment of the intervening week going through video footage and visitor manifests. He was looking for something he couldn't articulate but was sure he would recognise when he saw it. He was missing a link, some connection that would make sense if only he could access that part of his brain where the pieces would come together. He made another pint of coffee and spent three hours going over the previous day's CCTV and visitor data. Then he grabbed some lunch, got into his car and headed back to Wembley.

The first person he saw as he approached the staff security entrance was Simon Cauldwell. The two caught each other's eyes and nodded. It was the first contact they had had since the phone call in Qatar, and each recognised in the other the tell-tale signs of stress and fatigue.

'Anything?' asked the spook.

Alec shook his head. 'You?'

'We've had the usual crazies coming out of the woodwork, which is a relief I suppose. But there hasn't been a hint of anything bigger. Even with the reliable intelligence we've got, we're beginning to wonder whether we got it wrong.'

'I don't think so. I may not have seen Sheikh Abdullah, but his obsession filled that room like a scream. Something's going to happen. We just haven't worked out what.'

'What's your plan?' Cauldwell asked.

'I'm just going to sit in the stands and think and hope I come up with something.'

'You've got my number. Call me when you do.'

Alec was still sitting there as the floodlights came on in the early evening. He had toured the now-familiar danger areas hoping for inspiration and finding none. He felt the threat growing more solid as the moments passed and with it his frustration at seeing nothing that posed a security risk.

Being in a stadium on the day of a major international final is like lifting the lid of a beehive or an Amazon warehouse: everywhere there is purposeful activity going on, and no one can be diverted from their task. The bars were all open, the kitchens were in full swing and the marshals were getting their final briefing. Alec's attention was drawn to the cameramen and other media taking up their stations around the ground and he thought back to Madrid. As much for something to do as for any other reason, he spent the next hour looking under camera skirts and going up to bemused operators asking to look at their gear. There wasn't so much as a used coffee cup on the camera gantries and, apart from some strange looks, he got nothing from the steadicam guys or the snappers either.

He returned to the stands, this time on a different side of the stadium hoping that a change of perspective would yield some new ideas. His mind wandered to the players and what they were doing right at that moment. With under two hours to go until kick off, both team buses would be arriving soon, if they weren't already at the venue. The players would see the crowds outside and run the gauntlet of non-accredited photographers before being guided to their respective dressing rooms. From there it would be the usual routine of changing into practice kit, a warmup on the pitch, the manager doing some media and the team talk before finally being lined up at the top of the player's tunnel ready to run out in front of 55,000 roaring fans. With England in the final, it was hard for Alec to be neutral about the result, but he needed no reminders that it would all be for nothing if someone managed to execute the atrocity they had planned. He watched vacantly as the handlers with their sniffer dogs did a last circuit of the terraces and hospitality areas. There was no shout and forty minutes later they were gone again.

A few minutes before Wembley's gates opened to the public, the PA announcer went through a quick soundcheck, and the perimeter signage and giant screens were sparked into life. Marshals took up their positions as music filled the stadium and fans started filing in. Alec's chest tightened and his palms started to sweat at the realisation they were all on a trajectory to terror and he still had no idea how to stop it. He tried to control his breathing by watching the screens that were already spooling through sponsor's messages. He kept staring, aware of something just beyond the grasp of his conscious mind. Something about them didn't add up.

At seven o'clock, an hour before the starting whistle, that feeling was starting to crystalise into a suspicion, and he made the decision to go back to the operations area and security room. No one on the team had the time or inclination to engage with him, but he found a spare workstation and used his password to log into the CCTV archive. He pulled up footage from the second day after each of the Euro games. Forty minutes later, as the players were finishing their warmup routines on the pitch, he found what he was looking for. At ten o'clock on each of the mornings, two panel vans pulled up to the main entrance. Both carried the SE Consulting logo and artwork indicating their work with giant stadium screens. The driver of the lead vehicle got out, presented his credentials at the gate and the vans were waved through. Once into the get-in area, stadium security took the ID of the other crew members and conducted a brief inspection of the cargo bay of each van. The vans then parked off to one side and the crews disappeared from view. Two hours later they reappeared and exited the way they had come in.

Three days ago, following the second semi-final match, two identical vans appeared again at ten o'clock as before. This time they were in the stadium for over five hours before leaving exactly as before. Alec needed to find Cauldwell and Palme. Outside there was a roar from the crowd as both teams came down the player's tunnel and onto the pitch. The rousing chorus of national anthems got everyone on their feet, but from deep in the heart of the stadium, the noise was muffled. When the music stopped it was eerily quiet with flickering monitors the only indication that anything was happening at all.

He got Cauldwell first. 'I think I might have something,' he said, trying to keep his voice calm. He explained the anomaly and shared the times in question. 'Can you enhance the CCTV to see if it's the same guys? Go back through the quarter-final games. We know they were in the country so they could have done a trial run.'

Half an hour Alec saw a hassled-looking Rutger Palme walk through the operations area. He grabbed him and sat him down in front of screen.

'Alec, this better be important,' he said nodding towards monitors showing police and stewards struggling to contain the un-ticketed crowds outside the stadium. 'Have you seen what we're dealing with on Wembley Way?'

Alec walked him through the CCTV footage and looked to Palme for an explanation.

'I can't honestly tell you why they were here longer,' the head of security said, 'and I feel a bit embarrassed that we didn't notice, but I was there when we checked them in, and I can assure you they had all the right credentials. Perhaps someone in the digital team will know for sure what they were doing, so I think you can check with them. Mike never answers his phone, but you can get hold of him in the digital ops room.'

Alec hurried out of the room, his agitation rising. The whistle had just blown for half time and the walkways were rammed, making progress slow. He followed the crowd through the long corridors heading for a small door on the opposite side of the stadium. By the time he reached his objective, the break was almost over but he had located the room in question and hammered on the door for access. He spent an agonising five minutes before getting someone's attention and going through what he wanted to know. He barely noticed as the crowd exploded for a goal: at that moment nothing could have mattered less than knowing which side had scored.

'Tell you the truth, I'm hazy on the details,' said Mike, the frazzled techie. 'That's Rangit's thing only he's gone off sick, hasn't he? I mean, what a day to do it. It would take a lot to keep me away on a day like this.'

At that moment a call came through from Cauldwell. 'Alec, we've got the results back from the CCTV. You were right. It's the same van but the crew changed four matches ago. What are you thinking?'

Alec was growing panicky and kept Cauldwell on the line as he turned back to Mike. 'So, do you know what they were doing here for so long?' he found himself shouting.

'All I can tell you is UEFA are running a special video sequence in the gap between the end of the match and the trophy ceremony. We've uprated the electricity supply because it's going to draw more power than usual, and we can't risk an outage. The screen guys installed heat sinks behind the panels to disburse the extra energy, but that's all I know.'

A wave of nausea hit Alec like a tsunami. His legs went and he had to grab hold of the desk to avoid falling over. The music had started again outside – the game was going into extra time – but the blood roaring in his ears almost drowned it out. It was all he could do to hear his own voice.

'Are the screens controlled from here?'

'Nah, all that stuff is controlled from the comms room behind the media centre on the second tier.'

Alec forced himself into action and yelled into the handset at Cauldwell. 'It's the giant screens. They're the bombs.'

'Wait, that's not possible. We checked them just before the game and there's nothing there. No explosives, not detonators nothing.'

'I think the explosives are built into the units. They were only installed a month ago so maybe the explosives were already there then. And you wouldn't have found any wiring or detonators. They're going to be activated remotely by something in the video sequence. We've got to get to that comms room before they're triggered.'

The crowd's attention was fully on the game and Alec and Mike could run freely through the cavernous spaces inside the stadium. They reached the media centre as the first half of extra time kicked off.

Cauldwell was there to meet them. 'Right, Alec, we've got half an hour to sort this. It's going to be ok.'

The three of them ploughed through the ranks of startled journalists to reach the comms room. It was locked. Mike pulled out a set of keys, but the lock had been glued solid. Cauldwell hammered on the outside and yelled. Without waiting for an answer, he stepped back and flung a kick at the door. It opened outwards and he bounced off harmlessly with more of a dent to his pride than any mark on the barrier in front of them. He looked round into the faces of two hundred or more international media many of whom had their camera phones out. He thought about trying to stop them but decided it was pointless. This revolution, if it happened, would definitely be televised.

He got Palme on the two-way radio. 'Rutger, there's a problem. I need you to evacuate the areas around the big screens immediately. No need to start a panic but you need to get people moving away from there now.'

He pulled out a pistol and, indicating to those around to take cover, fired three rounds into the door around the lock.

'On my count,' he said to Alec, his weapon still drawn, 'pull the door open quickly then get out the way.'

Cauldwell braced himself to fire but there was no one on the other side. A bank of monitors blinked in the interior mirroring the feed going onto the screens outside. The smell was at the extreme end of normal for a techie's workspace and there was a chair in front of the control panel with someone sitting on it. Cauldwell kept his gun pointed at it and indicated to Alec to spin it round. As he did, an overweight Asian man fell forward, his torso a mess of blood, bone and torn flesh.

'Rangit,' said Mike, under his breath.

'Get him out of here,' yelled Cauldwell, stepping over the body. 'You,' he barked, pointing at Mike. 'Where's the kill switch? How do we shut this down?'

'We can't,' said Mike, shaking his head frantically. 'We bypassed the cutout when we uprated the power supply. The only way to stop it is to cut the power from the plant room.'

Cauldwell yelled into his radio again. 'Rutger, we need to cut the power to this area. I don't care what goes with it, just shut this thing down.'

The servers were locked behind grilles and these he started attacking with the broken table legs. Alec looked at his watch. They were deep into extra time with only minutes before the video would be triggered. He picked up a fire extinguisher and joined Cauldwell hacking away at the locks. The pair were still bashing when the final whistle sounded on the pitch and the system tripped over to the post-match sequence. Precisely forty seconds later the screens outside exploded.

Part Two

Chapter 14 August 2021

Knowing that it could have been much worse was no consolation to Alec. Their final desperate efforts to prevent the carnage were flashed across every international news channel. But far more painful were the images of Wembley Stadium, its iconic arch bent and buckled, both ends staved in like a crushed skull. There was no shortage of pictures, but one would go on to make World Press Photo of the Year. It was grainy, like a war zone. A snaking line of confused fans, their faces and England shirts blackened by soot, being led away from the smouldering wreck behind them.

The jury of public opinion was divided on Alec and 'Agent X' undecide between lauding them for their gallant efforts or lampooning them for their ineptitude. Familiar with the harsher mathematics of sport and security, both knew a failure to win for what it was: first among the losers. For Alec, the overwhelming feeling was one of guilt: guilt that he had not unravelled the plot earlier, guilt that he had done nothing to prevent it and guilt that he had survived when so many had lost their lives. The outrage and emotion that gushed from 24-hour rolling news channels were completely disassociated in his mind from the event he had experienced. That didn't stop him from sitting glued to the coverage in a state of self-flagellating penance, each new interview or angle another twist of the knife already plunged deep into his guilty heart.

First in front of the cameras were the politicians and public figures with carefully choreographed words spinning a self-promoting narrative of outrage, jingoism and sickening pride. They praised the dedicated security forces for 'running towards danger when the rest of us would run away,' and brave members of the public (Alec) who 'showed us the best of ourselves when those that mean us harm were doing their worst'. Every passing day brought a tidal wave of *thoughts and prayers, thoughts and prayers, thoughts and prayers* from a godless world; a world whose words were meaningless in the face of mindless, unprovoked terror. There were new memorials or candle-lit vigils in churches, mosques, synagogues and temples up and down the country. Each family buried its dead, their dignified calls for privacy ignored by a craven press desperate for ways to squeeze the last rattling breath from the biggest sporting disaster since Hillsborough.

The one group that was quiet, despite a reputation for inserting itself into every aspect of public life, was the world of football. Perhaps it was just too close to home; maybe the sport and its mouthpieces were shocked into silence by the knowledge that the England team had narrowly escaped with their lives. The usual suspects at the FA, the Premier League and assorted pundits with the different media outlets seemed to accept that their usually irresistible urge to comment was at odds with the public mood on one of the country's darkest days. The purdah was lifted at the last public memorial of that summer when the entire England squad, surviving players and managers dating back to 1966, and representatives of each of the seventy-two football clubs in the English league attended a vigil at Wembley. They linked arms as the deep bass of explosives shook the ground again and the desecrated stadium suffered its last indignity, collapsing in on itself despite standing seventy years less than its predecessor.

There was talk of a public inquiry at which Alec would be called upon to play a starring role. Families of the victims wanted answers, but he already had his verdict. His brain told him that an evil and remote criminal had commissioned and executed a wanton attack. His conscience taunted him, however irrationally, that he could have stopped the atrocity and failed, thus making him guilty of the deaths of 233 people.

While he struggled to connect with the public outpouring of grief, the many hundreds of private messages were much closer to home. The first WhatsApps arrived within seconds of the explosion and, together with cards and emails, did not stop for weeks. Word spread right around the football world bringing commiserations from every part of the globe. Most he took for what they were: a genuine expression of sympathy and solidarity. Harder to bear were the personal messages from bereaved families who had sought him out to express their gratitude at his efforts. One day, maybe, there might come a time when he could look them in the eye and accept their thanks. For that to happen he would have to find a way to make things right and that felt like an impossible circle to square.

There were a few messages that reached into his heart and helped him drag himself through the quagmire of despair that was sucking at his soul. One was a brief note from Nigel Rushbourne:

You may find it hard to accept, but your heroism saved hundreds of lives. You will come back from this and fight again on another day. When you are ready, I would like to talk to you about what form that fight could take. Until then you have my thanks and the thanks of all those families that are still together because of you. Nigel.

There was one message that, perhaps contrary to its sender's intentions, induced a response so violent, so visceral, that its energy fuelled the next part of his life and the events that followed.

When the text came in, he was sat in a bathrobe on his sofa, the only place other than his bed that he had gone to voluntarily for weeks. Although it was only early afternoon, the curtains were closed, and his face was puffy and pallid in the blue light of the TV. A large glass of vodka was balanced on the arm of the sofa beside him. He felt his phone buzz against his leg, picked it up and read three words: *doomed by hope.* He immediately recognised the Arabic literary reference and recoiled instinctively, dropping the phone and knocking his drink to the floor. He staggered to his feet trying to reach the bathroom but made it only halfway before collapsing to his knees and throwing up. He lay on the floor covered in vomit and convulsed by sobs. He howled with rage, surrendering himself fully to the grief of the hundreds of bereaved families.

Eventually the tears subsided, and the shuddering stopped. Then he picked up the phone and called Michaela.

'I need the number of your therapist,' he said, as calmly as he could.

'Why don't you start by talking to me?' came her gentle reply.

He didn't speak again and she waited, listening to his breathing. It wasn't the first time she had simply stayed with him, her silence saying more than words.

In the end, she tried again. 'I could come over.'

She had made the same suggestion before, almost every time they had spoken, in fact, but each time he had refused. This time he agreed. 'Ok, but not 'till tonight and I can't pick you up.'

The deadline forced him to summon up enough resolve to pull on some baggy joggers and an old t-shirt. He spent the hours until her arrival trying to dispel the impression that his house had been taken over by refugees with a drink problem. Michaela would be the first person to cross the threshold since the night of the Euros final, although by no means the first to try. The journalists had been sympathetic at first. Those he'd worked with tried to persuade him to put his story out there (through them and their newspapers of course). He refused all the offers and inevitably the doorstepping started. They had posed as Samaritans, utility companies, even JustEat delivery drivers but no one had got past the front door. At first it was a reaction against the pressure to talk but lately he had become aware of the state he was in. He was living in just two rooms surrounded by empty wine and vodka bottles and stacks of takeaway food boxes. These he bagged up to take to the local dump alongside the fetid contents of the fridge. He then spent a fruitless forty minutes trying to get the smell of stale food, alcohol and sick out of the carpet. It was soon obvious, even to him, that he wasn't going to succeed, so he ended up ripping it up and dragging it out to the back of his car. His sofa and mattress would have followed it if he had had the strength to move them. He judged, almost certainly wrongly, that he was in a fit state to drive and dispatched the rubbish at the tip. He spent the last two hours cleaning the kitchen, bathrooms and finally himself.

When the doorbell rang the house was disinfected if not exactly welcoming and he was still more or less sober. She tried not to let her shock at the sight of him register on her face. He'd certainly seen her looking worse. It wasn't just the full growth of beard or hair an inch longer than when she'd last seen him, he had gained several kilos and gone was any pretence that he had once been an athlete. In its place was a stooping shuffle that made him look at the same time heavier and smaller. He stood aside to let her in, scanning the street beyond for anyone who might be tempted to follow.

Michaela took in the kitchen with a quick appraising glance. The room looked as forlorn as its owner and the recently applied bleach merely masked the underlying fetor of something deeply unhealthy. She felt a sharp pang of guilt. Having parted company at the airport, she was out of touch for the entire week building up to the final. She justified the decision with the thought that she would have been no practical help and needed to preserve herself. She was never entirely convinced though, and on seeing his condition, desperately sorry. She was determined not to be a part-time partner again: this time around, whatever that meant, she would either be fully in or completely out.

He followed her into the kitchen and put his phone down on the breakfast bar for her to see. She took in the message then looked back to Alec. His hands were trembling as he poured another three fingers of vodka.

'I'm going to kill him,' he said, simply.

'That could be dangerous.'

'I know there are risks, for sure, but I'm going to do it.'

'That wasn't what I meant. Thinking you can take on one of the most powerful and protected men in the world is dangerous enough, for sure, but revenge, it could eat up the rest of your life. You could end up destroying yourself without getting close enough even to register on his radar. You asked about my therapist, well she would tell you that you have to start by forgiving yourself before...'

'I'm going to kill him,' he cut across her, his voice firmer and more resolute. 'I don't know how, but I'm not going to wait for years either. He's a dead man walking.'

'When was the last time you left the house?'

The question took Alec by surprise and knocked him off his stride.

'I thought so,' Michaela continued. 'I've seen that look before and when I last saw it it was staring back at me from the mirror. I wasn't drinking; my poison was fentanyl but the look was the same. By all means get angry at Sheikh Abdullah but use that anger to get yourself better first. That's the only way you'll be able to do anything about him or anyone else for that matter.'

Alec's defences came down. 'Do you think I should have therapy or check myself into rehab?'

She didn't reply straight away but opened the empty fridge then looked out into the back garden and the pile of bottles and takeaway cartons he'd missed.

'That's up to you, but you could do worse than starting with some healthier habits. You're not going to feel better until you've stopped trying to drown yourself in vodka and you're eating and sleeping properly.'

'Will you stay with me?'

'I'll stay,' she said, simply and crossed the room to take him in her arms. 'I'll stay with you as long as you need me, but you can't live like this anymore. We've got to get you back in shape.'

Alec buried his face in her shoulder and nodded, tears flowing.

'Hey, you can't start crying yet,' she said. 'You're going to feel like shit for the next two weeks. What are you going to be like when it really starts to hurt? Talking of shit, this place isn't actually fit to live in. We need to find somewhere else to stay for a few days while you get it professionally fumigated.'

He agreed to everything, of course, and within an hour they were in a taxi bound for an anonymous five-star hotel in Central London. In the end, the stay was a turning point. Alec went cold turkey on the booze and they ran every morning by the side of the river watching late summer turn into autumn. Lunch was sushi or fruit before they went their separate ways. He used the afternoons to punish himself in the hotel gym while she spent his money lining up a small army of suppliers to strip out, clean and complete a basic makeover of the Enfield house. At 5.30 they met up again for a swim, sauna and a massage before wandering into the West End to eat. Sleep was the hardest thing, but the exercise routine helped. By midnight each evening, he was at least too physically exhausted to do anything else. He spent many hours staring at the hotel room ceiling but progressed from short, broken nights to longer periods of undisturbed rest. Even with Michaela's support, the first few days were hell but, as she predicted, within two weeks he was starting to feel life was back under control.

His mind cleared too, and while he was lifting weights or pounding the pavement he also took the chance to think and to make some decisions. He was still determined to make the Sheikh pay for his crimes, but molten fury had cooled to diamond-hard resolution. As he started to channel his impulse for justice, the outline of a plan started to emerge. Michaela had deep misgivings. Her strong preference was to hand over everything they knew to Simon Cauldwell and walk away, but she could see that having a goal was also giving Alec the strength and motivation to get better.

The day after they moved back to Enfield, he shared some of his thoughts.

'My best chance, probably my only chance to get back in contact with the Sheikh is to put Southampton Football Club on the table as a real takeover prospect. When we met, he was genuinely interested in the club; he just won't break cover long enough to get the deal done. If I can take the club to him, literally bait the hook, then I think he'll bite.'

His first call was to the owners' representatives who almost bit his arm off when they realised a quick, oven-ready deal was a realistic prospect. Characteristically, their only sticking point was the share of the success fee that they would have to hand over to Alec if the deal went through. In the end they agreed on two per cent and he sent over the proposal he had brought back from Doha. Within minutes he was speaking direct to the owners themselves. They queried a couple of the Sheikh's points, but Alec knew they were desperate to sell and wouldn't quibble over anything except the price. Their one stipulation was a deposit of £100 million up front as a show of serious intent. Alec's first inclination was to try and talk them out of it but, on reflection, he didn't raise any objections. Having that sort of skin in the game would almost certainly mean the Sheikh himself would get involved and stay involved.

Having brought one side to the table and got another at least potentially interested in joining them, the next step was to try and engineer a meeting, then take his chances. He took a deep breath, picked up the phone and called the number which had sent the text.

'I see you've decided not to take my advice and walk away, Mr. Munday,' said the well-modulated voice which reverberated down the line. 'I think that is what they call the triumph of hope over experience.'

'On the contrary, Your Excellency,' he replied, controlling his breathing in an attempt to keep his tone steady. 'It's just that this way I walk away with a seven-figure sum in my pocket if the deal goes through.'

'Ah, you're a pragmatist and, if I understand you, it seems I was right about the club paying your expenses. What have you got for me?'

His cover story was swallowed readily, but then Alec had never met a rich man for whom the novelty of becoming even richer had completely worn off. What was more surprising was the relative ease with which the Sheikh agreed to put up the money. Raising the sum itself was clearly not going to present a problem, but he wasn't likely simply to send a wire transfer. In the end, the parties agreed to the money being held in international escrow, out of reach of both sides, until a deal was either concluded or abandoned. Despite the large guarantee, however, getting everyone physically around the table proved more difficult. Not only did everyone have seemingly irreconcilable travel schedules, but the Qatari kept throwing up a blizzard of objections. Alec thought back to his claim that constant vigilance was needed to avoid being photographed: perhaps his reluctance to be pinned down was part of the same paranoia.

After three weeks of conversations with a middleman in Doha, an arrangement was made for the reluctant royal's private jet to touch down briefly at Farnborough Airport where Alec would connect with him for the short hop to Geneva.

Michaela was predictably concerned when he told her about the meeting.

'Are you sure about this? she asked. 'It's only a few weeks ago that a text message from that man had you howling on the floor. Are you sure you're ready?

'I'm just taking advantage of an opportunity to try and gain his confidence. At some point my chance will come and he'll get what's coming to him.'

'You're not planning to do anything stupid, are you?' she asked.

'It's taken weeks to set up this meeting and I'm not going to back out now, he said. 'I'll be fine.'

He took a light grey suit out of the wardrobe and put it on over a white slim-fit shirt. The outfit felt tight as he bent down to lace up his Chelsea boots, but he put that down to muscle, not fat.

It was raining as Alec piloted the BMW around the M25. He tried not to take it as an omen. He told himself that the ceramic knife strapped to his arm was just his way of being ready if and when the time came, but the thumping of his heart as he approached the Hampshire airport told its own story. He passed easily through the airport's security but felt his knees start to weaken as he was shown to the plane. His host was still installed having not ventured landside. Alec checked the knife was still securely in place, climbed the short flight of stairs and stepped into the last word in luxury.

On a regular scheduled or charter flight, turning right is shorthand for the cramped, stuffy squalor of cattle class. The royal jet, part of the Qatari Royal Fleet, was the same in the way that Faberge and Golden Lay are both eggs. Only the crew turned left leaving the passengers to enjoy unparalleled aviation opulence. The traveling altitude might have been different, but in every other way the interior resembled a superyacht. The cabin was all burr walnut panelling and cream marine leather, subtly patterned with the same geometric designs Alec had seen in Doha. His eyes were drawn past the business area, with its personal reclining seats, to the lounge, decked out with wide sofas, a bar, subtle lighting and a state-of-the-art entertainment system. Two flawless crew members, modestly attired in matching uniforms, were in the kitchen creating an intoxicating aroma of coffee and baking croissants that filled the air. Beyond the kitchen the curtains were half open and Alec glimpsed a double bed which spanned almost the full width of the plane accessible via a short hallway. Off the corridor there was a room, presumably an ensuite bathroom, from which a large man with long crinkled hair and a week's worth of stubble now emerged.

Alec's stomach lurched as the Qatari beamed a smile of greeting, his presence filling up the space between them. He had discarded his traditional robes in favour of an open-necked shirt and tailored business suit which fitted snuggly over his heavy frame. His body language was open and friendly, but his lip curled and his eyes blazed with cruel humour. Having not seen his face before, Alec had no way of knowing at first whether he was meeting the genuine article. But the voice which welcomed him on board was unmistakeable.

'Mr. Munday, welcome. Please make yourself comfortable. We have one more person joining us and then we will be cleared for take-off.'

Alec lowered himself into a padded leather berth and accepted coffee from one of the stewardesses. As he did so the final passenger appeared in the doorway. They had never met, but Alec recognised the type. The chalk pinstripe double-breasted suit paired with brown brogues, school tie and signet ring all communicated a subtle code about school, club or college to the initiated. For the plebs, among whom Alec was happy to be numbered, they just screamed privilege. The newcomer shrugged off his jacket in the direction of one of the crew, revealing a flash of lime-green silk lining. His leather shoes creaked as he strode towards Alec, a manicured hand outstretched.

'Piers Seymour,' he said, shaking hands, firmly. 'I'm with Hubbard, the Investment Bank, and you must be our man Munday. I understand we have you to thank for setting this deal up. You and I must talk about who else you know.'

He glided smoothly on. 'Your Excellency, good morning to you. I trust the flight from Mustique was a comfortable one.'

Seymour took a seat across the cabin and engaged his client in some meaningful small talk while the crew prepared for departure. They had been on the ground less than ten minutes. As the plane accelerated along the runway, he opening his case pulling out a thin file.

'Our analysts have prepared this summary of the financial statements together with a costed plan for the expansion,' he said. 'As we're in the area, I've taken the liberty of requesting that the pilot takes us out over the stadium so you can get a birds-eye view of what you're buying.

He ran his fingers through swept back blonde hair as Sheikh Abdullah leafed through the papers. From his confidence alone, there was no doubt Seymour knew about finance, and from the cut of his suit it seemed likely that he and money were personally acquainted. But as Alec watched him in action, he found it hard to imagine him cheering on a team in a freezing stadium or having any understanding of the soul of a football club. They flew a couple of circuits of the ground during which Seymour used words like *double-digit returns* and *balanced portfolio*. It seemed the plan was to double the capacity of the 32,000-seater venue.

Alec, who had done some due diligence of his own, was tempted to point out that the Saints rarely played to a full house as it was. Instead he took the opportunity to pull out his phone. Before his host had chance to stop him, he had casually taken an eight second burst of video around the interior of the plane pinging it on quickly to Michaela while they were still within mobile range. The absence of a traditional Arab headdress meant the Sheikh's face was clearly visible and the way he snapped into action showed how unimpressed he was.

'Alec, you know how camera shy I am. Delete the pictures.' The geniality had gone from his voice, and he left no one in any doubt that he expected his request to be followed, unquestioningly.

Alec covered up his apparent error with what he hoped was breezy confidence. 'Just getting some ideas for when I get a plane of my own. I guess I'll just have to try and remember what it looks like.'

He deleted the footage and held up the phone to confirm before putting it back in his breast pocket. He felt the point of the knife dig into the crook of his elbow but, in truth, the prospect of it being used seemed a long way off.

With the banker's diversion complete, they changed course for Geneva where they set down for an hour to meet the Swiss and Chinese owners of Southampton FC. Alec had arranged a private suite airside within the terminal building and, as he had brought the sides together, it was down to him to make the introductions. Once his job was done, he sat back in the hope that he might learn about high-level negotiations. Instead, as with the conversation about his mobile phone, something in the Qatari's manner made it very clear there would be no deviation from the deal as presented. The price was on the low side of fair, but it was a take-it-or-leave-it, one-time offer making any haggling largely ceremonial. The sellers tried to extract some concessions and were rebuffed with exquisite politeness by the charming but menacing royal. In the end, they were motivated enough to sign anyway, and the unamended heads of terms were agreed well within the allotted sixty minutes. There was a quick handshake and the group parted ways, the Chinese to the business lounge to await a connection to New York and the Swiss into a waiting Maybach to be whisked back to the anonymity of their chocolate box retreat. Meanwhile, the royal plane had been refuelled and was ready to head for the Gulf with the owner apparent of Southampton FC onboard and his investment banker in tow. As they prepared to leave, Sheikh Abdullah let Seymour go ahead and placed a strong hand on Alec's arm.

'I'm glad you decided against using that knife up your sleeve,' he said, tightening his grip and pulling Alec in close to share the confidence. 'You would have been dead before you even had chance to draw it. Which would have been shame and possibly messy. This way you get to spend your money. Have a good flight home, Mr. Munday and please pass on my regards to Ms. Dagg.'

Chapter 15

Alec had always been a club man never abandoning the North London side he had supported as a boy and whose academy, juniors and first team he played for. Although his time as a professional had been short, he was still a season ticket holder. But when he killed a man in a far-off country in somebody else's war, he joined a new club, membership of which was for life. He may not have been an imposing physical force; his eyes didn't burn with the smouldering threat of violence, neither did men cower in his presence. He just knew that if it came to it; if push came to shove, he could and would pull the trigger again.

Members of the club for killers are not equal, however, and Alec was very much in the junior ranks. It was clear to him that anyone who could plunge a knife premeditated into another human in cold blood was multiple levels above or below him depending on your perspective. How Sheikh Abdullah could have known about the knife was anyone's guess, but it didn't take a psychoanalyst to know that Alec would never have used it, no matter how obsessively he wanted the man dead.

His newly toned muscle chaffed against his suit as he sat in the airport rehearsing in his mind how the conversation with Simon Cauldwell would go.

So, let me get this right. You were in the same room as the Sheikh. Again. And he was unarmed and unprotected. You were carrying a knife and all you bring back is the same deal to sell the same football club. Oh, and a few seconds of video.

Alec had to face it: yes, he was a killer but a killer by default; a shot-in-the-dark kind of killer, very much a peripheral member of the club for killers. For him to graduate to Call of Duty prestige level, cold, hard killer status would take more killing than he had the time or the stomach for. If he wanted the Sheikh dead, he was going to need help. He scrolled through the contacts on his phone and pressed the call icon under Nigel Rushbourne's name.

'Alec, I wondered when I might hear from you. How have you been? Do you want to get together? I could have a driver pick you up tomorrow morning as before. I do hope Michaela will be accompanying you. Thoroughly looking forward to a little chat.'

The conversation was over before it began. Alec hung up feeling, not for the first time that day, like he was an observer in someone else's game. He would need to be better prepared before tomorrow's meeting.

Michaela stayed true to her word and was beside him in the car as they arrived at another nondescript office building, this time on an industrial park in Stratford, East London. While his guests were dressed casually, Rushbourne looked exactly the same as last time Alec had met him: a crumpled suit, cheap white shirt, tie of indeterminate provenance and scuffed black shoes. He could have been an aging IT consultant or the store manager of an out-of-town electrical retailer. Maybe it was the perfect way to hide in plain sight, but he didn't inspire confidence. He looked at them both carefully as they entered the otherwise empty reception. Leading the way to a meeting room, he shut the door and addressed Michaela first.

'We've not been introduced,' he said, watching her reaction, 'but I feel I already know a lot about you. How have you been? Is the therapy helping?'

His tone sounded sympathetic, but it was a loaded question and she bristled at the intrusion. 'You sound like you would know better than me,' she said, stiffly.

He smiled, bitterly then turned to Alec, acknowledging him with a nod and a look that betrayed years of painfully accumulated memories.

'You got my note I hope, Alec. It's good to see you again. I had reports that your Wembley experience had been distilled into a bottle you were determined to keep drinking from. In that case you're looking remarkably fit. That's good; you're going to need to be.'

It was only the second time the two had met and the first since Wembley, and memories of that experience came flooding back. Millennials would no doubt call it being triggered: for Alec it went way beyond an ill-judged micro aggression.

'How's Simon?' he asked.

'Simon, yes. You must wonder about what happened and what we've found out subsequently. Do you know what rankles with me? We had everything; all the dots were there, we just didn't join them up them in time. You came closer than any of us, which is to your absolute credit. Nut it goes down as a terrible loss. Questions have been asked, inevitably, and Simon, well, let me say that nothing that took place changes my opinion of him. He is still an exceptional officer.'

'Did any of the leads we found go anywhere?' Michaela asked.

'Well,' Rushbourne paused, a pale hand pushing up into his grey hair and down over tired eyes. 'The Russian connection was a blind. They were a legitimate company, but the screen panels were manufactured in China and arrived in the UK via a stop off in the Gulf. We think they were probably packed with plastic explosives there. We found the bodies of four unidentified males in a burned-out car, not too far from here as a matter of fact, and we suspect this was the regular maintenance crew. They'd been shot and burned to hide their identities. We gave the Russians the option to repatriate the bodies, but they declined, so that was a dead end. As for the terrorists themselves, we have no indication that they are still here but no specific intelligence to indicate they've left either. It was a very sophisticated operation and it's a concern that a group of their evident talents is still on the loose. We've shared the details, such as we have them, with other friendly agencies and now we have to wait until they surface again. It's rare that a cell like that stays unemployed for long especially after their calling card was embossed so spectacularly. And as for Sheikh Abdullah.' Rushbourne shook his head. 'I'm afraid the wheels of justice turn very slowly if at all for individuals like him.'

Alec interrupted. 'I'm going to kill him,' he said, in a matter-of-fact tone, 'but I need your help.'

Rushbourne nodded slowly, adopting the look of a benign uncle patting the head a nephew at a family Christmas.

'It's a lovely thought, isn't it,' he said. 'And I admire your intentions, believe me. It would lay a lot of ghosts for all of us. It may be that there are ways we could help you achieve your aim, but it won't be easy, and it won't be quick. Do you know, we don't even have a single recent photograph of him? There are some who speculate that he doesn't exist at all, but I do have a university photo that seems to match. It's from Sandhurst actually: he joined the University Officer Training Corps whilst studying at Nottingham seventeen years ago. We really could do with something a bit more up to date.'

'I can help you there,' Alec said. 'When I called you yesterday, I had just come out of a meeting with him. I sent some images to Michaela.'

She handed her phone over to the middle-aged spook who seemed quietly impressed.

'I take it we're about to read that one of our Premier League football clubs has been taken over by another foreign owner. Ah Simon, come in.'

Alec and Michaela looked round, sharply as Cauldwell entered the room.

'Oh, ok. I assumed…'

'Yes, well I needed to know what was in your mind before involving Simon.'

Cauldwell took his seat at the table. If he had been affected by their ordeal of a few weeks ago it was not evident from his manner.

'Now that we're all here,' Rushbourne continued, 'let's talk about how we might work together to achieve some mutually beneficial goals. I was just explaining that it's going to take a very long pole to reel in such a senior member of Qatari royalty.'

Cauldwell had obviously been listening to their conversation and took his cue when Rushbourne handed him Michaela's phone.

'Very useful,' he said, to Alec's surprise. 'With this we can flag him in face recognition systems anywhere in the developed world. And, if we know the locations he visits, we can start matching his movements with suspected associates and triangulate his mobile devices. Hopefully from there we can start to penetrate his network of financial interests and all the time we're gaining intelligence which we can act upon.'

'Yes, well thank you, obviously,' said Rushbourne. 'As Simon says, it is useful, and you took a considerable risk in getting it. Now, you could walk away but that's not going to get you any closer to bringing our royal terrorist to justice. So, we are rather hoping you'll stay and help us with another project we've been tasked with. It's not often that so many stars align, but this may be one of those serendipitous occasions when you could get a chance to achieve your goal, we get to further our security aims and the country scores some valuable points too.'

Alec looked sceptical. 'A win-win-win: what are the chances?'

Rushbourne wasn't put off his stroke. 'It may interest you to know that Sheikh Abdullah has recently become part of another powerful but shady international group that we have in our sights.'

'What we talking? Bilderberg or the Illuminati?'

'You really should stop visiting those conspiracy websites, Alec. No, this group is only too real, I'm afraid. You'll have heard of the FIFA Council?'

Alec nodded.

'He has just been elected.'

Alec was incredulous: 'You are fucking kidding me. That venal bunch of bastards? They're the worst of the lot, so he's going to be right at home. But where's the security angle?'

'There's no doubt that the nation's security would be strengthened if we could get closer to certain members of the Council, but we also have another objective: one that's more about soft power.'

'Now you've really lost me. Why the sudden interest in football, and where do we fit in?'

Simon Cauldwell took up the story. 'Just over ten years ago, England submitted a bid to FIFA to host the World Cup in 2018. I'm sure I don't need to go over the details. Suffice to say that despite government backing and the combined appeal of Prince William and the two Davids – Beckham and Cameron – the whole thing was a disaster. We got only two votes from Executive Committee members, as they were called then, and we were ejected in the first round, returning home with our tails between our legs. It was a national humiliation.'

'The whole process was corrupt though, wasn't it? We just didn't have the war chest that Russia and Qatar had.'

'Up to a point, yes, and there's no doubt that the Qataris effectively bought the competition in 2022. If it were just about that we could argue that there is no disgrace in losing to a bidder who has no price ceiling. But the Russian bid was different. There were some sweeteners paid, no question, but it was a fraction of what came out of Doha. The Russian bid was widely acknowledged as being weak, but their ground game was a triumph.

They twisted arms, greased wheels, sweetened deals; they had more tricks than a Nevada brothel and it was all supported, of course, by the GRU, the Russian military intelligence service.'

Cauldwell's voice became louder and angrier the longer he spoke.

'We were played and betrayed, lied to and outmanoeuvred. It was an expensive and very public lesson in how irrelevant we are in the new world order and the depths to which our international influence has sunk. The era of British diplomacy, fair play and 'word is my bond' deals sealed with a handshake is over. We were shown up as a has-been nation trying to navigate the world as we would like it to be rather than how it is. David Cameron, the prime minister at the time, summed it up when he said, "According to FIFA, we had the best technical bid, the best commercial bid; no-one could identify any risks coming to England. It turns out that's not enough."'

Alec frowned at both of men across the table. 'You've changed your tune, Nigel. When we first met you were dead against hosting major sports events. Something about the great unwashed spilling their beer in our streets, wasn't it?'

'Circumstances change and, as I say, we've been asked to get involved.'

'As for Simon, I've stood beside you as the bombs were about to go off. I saw grim determination to fight to the end but nothing resembling this kind of passion. Why is this so personal?'

'Let me put this in language you'll understand,' said Cauldwell. 'In the last year of Sir Alex Fergusson's reign as manager of Manchester United, his aging squad won the Premier League title by over ten points. The year after he retired, they won nothing, and apart from the odd one-off, they've barely picked up any silverware since. Yes, they're doing better than Spurs, but this is Man United we're talking about: the most successful team in England for twenty or more years. Well, the same is true of British influence. There was once a time, albeit a long time ago, when Britannia really did rule the waves and no country on earth would have dreamt of challenging us. Things came close in the Second World War but, with the help of the Americans, we won, and we've traded on that victory ever since. That sort of currency keeps our country safe; it's like an extra layer of battle armour for our troops in the field and it's a platform for trade and everything else that's meant we're not just another France or even a Germany. But now look at us; we're weak and vulnerable, able to be pushed around and the vultures are circling. Losing that bid may have seemed unimportant, but it gave our enemies the confidence to mount attacks like the one on Wembley. And it won't stop there. Whether it's on the battlefield or in the boardroom, we're wounded, able to be picked off or, worse, just ignored.'

'I get it, but why Man United?' asked Alec. 'Why not the England football team? I mean, we haven't won anything as a nation since 1966.'

'I maybe patriotic but I'm not a fantasist,' Cauldwell shot back. 'Since World War II our role on the international stage has diminished and not unreasonably. Against the likes of America and China it's not realistic to expect that we can be the dominant empire that we were in the 19th Century. But in recent years our weak and incoherent politicians have squandered what little residual influence we had. We were never natural bedfellows of the Europeans, but Brexit basically cut us off at the knees. Now we're losing even the smallest diplomatic battles and we need to do something to rebalance the odds.'

Alec and Michaela exchanged glances. There was no doubting Cauldwell's sincerity. Alec was about to enquire who he would cast as England's new Alf Ramsey or Alex Fergusson when Michaela asked a question.

'So, I take it we're bidding again. Why do you think it's going to be different this time around?'

Rushbourne jumped in. 'Because,' he said, with a flourish, 'we're going to do three things. First, it goes without saying that we'll have a first-rate technical bid that's stronger than the others; second, we'll win hearts and minds in a ground game to beat all ground games; and third, of course, we'll cheat.'

'People say that sport is war minus the shooting. Well, in this instance they're spot on, except perhaps for the no shooting bit,' said Cauldwell. 'This is the ultimate challenge and a way to get back some of that lost national pride. We get to go head-to-head with the world's covert agencies and show that we're smarter, more resourceful and more ruthless than the rest. It's no holds barred, winner takes all and the prize is the World Cup in 2030.'

Michaela was unconvinced. 'It just sounds like willy-waving.'

'Bragging rights, I think is how it's usually described,' said Cauldwell, coolly.

'But with highly trained operatives and access to deadly weapons. What could possibly go wrong?' she shot back.

Cauldwell laughed and turned to Rushbourne. 'She's right though, Nigel. Just because the prize is unconventional, doesn't mean the stakes are any lower or that our opponents will fight clean.'

'What are the rules of the game?' Alec asked. 'No holds barred suggests win at any cost or die trying.'

'I've given Simon some parameters to work within,' said Rushbourne. 'There is to be no physical violence unless we are attacked by a member of another agency, and no financial inducements are to be paid.'

Alec raised his eyebrows. 'No bribes? That narrows down your options, doesn't it?'

'You forget that the system has changed. The FIFA Council now has 37 members, and the final decision is taken by the FIFA Congress where every member federation has a vote. That's 211 football associations, so bribery is not really an option anyway.'

'You've done your homework, Nigel,' said Michaela. 'Do we know whether there is any block voting? I mean, look at the Eurovision Song Contest; that's basically impossible for a UK song to win.'

Rushbourne saw a buying signal from the former policewoman. 'There has only been one vote under the new system, so it's a bit too early to tell, but there were some clear and predictable patterns. In reality, though, the FIFA President and the Council engineer things so they get the outcome they want. The bidders have yet to be approved by the Council, but we're likely to be up against Morocco, who came second last time, a combined Latin American bid, a similar grouping from Eastern European and a bid from Spain and Portugal. Azerbaijan and China are also interesting. Azerbaijan is using major events to sportswash its environmental and human rights record and they have the money to back it up. But with so many other European bids, they're not really a serious threat. No, it's China we need to watch. Under FIFA rules no Asian country can bid as they're in the same region as the next World Cup hosts, Qatar. But this is where it gets interesting. There are rumours flying around that FIFA will bend the rules to let them in and, being generous, there is a strong argument for doing so. After all, Qatar is closer to London than it is to Beijing. Putting a less positive gloss on it, China has a reputation for spending to achieve what they want, so FIFA would have an obvious motivation.

He paused to let the implications of his analysis sink in.

'As for our bid,' he went on, 'it's not going to be England on its own but a Home Nations entry, which could work for us. There's a lot of sentiment in these decisions, so if the vote were to be held today, there's a good chance we'd win as a gesture from world football after the Wembley bombing. Whatever anyone thinks about them, FIFA sees itself as a benign and positive influence on the world, hence the choice of 2026 World Cup in Canada, USA and Mexico. With the Scots determined to keep re-running their independence referendum, would FIFA see the World Cup as a chance to keep the United Kingdom together? Who knows, but that's the realpolitik of bidding and someone else's responsibility. I'm more interested in what we can do behind the scenes to tip the scales decisively in our favour and I'd be interested in your ideas.

'What's the timeframe?' asked Michaela, practical as ever.

'That's already been given to us,' Cauldwell jumped in. 'The final decision will be taken at the FIFA Congress held during the World Cup. Ordinarily, that would have been in July but, as we know, Qatar is hotter than Satan's arsehole during the summer, so it's been put back until late autumn. There are a few obvious milestones along the way, though. The FIFA Council meets next month to confirm the shortlisted bidders so at least the opposition will be a known quantity. They'll also decide the members of the Evaluation Task Force, the team that goes and visits each bidding country. As you can imagine, these visits are an industrial-scale honey trap for FIFA with more brown envelopes flying around than your average post office, so that feels like an opportunity. The Task Force will report back to the Council at their March meeting and there'll be two further meetings – in July and October – to thrash out which bid or bids they'll recommend to Congress. If they were to go for the Chinese, Congress would also have to approve the change to the continental rules. That's a big ask as it would mean members agreeing to a rule change and deciding a bid at the same time. However, the FIFA President has a way of getting what he wants, so don't rule it out.'

Cauldwell went quiet and Rushbourne looked directly into the faces of Alec and Michaela.

'So, what do you say?'

Chapter 16

'For the benefit of our guests, I should explain that there's a reason The FA is called *The FA* rather than the *English* FA; at the time it was set up, in 1862, it was the first and only football association. We created the game, decided its rules and gifted it to the world. Is it too much to ask that we host its World Cup from time to time? I think not…'

The GB-2030 Bid Committee had been meeting like this every few weeks for almost three years and, it is fair to say, progress had been depressingly slow. Ten minutes in, some around the table already had their heads in their hands while others smothered yawns. But the speaker, FA Chairman Lord Cheeseman, was undeterred.

'Despite being forced to gather in temporary headquarters, our meeting here in Wembley is auspicious. Before the building of the first Wembley Stadium in 1923, this was the sight of the Watkins Tower which opened in 1896 as a visitor attraction to encourage travellers to ride on the new Metropolitan Railway…'

'Roger, I hate to cut in, but could we get to the point please.' The interruption was from Damien Scott, MP, whose job as Chair of the committee meant it fell to him to keep the meeting on track.

'Yes well, my point, if I'm allowed to make it, and without upsetting our friends from the Home Nations, is that the pillars of world football were built on the enterprise and effort of notable Englishmen. I'd like to say for the benefit of our newcomers that we should be mindful of the debt which we owe them and of our duty to one another and to English, sorry,

British football fans. This is not a place for egos; in modern football parlance, there's no 'I' in team…'

'But there is a 'u' in cunt.' This time it was the mumbled voice of Mike Deighton, inventor, entrepreneur, club owner and main financier of the bid to stage the 2030 FIFA World Cup.

Cheeseman flushed, angrily. 'You may consider me an old fart, Deighton,' he hissed, 'but cross me and you'll have made a powerful enemy.'

Scott jumped in again. 'Gentlemen, please. If we can't even get through the introductions, then this bid really is beyond revival. Can I remind you that our main order of business today is to try and address our lack of progress to date and these exchanges are just another example of how disjointed we are.'

'He started it; calling me a cunt.'

'You wouldn't shut the fuck up…'

'Enough! Now, to save time I'll go around the room for Alec and Michaela's benefits. You've already heard from Roger Cheeseman of the FA and Mike Deighton, then we've got Bill Williams from the Welsh FA, Dodie Fyfe, Scottish FA and Jim O'Neil from Northern Ireland. There's Gill Andrews, our new man on the FIFA Council, Sir Keith Hale who chaired London 2012, Debbie Evans-Pugh who worked alongside him, Gabby Gallacher I'm sure you know already from her media and TV work, Dame Annie Brown-Trevis and Ade Chaponda. On the professional side I'd like to welcome back Andy Small from Big Bad Events and Malcolm Tonghe from Silver-Tonghe, our PR agency, both of whom we'll be hearing from today. Now, I'd like to introduce former footballer Alec Munday who has a bit of a reputation for getting under the skin of the various goings on in world football. The latest avenue for his talents is as a journalist and I think it's fair to say that he puts the rat into narrative with various media outlets. If that wasn't enough, you'll no doubt be familiar with the role he played during the Wembley bombing. His status as have-a-go hero catapulted him to fame across sport and beyond. With Alec is Michaela Dagg who, among many other things, is a former senior policewoman. I was introduced to these two about eight weeks ago and they volunteered to help. So, I gave them a wide brief to look at how we're doing compared to the other bidders. Chatham House rule applies, of course, so we can all speak freely, but I'm hoping they may be able to offer some insights as to where we have ground to make up.'

Scott nodded to Alec who took his cue. 'Thanks, Damien, for the invite and the introduction. It feels more like I've spent my journalistic career putting the twit into Twitter, but I'm grateful for the mention.' He looked around the room, mentally ticking the boxes in his own private game of diversity bingo. 'As for the other business, that was really a case of right place, right time or wrong time depending on how you look at it.'

His attempt at self-deprecation was appreciated, although one or two looked at him with a quizzical squint.

Damien Scott pressed on. 'We shall hear a bit more from Alec under agenda point seven but, with the introductions done, let's move to point two: security. One of the action points from our last meeting was to ask Big Bad Events to look at the range of risks the bid and any subsequent tournament will face. Perhaps Andy, you could update us.'

'Sure, Damien and g'day everybody,' Small said, standing up in front of a powerpoint deck labelled slide 1 of 47. 'As we identified last time, the world has changed and that means the nature of the threats we face has changed with it. The piece of work we've carried out was prompted by the Covid-19 pandemic of 2020 and the recent devastation of Wembley Stadium. We asked whether we should factor in the possibility of a major catastrophe to our bid planning and, look, it's a fair question. Taking the pandemic possibility first, the good news is that the world is much better prepared for a future virus having just had to wargame the last one in real time. On the flipside, our awareness of the damage a pandemic can do is now much higher so, paradoxically, although the risk of major disruption is lower, the cost of any kind of insurance policy that would help mitigate it is significantly higher.'

Andy Small was small only in the sense that Little John was little, but his impressive stature did nothing to relieve the monotonous Strine in which his presentation was delivered. Alec felt himself drifting and, looking around the room, could see he wasn't alone. The National Football Association representatives were committee meeting veterans. Uniformly dressed in blazers, FA ties and thick-lensed glasses, they seemed to enter a dormant state, hovering on the verge of consciousness while retaining just enough grip on their surroundings to respond if addressed directly by name. The others around the table were not as practised in the art and there was an audible exhalation of breath as, barely an hour into his presentation, Small wrapped up and sat down.

'That's tremendous, Andy,' said Damien Scott, trying to inject some energy into his voice. 'I'd like if we can, to knock off the next three points before we break for coffee. Let's go round the National Federations for a quick update on local support.'

The coffee came forty minutes later by which point some of those who hadn't yet spoken had to be physically roused. Although never a smoker, Alec followed his habit of joining those who were on the basis he'd probably get a truer read on the way the meeting was going. He wasn't disappointed.

'Hello stranger,' came Gabby Gallacher's lazy drawl. 'What the hell are you doing here?' she said, taking a long drag on a Sterling Superking and mwah, mwah'ing three inches away from each of Alec's cheeks.

'Hi Gabby. Great to see you too, although I could ask the same question.'

'I thought I might be in line for the presenting gig, but I can't see us ever getting that far. We are *so* not going to win this thing, not in a million years.'

'It doesn't exactly feel like we're serious contenders if this morning's anything to go by.'

'They say laws and sausages are two things you don't want to see being made but I'd add World Cup bids to the list. Fortunately, this is just the politics; the actual work on the bid is being done by the executive team but, I have to say, another five minutes of that and I would have stabbed my own eyes out. What did you think, Debs?'

Debbie Evans-Pugh gave a resigned shrug. 'Par for the course, I'm afraid. I did four sodding years of this in the run up to the London 2012 bid, and don't think it was any better just because we won. The Dame does his best,' she said, referring to Damien Scott by his parliamentary nickname. 'But it's like pushing water uphill. And Mike Bloody Deighton doesn't help either, winding Roger up all the time. He may be richer than Croesus but he's only here because he came out for Brexit and they couldn't give him a 'K' on account of him being a non-dom. Anyway, Alec Munday, journalist and fully paid-up national treasure, what desperate urge brings you to this shitshow?'

'I was approached, and they made me an offer I couldn't refuse but I suspect after they hear what I've got to say, I won't be asked back.'

'Ooh, that sounds juicy. Do share,' said Gabby.

'You'll have to wait 'till agenda point seven, I'm afraid. Until then my lips are sealed.'

'Oh well, in that case piss off and let me have a word with Gabby,' was Evans-Pugh's caustic dismissal.

Alec glanced towards Michaela who had been trapped by the FA blazers. He could have rescued her but where was the fun in that. Instead, he wandered over to Malcolm Tonghe, the PR man. 'Hello mate. How's tricks?'

'I'm in fine form, but how are you?' came the languid tones of an expensive education. 'It's *so interesting* to see you. I thought to myself when you came in earlier, I wonder what the author of *Direct from the Dressing Room* could possibly be doing here. A bit off your patch, aren't you?'

Tonghe was a seasoned pro but hardly known for keeping his ear to the ground. However, on this occasion he had hit the jackpot; *Direct from the Dressing Room* was Alec's anonymous *Guardian* column where he drew back the curtain on the intimate lives of famous footballers.

'You shouldn't believe everything you hear on the grapevine, Malc. Anyway, I thought it was Paul Merson that wrote that.'

Tonghe looked direct into Alec's face, waspish disbelief obvious in his eyes. 'If you say so. Anyway, what are you doing at this shitshow then?'

'Funny, you're the second person to call it that in the last two minutes. So far, all my energies have been focused on trying to stay awake, but you're up next so I'm hoping things will liven up a bit. Break a leg.'

To call Malcolm Tonghe a smooth operator was hardly to do justice to the man who stood to command the floor. A lifetime's practice in the alchemic art of porcine lipstick application made it impossible for him simply to pass on information. He could not utter a sentence without first calculating in minutely gradated detail how it would be received. Each word was weighed, every phrase refined in real time and delivered with what he judged to be perfect emphasis. If he was expressing sympathy, emotion would ooze from every pore. If he was appealing to patriotism, his audience could feel his inner struggle to keep his right hand from moving to his heart. And his range when it came to anger was legendary. Industry insiders claimed his trick was to conjure up a mental picture of someone he felt embodied the message he was delivering. Whether this was true or not, his approach generally worked and today he felt the need to inspire confidence. His heels left the ground and his chin jutted forward as he channeled cricketer Ben Stokes at the crease projecting 'I've got this' with every nod and inflection. He proceeded to swat the ball all around the ground, hitting sixes and fours off every delivery, chasing down an impossible total before sinking spent into his seat.

It was a bravura performance and left his audience feeling that there might, just might be a chance: that football could be coming home after all, and the World Cup would be staged in the Britain for first time in over sixty years. In the pause after Tonghe sat down, at least one person in the room had to restrain himself from applauding. There were smiles on the faces around the table even if only at the chutzpah of a master of his craft.

Mike Deighton was the first to comment. 'That's what I'm paying for,' he said. 'Someone who believes in this bid rather than kicking a gift horse in the mouth. Deliver it like that, Malcolm, and FIFA will give you a standing ovulation.'

Alec had heard of Deighton's gift for malapropisms yet couldn't fail to be impressed by the casual confidence with which he delivered his verbal gaffs. The committee had obviously moved past his faux pas and took on an air of positivity for the first time since the meeting started. There was enthusiastic nodding and mummers of assent from most of the members. The trouble was, Alec didn't believe a word of it and he was up next. He waited while Damian Scott moved the agenda on and then all eyes turned to him.

Alec stood up on cue. 'Thanks again for the introduction, Damian. Look, I won't take up your time. Aside from being an England fan, I've got no dog in this fight, and you can take what I'm about to say and do whatever you like with it. How we got involved isn't really important, but as you've heard, we were asked to do a bit of digging into how the GB-2030 bid was going down with the insiders at FIFA. I have spent a busy few weeks watching your rivals and Michaela has done some very preliminary research into their finances to see what they would reveal and, long story short, you're being outgunned on all fronts with the possible exception of one.'

He handed out spiral-bound copies of a thin report.

'We started with the declared list of runners and riders: Azerbaijan, Morocco, China, Spain/Portugal, Argentina/Uruguay/Chile/Paraguay and the Balkan States. I'm sure you've got thoughts on the strengths and weaknesses of each bid, but obviously the UK's existing stadium infrastructure and experience means we've got to be top of the pile technically. We've got a stronger football culture than most of the others and there'll be enough media and sponsor support to cover off the commercial angles. But, as you know from 2010, that doesn't get us across the line. So, I've looked at how each bid is campaigning and tried to judge what effect they are having on those who are going to decide the final vote. To do that, I grabbed my NUJ lanyard and headed for the airport.

'First stop was Africa, Burundi to be precise. I was one of the foreign press invited to the inauguration of a new football centre in Bujumbura paid for by SOCAR, Azerbaijan's state oil company. Now, you'll tell me that UEFA is only going to support one European bid and the public backlash from the Euro games staged in Baku would make them an unpopular choice, but I wouldn't be so confident. UEFA clearly wants to encourage them, and FIFA has shown it doesn't care about public opinion. For what it's worth, I'd say they are a long shot, but win or lose, the publicity alone means it's good value for them. So, if you assumed they'd drop out, I'm going to predict they will be muddying the waters right up to the end. The FIFA Council can only recommend a maximum of three bidders to their Congress, but I'd say they have to be considered a threat.

From Burundi I went on to a conference of the African football federations chaired by one of FIFA's Senior Vice Presidents in Senegal. It turned out I was the only who paid for my flight as all the delegates' travel was covered by the Chinese. China can't host under the current rules, but I think we all know that FIFA won't block them just because Qatar is technically on the same continent. The conference hotel was paid for by the Moroccan Government who handed out goody bags with some chunky reminders of their view that it's time for "exotic Africa" to stage the World Cup. The opening gala dinner was a grand affair sponsored jointly by the Latin Americans. They used their welcome address as hosts to promise that the benevolence of FIFA would be richly repaid should they be chosen. Blatant, yes, but no one can accuse them of not putting themselves in the running. From there I flew to Madagascar – lovely place by the way – for the visit of the Spanish national team who played a friendly against the locals and went on a charm offensive in local schools, which was all over their media.'

'So that was Africa,' he went on. 'Then I headed for South America, to Bogotá where the Moroccans and Balkan states were hosting the CONMEBOL equivalent of the Balon d'Or. Then the circus moved on to Paraguay where Argentina, Uruguay and Chile had brought their respective women's teams to play the Copa América Femenina, which was a nice touch I thought. I didn't go myself, but I heard there was an Azerbaijani delegation there too, apparently exploring err, trade opportunities, whatever those might be. And the common factor to Burundi, Senegal Colombia etc.? They each have a representative on the FIFA Council and some of them are already being touted as part of the team that will assess the bids on the ground. Love them or loathe them, these are the decision makers, and they are being actively wooed by your rivals.'

'This is all highly irregular,' said Cheeseman, licking the end of his thumb and rifling through a pile of papers. 'FIFA rules state no campaigning and no direct contact with Council members until after the bidders have been approved. There are very strict rules on football development projects and funding has to come from recognised national interests. So, I think we have several reasons to complain.'

'Never mind who's circumcising the rules,' said Deighton. 'What I want to know is how much this is all costing?' He gestured at Alec. 'We can't have him flying around the world like a wolf in cheap clothing if we're going to need every penny to promote the bid.'

Alec looked exasperated. 'Sorry gents, you're missing the point. Whatever the rules, I'm telling you what's actually going on and this is just a snapshot. I'll leave it to you to find out what happened before the past couple of weeks and but I'd say they've got a lot planned for the run up to the decision. And as for the money, even if you were paying my expenses, which you're not, by the way, they're a drop in the ocean compared to what the other bidders are spending. Michaela will give some more details on finance, but as it stands, the GB bid is dead in the water. Anything you're spending is a waste of money because you're going to lose.'

Alec handed over to Michaela to summarise the financial information she had unearthed.

'I conducted a very superficial trawl,' she said, 'through publicly available information and did some rooting around in a few of the darker digital corners too. It goes without saying that the Azerbaijan bid is heavily backed by the government although the actual cash is being put up by SOCAR and shows up in their books as sponsorship. I ignored China for now as there's no question they are in a strong enough financial position to fund a tilt at the World Cup. And, as Alec said, they're definitely on the bid trail.

The others are bit less obvious, although I did have some luck with Morocco where I found an account held in the same bank and with the same signatories as the main Moroccan FA account. In the last six months they received a five-million-dollar deposit from a Russian mining corporation which is seeking a licence to operate in the country. That's in addition to a windfall of eight hundred thousand dollars direct from FIFA which they diverted from the football development account. That adds up to a decent fighting fund as far as campaigning goes, but it's unclear where the money would come from to stage the World Cup itself, particularly in the new 48-team format.

'Spain and Portugal, or SpaPo2030 as they've called their bid company, are on the back foot financially. They know they are not going to spend their way to success, but they have siphoned off a large slice of their European Structural Fund allocation on the basis that a successful bid is a key part of their response to Covid. As for the Latin Americans, their bid seems to have been one of the main beneficiaries of recent changes to tax laws which have repatriated billions that had been squirreled away in Panama. As a result, they are not only well funded for the bid but for the infrastructure they would need to stage the competition too. As for the GB bid, you have been the most transparent financially, but I did find that small slush fund – yes, if I can find it then so will the other bids – totalling around two hundred thousand pounds. I'm sure you don't need me to tell you that's barely going to scratch the surface. There are more details in your reports, but, in summary, if money is the answer, then I'm sorry to say, you're not asking the right questions.'

'You mentioned that, aside from our technical bid, there was one other area where we were winning,' interjected Scott, hopefully.

'Oh, yes, you're definitely winning the PR battle,' Alec replied, to visible preening from Tonghe, 'but not in the way you're hoping, Malc. Everywhere I went they were all talking about GB-2030, singing Football's Coming Home and either fuming about White Imperialism or laughing like it's the biggest joke they've ever heard. So, you've got the story out brilliantly, but it's completely at odds with the reality. The chances of football coming home to the UK are somewhere between those of me getting pregnant with twins and hell freezing over.'

There was a stunned silence around the room broken only when Damian Scott said: 'Well, this has been extremely informative. I'd like to thank you on behalf of the group.

Perhaps Gill, you'd like to respond from the perspective of a FIFA Council member, then we'll take questions for Alec.'

'Erm, yes well, I have no reason to doubt the veracity of reports although to have reached this sort of fever pitch so early in the process is unusual. They could all be viewed as contrary to FIFA rules, but no doubt the bidders will have a plausible explanation. As we've said before, this is a marathon, not a sprint, and we have seen plenty of bidders run out of steam by turning on the money taps too early. My advice would be to hold our nerve. I continue to work on my FIFA Council colleagues and I'm quietly confident we're making headway.'

'I'd love to share your confidence, Gill,' said Sir Keith Hale, 'but in my experience what you actually discover is the tip of the iceberg. Alec and his friend have found out some useful information, but I suspect there's a lot more that they don't know about. I do have one question for you though, Alec. Do you think there's a chance we can win?'

It was Alec's turn to be silent as he considered his response. 'Obviously, that's one of the things we have been asking ourselves. And our answer is 'it depends'. I don't think anyone's expecting a GB bid to outspend the others, but there is more than one way to win with FIFA and I'm not talking about playing the odd friendly or sending crocodile handbags to Council member's wives. So, yes, I think we could win, but the question I'd like to leave with you is 'do you have the stomach to do what it takes?'

Chapter 17

Damien Scott's driver was impassive as he piloted the official Vauxhall Insignia through the Wembley streets and back towards Westminster. Michaela sat beside him while Alec and the MP sat next to each other in the back.

'A driver is normally only for Secretaries of State and above,' Scott said, 'but there are a few perks of being the PM's bagman. Sorry about all that back there. How we ever came to have an empire is beyond me.'

Alec sympathised. 'I'm not been a committee man,' he said, 'and I don't know a footballer who is, but that lot couldn't organise a panic in a leaking submarine. Do you need them all on the team?'

Scott sighed heavily. 'Individually they're impressive – Cheeseman is ex SAS wouldn't you know, Deighton made his first million in Lebanon of all places and I boxed for Eton – but put us in a room and call us a committee and we revert to behaviour that gives democracy a bad name. There are so many footling points of order and grandiose statements 'for the record' that I despair sometimes. Part of FIFA's criteria though, is that a bidder has to show they've got political and public support back home, so we need to keep working to create a united front. One of the things our rivals have in the Azerbaijans of this world is total adherence to the diktats of their ruler. If I say 'the Prime Minister really wants this to happen' it means something completely different here from what it would in Baku. Anyway, I wanted to ask what you meant by having the stomach to do what it takes to win.'

Alec looked directly at him. 'I think you know exactly what I meant otherwise you wouldn't have had your spooks bring us in.'

'Don really does want this, you know. He saw what London 2012 did for Boris's popularity. That's unicorns and fairy dust to a Prime Minister who's trying to persuade everyone he's got a plan to build back better after Brexit and the pandemic. He'd be prepared to sanction almost anything to get that kind of a win at the moment.'

Don was Donald Ellington, Boris Johnson's successor as PM after he was skewered by his party. Once they worked out that their leader's arms-length acquaintance with the truth was an electoral liability, the knives were out. The new man was a chancer and an opportunist who was blessed with the demeanour of someone quietly competence. He knew his limitations, though. Having not had to win an election to get the top job, he realised it would take more than a safe pair of hands to head off an emboldened opposition. Short of war with France, a World Cup, however far into the future, would do the job, but he was determined not to be embarrassed by FIFA a second time.

'He knows we call him Ducky: drives him crazy. Not a gay reference, you understand, but even so. He was shooting for Duke, as in Duke Ellington, but it was *The Mirror's* headline that did for him on that score with "Donald Ducks the Question". It didn't even matter what the question was, he was always going to be Ducky after that. Anyway, cutting to the chase, what do you have in mind?'

'In football it's called shithousery but dark arts, dirty tricks, call it what you like, we'll need to get some dirt under our fingernails if you're to stand any chance of giving your boss his unicorns. We know the bids are all cheating but that's not going to cut any ice in Zurich. You might be able to pull some diplomatic strings, but if we're going to have any real chance of success, someone's going to have to go after the Council themselves. The Congress has the final say but it's those 37 members who make the decision. They're going to have to be threatened, discredited, attacked and undermined so that in the end FIFA is either bullied or embarrassed into giving us the World Cup.'

'The other bidders won't take it lying down either,' added Michaela, 'so inevitably, things are going to get messy. There'll have to be clear blue water between whoever's dishing the dirt and the bid itself, particularly if the PM's backing it. We're talking about fighting a whole separate campaign while the official bid bumbles along doing just enough to seem credible. Behind the scenes, FIFA may suspect who is responsible and, more to the point, who can make it stop, but officially, there will have to be complete deniability. Which is, I'm guessing, why we're here.'

Scott looked first at Alec and then at Michaela. 'I was impressed with you both when we were first introduced, and I have been no less dazzled by your formidable talents since. Nigel Rushbourne has hinted at what your involvement at Wembley was, Alec, and filled me in a bit on your previous brush with organised crime, so I guess we all know what we'd be getting ourselves into. He'll help where he can, but this isn't a stage they are used to performing on. You'd effectively be running the show and if you take it on, you'll be on your own. No one, not me, and certainly not the Prime Minister, will know the full extent of your actions and whatever the result, your efforts won't receive any official recognition. Nigel also implied that you'll be finding ways of funding your activities. I'm not going to ask, but you will, I imagine, be putting yourselves to considerable personal inconvenience and no small risk.'

'That's some sales pitch,' Michaela said. 'Why would we do it?'

'I don't know, but I'm hoping you will anyway.'

'Give us a week to think things through then, if we're in, we'll give Rushbourne a shopping list of what we think we'll need. Let's see if we're all still on the same page at that point.'

The ministerial car pulled into a side street near Paddington Station and dropped off two of its passengers before continuing on its journey. Alec and Michaela headed for the Frontline Club. He had first taken her to the war reporter's hangout early on in their relationship, and it had become their first choice for a quiet lunch when they were in town. They took up their regular spot at a table near the bar and ordered some food.

With the waiter dispatched to search for some Seedlip gin substitute for Alec, Michaela was the first to speak. 'I think we should do it. It's dodgy, potentially dangerous and probably pointless, but it sounds like fun. Right up our street, don't you think?'

Alec was amazed. 'You've changed from when I first met you, and I'm not sure it's for the better. I thought you'd be dead against.'

He stopped and considered the idea carefully for the first time. 'I'm not sure,' he said, in the end. 'It reminds me of when my nan used to bring presents round at Christmas. I'd fall for it every year; I couldn't help it. I'd get all excited, but when I tore through the wrapping, she'd outdone herself with some handmade horror. And the worst thing was I had to try and look grateful. I remember my mum told her one year we were learning about the Romans in school, and she knitted me a centurion's helmet with the full red Mohican and chinstrap. They made me wear it right through dinner.'

'Your nan sounds great,' laughed Michaela. 'You know she did it deliberately, don't you?'

'Yeh, probably. Anyway, it taught me to look past the shiny paper, and I can only see disappointment with this one.'

'Go on,' she said. 'I still think it sounds like fun.'

'Think about it, we're going to have to cross all sorts of lines with FIFA and the other bidders. And when we lose, which we almost inevitably will, we're just going to get the blame for stirring things up. And if, by some stroke of luck, we did get a result, the members of that bloody committee will claim the credit. I mean, the state of them; more dinosaurs than Jurassic Park. I'm with Simon and his vision of Britain's place in the world, but frankly the other bidders have more to gain than Team GB and that's not going to change.'

Now it was Michaela's turn to look surprised. 'Wow, what happened to giving the Sheikh the shakedown? As for losing, we know the bid's going to lose if we're not involved, so it's up to us to get it done. The way I look at it, we're completely deniable so no one can ever blame us whatever the result. I've spent a career following procedure only to have the courts throw out my cases on a technicality raised by some smart-arsed barrister. This way, we make our own rules and deliver our own justice, and I'm looking forward to some payback.'

'Maybe that's it. I was always brought up to work within the rules. Yes, footballers try and bend them and get one over on the ref but, at the end of the day, if there aren't any rules, the game's not worth playing.'

'It's a great speech but I'm not buying it, and I'll tell you why. You of all people should know the buzz you get from winning is like a drug and you're hooked the same as every other footballer. I saw the look on your face when that plane took off from Serbia; it was like you were right back in the game. I know Wembley didn't go well for you, but you can't deny that while it lasted, you were operating in full colour on Ultra HD with the sound turned up to eleven. When you've experienced that, it's impossible to be satisfied with the dull, grey realities of a normal life.'

Alec took a slug of his alcohol-free gin and put it back on the table in disgust.

'Maybe,' he conceded, then more decisive. 'Yeh, who am I kidding? At the end of the day, I'm bored. I've got more money than I could ever spend and my only use to society is advising footballers on how to keep their dicks in their pants and their skeletons in the cupboard. Since I stopped drinking, I feel like I'm living life at half speed. I need the next high and this sounds like the best offer we're going to get, if you're onboard.'

Michaela smiled and shook her head, amazed at his willingness to apply a handbrake turn to his arguments. 'Don't you worry about me; I'm ready for a bit of excitement in my life and, before you ask, my therapist agrees. I told you that I would either be fully in or completely out and I meant it.'

'All right,' Alec said, with enthusiasm. 'We should take that week to think the unthinkable and see what sort of plan we can come up with between us. Let's give Damien Scott something that really will turn his stomach, then see how much he wants it.'

'While we're on the subject of the unthinkable, there was something else I wanted to talk to you about.'

'Ok,' he said, a question mark forming in his eyes.

She picked up her drink and played with the glass before ploughing on. 'I think you should move.'

The question mark deepened. 'Go on.'

'Yes, you know, make a fresh start somewhere else. I know we cleaned the Enfield place up a bit, but it's got too many ghosts, Alec. There's nothing keeping you there and it's nice and clean so it should sell easily enough. Just draw a line and move on.'

Her suggestion didn't take him completely by surprise. She had been avoiding his house for weeks and all their last few overnight dates had been in hotels. 'Ok. Where do you fancy?'

'What makes you think I'd be coming with you?'

'I'd like you to, if you wanted.'

'Where has this come from? She asked, with faux outrage. 'I mean, I make a casual suggestion that you consider a change of scene, and you're jumping to the part where we move in together.'

'This isn't anything new, at least, not for me,' he said, seriously. 'We've done stuff that most people wouldn't be able to comprehend, you know how I think and what I need and I can't imagine sharing my life with anyone else. I also think I'm good for you too, so what do you think?'

Michaela looked down at her drink again, taking time to choose her words. 'There would need to be some changes.'

'What like? You've already told me I have to move house.'

She looked directly at him, her large brown eyes unusually hesitant and vulnerable. 'I need two things: I need you to be committed and I need a stake in our partnership. If we're going to do this, I'm going to put my flat up for sale, and I'll put what I get for it into a place with you.'

He nodded the kind of nod that said he was listening rather than agreeing. 'You know, this whole arrangement where I pay for your therapist isn't working for me, and it's got nothing to do with the money. I want you to be able to pay for your own therapist or whatever you need but I want to be part of the outcome. So, don't put your flat on the market; no one sells these days unless they need to. We'll rent out both properties and get somewhere new together.'

'Yes, but I need to feel I'm making a contribution to what we're building. I've seen what happens with your football mates and their WAGs, and I'm not going to be a kept woman who can be discarded in a year or so if you lose interest.'

'It sounds like you want a pre-nup or a non-nup, or some other sort of contract...'

'Don't be like that, Alec. You make it sound like I'm trying to tie you up in legal knots when all I want is an equal partnership.'

'You didn't let me finish. I agree with you, and we don't need to get any lawyers involved. I'm going to sign two blank cheques and give them to you. You know how much money I've got so you can fill them in for as much as you like and that's your money. We made it together so it's rightly yours anyway. If you choose to use part of it to invest in a property with me that's fine, but either way it's yours on the basis that we're going into this as partners.'

She sat in silence, working her way through the implications of what he was proposing. In the end she said, 'I accept, I think. But why two cheques?'

'You'll get the number wrong first time and I want you to have the chance to go back and change it without us having this discussion again.'

Her face cracked into a smile. 'You're full of surprises. I've never had a live-in partner before.'

'Well, we better start practicing being a full-time couple back at the hotel.'

Chapter 18

Locals can always tell when the Old Man is in residence. It isn't that any additional flags are flown – they fly 365 days a year unless lowered to half-mast upon news of the death of a Council member – or that the place bustles with an extra urgency or sense of purpose. This is Switzerland, after all, where suits are grey, spectacles gold-rimmed and business is conducted in ways that attract as little attention as possible. Security is discretely increased, it's true: there are two guards on the main entrance and dogs loose in the grounds around the shrouded granite and glass structure. But only the keenest eye would see the difference. For those who care to notice, there is a sharp increase in the number, up to ten or even more every hour, of large German-made limousines ferrying supplicants from Zurich Airport. Even so, Swiss timekeeping being what it is, there comes a moment each evening when the steady two-way flow of chauffeured saloons turns into a one-way exit of French hatchbacks as the staff at FIFA Headquarters clock off.

The number of vehicles heading southwest on FIFA Strasse seems out of all proportion to the capacity of the three-storey building behind them, leaving the out-of-town visitor to imagine workers packed in like commuters on the Tokyo subway. The reality is as logical as it is absurd. In a glorious metaphor for his client, the building's architect decided to invert the structure and bury it underground creating a vast cavern of subterranean offices thrusting down some thirty metres below the surface.

The Old Man's working day is spent in his office two floors below ground, but once it is over, he waves his unique fob at the elevator's control panel and rides up five floors to the top of the building. One by one, the other parts of FIFA HQ go dark, but lights in the penthouse show, as surely as the Union Flag fluttering over Buckingham Palace, that the FIFA President is in his suite.

He rarely uses the luxury apartment having a perfectly serviceable lakefront mansion just a few minutes away. But the Old Man has made it a habit of his long and successful presidency not to leave the seat of power in the run up to Council meetings however sure he is of the agenda. Today he sits alone at a large, kidney-shaped desk made of polished wood despite the clock on the shelf beside him showing almost eight-thirty in the evening. The timepiece is a gaudy affair with an inlay of the South Sudan flag surrounded by jewel-encrusted footballs. It was a present from the Association when it became the latest to join the FIFA fold in 2012. It is barely noticeable amid the myriad spurious trophies, medals, commemorative baubles and other expensive tat jostling for position.

There is no computer on the desk although the plastic-lined hole at one end is evidence that there might have been once and could be again. But, for this president, a desktop machine would be entirely redundant. His legendary IT phobia is a myth that he encourages to provide the perfect justification for his rule never to reply to messages. In fact, he uses an iPad to receive communications by email or instant message and, if he considers that a personal response is required, he picks up the phone. The logic behind his choice is faultless; the subtlety of the human voice, he claims, conveys both the content and intention of the speaker much more powerfully and succinctly than any written communication. On this point he can never be challenged leading some to suspect a different reason. His real purpose, they conclude, is to avoid a paper trail connecting him personally to the misdemeanours of the organisation he presides over.

Alongside his iPad lies a sheaf of papers prepared for him by Secretary General, Guillermo Salz. He perused the agenda earlier in the day but now takes a final glance through each point, satisfying himself that there are no political or administrative man traps he must navigate. The financial picture was almost embarrassingly rosy, and he was directing some of the surplus to Council members on whom he needed to rely. As ever, the money was earmarked for football development, but he was not foolish enough to imagine that any more than a fraction of it would be transmuted into 3G pitches or changing facilities. Which is exactly how he likes it. In fact, like the match fixers he regularly denounces, his position is made more secure by the knowledge that his Council colleagues are skimming, syphoning or out-and-out stealing national federation funds. Once he knows their fingers are in the till, he gently but ruthlessly controls them suggesting either that the money tap could be turned off or that their embezzlement could be made public. Following the money and how it is spent has proved an extremely reliable way of cementing his grip on power whilst giving the appearance of an open democracy. This cosy arrangement has only ever been tested when countries channel state funds through their FAs to support a bid for a major football tournament. A huge influx of cash could in theory make local officials less reliant on his largesse. In reality most of the surplus was destined to come to FIFA one way or another and, when it did, he was in a position to reward the federation in return. He has spent many a quiet moment reflecting on whether his system might be improved, and every time he concludes, with some pride, that it cannot.

Beyond money, there was nothing controversial on tomorrow's agenda amid ample evidence that all is for the best in this best of all possible worlds. After a triumphant Russia World Cup, sponsors were flocking round, Qatar had grabbed the media narrative and was even holding out an olive branch to its quarrelsome neighbours. Football spreading peace in the Middle East: the world should be grateful.

He knows better than to let an opportunity go to waste, however. A Council meeting with few discussion points is the perfect moment to bring up a subject close to the Old Man's heart. Which is why this evening his attention is directed to a large map of the world projected onto the wall opposite. It resembles the old maps of the British Empire with its dominions shaded red. In this version, a large slick of FIFA blue dominates Europe, the Middle East, Africa and Latin America. These are the territories where football is the most popular sport. Stubbornly large land masses in North America, the Indian Sub-continent and elsewhere are coloured white. These have yet to succumb to football's advances. A third, smaller but still numerous collection of orange-shaded countries are those where football is in the top-three sports. These are the Old Man's top targets and rich praise is lavished on federation bosses who turn their countries from orange to blue. To support their efforts his definition of popularity is extremely malleable. In the US, grassroots participation is the most favourable statistic, but it is still a long way from moving out of the white zone. In Australia, the high value of media rights was enough to turn it orange a few years ago. But the baffling popularity of Aussie Rules and rugby league looks set to keep it there.

The map is to form the centrepiece of his set-piece presentation to the Council. As he looks, his intense gaze is drawn to Asia, the only cloud on his otherwise sunny horizon. Straddling both hemispheres and containing over half of the world's population, it is just too big. China is the main goal and a rich prize for FIFA and the president personally. Support from the Xi Jinping took the country from white to orange in 2015. All it would take is a major tournament to turn it blue. Why had his predecessor not noticed how big it was? The decision to award the World Cup to Qatar had been a bold (and very lucrative) one, but now the rules meant it was blocking bids from other more important nations. He pondered trying to engineer a breakaway of countries from the Middle East and North Africa. It was the long-term solution but meant conversations with twenty fractious members. They would have to be dragged kicking and screaming to the table and it would all take too long. And cost too much.

The only possibility was a one-off exception to the rules but that wasn't easy either. The Asian Football Confederation would be delighted with the prospect of another World Cup within its borders. That was the problem: there were already signs that the AFC president was flexing his muscles. Being a Indian billionaire meant he was largely, although not completely, immune to financial persuasion. He craved power and, while there was no realistic chance that he could challenge for the top job, his wings needed clipping.

Ordinarily, the solution would be easy: send him to the Chinese with a promise that not only can they bid, but they would also be favourites for the 2030 World Cup. Then snatch the prize away denying that any such promise was made. That would diminish his currency among his membership and undermine his credibility as a future FIFA President. The Old Man possesses the foresight of a chess grand master, and he has seen two problems with this approach. First, it would embarrass the Chinese, upsetting a delicate relationship in which he has invested many years' work. And second, it would put the British in poll position. They have been a thorn in his side for years with their sanctimonious arrogance and sense of entitlement. The last thing he is going to do is let FIFA's crown jewels go to GB-2030 on his watch. But, what to do? If only people realised how difficult his job was at times.

After some consideration he decides to sleep on it and instead reviews his secretary's notes of the day's meetings. A courtesy visit from King Philippe of Belgium won him the promise of support for FIFA's bid for observer status at the United Nations. It helped that his country was about to take over the presidency of the UN Security Council. In exchange he would use his influence to encourage France to agree to a combined bid with Belgium for the Club World Cup. Naturally, the French will never agree, but the prospect of some kind of parity, however unlikely, was enough for the anaemic monarch.

A dozen pre-positioning meetings had followed with Council members where assurances had been exchanged and alliances crystallised ahead of tomorrow's meeting. Everybody knew that the important decisions were already taken behind the scenes but that didn't make the strategy any less effective. In fact, it was a badge of honour among members to be called to these preparatory meetings. So proudly did they wear their badge that the Old Man had taken to calling some of them in whether he needed to or not, just for the loyalty it bought him.

The final meeting of the day had been with a fellow Swiss, the President of the International Committee of the Red Cross. He had brokered an arrangement with the Red Cross to channel development funds to Haiti after the Haitian FA proved so embarrassingly corrupt that even FIFA had to distance itself. It was a good piece of business and secured him a fig leaf which would, no doubt, be useful in the future.

There were too many people in town for any commercial deal making to have been done, even from the hermetic bunker of his office. That would wait until the media spotlight that followed Council meetings had moved on. But all in all, it had been a good day's work and now it was time to relax. His chef had been given instructions to prepare something light, but first he needed a massage. He pressed the handsfree button on his desk phone dispatching his driver to a downtown Zurich address. He would be back in twenty-five minutes which was enough time to pour himself a glass of chilled Montrachet and take a shower.

He is padding around the apartment in a kimono when the buzzer goes and he lets in Sandrine, his masseuse with benefits. The Old Man's relationships have followed a pattern: a few good months followed by several bad years and an expensive fight at the end. He puts this down to his dedication to football. Women just couldn't understand that the sport needs him; he is its servant, and when it calls, he must answer. The arrangement with Sandrine gives him the benefit of some personal attention without any expectations or complications.

She is not a first-time caller and knows her client's preferences. She leaves an hour later having teased his flaccid dick into a reluctant climax. In her pocket is an extra fifty Swiss francs and his assurance that he will need her services again soon. He pours himself another glass of wine and sits down to a salad of rocket, tomato and buffalo mozzarella before turning to the final task of the day.

As well as an invitation to attend a personal meeting, there is one more favour in the Old Man's gift. The Council sits cabinet-style around a large hollow table surrounded by translator's booths. Most can get by perfectly well in the lingua franca, but protocol dictates that simultaneous translation must be available. And the translators take the blame for any otherwise awkward lost-in-translation moments. The top seats at the table are allocated according to rank. The Secretary General sits to the left of the President with the Senior Vice President on his right. The seven Vice Presidents fan out on either side followed by the heads of the Continental Federations. Their order is decided by the number of national federations under their patronage. The task of seating the ordinary members is a thorny one which has caused the Secretary General more than a few sleepless nights. Inevitably, it is the President himself, with his finely calibrated political antennae, who makes the final decision. He is quick and decisive, like a mediaeval king, not hesitating to promote one and downgrade another, scribbling initials on a printed table plan. He has no time for political correctness unless a member's propensity to take offence suits his purpose. His only rule is expediency: members who he wants to speak sit along the sides, his loyal henchmen are in opposite corners and those he wants to pressurise are positioned directly in his line of sight. Anyone in danger of getting above themselves is dispatched to what he likes to think of as Council Siberia: outside the Vice Presidents at the extremities of the same long side of the table that he occupies. The decisions made, he goes through the double doors into the Council chamber.

He leaves the plan on the table for a minion to deal with in the morning and strides back into his private apartment going directly to bed and sleeping the sleep of the innocents.

The following morning, he has scheduled a succession of brief one-to-one slots between his Secretary General and four Council members who will be called upon at strategic moments for endorsement. Then, at the appointed hour, a fleet of black Mercedes brings the rest of the Council members from the Baur Au Lac hotel while the puppet master watches on from the privacy of his penthouse. Others may consider them a wretched cabal, but he sees only a complex machine which he alone can control. They are his creation, the result of planning and manoeuvring going back decades; of palms greased here or crossed with silver there. They are not friends of course. At a personal level he would happily see most of them dead. But each one has a part to play in the complex mosaic of the world's favourite sport and he views them with pride if not affection.

From his vantage point he can see them jostling for position in the line for security. He is particularly interested in the behaviour of the newest member of the group, Sheikh Abdullah al Thani. The Qatari royal is dressed in a regular business suit but with oversized sunglasses and a baseball cap completely shielding his face. The Old Man has spent several fruitless hours worrying away at the problem, but has yet to find a way that he might control the powerful Arab. He consoles himself with the thought that he has never met a man without weaknesses. There would be time enough to identify what they might be, for now, he has a niggling feeling that he should tread warily.

Only when all the Council members are seated and order is established, do the double doors open for the President's entry. He completes a half circuit of the table feigning surprise at the way the room is arranged. He will often single out a member he himself has consigned to Siberia with a warm squeeze of the shoulder before taking his seat. When he is comfortable he gives a nod to the Secretary General who announces that the FIFA Council is in session.

Chapter 19

A dreamy new apartment in St Katharine Docks was a great place to imagine ways to twist the arm of the FIFA Council. It was still kitted out like the show home it had been, complete with inoffensive artwork, display cabinets with monochrome crockery and fine cut crystal glassware and a full complement of soft furnishings. If they ever got bored of staring at the Thames through panoramic windows, there was a state-of-the-art audio and home cinema system. Alec felt he had finally reached level par with the footballers whose palatial properties he had so often been a guest in. He and Michaela had viewed the top-floor condo within a week of their decision to move in together and picked up the keys three days later. It was rented but with an option to buy and, right now, it felt like an safe bet that was what they'd do.

The November sun was setting over Tower Bridge and the deepening blue dusk that followed gave a few early Christmas trees their chance to shine in the surrounding office buildings. The pair looked like a couple from a magazine drinking coffee from white, gold-rimmed mugs and looking over London's arterial waterway beneath them. Although their lives had followed very different pathways, they had both lived in London long enough to call it home. They remembered childhood trips down the Thames staring at the old wharves and wondering what kind of people lived behind the reclaimed facades in newly gentrified residences. Now they were those kinds of people, and it was taking some getting used to.

'This is a bit mad, isn't it? I mean, how did we get here?' Alec said, putting his mug carefully onto a coaster.

'I know, look at you using a coaster. You're all grown up.'

'Don't pretend you're not blown away by it too.'

'I just don't want to touch anything in case I break it. How do people live like this?'

'We could scuff it up a bit like I used to do when I got a new pair of Stan Smiths.'

'Don't you dare. I just want to keep it perfect.'

They channelled the feeling they were living another couple's life and wasted the next couple of hours on an increasingly outlandish shopping list to present to Nigel Rushbourne and Damien Scott. Inevitably it was Michaela who burst the bubble.

'You know what, this is fun and all and I hate to break it to you, but there's going to be no fully loaded Aston Martin, no 3D printer which can produce a lifelike rubber mask, no VR glasses with facial recognition, no window climbing sucker pads and not even a watch with a laser beam.'

'Don't tell me, my Mission Impossible dream is over.'

'Sorry. Time is ticking away, so we better start getting real. We know there's no money on the table so let's try and focus on things we're actually going use and which Rushbourne's likely to be able to deliver.'

In the end, their wish list was disappointingly short. They asked for two legends each with fully back-storied passports and credit cards. They were under no illusions about their spy credentials, but the chance to come and go without leaving a trail of incriminating personal data was worth having. Apart from those, the most they could come up with was a digital listening bug, the latest set of rainbow tables and a decryption device. They also requested the services of a hacker if those weren't enough to get them into whichever digital dungeons they wanted to explore.

It turned out the most useful resource they were given was manpower. Michaela spent two weeks with a team of analysts turning over as many rocks as they could find. They joined up the financial dots of FIFA's finances, those of its Council members, and all the bids. When they were done, she pulled the information into a single report and stood the team down. Needless to say, the dodgy dossier she produced was a real page turner. It may have lacked some of the Old Man's intimate insights, the picture it painted of his band of FIFA brothers was no less scandalous. Their original motivation may well have been a desire to promote the game. Now, however, the world's top football administrators were almost without exception chasing the two desires of ambitious men the world over: money and power.

Sat at their sculpted white breakfast bar in the early evening, she walked Alec through the findings.

'The charge sheet for this lot got longer and longer the more we looked,' she said, taking a slurp of coffee. 'Even reading my own report back I'm still shocked and if the media ever got a sniff of what was going it would fill the papers for weeks. Some of the Council are already rich beyond the imagination of most people, yet they're still prepared to do almost anything to stuff their pockets. And the worst thing is, they don't seem to care who knows it. I mean, a few of them have created a property portfolio hidden inside a shell company or squirrelled money away in an offshore bank, but the rest are doing it in plain sight. They're either stupid, utterly shameless or feel they're untouchable.'

'Rushbourne was right then,' said Alec. 'The amount of money it would take to buy off the Council is well out of the UK bid's price range. But it sounds like they might be more open to persuasion if they felt their cash was at risk. Can you just hack into their accounts and steal their money?'

'Theoretically, I suppose, but why would that make them vote for a British World Cup? There are seven with money or property in the UK and I was thinking we could tie them up with an Unexplained Wealth Order.'

Alec nodded, then gave up pretending he knew what she was talking about. 'Go on, then. I know you're dying to enlighten me.'

'A UWO, popularly known as a McMafia Order, is a power the courts have to freeze an individual's assets if they can't explain how they acquired them. So, if someone with no income owns a twenty-million-pound Chelsea mews house the law can grab it. They are difficult and expensive cases to win, but we're only looking to twist a few arms. Assuming Rushbourne can get the courts to play ball, we wouldn't need to do much to cause them a whole lot of inconvenience and expense.'

He caught on quickly. 'So, once we've got their balls in a vice, we tell them we can make the pain go away if they do what we want. Sounds good. So that's seven dealt with, but we've still got a way to go. I reckon we're going to need at least twenty-five to vote for GB-2030 to secure the Council's nomination unopposed.'

Michaela looked down her list. 'I don't think we'll find it too hard to blackmail the greedy ones. There are at least two here with serious gambling debts, so if we could arrange to serve them up a run of bad luck they'd soon be desperate and I'm sure the others will be just as open to persuasion.'

'But that still leaves a dozen names on the list. Anything we can do with them?'

'I've dug into their personal finances and, from what I can see, I'd say money isn't their main priority. They are all well off or even rich by most people's standards, but there are no superyachts, big cocaine habits or even alimony bills burning through the cash. They live within their means and haven't had big handouts from FIFA that I can see. They just seem to be in it for the lifestyle.

'I suppose, the chance to travel the world on FIFA's dollar isn't a bad life. You know, business class flights, five-star hotels, tickets to any football match you fancy and all the chicken dinners you can eat? It wouldn't suit me, but there are worse ways to spend your retirement. At least if they're actually in it for the good of the game, they are likely to support the strongest bidder and swing behind a host who guarantees security, plenty of fans in the stands and a decent hotel for Council members.'

Michaela shook her head. 'When I say *lifestyle*, a platinum airmiles membership, suite at the Ritz Carlton and limitless supplies of matchday hospitality isn't really what I meant. I mean, look at these two.' She showed Alec the various websites she had been researching. 'This bastard makes the headlines wherever he goes, and not in a good way. He's been accused of raping young girls and boys and only seems to have evaded prison by using FIFA as cover. The other one's not much better either. There's an open investigation into the death of a prostitute in Portugal that's got his name all over it. So, don't expect him to be on the evaluation commission for that bid.'

'Dealing with this lot really is like trying to pick up a turd by the clean end, isn't it? How can we get at them? I mean they should be vulnerable, but they behave as if they're immune.'

'The first rule of coercion is to find something they really care about. We just need to keep looking until we find out what that is, then threaten to take it away.'

'Ok, I guess. Who else have we got?'

Michaela flicked through the open tabs on her laptop. 'Two of the other names are presidents of continental federations. They look squeaky clean but, given the company they keep, that's suspicious in itself. Maybe they have ambitions to take over the top job and are playing a longer game.'

'I know some FIFA members make Jimmy Saville look like your model babysitter, but there's no way anyone's going to get the top job if they're as cloudy as a Russian wrestler's urine sample. As for your rule, that should mean they really care about their reputations. The prospect of some carefully slung mud could well be enough to bring them around to the virtues of a British bid. I should be able to work the media angles on them. Who have we got left?'

'Ok, there are still three we haven't talked about,' Michaela said. 'First there's the President himself, although he doesn't vote on the Council.'

'That doesn't mean anything. He pulls the strings of all the voting members and it's not in his nature to allow a vote where he doesn't control the outcome. Unless he's firmly behind a UK bid it's not going to fly. There's got to be some dirt on him, though, hasn't there?'

'Not really, in fact, there's very little of anything. He has a real aversion to putting anything in writing, so he's got almost no digital footprint: he's like one of those Olympic divers who enters the water without a splash. There have been plenty of accusations made against him over the years and the Americans really got their claws into him for a while, but no one's ever got anything to stick. He pulls in a chunky salary, and he's built up a modest fortune with a lakeside house in Zurich and a few other investments, but I can't find anything that breaks any rules. I've been through registers of Swiss and overseas companies, done a trawl of beneficial owners in the main tax havens and even accessed a highly classified database of safety deposit box holders and he doesn't turn up anywhere. If he's on the take personally, he does a good job of keeping it quiet. The only thing I've found is a five-million-dollar trust fund set up fourteen years ago with a single beneficiary; his granddaughter, Alexa.'

'I didn't know he had children let alone a granddaughter. She sounds like someone he really cares about.'

'Maybe. The girl's mother was his daughter by wife number two. Both women died in a freak skiing accident when Alexa was tiny leaving her to be brought up by her father. Apart from the trust fund which she'll get access to when she's eighteen, I'm not sure there is any contact between them. And I can't find anyone else who he's involved with.'

'He's always claimed to be married to the job: maybe it's true.'

Alec stared out at the ever-changing view of the Thames. The sky was now dark, and Tower Bridge was lit up by huge arc lights which reflected off the oily surface of the river below. 'Let's park him for now,' he said, 'although we will have to dig up something. You said there were three we hadn't talked about. Who are the other two?'

'Next to the President we have our friend Guillermo Salz although I really don't know what influence he's got. From what we've seen, the Secretary General job description seems to consist of being PA and bodyguard to the Old Man, so he could be either a complete non-entity or the power broker behind the throne.'

'He was a player back in the day, wasn't he?' Alec asked.

'He was but he seems very different from the kind of footballers you're familiar with. He retired in his late twenties and has engineered a slow but relentless slither up the greasy pole of football administration. I suspect he's quietly ambitious and biding his time ready to take over the top job when his moment comes, but he's been completely loyal to the Old Man for years.'

'So, he's not going to be easy to control but neither does he have much power. I guess we park him too, for now. So now we get to the last one on the list. Why do have a feeling I won't like this one?'

'Yes, you guessed it. With practically limitless resources, no public profile, a 30-strong security detail and a reputation for violence, Sheikh Abdullah is officially the toughest nut to crack.'

'Did you find anything at all about him?' asked Alec, happy to move on from the Swiss fonctionaire to the Qatari royal.

'Cauldwell pulled his British Security Services file and Rushbourne wasn't kidding. It's no wonder some people don't think he exists; he's like a ghost. Even with their access, I couldn't get close to pulling together a picture of his finances and as for his personal life, I'd be lying if I said I'd got much more than that photo of him at Sandhurst from thirty years ago and our video clip. It's like he decided in his mid-twenties that life was best lived off grid. There used to be occasional rumours in the press, but they're shut down so brutally that none of the media go there anymore. With his reputation for supporting terrorism, you'd have thought the Israelis would have taken an interest, but Cauldwell says even they only have fragments.'

'What about the money for Southampton? That must have come from an international bank account somewhere.'

'That was paid by Al-Gharafa, his Qatari club and they don't have any revenue beyond what you'd expect from a football business. They took out a loan from a local Qatari bank to pay for the deal and that's now been loaded onto the South Coast club. Either way, Sheikh Abdullah's name isn't connected to any part of the transaction.'

'And yet, I've apparently met him twice in that past six months and here is popping up at FIFA. Doesn't it all strike you as a bit unlikely?'

'What do you mean?'

'I don't know, but think about it. This is a guy who's apparently lonelier than a Chelsea fan in the Cop end of Anfield who just happens to invite me to his place for a chat.

Then a few months later, I've been on his private jet and here he is on the committee we're trying to infiltrate.'

'It might explain why Rushbourne is so interested in getting you involved.'

'Or it could be that we're being played. Something doesn't add up to me.'

'I'm not sure. Think about it: how much did you make from that Southampton deal?'

Alec looked sheepish. 'Erm, I got a two per cent introduction fee.'

'So, on a-hundred-and-fifty million, I make that three million quid. Correct?'

He nodded, evasively and she carried on, 'Well, who do you think put up that money? I know the club paid you, but if this was all an elaborate ploy, someone had to have paid them. And, in case you've forgotten, someone did actually blow-up Wembley Stadium. That's a whole lot of trouble and expense to play some sort of game with FIFA.'

'Maybe you're right, and you're usually more suspicious than I am. If it was just about the bid, all we'd need is the President's support and a working majority of the Council: not easy, as we know, but it's achievable. Maybe Rushbourne's out of ideas and this is his way of getting someone else to do the legwork on that Qatari bastard.'

'I think you're overestimating what he thinks we're capable of. Anyway, at least we've got the start of a plan for most of them. I'll keep following the money trail and look at ways to pile the pressure on the greedy ones…'

'…and I'll have a think about how we hit the pervs and paedos. I can't really use historic cases, so I'll need to find some new ways of bait the trap. They seem to feel they're so far above the law that I don't suppose it will be too hard. What a bunch of fucking creeps, and we have to keep them in power rather than expose them. Once this is all over, though, they are ripe for a takedown.'

Alec was starting to come over all self-righteous and Michaela knew better than to point out that the source of his own wealth was also something he would have trouble explaining. She just nodded and left space for him to refocus.

'Anyway, moving on,' she said, after a pause. 'I'd like to start down the legal route and get my old colleagues at City of London Police to apply for McMafia Orders against those with assets in the UK. I may not be flavour of the month, but if the cases are presented to them on a plate, they'll find it hard to resist. Even so it will take a few weeks to submit the paperwork and argue with the City Bailiff. If I start now, they should start to feel the heat by spring which feels about the right timing. Meanwhile, the Evaluation Task Force visits start in January which gives us a whole new set of characters to look at. Have you thought of any ways we could undermine the bids?'

Alec pulled open a box file full of notes grabbed from various media analysts.

'Their faults are glaringly obvious for the most part, but it's actually quite tough to predict the Council's reaction when the problems are pointed out. They have a habit of turning weaknesses into a reason to offer their support. Like seeing bids from autocratic or disunited countries as a way of spreading democracy or peace. There's many a failed bidder who thought they had landed a knockout blow by describing their rivals' plans as unaffordable vanity projects only to find FIFA loves the idea of being at the heart of a new era of enterprise.

'By that logic, they could say that a World Cup on the moon is pushing forward the boundaries of human science.'

'That's FIFA for you.'

Chapter 20

Although he was undoubtedly a player, the Old Man had never been a footballer or even a coach, and his familiarity with the sport's more arcane rules was famously sketchy. But in his imagination, this moment was how a manager felt when he sent his team onto the field. They had been training together for weeks, they had been individually briefed and now he had to trust the heroically named Bid Evaluation Task Force to do its work. These were treacherous waters. The team – three former players, a retired judge and a Swiss lawyer – was embarking on one of sport's sternest tests of character: one with consequences only he could foresee. There was no way to disguise it: each of the aspiring World Cup hosts was preparing the sweetest and most elaborate honeytrap they could dream up. They would attempt to corrupt the five men with all the means at their disposal. The visitors would meet nobilities, celebrities and football legends, they would dine on sumptuous foods washed down with the finest wines and, when nightfall provided a discreet shroud, they would have their darker appetites sated. There would be gifts, girls, money, promises and threats, all to achieve one aim: to ensure a favourable evaluation report.

This was a test that all five would certainly fail, indeed it was for exactly this reason that each had been chosen. There was a place for incorruptibles in world football (although in his opinion, the limits of their usefulness were reached ever more regularly), but this was definitely not one. It was vital that the Task Force be seen to be enjoying the full rewards of their influential positions otherwise their hosts would feel cheated, their hospitality snubbed, that they weren't being given the opportunity to play to their strengths. The Task Force had to have stamina, an iron constitution and an appetite for a party. But when the music stopped, they had to submit a report which was a reasonable reflection of the technical strengths of each bidder. And it was in that key phrase, *reasonable reflection*, that the hooks and snares lay.

Imagine, the Old Man had told them, they were in week four of their five-week mission. They had spent every day of the past twenty-eight travelling, visiting stadiums and other venues comparing the reality on the ground with the glossy pictures in the bid book. Almost every night they had been royally and expensively entertained and by now they were feeling exhausted, dissipated and in dire need of a detox. It was at this precise moment that they were at their most vulnerable. This was the time, he urged, when they needed to be on their guard against the temptation to skip that last site visit of the day. They needed to maintain maximum vigilance in case a bidder tries to pass off an old training camp as novel, keep locals off their otherwise overcrowded metro system or take the scenic route to avoid placard-waving protestors. This was when their characters would be tested to the full, and it was a test they could not fail.

The Old Man stood in reception as his handpicked ambassadors trundled their wheely cases past him towards the waiting limos. For the security guards who stood just metres away, his routine was familiar. They stood by impassively as he clasped the hands of his protégés and gurned in a display of brotherly affection they knew would evaporate the second his envoys were out of sight. Before the convoy was halfway down FIFA Strasse, he had clicked his fingers at the receptionist with orders that Salz, his Secretary General be summoned, then descended to his subterranean office once again.

The attention members of the Bid Evaluation Task Force received on the first stop of their tour set the tone for the entire trip. They had chosen Barcelona to ease their way in gently, but on arrival they made the mistake of speaking to the media. This should have been fine except that it was seeded with journalists from the other bidding nations.

'Will you be investigating reports that terrorists have said they will target a World Cup in Spain?' The questioner was ethnic Chinese in a cheap suit and glasses, holding a notebook but no pen.

'Is it true that someone on the Spanish bid has been implicated in an embezzlement scandal?' came a North African voice.

The Spanish bid team finally rescued their shellshocked guests but not before a partisan press corps had subjected them a full ten minutes of mudslinging. The staff at the Task Force's luxury hotel had lined up to welcome them, but in their rooms they found files of allegations and insinuations planted by rivals.

That evening they were scheduled to attend a reception at the city's Estadi Olímpic and had agreed to reconvene in the hotel bar half an hour before they were due to be picked up. As a member of the media, Alec had already got a good look at the visitors: now it was Michaela's job to get closer still. She wandered into the bar glancing casually in their direction. The Old Man had made it a habit to choose smaller footballing nations from which to pick his representatives. He argued they were less likely to side with one of the candidates, but the reality was they all had their alliances. He just found the smaller federations easier and cheaper to control.

The men were all in their late forties or older and there was only one brown face among them. The footballers were Macedonian, Turkish and Slovenian and easy to spot. All three were large, physical men, sharply dressed and well-groomed. They sat confidently in their seats, legs spread. The retired judge was Indian and had the wide girth and magisterial bearing of a man who had spent his life on the bench high above contradiction. The grey-suited Swiss lawyer was small and angular. His sharp features and precise movements made him look ill at ease in the warm conviviality of the bar.

Dressed anonymously in standard off-duty uniform of mid-blue jeans and a hoodie, Michaela attracted no attention as she sat down in a high-backed chair facing away from the group. She leaned forward, hair falling around her face to reveal the white stems of her AirPods. If they registered her at all, anyone looking on would assume she was another a young woman completely absorbed in the contents of her phone. What they wouldn't see was a tiny and highly directional UHF microphone tucked invisibly behind one ear. The device, the one piece of spy kit Cauldwell had been able to supply, filtered and amplified the group's conversation relaying it with remarkable clarity via her mobile.

FIFA business is generally conducted in English but, like many other sports federations, its official language is French. In an attempt to keep their conversation private, this was the language the team now chose to speak. Unbeknown to them, their eavesdropper was fluent although, to be fair, none of the other languages they had in common would have proved a hindrance to her either.

Even though he was speaking French, the first voice Michaela heard was unmistakably Turkish: Hakan Oktay, former centre back for Galatasaray. His accent took her back to her earliest days as a WPC when she had cut her teeth among the rival gangs policed by Tottenham Nick.

'I expected the Spanish to do better.' he said. 'If I was judging on their media management, I'd say this bid isn't going to make the cut.'

'And as for that report,' came the native French tones of the lawyer, Willi Metz. 'I assume you were given the same thing. I am shocked that they could gain access to our hotel rooms when surely it is obvious we should be protected as special guests.'

The next voice was Judge Amdani who brought the singsong inflections of India to his Franglais. 'Interesting observations, all the same, what? I would like to know where is the source of their information. If half of the allegations are true, then SpaPo 2030 is in deep water.'

'Maybe,' said the Metz, raising an eyebrow at the judge's syntax. 'But I have to remind you of the President's strict instructions that we should be led by our hosts rather than launch investigations of our own or prompted by anyone else. We must disregard this information and we certainly should not raise questions in any official meetings.'

In this spirit of determined inquiry, the group drained their glasses and hurried off to a pair of waiting limousines ready to throw themselves into the evening's entertainment.

Michaela had dinner with Alec, bringing him up to speed, before retaking her place in the bar. When the team returned they had female company in tow and the volume of their conversation suggested the drink they shared earlier had been the first of many. The concierge gave the girls a glassy stare but did nothing to stop the party as they tottered across the marble-floored reception. The men shepherded their partners enthusiastically into the lifts leaving the lobby quiet again.

At breakfast the following morning Michaela sat a couple of tables away, her hidden microphone doing its job once again. From their talk around the table, she could tell most in the group had felt the evening had been a success.

'That, my friends, is why we agreed to be on the Task Force,' declared Radovan Hribar, the Slovenian former footballer, with relish. 'Man, if my ex-wife had got up to a few more tricks like that, she wouldn't have ended up abandoned and alone in a Ljubljana apartment.'

'Yeh, that fahişe was so hot, she would have melted my credit cards,' said Hakan Oktay. 'She was worth every lira but I'm glad I wasn't paying.'

The players laughed and even the judge had a smile on his face. He was trying hard to be more circumspect, although, as Michaela could testify, he hadn't been so reserved last night.

'I hope we all have the energy to do our jobs today,' he said, getting his excuses in early for the days and nights to come.

'Don't you worry about that,' said Oktay. 'I'm fully match fit, so if you want me to stand in for you tonight, just let me know. I'll even let you watch.'

Amdani winced, but his reaction was nothing compared to Metz whose body language betrayed a man struggling with an internal conflict. He slammed his coffee down, sending a tiny brown tidal wave across the breakfast table, and his eyes twitched behind gold-rimmed spectacles.

'I am a man of integrity,' he snorted. 'I cannot allow myself to be drawn into a compromising position.'

The group went quiet and looked at each other, not knowing quite how to take this outburst.

'So, you were happy to join in last night, but now you're a man of integrity,' said one of the players. 'I bet you even asked for a receipt.'

The rest of the group laughed as the lawyer went crimson, squirming furiously. Michaela suspected his hang ups were more deep-rooted than just the risk to his reputation. She had seen his partner of last night leave the hotel, her lip split and her face clumsily made up to cover a rapidly bruising cheek. She wouldn't be working again for a few days.

What's on the agenda today?' asked the judge, keen to change the subject.

The lawyer saw his salvation and pulled out a schedule. 'We're putting the public transport system to the test with a train ride to Zaragoza. Then this evening there is a reception with the Barcelona President and his guests.'

'I'm looking forward to it already,' said one of the other players, although his face didn't look quite so enthusiastic as they stomped off towards the station.

Michaela watched them go then caught up with Alec.

'It's going to be a very long month if we have to spend it trailing around after this bunch. Remind me what we're hoping to achieve?'

'We're not interested in their sex lives or even the bribes or offers of fake consultancy work. We need evidence of under-the-counter deals done in exchange for support from the FIFA Council. We know the Old Man uses the evaluation process to get close to bidders. It's a delicate business trying find out how much they or their connections are prepared to stump up. It won't be the whole Task Force, but there will be at least one person on the team whose job it is to make the approaches. The bidders will probably offer some sort of kick back, whether that's from the construction companies building the stadiums or the agency with exclusive rights to sell match and hospitality tickets. Whoever's involved locally stands to make a lot of money and FIFA sees it as its God-given right to grab a share. They won't go so far as to ask explicitly for money; they'll just drop unsubtle hints. Things like a pledge of funding for their development projects would be viewed very favourably by the Council. What happens after that could go several different ways, but most likely they'll look to recruit a fixer; someone on the bid team who can be cut in on the deal and make the exchange. When these things have come to light in the past, investigators have found links to offshore licensing companies selling World Cup marketing rights. In return for being able to use the FIFA World Cup logo on their products, companies pay a license fee which ends up in an account controlled by a relative or close associate of the Old Man. Along the way there's a skim off the top for the go between.'

Michaela looked impressed. 'So that's where those offshore funds originated and no wonder it's so hard to tie them to any individual. You've got to say, it's a neat way of covering up what is effectively a bribe. And it's almost a victimless crime: the only people that suffer are the fans who will pay a small premium on their tickets.'

'Don't assume it's that small,' Alec said. 'The sums of money involved can be huge.'

'Ok, so how are we supposed to identify when the deal is going down? They've pretty much worked as a team so far.'

'At some point one of them is going to start to fly solo, setting up meetings or attending a private dinner, so we just have to watch and see when that happens. They probably won't even meet someone working for the bid but maybe a senior person in the Football Association. We won't get to see the actual approach but if we could identify who's making it, then we can start building up a picture of what they're doing.'

'That sounds easy enough, but how does it help us control the bidding process? It would be useful information to pass on to the UK bid, but ultimately it could just reinforce how far off the pace they are.'

'True enough, but you shouldn't underestimate the impact of FIFA's double dealing being made public. When details of their dodgy TV rights deals came out, both the Swiss and Americans brought criminal charges and several execs ended up going to jail. No bidder's going to want to take those kinds of risks. The challenge is always to make it stick to the Old Man himself, and if we found that kind of information it really would be a game changer. Imagine if you could go to him with evidence he's personally behind FIFA corruption. He'd probably let you host the World Cup in your garden.'

Two days later, their moment came. The Task Force had moved on to Lisbon to evaluate the Portuguese side of the joint bid. They checked into their hotel and were confirming evening plans when one of them, Hakan Oktay, made his first play.

'I'm not going to be joining you tonight, I'm afraid,' he said to the group, as Michaela listened in unobserved. 'I have a standing invitation with João Nandes to get together whenever I'm in town. Frankly, I'm not going to trade a night out with him for anything.'

The name meant nothing to Michaela, but she made a note while the others shrugged, somewhat resentfully and moved on. The Portuguese FA had laid on a night out at a fado club for a performance of local folk music. The unofficial guidebook described it as 'flamenco for depressives' so it was an evening to be endured rather than enjoyed. They steeled themselves and she watched as they gravitated towards the hotel bar for something to numb the pain.

When Michaela mentioned Nandes to Alec, it was his turn to look impressed.

'The super agent? Blimey! He looks after some of Europe's top players so what he doesn't know about doing deals in football isn't worth knowing. I met him once; all perma-tan and whitened teeth, but he's a real piece of work. He wouldn't piss on your granny if she was on fire. He could definitely be our fixer, but it would be like giving a vampire the keys to the blood bank. When he's done there probably wouldn't be much left for anyone else.'

Alec spent a few minutes Googling agent and player. 'I can't find any connection between them,' he said, 'other than general football interests. They're about the same age, so Nandes won't have represented Oktay and I can't find any club they've both had dealings with. This looks like it's got the Old Man's fingerprints all over it which would make Oktay his emissary. I wonder what's in it for him.'

Whatever the Turkish footballer thought he was going to get from the deal, neither Alec nor Michaela could have predicted that tonight's rendezvous would be his last.

Chapter 21

There are many ways to die in a hotel room and the Old Man had first-hand experience of more than he would have liked. There was the Icelander, Gudjohnson, whose flushed complexion and passionate embrace of whisky and cigarettes telegraphed the heart attack which did for him in Lima's 5-star Miraflores hotel. Laurent Bonammi was scrupulously clean living apart from the occasional alcoholic bender which accounted for the rock 'n' roll nature of his death, drowning in his own vomit at the World Cup in South Africa. The American, Chubby Chester, was more of a surprise. The Old Man had him down as a pervert and possibly a paedophile, but that didn't even begin to cover it. The snuff porn on the floor as his naked body hung lifeless from an autoerotic choker proved his demons were even darker.

Despite the blizzard of allegations against the organisation, there had been only one actual murder of a FIFA official in his twenty-seven years at the helm. The press release had said that Prince Abeidi Suleman had slipped in the shower, but the coroner's report described over fifty injuries. Everyone on the inside knew that unpaid debts to Russian Mafiosi were the cause of his brutal extinction.

The Old Man despised them all, each one more dissolute than the last. Always the men; never the women. Not a single suicide though, at least not a deliberate one. Perhaps it just didn't go with the personality required to ascend to the FIFA Council. They all had a rat-like instinct to survive; to twist a situation to their advantage against impossible odds. Which is why he refused to believe that Hakan Oktay had killed himself. The pair had met several times over the past months and there was no indication that the Turkish player was anything but happy with life. He had a wide circle of friends, money in the bank and enjoyed semi-celebrity status at home in Istanbul. His wife and children were beautiful, but he had what the Old Man considered to be a healthy appetite for the other pleasures that came his way. And yet the empty packet of OxyContin beside the body was labelled up with Oktay's details, and there was no sign of anyone else's involvement.

The other members of the Bid Evaluation Task Force didn't believe it was suicide either, as Michaela learned from eavesdropping on a conversation between Judge Amdani and Radovan Hribar after the body was discovered.

'The paramedics tried to revive him, but he had been dead too long,' said the judge. 'I called the President as soon as I received the news, reporting to him that suicide is suspected. The Old Man was unconvinced to say the least. Does an overdose sound likely to you?'

'No way. I know you can never fully understand what is going on inside someone's head, but Hakan? No chance.'

'Do we know if he even made it to his night out with João Nandes?'

'According to the hotel manager, he left the hotel an hour or so after we did and got back just before one a.m. He gave a wave to the night porter who reported that he seemed completely fit and well.'

'So, what's your explanation for his death?'

'I don't have one, but I don't buy the suicide theory, not for a minute. He was saying only yesterday how much he was looking forward to visiting the new Benfica stadium. Apparently, he played in the Champions League at the old stadium in the early 2000s. I know he was also meeting someone in Madrid tomorrow too. It just doesn't make any sense.'

The elderly Indian thought for a moment then spoke, choosing his words with care. 'I did not know him well but, from what I saw, I agree with you, that suicide would be most unexpected. However, if we assume the medication played no more than a minor part in his death, the only other explanations we are left with are a tragic accident or foul play.'

The other two members of the Task Force joined the conversation. 'This is terrible news, indeed,' said lawyer Willi Metz. 'What do you think we should do judge?'

The Indian had acted as a father figure to the group since the news broke, so Michaela was not surprised when she heard him take the lead. 'I think it is not for us to investigate what happened to Hakan. We have a busy day ahead of us and we fly to Madrid tonight and it seems to me there is nothing to be gained from changing our schedule. I have spoken with the President, and he is sending a member of his personal staff to pick up the pieces here. He has also arranged for someone to inform Hakan's wife. I have left instructions with the hotel to pass our details to the investigating officers if they are needed. If anyone has information of value to the Police, then let's be as cooperative as possible. Otherwise, I propose we carry on.'

The rest of the group were reluctant but saw the logic of the judge's argument. After a brief discussion, they agreed and fifteen minutes later were boarding the minivan which was already waiting outside.

Michaela watched them go then reported the conversation to Alec who was equally suspicious of the circumstances surrounding the footballer's death.

'It seems unlikely, but could those pills have killed him?' he wondered.

'There are plenty of accidental opioid overdoses each year but they're mainly in people injecting the stuff. It's not impossible, but just the quantity alone means you'd have to be very confused to accidentally OD using tablets. The fact that the night porter said he seemed fine suggests he wasn't staggering drunk and no one seems to think he killed himself.

It would help to see a toxicology report but, if I had to commit, I'd say someone killed him and did a superficial job to dress it up as a suicide.'

'Superficial, as in they knew they'd get found out?'

'Pills are not a great murder weapon. Hard to administer and they take too long to work. If it is foul play, the tox report or the PM will flag something up, but I'd be willing to bet they'll find undigested tablets in his stomach.'

'I think there might be more to this than a hotel room robbery gone wrong. I suggest we give ourselves the morning to see what we can find out. I'll try and contact João Nandes if you can talk to the hotel staff. ASl if anyone saw anything suspicious or, better still, has any CCTV footage of someone going into Hakan's room.'

Two hours later, they had what they needed. Nandes was screening his calls but picked up when Alec said what had happened. He was shocked and started by denying that the two had ever met. After some persuasion, he confirmed that he and the footballer had eaten at a local seafood restaurant then spent a few of hours at the Sky Bar on the roof of the Tivoli hotel. His driver had dropped Oktay at his hotel in very good spirits at around 12.30 – one o'clock and, in his view, it definitely wasn't suicide.

Michaela spoke to the front desk and the hotel system confirmed that a new keycard had been made just before ten p.m. A junior member of staff eventually admitted that he had been asked for a replacement key by someone claiming to be Mr. Oktay and quoting the correct room number. There was CCTV in the lobby and they brought up footage of a man in his forties approaching the desk at the time in question. The same character outside the room several hours later. Portuguese police would follow up to try and establish an ID, but there was no doubt in Alec and Michaela's minds that Oktay had been murdered.

'So we've got another hotel and another dead FIFA official,' she said.' What are the chances?'

'Yeh, it's like déjà vu all over again,' he agreed, with a touch of irony.

Alec spent a few minutes huddled over his laptop, scribbled a few notes and said, 'I think it's time to call Guillermo Salz.'

The FIFA Secretary General was reluctant to take the call but relented when Alec told him he was sitting in the lobby of the Valverde Hotel, Lisbon.

'Mr. Munday,' said a clipped voice as the Swiss-German came on the line. 'I understand you're on the scene of a death in the FIFA family once again. Should we suspect a connection?'

'Don't think so, especially as I wasn't there at the other four incidents involving FIFA staff or property since our last conversation. I mean, your brand-new training centre burns down killing the groundsman; the bank holding your main cash reserve is cleaned out; even the FIFA videogame has been a target, with players' personal details being hacked. And in each case, the details of the story end up all over the media. So, if we're talking about connections or coincidences, I'd say we both know I'm not your man.' There was no response so Alec pressed on. 'Do you know what I think, Mr. Salz? I think FIFA is under attack.'

Salz was quiet, giving himself time to think, then he said, 'Mr. Munday, the last time we spoke you offered me a trade for information. Can I assume you have another similar proposition in mind? And if I might also make a logical jump, the fact you are in the same hotel as the Bid Evaluation Task Force suggests your proposition has something to do with GB-2030. Am I correct?'

Alec took the comment as confirmation he was on the right track. 'I do think we might have something to talk about.'

'And that is where I think this conversation ends. You see, last time we met you told me you were with British Security Services. Naturally, I tried to verify this claim but all I found was a former footballer turned journalist who makes a habit of getting into trouble. I was certainly surprised to see you reappear at Wembley on that terrible day, but it fits the same pattern, I'm afraid.'

It was Alec's turn to take a moment to think. He decided to roll the dice. 'We can't bring back your groundsman or Hakan Oktay, but how about if we got you your money back? I read it was seventeen million Swiss Francs. Is that the correct figure?'

'I have to admire your persistence, Mr. Munday. That was the reported figure, and as you say, the confidential details of our recent troubles somehow found their way into the media, so let us take that as close enough. I don't know what you have in mind but if the sum was somehow to be returned to FIFA, then the President would be very pleased. So pleased, he would probably invite you to a meeting to acknowledge your support and thank you in person.'

'How do you think we're going to be able to get their money back?' Michaela asked, when the call was over.

'It doesn't have to be the same money that was stolen, does it.'

'Ok, let me put it a different way. How do you think we're going to be able to get hold of...' she searched on her phone for the latest exchange rate. '... fourteen million quid?'

'I know you like a challenge and I'm sure Hugo would be happy to help, for his usual percentage. But...' he shrugged, 'if we can't, we can't. We haven't lost anything.'

Hugo was Hugo Ashburton, a founding member of the Flaming Ferraris, City hellraisers in the late 90s. Now he was the owner of NumbersGame, an algorithmic betting service. His talent for making money combined with the morals of an Oligarch's daughter made him an interesting person to know. He had been extremely useful to Alec and Michaela in the past, and this would be right up his street.

'I'm assuming we can't just login and help ourselves,' Michaela said, when she told Hugo why she was calling.

'*We* can't, Mickey, but I may know someone who can,' Hugo said. 'One of my clients, or should I say former clients, an extremely wealthy man but tight as a submarine door. Anyway, we'd made him another pile of filthy lucre, but he was being coy about parting with our commission. The usual representations went un-responded to, so I decided to take matters into my own hands. After a bit of due diligence on my side, I engaged the services of Wolverhampton's answer to Lisbeth Salander.'

'You mean you hired a hacker?'

'Not just any hacker. You should see this girl work: fingers dancing over the keyboard, eyes ablaze and smoke pouring from her laptop. Within seconds I had my money plus a sizeable chunk of change to cover her expenses and my inconvenience. She installed a web of security over the NumbersGame vaults so the chap in question couldn't hit me with a reverse ferret, so to speak, and everyone's happy. Well, everyone except said client who is still breathing murderous threats, but such is life.'

'And you think your hacker could help?'

'I'm sure she'd be delighted. Just cross her palm with silver and point her in the right direction.'

'Ok, it might take some time to set up, but I'll let you know when we're ready.'

Back in London, following the money trail from FIFA's bank to an account with enough funds to cover the stolen amount yielded a quick result for Cauldwell's analysts and within hours she called Hugo with the details.

'I'd like to see your friend in action, if that's ok,' she said, then hung on while Hugo wriggled.

'Ermm, she's working remotely and she, err… doesn't like to be watched. It's a hacker thing.'

'Hugo, you have actually met her, haven't you?'

'Not as such,' he squirmed, 'but she came highly recommended and, as I told you, she worked wonders on my behalf. Between you, me and Cambridge Analytica, I'm only assuming she's female because she goes under the handle Trix. Leave it to me, Mickey. I'll let you know how she gets on.'

Hugo called twenty-four hours later with good news and bad news.

'So, the money is in Alec's offshore account as instructed. Trix helped herself to slightly more than the amount in question to cover expenses at this end, so we're all square. As ever, it's a pleasure doing business with you. I should tell you though, Mickey, she took a quick look round while she was in the account and followed the trail a bit further too. I'm sure you probably know this already, but you're mixing with some very unsavoury types. As well as the usual tangled web of brass plate companies there's a structure which looks suspiciously like the Russian Laundromat.'

'That phrase takes me back, Hugo. You mean the industrial money laundering operation I was trying to shut down a few years back.'

'The very same, except there doesn't seem to be anything linking this one to Russia. It's always hard to be sure, of course, but Trix suspects Middle East connections either in Saudi or Qatar. Does that make any sense to you?'

'That's a hell of a coincidence,' Alec said, when Michaela told him about Hugo's findings. 'I think I was right: FIFA is being targeted and, while the attackers are all different, their orders all seem to come from the same place. There are a couple more things I'd like to try before having another conversation with Salz and I think our new acquaintance could help with that too.'

Two eventful weeks later, the pair were sitting in the FIFA reception area having been relieved of their mobile phones again. Guillermo Salz beamed as he walked towards them.

'The Old Man really is impressed,' he said, smiling widely. 'Not only that, he would also like to discuss other ways a team of your talents could be useful to FIFA.'

'Then this should be an interesting conversation,' Alec concurred.

Salz directed them to the elevators and the three of them took the short trip down into the depths of the operation. The lift opened onto a corridor of blank doors. A nameplate on each one bore the name of a footballing legend but otherwise there was no indication of what was going on in any of the rooms. Their host led the way to a door marked Pelé, ushering Alec and Michaela ahead of him into a windowless boardroom with fresh coffee on the table. He encouraged them to sit at one side while making busy with the coffee and giving a well-practised spiel about the building. After ten minutes his small talk was starting to run out, so it was a relief all round when the door opened and the Old Man walked in. Alec glanced up to catch the exact moment when his face switched from tired, pinched and worried to the 1000-watt politician's smile. He knew they were on to something.

'Mr. Munday, Miss Dagg,' the Old Man said, an open-handed gesture calculated to convey his affection. 'My Secretary here has told me a great deal about you already, and it is a great pleasure finally to meet you.'

Salz winced at being referred to as a secretary, but the Old Man breezed on taking his seat at the head of the table and dismissing the offer of coffee.

'So, tell me,' he said. 'Do you know who stole our money?'

'That is not an easy one to answer,' Michaela began. 'We followed the money trail through various accounts to one registered to a company in Panama. This turned out to be a modern-day marshalling yard. Money is brought in, turned around and moved on from shell company to subsidiary. Then on further to tax havens in all corners of the planet. It is a practice I have seen before, and it's always designed to obscure the identity of the ultimate beneficiary. So, the short answer to your question is 'no' we don't know who stole your money. And even if we could trace it back to an individual or organisation, it's practically impossible to prove that they had anything to do with the theft.'

The Old Man struggled to mask his relief. 'Well, no matter,' he said, quickly. 'The important thing is that we have the money back. This will make an enormous difference to the success of the global game, and we are very grateful to you for your efforts on our behalf. You will be well rewarded when the money reaches our account. I assume there is no reason to delay the transaction.'

'The money should have hit your bank by now,' said Alec, 'and I assure you we are not looking for any kind of reward.'

The Old Man gestured impatiently towards his underling who hurried out of the room.

Alec took his chance. 'In Mr. Salz's absence, this may be an opportunity to discuss some of our other findings. As Michaela said, we have not been able to determine conclusively who took your money, but we have a good idea who it is. As, I suspect, do you. Before we get to that, we've also been having some fun on your behalf.'

The Old Man's face froze. The smile was still in place, but it was glassy and forced.

Alec ploughed on. 'You'll know, I'm sure, that many Premier League footballers are keen players of the FIFA video game. What you may not know is that several of the big Premier League clubs also run an e-sports team. When we saw that EA Sports had been hacked, we sent in one of those teams to see if they could draw the hackers out. The challenge proved irresistible, and we ended up with sort of an unofficial League of Legends tournament. As expected, the hackers totally dominated our boys in the game, but they had to reveal enough personal information to show where they were vulnerable. That meant we were able to set up some hacks of our own. Without going into detail, we emptied their bank accounts, trashed their credit scores, foreclosed on their properties and had their cars impounded. In less time than it takes to fix a World Cup qualifier, we ruined their lives. Then we turned off the game and talked to them direct. We told them we would reboot their finances, but they had to tell us who'd paid them to hack the game in the first place. Their reaction was interesting.'

Alec held the Old Man's gaze. He saw hesitation in his eyes but also a calculating brain behind them.

'They were clearly terrified,' he went on. 'At first, they denied everything even when we showed them their digital fingerprints on the original hacks. Once they knew they were caught, they tried all sorts of tricks rather than reveal who had put them up to it. Bear in mind their lives were in tatters by now: it would have taken years for them to recover, but they still wouldn't open up. In the end we went silent on them for twenty-four hours just to let the reality of their situation sink in and, one by one, they started talking.'

'It was immediately clear they didn't know who they were working for. So, we sent them off to find out, which was basically like recruiting some of the world's best hackers onto our team. They went back to the initial contact, found out where communications had come from and how money had been transferred, and every one of them drew a blank. The most they could get was what we already knew: nothing definitive, no smoking gun, just a series of straws in the wind coming from a certain direction.'

It was Michaela's turn to pick up the story. 'We also contacted the Swiss police who investigated the incident at your new training facility. They were very cooperative and gave us their report. Obviously, it is tragic that a man died, but it meant that the inquiry was more thorough than it would have been for a normal case of arson. The CCTV and witness statements pointed strongly to a criminal outfit from Stuttgart, less than 200kms away. With no obvious personal gain, the police could find only circumstantial evidence linking the gang to the fire. They filed a report with German prosecutors, but the decision was made not to press charges. I used my Interpol connections to get them to pay a follow up visit, which they did using an uninsured vehicle as a pretext to rattle a few cages. As you can imagine, the gang was uncooperative although they did claim that they weren't in the business of starting fires and, hypothetically speaking, would only have done so if they'd been paid. To their credit, the police were quite persistent, threatening their operation until they remembered who their hypothetical client might have been. But the gang brazened it out, and in the end, the police just seized the illegal car and left them alone.'

The Old Man's smile had faded, but there was an intensity in his eyes as he absorbed what the pair opposite were saying. 'You have certainly been busy,' he said, 'although it seems all your efforts have been in vain. Maybe these incidents will have to remain mysteries.'

Alec pressed on regardless. 'Possibly, except that then I had a lucky break when I investigated the media leaks. We thought it was odd that all these stories had found their way so reliably, quickly and accurately into the press. So, as it's my area, I made a few calls. As you know, most journalists are very protective of their sources and would risk arrest and even imprisonment rather than give them up. Most, but not all. I would have thought one of the tabloid lowlifes like Andy Grubber at *The Mail* would be on the take. But in the end, it was *The Telegraph's* football correspondent, Charles Farbrace, who found the temptation of a trouser full of cash too hard to resist. He spoke to us on condition that it would never be made public.'

The Old Man continued to look friendly, but his confident demeanour was starting to slip.

'Of course, it is hard to verify, but Farbrace claimed the leaks originated from the offices of the Al-Gharafa football club in Qatar. When he called to stand up the stories, he was told by none other than club president, Walid Al Kubaisi, that they were true. That name rang some bells with us as we had dealings with Squalid Walid and his boss a few months back. On that occasion it ended up with the destruction of Wembley Stadium.'

At that moment, Guillermo Salz opened the door giving the Old Man the chance to change the subject.

'Ah, Salz,' he said, quickly. 'Good news on that returned money, I trust.'

'Very good, Mr. President.'

'Good, that is good. Mr. Munday and Miss Dagg were just telling me they have done some business with the newest member of the FIFA Council, Sheikh Abdullah.'

'Ah, were they?' Salz said, his brain quickly computing the multiple chains which could have led their conversation to Qatar. 'He is, indeed, one of the more enigmatic Council members. But, if I may ask, why your interest and, perhaps more to the point, why a British security service angle to the UK bid?'

'When we last spoke, you didn't seem to believe a security service connection, but we'll let it pass. I said then that we thought FIFA was under attack. Now we have evidence that the source of those attacks is centred around the Middle East and most likely Qatar. We're offering to help.'

The Old Man started to speak but Salz cut across him. 'And I must repeat what I told you then: we cannot get into a conversation about FIFA's internal governance with a representative of one of the bids, particularly one which is trying to use its secret services to gain an advantage.'

'We were brought in by the UK bid to keep FIFA honest, an understandable sentiment, I think you'll agree, after the, err... unpleasantness the last time the UK was involved. In doing that, we have discovered the trouble you're in and we genuinely thought you would be pleased with our offer of help.'

'Mr. Munday,' the Old Man interrupted, 'I am grateful to you for what you have done on FIFA's behalf and your offer is duly noted. We know where to find you if circumstances change. But now, you'll have to excuse me. It is time for my next appointment.'

Chapter 22

The UK was the last stop on the Evaluation Task Force's epic tour of bidding

countries. They were all more than ready to finish their mission and get home. The surviving

original members – a retired Indian judge, a Swiss lawyer and two former footballers – had

seen their number restored to its original five. Their new colleague was a large silent man

with a wide neck and suspicious bulges under an ever-present black suit jacket. They might

have felt more reassured had they known that Simon Cauldwell and an armed, twelve-person

Security Services unit were also keeping a discreet twenty-four-hour watch.

The Task Force's first set-piece event was a welcome reception on their arrival in

London arranged by PR man Malcolm Tonghe. Dinner was in the panoramic banqueting

room high above Tower Bridge and jointly hosted by Sports Minister Damien Scott and the

Lord Mayor of London. The office of Lord Mayor is, of course, completely different from the

London Mayor and his inclusion was Tonghe's idea. He felt the ceremonial figure with his

tricorn hat would play rather better than the dreadful little man whose actual responsibility it

could be to guarantee the safety of the World Cup in London.

On Alec's advice, Tonghe was determined to show that his town could deliver

something more creative than the tedious receptions the Task Force had endured elsewhere.

London is a melting pot for all the cultures of the world and Tonghe set out to make an

impression. He ruled out the keepie-uppie act opting instead for two performers from the

Cirque du Soleil acrobatic troupe performing that week at the Royal Albert Hall. Their spectacular floorshow would be followed by street magic from the almost supernatural Dynamo. And the entertainment would conclude with him conducting an orchestra of fireworks over the Thames. The menu was equally exotic. Rather than traditional British fare, he researched the favourite dishes of each visitor and combined them into a tasting menu which he briefed to one of the city's Michelin starred kitchens.

As well as members of the bid committee, Tonghe had also invited three former top-flight players. Mark Hughes and Eddie Howe were picked not just for their availability, but also because they had each played alongside the former footballers on the Task Force. Some might have detected in Paul Elliott's presence a politically correct nod to the Black Lives Matter movement. But the reality was much simpler and surprisingly refreshing: the former Chelsea defender was just a great lad to have around on a night out. Having left nothing to chance, Tonghe formed a one-man reception committee as his guests arrived.

Alec and Michaela were planning a low-key entrance towards the end of the pre-dinner drinks, but their attempt to slip in discreetly was foiled as soon as she stepped out of her coat. Dressed in a grey satin Givenchy dress which fitted like a sheath, Michaela outshone even the spectacular view from the bridge and turned every head in the room. Despite admiring every inch of her, none of the Task Force showed the faintest sign of having seen her before even though the pair had been on every stop of their tour.

In Beijing, Alec had noted that Slovenian former footballer Radovan Hribar had replaced Hakan Oktay as the Old Man's go between. Alec's objective was to make initial contact and secure a one-to-one meeting. He started working his way around the room. That gave Michaela the opportunity to use her charm and command of almost all the languages around the table to demonstrate London's multi-cultural welcome. A deferential incline of her head to the judge and use of the affectionate Amdani-ji soon had him twinkling with delight. Metz, the Swiss lawyer was practically salivating as she shook his hand although having seen the damage his affections could inflict, that was as close as she was going to get.

Despite the unusual blend of curried okra, fondue and buckwheat dumplings, the dinner went well. Damien Scott made a brief welcome speech and the judge, who had assumed the role of chair, made an equally brief toast of thanks after the meal. No one was surprised when he announced he was retiring to his suite at the next-door Tower Hotel. Scott and the Lord Mayor also made their excuses, leaving those members of the party who still had reserves of energy ready to move on.

To the north of Tower Bridge is Minories, an ancient parish once as colourful as any in the City of London. Over the ages, it has counted among its residents the Franciscan Order of St Clare in the 11th Century and the City's largest Jewish community 500 years later. Today, it has all but lost its unique identity with one important exception: it is home to London's largest transgender nightclub, which was where, wittingly or otherwise, Tonghe decided to lead his guests. The WayOut Club almost shut its doors for good during the Pandemic but came roaring back when the restrictions were lifted, adding new club nights to its normal Saturday night riot of drag and burlesque. To say that the experience was like nothing else the Task Force had encountered was an understatement. But it turned out to be a stroke of genius from Tonghe. Alec stood back and watched two worlds collide as the former players, with more drinks than inhibitions onboard, threw themselves enthusiastically into the fray. The atmosphere made life difficult for the security crew, but by the time Alec finally got close enough to Hribar to make his approach, he was pushing at an open door.

'How did you know we love drag in Slovenia,' the player said, voguing, provocatively. 'Everyone remembers Conchita when she won Eurovision, but we had the first act way back in the early 2000s. I just wish I had one of my wigs and some heels. Come on Alec, let's see what you've got.'

'Dancing as good as yours deserves an audience, mate,' Alec replied, keeping his arms firmly by his sides.

Hribar gestured towards Metz who was hitting aggressively on any of the punters who came his way. 'Maybe, instead of watching me you should look out for the Alpine arsehole over there before he makes trouble.'

'What's his problem?'

'I don't know but he acts like his parents forced him to marry a nun. Every time he leaves the convent he goes crazy.'

Alec shared a nod and a glance with Michaela who took the hint and steered one of Cauldwell's men towards the unpredictable attorney. There was the briefest of movements before the security man was apparently helping the out-of-town guest to his feet having fallen. He didn't try his luck again, but Alec had more success.

'I'm told you're the man who can make things happen,' he said.

'You're really asking me that in a place like this?'

'I mean about the bid. I understand you're the deal maker.'

'Well, tonight I'm the dancer, but let's talk tomorrow.'

He handed over a card with a name and mobile number and strutted back to join the party. Alec and Michaela stayed a while longer then headed for home a convenient two-minute walk away. They had discussed security with Cauldwell, hence the deployment of his team, but it was still a surprise when Alec's mobile went off less than an hour later with the spook on the line.

'Nothing to worry about, Alec, but I thought you'd like to know someone tried to kill one of our visitors tonight. We stepped in and have the guy in restraints. Well, I say *guy*, I'm not sure he'd really pass for any gender at all in his current state. Fair play for having a go, though; it can't be every day you have a to play a cross-dressing assassin at short notice.'

'Fuck, what happened? Is anyone hurt?'

'No, everyone's fine. Your man Radovan didn't even notice, although he was a bit shocked when I told him it might be safer to call it a night.'

'Good work, Simon. So, are you going to interrogate him tonight?'

'Oh, yes. I just thought you might like to be there when we do.'

'Give me five minutes,' Alec said, making a grab for his clothes. 'I assume Michaela's invited too.'

'Don't take this the wrong way, but I think she's likely to be more use than you are. See you both out front.'

They pulled on jeans, hoodies and trainers and got downstairs just as Cauldwell's standard issue pool car swung round the corner. He was followed by a black panel van whose rear doors opened as it pulled up. The officer inside introduced himself as Mike and the convoy sped off. The gloomy dome light of the interior was not the most flattering, but the sight of their prisoner would have had Tyson Fury edging away, nervously. He was a giant of a man who had clearly stolen the first dress and wig he had come across. The outfit, a violent smear of red lipstick and a very intimidating stare were enough to get him across the club's threshold. Now he squatted opposite them his tattooed arms and huge shoulders straining the thin fabric to breaking point. His face was bloodied and the flimsy cable ties securing his wrists to restraints in the van were not reassuring. Especially as the expression on his face said that his instinct was to rip the three of them apart.

'How did you spot him?' Alec asked, to Mike's amusement.

'It was the shade of lipstick,' he grinned. 'According to the boss, it's very much last year's colour.'

'Have you got any information out of him yet?' asked Michaela, typically more matter of fact.

'Nothing ma'am,' came the reply. 'We're not even sure what language he speaks. That's where the boss thought you could be useful.'

Michaela took a closer look and made her choice.

'Skazhi mne, na kogo ty rabotayesh, ili my otrezhem tebe yaytsa.'

The thug strained at the cable ties and tried to spit in her face.

'Bingo. He's Russian,' she said, 'or at least he speaks the language.'

'What did you tell him?' Alec asked.

'I told him we'd cut his balls off unless he told us who he was working for. As you saw, it got a response although getting the actual answer may be more difficult.'

'Don't you worry about that, Ma'am,' said Mike. 'The boss has all sorts of tricks, but he'll appreciate having you along to translate.'

The van followed the Limehouse Link through the City and struck out towards Essex on the East India Dock Road. After a couple of miles, they turned north and another five miles further on, Alec recognised the industrial estate where they had last met Nigel Rushbourne. Cauldwell's men swung into action and manoeuvred the overinflated Russian into a lockup facility behind blank steel gates. Inside it looked like a long-abandoned garage workshop but the chain and padlock on the entrance were both new. More cable ties were used to secure their prisoner to a steel bench then Cauldwell started to relax. He took Mike outside.

'Good work, mate. Do me a favour and I'll take it from here. There's an all-night café about half a mile away. Take the van and Alec here to buy us all some teas then get back to the Tower for the rest of your watch. I'll brief the change-over crew before they start, so you should be away by six. See you tomorrow night.'

The Russian proved surprisingly easy to break down. The ties held against a surge of roid rage that hit just after three a.m. and by five he was curled into a foetal ball, groaning and shivering.

'I'd say Sergei here has been popping more than aspirins,' Cauldwell said. 'We'll leave him for another hour and then I reckon he'll be ready to trade the keys to Putin's dacha for a bacon sandwich and a cigarette.'

Predictably, the Russian was a long way from the top of the food chain, but he did give Michaela what limited information he had about those above him. By 7.30 they had all they were going to get. Twenty minutes later, as the first arrivals pulled into the industrial estate, he was being carted off by the Met Police's Counter Terrorism Command. By eight a.m. Caldwell and his unit were ready to call it a night.

'He's basically a hired thug, but CTC will turn him upside down and shake him to see what falls out. Meanwhile, it's job done. Our guests will presumably have had chance to think about what nearly happened. I suggest you get back to them and see how they're feeling.'

It was late morning by the time Alec and Michaela were ready to face the world again and the Task Force was already out on site visits. Alec pulled out Hribar's card and called him to arrange a meeting in the hotel bar that evening. When he arrived, the group was together and last night's narrow escape was the main topic of conversation.

'You look like you could all use a drink,' said Alec, gesturing to a waiter. 'How has it been today?'

Judge Amdani spoke first. 'I have to confess we are feeling that Europe is not a safe place to be holding a World Cup at the moment. We had no difficulties in China or Latin

America but an unexplained death in Lisbon and now an attempted murder here? It is unsettling, to say the least.'

'Have you considered that it may just be a lot easier to organise a hit in the UK or Portugal than it is in China or Venezuela?'

This time it was the Swiss lawyer who answered.

'A hit? Are you suggesting that we may have been the target?'

'It must have crossed your minds,' Alec said. 'After all millions of tourists pass through London and Lisbon every year without incident.'

Metz fixed him with a stare. 'And what do you think could be the explanation for such unprovoked attacks?'

Apart from the man with the large neck, the group looked at Alec keenly, and he could see in their faces that there was more going on than they were revealing. 'I'm sure you've got a better idea than me, but I'll tell you what I told Guillermo Salz recently: I think FIFA or elements within it are under attack and I think I know the person behind it. What I don't know is why, but it's obvious the stakes are high and getting higher.'

The faces around the table looked genuinely shocked.

Alec paused then pressed on. 'Tell me, what do you know about Sheikh Abdullah?'

Judge Amdani was the only member of the Council around the table, and the others looked to him to reply.

'His Excellency is a very senior member of the Qatari Royal Family and a valued member of the FIFA Council. His appointment was a natural part of preparations for the World Cup in his country.'

No one spoke and Amdani couldn't resist the urge to fill the silence. He spread his hands. 'I'm not sure what else I can tell you. He is quite different from the other members, and no one is entirely sure why such a private man would take up the role. He also seems quite unfamiliar and, if I may say, uninterested in the FIFA way of doing things.'

'You've met him, then,' Alec confirmed. 'How does he seem to you?'

'Our acquaintance has been brief and limited only to two or three Council meetings. As far as I can recall, he has not made any contribution at all. He seems only to stare at the President, as if his attendance is designed to intimidate.'

Alec sensed he had taken the conversation as far as could but was sure enough seeds had been sown. 'Well, gents, you'll have the benefit of British security for the rest of your visit so do enjoy it. When you return to Zurich, do please remember me to the Old Man and let him know that our offer still stands. If you'll excuse me, I just need to cover off a few details with Radovan.'

Chapter 23

The GB-2030 bid team invited Alec and Michaela to a washup meeting forty-eight hours after the Task Force had left town. The mood was bullish and Damien Scott opened proceedings with congratulations.

'I don't think that could have gone any better, do you? Excellent hospitality, some stardust from our footballers and, if my spies are correct, Malcolm, The WayOut Club was a masterstroke.'

Tonghe preened while FA chairman Lord Cheeseman seconded Scott's assessment.

'I think we showed them what they needed to see, Damien. After all, we do have the best football infrastructure of anywhere in the world. And they will want to be associated with a bid that sees one of the temples to football rebuilt with their name all over it. That said, we could do well to think back to 2010: we were well ahead at this point then too.'

Bid backer, Mike Deighton didn't share his colleagues breezy confidence. 'Yes, well before we go off on a tandem,' he said, 'what about the nightclub incident? It sounds like one of them is plucky to be alive.'

The bid committee had taken to looking to Alec for advice on security matters and he chipped in uninvited. 'I don't think it was anything really, Mike. Just one of those misunderstandings that can happen when all the men are wearing dresses. I'm sure we've all been there, haven't we? Someone won't take 'fuck off' for an answer and one thing leads to another.'

Deighton huffed. 'Sounds like it was a bit more than someone getting the wrong end of the prick.'

'Anyway, no harm done,' jumped in Scott. 'Now moving on Roger, assuming we've got full marks in the evaluation report, what's next for the bid?'

Cheeseman took an unnecessarily ponderous fifteen minutes to summarise the next stages of the bidding process. But he did pull a rabbit out of his hat towards the end.

'Now that England has qualified for the World Cup in Qatar,' he said, with obvious satisfaction, 'I'm pleased to be able to announce that we've agreed with the Saudi FA that the England team will travel there for a series of friendly matches. The tour will be in the international break in mid-April and I'm sure you don't need reminding how strategically important the Middle East is. We're still working out who the opposition will be, but it should be a great way to show our support under the guise of World Cup acclimatisation. And Gareth Southgate's all for it.'

Alec was immediately on the alert but, seeing the approving nods around the table, decided to keep his own counsel, and the meeting fizzled out an hour later. Once it was over and most of the members had gone their separate ways, Damien Scott bent Alec's ear.

'How's it going, Alec?'

'Are you sure you want to know?'

'Not the details, obviously. Just the general gist.'

'We've come across the usual shenanigans during the Task Force's evaluation visits to other host countries but nothing you'd be surprised about. I spent part of their last evening here with a well-oiled Radovan Hribar, the Slovenian ex-player on the team. We identified him as the President's envoy at previous stops on the tour and he wasn't shy in setting out what we're up against. He as good as told me what the other bidders are promising to funnel in FIFA's direction by way of kickbacks, and it goes way beyond a few brown envelopes of cash. Qatar apparently set the pace and now it's pretty much an open secret that FIFA feels it deserves a greater share of the benefits its events bestow on host nations.'

'I don't know how we'd ever be able to make that work in the UK,' Scott replied, glumly. 'We had the sports team from Deloitte do the sums and I'm afraid it's all rather intangible. I mean, how are we supposed to put a value on British teenagers being marginally less obese, let alone give FIFA a cut?'

'That kind of calculation's above my paygrade, I'm afraid,' said Alec. 'There's something bigger going on, though, which may be useful. You know about the knife attack in the nightclub but that's not all we've found out. Michaela and I did some digging into Hakan Oktay, you know, the Task Force member who died in his hotel room in Lisbon?'

'Yes, I saw the reports. Tragic.'

'Well, no one's convinced it was natural causes and he hadn't taken enough pills to kill himself, so it definitely looks like foul play.'

Scott looked concerned. 'Surely, you don't think it was a rival bidder.'

'Unlikely. We suspect it has more to do with the Qatar World Cup and we're trying to find a way to turn it to the advantage of our bid. If we're successful it would be decisive and save the bid a fortune too.'

'That sounds very positive.'

'Maybe, but I have a feeling the cost will hit somewhere else.'

'Well, I'm sure Nigel will update me if it's anything I need to be aware of. Oh, by the way, what did you think of Cheeseman's little coup, arranging a friendly series in Saudi?'

'Mmm, I can see why he's happy. He swerves FIFA's rules on using friendlies as part of a bid, but I'm worried. There's something brewing in that part of the world and football's at the heart of it. My advice is to let another country take that risk.'

Scott breezed over him. 'Nonsense, Alec. The PM's all for it. We're overdue a trade mission to the region and it means we're well positioned ahead of the World Cup too, so you and Michaela better get packing.'

'What? Why would we be involved?'

'You're the closest thing to an international spy couple since Brangelina, and you're working for us. We need you on this trip.'

Alec was still turning the proposition over several hours later. He brought it up at dinner with Tyrone and his partner, the supermodel Maya, their neighbours from across the river.

'I don't know what he's expecting us to do,' he said.

'Come on, man, it'll be a laugh,' said Tyrone, who was going anyway in his capacity as FA ambassador. 'I've been on a few of these trips. We just fill in for the players when they're training, you know, shake a few hands, take a few pictures. Otherwise it's like being back in the squad again.'

'You're not going are you, Maya?' Michaela asked.

The ethereal beauty was much more down to earth than her acolytes let on. 'Not fuckin' likely,' she said. 'I'm going Dubai with the girls. After Tyrone's done, we're 'avvin a few extra days there. You should both come.'

'Tell you what,' Michaela said, 'I think I'll come with you from the start. A dry week in the desert with a bunch of footballers? I'd rather still needles underneath my toenails. Alec, you can tell the spooks that I'm doing desk research but in region if I'm needed.'

He couldn't think of a good reason for her to change her mind, so on a Tuesday evening three weeks later they were both headed in broadly the same direction. The taxi took them first to passenger drop off at Terminal 2 where Alec loaded half a dozen of Louis Vuitton's finest onto a trolley while Michaela located the Emirates desk.

'Have a great time,' he said, 'I'll see you in a week.'

'I'll be fine, but I'm worried about you. Don't do anything stupid.'

'According to the guys at the FA, there shouldn't be anything for me to do, so you've nothing to be concerned about. Go on, get stuck into that business lounge.'

Alec kissed her long and slow on the lips then watched as she wiggled her trolley towards check-in. He was still in the taxi to Terminal 5 and a British Airways flight to Saudi when he received an alert on his phone: Guillermo Salz had been arrested in Switzerland for fraud. It seemed the pressure on FIFA was continuing.

It was a six-hour flight from London to Dubai during which Michaela and Maya indulged in the full Emirates business class experience then dozed in the flatbed seats. The journey time was almost exactly the same to Saudi although the young England squad were too excited to get much sleep. The old hands tucked into the hospitality knowing it would be their last alcoholic drink for a while. Not since the nineties have hotel mini bars contained anything but soft drinks for England football tours. Any would-be hellraisers were going to be disappointed when they encountered the Kingdom's famously sober nightlife.

By pure coincidence, as both the Emirates and BA flights glided across the skies of Europe and on towards the Middle East, 30,000 feet below them the FIFA Council was in session. The debate had been heated for several hours and Alec and Michaela's ears would have burned had they been able to listen in.

'It is harassment, pure and simple,' said one voice, his accent giving away central African roots. 'I had assumed I was suffering a unique experience but to learn that many of us have suffered the same indignities. Well, it looks like a campaign of intimidation.'

Others around the table echoed his frustrations and the simultaneous translators struggled to keep up as the Council members spoke over one another determined to add their voice to the clamour for action. In the end, it was the normally reasonable member from Germany who stood up and raised his voice, his ire focused directly on the President.

'The situation is unacceptable,' he said, spraying saliva as he shouted, 'and we want to know what you are going to do about it.'

The Old Man looked strangely alone as he absorbed the full force of the criticism. The seat next to his would normally have been occupied by the deflective shield of Guillermo Salz. His absence was inconvenient rather than unexpected, of course. Indeed, the information leading to his arrest had been leaked by the President's office. But for the man responsible, there was a tinge of regret over the timing. He addressed the room with none of his customary vigour.

'My friends, my brothers, there are many who do not understand our work and we suffer more than we deserve the slings and arrow of those who oppose us. Through all of these unfortunate situations, FIFA has survived, and we will come through this new battle. The FIFA project can never be stopped.'

The room was monetarily stunned into silence until the same clamouring voices erupted again.

'Mr. President, you are missing the point,' came the African voice again. 'This is not about FIFA; it's me that is being attacked. And not just me. Members around this table are seeing their reputations damaged and their personal wealth plundered, and you need to take action.'

Some of the wiser heads on the Council began to see the trap that had been set and sat on their hands, but most were even more vocal than before. The Old Man waited for a few more agonising seconds before rising sharply to his feet, his eyes blazing.

'Do not talk to me about reputation or plunder,' he boomed, his voice appearing suddenly much larger than his diminutive frame. 'Most of you shouting the loudest have the reputations you deserve, and as for plunder, you are like rapists plucking the wives of your fellow countrymen and our beloved sport. You owe everything to FIFA and yet you put yourselves, your squalid characters and your stolen fortunes ahead of your loyalty to me or to this organisation.'

His gaze swept the room, locking eyes with the dissenters on the Council, daring them to challenge him. The faces that stared back suddenly very aware that he knew details of every FIFA dollar they had received and, more often than not, how they had spent it. And as for their reputations, none of them would stand up to any kind of public exposé: most had half-buried skeletons that could destroy them and the Old Man had made it his business over the years to find out what they were.

He lowered himself into his chair speaking as he did so, calmly but pointedly. 'Action under English law targeting unexplained wealth does, I am told, require a high evidential threshold which suggests the authorities are very confident of their position.'

He paused again, allowing his message to sink in.

'Nevertheless,' he continued, as if thinking aloud to himself, 'it is possible there may be some mischief making going on.' He directed his gaze at Gill Andrews, the British representative. 'Would you know anything about that, Gill?'

The FA man huffed and puffed, ineffectually. 'Mr. President, I hope you're not suggesting this has anything to do with the UK bid to stage the World Cup. I should like to refute such an allegation in the strongest terms. Other than vague gossip, this meeting is the first I have heard of any legal action. I would like it put on record that our committee had no involvement or knowledge that any proceedings were being put in motion.'

He ran out of steam and the Old Man let the silence expand to fill the room, making his point for him. He gazed around the table, his focus alternately singling out an individual Council member then staring off at a spot just below the ceiling. His eye caught that of a member who had been silent up to that point, and a thought seemed to take him by surprise.

'Sheikh Abdullah, we haven't heard from you on this or, to my recollection, any other subject. Do you have any thoughts?'

All eyes turned to the robed figure who looked surprised to be single out.

'Do not concern yourselves with the English,' he responded. 'They will not be a problem for much longer.'

Gill Andrews spluttered: 'Should I be taking that comment as a threat, your Excellency?'

The Arab just stared back, his face a mask, but no one around the table was in any doubt what he was capable of.

Chapter 24

It was the equivalent of four a.m. London time when a now sleepy England squad touched down in Jeddah on Saudi Arabia's Red Sea coast. The modern resort town is the country's answer to bright lights of Dubai and claims the crown as its most liberal city. Although at just forty miles from Mecca, the fountainhead and cradle of Islam, everything is relative. Fortunately, the day ahead was set aside for orientation with only a brief media appearance at sunset on the manicured lawn of their luxury five-star hotel on the city's waterfront. The team's visit had generated a lot of local interest and a large crowd of photographers and reporters from TV news and sports channels were assembled for the official photocall. The photographers were polite and happy to snap away at the group, but the journalists' focus was on the players from Liverpool and Chelsea. Not only were their two clubs battling it out at the top of the Premier League, they also played alongside prominent Muslim players Mohammed Salah and Antonio Rüdiger about whom no detail was too trivial to report.

The first match was scheduled for Thursday evening, the start of the weekend, with a strong England line-up playing an all-stars team drawn from the two local Saudi Pro League clubs. The result was never in doubt and most of the first team were pulled off at the break with the hosts already trailing by six goals. At the end of the game the cameras kept rolling as the players dutifully signed autographs for good-natured fans in the King Abdullah Sports

City Stadium. While the players changed into their official M&S tour suits, the cameramen moved their gear to the beach where there was a reception with local celebrities.

The following morning, the players, coaches and management were back at the airport for the ninety-minute hop to Riyadh, the Saudi capital. Once there, their hosts had arranged an exclusive visit to the Kingdom's newest attraction, the Six Flags Qiddiya theme park. Southgate's men were some of the first foreign visitors to experience this spectacular combination of funfair, water park and F1-standard motor racing circuit. The sun shone and the lads blew off some steam on the rides duly Insta'ing everything in sight. The resulting publicity was a big boost for the park and more than covered the cost of the tour.

That evening they trained for the first time at the King Fahd International Stadium, venue for the showpiece event of the tour: a match up against a visiting Brazil team. Such was the excitement that each of the venue's 67,000 seats could have been sold three times over. There were a few hundred travelling England fans and the international press pack had also made the trip. That Saturday night in April was as close to cosmopolitan as Riyadh ever got.

Most of the England fans had travelled overnight on Thursday and spent Friday on slightly world-weary tours of the cultural heritage at the heart of Arabia. An evening drinking Coke left many of them with a raging thirst and they were determined that the day of the game would not be a dry one. Many had already skipped work, lied to the wife, borrowed the money for flights, smuggled six into a twin room past a hotel concierge and bought match tickets on the black market. Sourcing alcoholic drinks then evading arrest, imprisonment or deportation for consuming them were just more challenges to overcome. They were on a quest, and there are very few more focused individuals than football fans on the hunt for a drink.

Touts outside the stadium may have waved a handful of what appeared to be tickets, but the hot money was chasing supplies of liquid refreshment for before and after the game. A community of expats, billeted discretely in gated communities, had been working on the homebrew since the England visit had been announced. Tonight was what they had been building up to. Phone calls were made, deliveries arranged, and all over town drivers were dispatched to ferry the valuable liquor to eager customers. Some of it never arrived, some was as different from amber nectar as it was possible to imagine, and most was so weak it would have been classified as alcohol free back home. But the warm night and the buzz of the illicit operation meant the moonshine had the desired effect, at least temporarily.

Connor Flynn of SAS Dagger notoriety was always going to go one better. He approached the task like a military exercise. Which was how Alec found himself at four the following morning playing poker with a drunken dozen of England's finest. He and Connor had stayed in touch since that day in Hereford almost a year ago, and it was one of the bright spots of the tour to discover that his former patrol leader had been called up for England duty. Connor had taken Alec aside to bring him in on the arrangements. While the players were being ferried to the pre-match warm up, Alec was waiting in the shadows of the hotel service entrance to liaise with their bootlegger. Supplies secured, he grabbed a taxi and made it into his seat just before kickoff.

The game was a raucous affair with hatfuls of goals from both sides and a crowd that went wild for everything. It ended five apiece with Connor earning two assists, so he was buzzing when they got on the coach back to the hotel.

'I watched the replay, man,' he gushed. 'Clive Tyldesley called that first cross sublime and said I played the Brazilians at their own game. I'm surprised I didn't get man of the match.'

'Put the ball away, Con,' said one of the old hands. 'You should've come up against the old Brazil team. Now, they really were something.'

Connor was undeterred and bounced on to Alec. 'Did you get the supplies, mate? I'm fucking dryer than a Camel's hump.'

'All set up in my room, but keep it under your hat, eh? You know what they're like round here. Who else knows about it?'

'Only Darren, Ryan, Wozzer and Calvo. With you and me I thought we'd have a decent poker game.'

'We could do with a few more to make it interesting and there's a crate load of booze. What about Jermaine? He deserves a good rinsing and I reckon we'd take a few quid off Tripps and Stoney. I'm not saying they're stupid, but between them, they spent less time in school than Greta Thunberg.'

'Alright, I'll sign them up,' said the excited player. 'What about girls? Reckon we could get us any bow chicka wow wow?'

'You're joking, aren't you? You've got more chance getting a blowjob off the Pope round here. They'll chop your knackers off if they catch you so much as sniffing a local girl.'

'Ok, no girls,' Connor said, bobbing towards the back of the bus. 'L8rz.'

As they arrived at the hotel, England team director of operations Helen Bell came aboard and grabbed the microphone. The squad groaned as her voice boomed through the PA: they knew what was coming.

'Right lads, nice job tonight. Well done. Ordinarily, I'd be telling you not to go too wild with the celebrations but, and I can't stress this enough, we're relying on you to make it a quiet one. You must not ask the hotel staff for booze, proposition anyone for sex or hit the streets in search of drugs. Basically anything the folks back home would tolerate as just lads having fun is off limits. Do I make myself clear?'

'Can't we just get stoned?' came a voice from the back, followed by gales of laughter.

'Very good, thanks Darren. Seriously, a sense of humour bypass is one of the main requirements of the religious police. They have long faces and short fuses and the penalties they hand out range from lashes to amputations or prison sentences. Please, for your own sakes, stay in the hotel and keep a low profile.'

Alec's first mistake of the evening was to invite the guys to his room rather than simply handing over the stash.

'The locals call it Siddique' he said. 'It's stronger than rocket fuel so I've got in a load of mixers too. Drop your gear off then head to mine with a glass and it's game on.'

Two hours later, word had spread and fifteen lads were crowded into his now steamy hotel room. The poker game was in full swing. As ever, there were some big winners and some sore losers. Connor and Alec were sitting on large piles of chips repeatedly using their muscle to bully the others into folding before sharing the spoils on the table. With each round of moonshine, the decision making became more reckless with players going all in to try and bluff their way back into the game. Worse, most had taken their poison with Red Bull or Monster, so they were wide awake drunk and getting lairy. Alec had ten years and a lifetime's experience on most of them, and he did his best to keep a lid on things. He cajoled, warned and argued with the players, but in the end, he was physically incapable of holding them back. Once they got bored of chasing their losses the cry went up to *hit the pool*. He thought about calling Helen Bell but chose instead to stick with the crowd, try to reign them in and bail them out if necessary. He brought up the rear as they crowded into the lifts heading for the basement.

It was four in the morning, the spa was deserted and everything would probably have been ok. Except that they went through the wrong door and ended up in the women-only pool. Even then they would have got away with a chastening word had all the lads not insisted on getting naked. Within minutes the hotel's night manager and three security guards burst through the doors yelling and brandishing batons. They were met by fifteen pissed men giving it the universal wanker sign from middle of the pool and singing *'come and 'ave a go'*. It was not the most conciliatory response. Despite Alec's remonstrations, the manager replied in the only way he knew: by calling the police.

Chapter 25

By dawn the only thing standing in the way of the shamefaced lads and the Mutawa's lash was the hotel manager's reluctance or inability to finger the individuals concerned. Once they realised the police were on their way, the boys panicked, grabbed what they could find to cover their modesty and made a run for it. When the authorities arrived, the night manager had no option but to select all the names from the hotel guest register. With the hotel now quiet, staff tried to smooth things over, but the religious police were determined not to leave without dispensing some summary justice. The entire squad was woken up and summoned to a conference room where a large man in a clerical robe subjected them to the Arabic equivalent of Sir Alec Fergusson's hairdryer. By the time he'd finished, everyone, including the manager, was shaking guiltily in their tracksuits. It was only Alec's suggestion that they make a sizeable donation to a local sports charity that finally took some of the heat out of the situation. Even so, they found their luggage had been brought down and dumped unceremoniously in the street outside. Although it was only seven in the morning, the entire party was forced to line up next to the pile while a furious Helen Bell settled the bill and called the coaches.

Most of the squad put on outsized headphones and used the drive to catch up on their sleep. But in the management seats the recriminations started.

'I'm holding you two responsible,' Bell said, sharply to Alec and Tyrone. 'This isn't over and you're the ones who are going to take the wrap for it, not me.'

'Don't blame me,' said Tyrone, innocently. 'I was nowhere near.'

Alec decided to go on the offensive. 'I did you a favour, Hells,' he said, conveniently forgetting his role in obtaining the alcohol. 'What did you think was going to happen? For some of these boys that was one of the biggest games of their careers; going toe to toe with Brazil in front of nearly 70,000 people. They all played a blinder, scored loads of goals, defended for their lives and what did you do? You put on a Coca-Cola reception for an hour then asked the boys to tuck up quietly in bed. I don't care whether we're in Saudi or on the fucking moon; you've got to do better than that.'

'What were we supposed to do? We're in a dry country. How would it look if the England team management were caught buying black market booze?'

'So, you did nothing, and the boys made their own arrangements, and if I hadn't been there it would have been a helluva lot worse.'

'Worse? How exactly could it have been any worse? You're just lucky we were on a coach and on our way out of the city before any media turned up.'

In the end the argument fizzled out, and they all sat back in their seats as the dusty suburban scenery outside gave way to scrub and then sand. The final stage of their Saudi tour was four hours away along a highway which carved a dead straight line across the desert. Black gold had been discovered here in vast quantities in the 1930s and been extracted ever since. In the process it had turned a fishing hamlet on the country's northern coast into a city of over a million souls. Dammam is now a vast industrial complex of, refineries, pipelines and a commercial port. Beyond the city limits lies Rub al-Khali or the Empty Quarter. This arid landscape of dried-up lake beds, gravel plains and endless fickle dunes stretches for 250,000 square miles making the highway the only land route to civilisation.

The England team were scheduled to train that evening with local journeymen Ettifaq FC before playing an exhibition match against them the next night in front of 40,000 locals.

Dammam was not exactly on the circuit for visiting celebrities, but word had got around, and the entertainment-starved city dwellers were clearly expecting a show. As the coaches entered the downtown area, welcome banners hung from every lamp post and the players grabbed their phones to snap the huge billboards of their faces which lined the streets.

'It's like a Primark version of the Champions League finals,' said one, whose picture had not been used to promote the visiting team. 'Calvo, your face looks like it was made on FIFA.'

'There's a reason the sponsors never use your face, Stoney. I mean, apart from the acne, your nose looks like it was made for a much bigger person.'

The banter was interrupted by Helen Bell's voice on the microphone.

'So, you'll be coming back here to train this evening. As you can see, the locals have rolled out the welcome mat for us so clean underwear please. For the moment we're going to the hotel which is a beach resort a few miles out of the city. Lunch will be waiting for us and then the afternoon's your own.'

The coaches trundled along wide thoroughfares lined with the usual mix of malls, banks and fast-food outlets interspersed with low-rise apartment buildings. Pavements fringed the boulevards, but nobody walked. The few people they did see were on the street only for as long as it took to move between their cars and the shops. There were no women. The camera phones soon returned to their owners' pockets, and everyone settled back into their seats. With the city receding into the haze, the coaches followed the coastline for twenty minutes before turning off the main highway onto a single-track road towards the sea. The horizon stretched away unimpeded in every direction across a grey, sandy wasteland smeared with patches of surface oil.

The hotel, when it finally appeared, was behind a high fence and offset security gates. Alec wasn't paying much attention, but he sat up as the coaches weaved their way through the checkpoint past four uniformed guards with automatic weapons hanging across their bodies.

The initial impression may have been like entering an army base, but there was no denying the luxury that lay beyond the fence. The hotel building was curved, its three floors of rooms overlooking a central atrium with formal gardens and a fountain. The grounds were verdant and studded with palms. To one side of the hotel there were tennis courts and a kidney-shaped swimming pool overlooked by the tall windows of a fully equipped gym. When they got to reception it soon became clear they had the place to themselves. After the incident in Riyadh, this was a welcome chance for some privacy. The hotel staff were attentive and invited everyone into the main dining room for lunch where, having missed out on breakfast, the entire camp piled in enthusiastically.

Once he had filled his tray from the buffet, Connor winked at Alec and gestured for him to sat down at his table.

'I'm not sure we should be seen together, mate,' Alec said. 'We're in enough trouble as it is.'

'Don't worry about that. Now, did you get the booze out this morning? That lot cost me a fortune.'

'Are you sure this is the time? We very nearly caused a diplomatic incident last night.'

'Relax, won't you? This is supposed to be about team bonding, and I can't think of a better way to do it than with a few sherbets and a card game. How much have we got left?'

'There's plenty but let's keep it 'till after training this evening, yeh?'

The squad spent the afternoon racing the now standard issue inflatable unicorns in the pool under the watchful eye of Helen Bell, hovering around like a new grandmother. Most of the lads were fine with the spring sunshine, but a couple were so pale skinned they'd get sunburn from their phones. Despite Bell's frequent applications of sunblock, they were the traditional British lobster red by the time the sun went down.

Alec decided to spend a couple of hours checking in with clients rather than go with the team to training. He strolled through the lush greenery and down to the empty beach beyond. The absence of footprints and loungers told him that few people came to the resort to build sandcastles. Although, beyond a few ornamental rocks, it wasn't immediately clear why would come at all. As the sky turned from orange to azure then inky blue, he put a call through to Michaela describing the scene as the twinkling lights of Bahrain island appeared a few miles offshore. Soon, the beach was almost black, and he tried to retrace his steps toward the lights of the hotel. Distracted by their conversation, he missed the main path and stumbled into a service area to one side. He was about to turn around when movement at the opposite fence caught his attention. He lowered his voice and watched unobserved as a security gate slid back and a white minivan drove into the yard. Four uniformed men emerged from the passenger seats. They picked up weapons, clips of ammunition and what looked like overnight supplies of food and water before disappearing into the gloom in the direction of the security gate. Five minutes later four identically dressed men completed the same exercise in reverse.

'Have you ever stayed in a hotel guarded by men carrying semi-automatic weapons?' he asked Michaela, who was still hanging on.

'Obviously not,' she replied. 'Maybe they're concerned about the celebrity status of their guests.'

'Maybe, but there's something weird about this place. It's literally in the middle of nowhere and we're the only one staying. I tell you what it reminds me of: a miniature version of the Sheik's palace in Qatar. In fact, it looks exactly the sort of place you would use as a prison for a maverick royal who refuses to tow the party line.'

'Doesn't the Crown Prince have form in that area?'

'It would explain the complete lack of tourist amenities. Still there are worse places to spend a couple of nights.'

'As long as that's all it is.'

'Well, if you don't hear from me, at least you know where I am. Hello, are you still there?'

The phoneline was dead and his mobile registered no signal when he tried to call back. In the hotel the wifi was still apparently going strong, but when he tried to call over WhatsApp all he got was an error message. He walked through the corridors looking for a member of staff, but the place was seemed completely empty. He zig-zagged from one floor to another and still hadn't come across anyone by the time he found himself back at the deserted reception. Behind the desk, computers blinked away purposefully but all he got was a pixilated dinosaur and a 'no internet' message when he tried to connect. The phones were equally unresponsive. He thought about trying the kitchens but opted for the gatehouse where at least he knew there were some other humans. The four guards were huddled around a portable TV set smoking and clearly not expecting to encounter one of their guests. They jumped up as he approached but their weapons remained on hooks behind the door. They were polite enough when Alec asked to borrow a phone but their access to the outside world seemed to be as limited as his own. By way of explanation, they simply shrugged, their slightly awkward body language implying that this was not an uncommon experience. He tried to negotiate for one of the men to drive him somewhere with a mobile signal but at that point their ability to interpret his hand gestures ran out and he received only apologetic smiles.

By now Alec's suspicions were well and truly alerted, but with no sign of any immediate danger and no way of contacting anyone else, he was left with very few options.

He was still wondering what they were involved in when the buses carrying the players, coaches and support staff arrived. From the grumbling within the group, Alec assumed they were already missing internet access. He took Connor Flynn to one side.

'Do you know where you lost signal, Connor?' he asked, as the buses disappeared back through the gatehouse barrier.

'I was chatting, so I don't really know, but Darren was on Spotify and he started complaining a good few miles back. What do you think's going on?'

'Your guess is as good as mine, mate. I was on a call when the line went dead, and I can't get any joy out of the landlines either. At least there's some people around now,' he said, indicating the sudden appearance of three uniformed reception staff. 'Perhaps they'll be able to help.'

He had better English but were ultimately the concierge was as unhelpful as his colleagues on the gate.

'These things happen, very sorry, sir, sure it will be restored by the morning. Meanwhile can we get you anything to make your stay with us more comfortable?'

'Can anyone give me a lift or lend me a car so I can drive to get a signal?'

'Very sorry, sir. The staff tonight is all residential. We are brought here by minibus which will collect us and drop off the day staff after the waiters serve brunch in the morning. No one has a vehicle until then, sir.'

Alec sensibly ducked out of any after-hours antics so was up early the following morning. His phone and laptop still registered no signal so he spent half an hour going through the hotel, talking to staff and visiting the kitchen. The chamber maids were happy to say that all laundry was done on site and the chefs proudly showed off their food store with enough fresh and store cupboard ingredients to last at least a fortnight. Outside, he confirmed the information received the night before; there was no transportation on the site. Having exhausted the alternatives, he decided to see how far he'd have to run to get a mobile signal. He changed into shorts and trainers, picked up two large bottles of water and walked out through the barrier. The guys on the gate put up no resistance and he figured they couldn't raise the alarm either so he would be undisturbed, for the moment at least. The road went in only one direction and at a jog it was forty minutes before he reached the main highway and turned right towards Dammam. Another half an hour later he felt his phone vibrate and pulled off the road sheltering out of site behind a low brick building. The buzz was a message from Full English, a journo-cameraman duo who follow the England team and had his number from previous encounters. Having paid for their own flights, they wanted to make the most of the trip and had decided to travel to Dammam to watch the game. They were trying to tap up Alec for tickets.

He hit call-back. 'Hi chaps, where are you?'

'Alec, good to hear from you mate,' came the response on a very noisy line. 'We're in a hire car on the road out of Riyadh. Can you get us press access to the game?'

'I'm sure someone can, but listen, we may be in a spot of bother.'

As he was talking a blacked out 4x4 pulled off the highway and headed straight towards him. He made his decision.

'I can't talk but I need you to raise the alarm,' he said urgently. 'I'm going to text you roughly where we are and a number I need you to call. We're relying on you. Gotta go.'

Alec had only enough time to text the approximate location of the hotel and Michaela's mobile number before the car pulled up and two men wearing dark suits got out. He protested but had little choice but to go with them. Inside the car he tried to find out what was going on, but the men didn't speak, just drove back to the hotel and handed him over at the gate.

Inside the hotel the staff had changed. The relief crew were impeccably polite, but they were no more able to fix the lack of signal than their nocturnal colleagues. The players had appeared for mid-morning brunch and were now waiting for the buses to training. When nothing turned up, the coaches took them off for some gentle S&C work on the beach leaving Alec with the chance to catch up with Helen Bell.

'How's it going, Helen?' he started.

'*Helen* is it now? Everyone calls me *Hells* unless they want something. Knowing someone's about to ask me for a massive favour is about the only plus point to my parents' stupidity in the naming department.'

'It could be worse. Out there somewhere, Mr. and Mrs. Back are looking at each other and wondering what to call their new baby daughter.'

The look she gave him was a skin flayer. 'What do you want?' she asked, acidly.

Alec ploughed on undaunted. 'Anything about this setup strike you as weird?'

'I really don't have the time, Alec.'

'Yeah, right. Always be hustlin' eh? ''Cept without any phone or internet, you're faking just like I am, and I think this is weird. Did you choose this hotel or was it presented by our hosts?'

She sighed and picked up her bag. 'You're persistent, I'll give you that. Come on, I need a fag. Now, what's your problem?'

They walked in the grounds where he took a few minutes to share his concerns.

'I was on the phone to a friend of mine last night speculating about the kind of place this was when the line went dead. This morning, when I finally did get a signal, I was picked up in a matter of minutes and brought back here. That isn't normal. So, did you actually choose this hotel or did our hosts select it for you?'

'This bit of the trip was tagged on as an afterthought so I'm hazy. I think it was one of a number of choices but billed as a retreat for the squad and the chance for some team bonding.'

'A strong steer, then.'

'I suppose so, but I don't remember being under pressure to pick it.'

'So, as it stands, we're a long way from anywhere and dependent on the transportation coming back for us. From what I remember of the itinerary, the buses to take us to the stadium were due an hour ago, so what do you plan to do?'

'I don't know, Alec, but you've obviously given it some thought. What do you think I should do?'

'I'm not sure I need to be telling the FA director of operations her job, but if it were me, I'd be banging the desk at reception insisting they tell me what's going on. If they can't find a way to get in touch with the outside world, then you need a car to take you somewhere where there is a mobile signal. Then, when you've got it, you need to take matters into your own hands. You need the buses back here, the team at the stadium and, when the match is done, for everyone to be on our way home.'

She may have been known by all as Hells Bells, but Helen Bell was rarely called on to give it the full eternal fire and brimstone. However, she took Alec's suggestions on board and strode purposefully to reception. He was still sat in the grounds when she returned twenty minutes later, red in the face and very frustrated.

'They're completely stonewalling,' she protested. 'I even insisted on them showing me the goods entrance to check for a vehicle but there's nothing there, not even a bike. I think we're stuck and I'm beginning to worry'

'Alright, you carry on with the team. I'll dig around and see what I can come up with. They must be getting deliveries in even if it's only fresh fish.'

By mid-afternoon, he was rather less confident, and the camp was getting restless.

Chapter 26

Alec reported what happened next to a joint committee of suits. He was told they were from the Foreign Office and the FA but was as sure as he could be that it was a British security services debrief.

It would have been about six-thirty in the evening. I was sat on the beach when Full English appeared over the dunes. Their hire car was a classic open-topped Suzuki Jimny which was why it had been so noisy on the phone. It turned out to be a very useful choice. They had found the front entrance to the hotel but were turned away by security. They'd gone back to the main road, headed north for a couple of miles, and come in over the sand. They told me they'd spoken to Michaela who immediately put two and two together when she got my message. She said she would try and set up a rescue mission if they could attempt to make contact with me again. What none of us knew at that point was that after their first conversation, Michaela had taken a commercial flight from Dubai to Dammam. We decided that it was best for Full English to go back to where there was a mobile signal and get another message to Michaela. I briefed them on the information I thought she'd need: details of our situation, the number of guards, access points; anything I could think of that might be useful. They promised to come back between eleven o'clock and midnight then headed off along the beach. As we know those few hours turned out to be quite busy.

Calling the time between seven in the evening and two o'clock the following morning 'quite busy' was typical British understatement. As soon as they were within range of a mobile signal, Egg, the journalistic half of Full English called Michaela saying they had 'located the cargo' and that it would be 'ready for pickup' later that night. Only then did she tell them she was in already Dammam and the three arranged to meet. She wouldn't say anything else on the phone, but when they connected in the city, she revealed that a special forces unit had been scrambled from Akrotiri in Cyprus. The eight-strong extraction team were on board a C130 Hercules transport plane prepped for a boat drop operation. Their expected arrival time was one a.m. and she would be organising the welcoming committee.

I've been trying to construct a timeline of events for that evening. I remember looking at my watch when I got back to the hotel: it was 7.45, but it was immediately clear something had changed. The team, coaches and support staff were eating in the dining room and seemed to be in good spirits judging by the noise. Outside the place was deserted, reception was closed and there was no sign of the regular staff. I poked my head into the dining room and called Tyrone over. He had been looking for me as he was also starting to worry about what was going on. I told him about the casual change of guard at eight p.m. the previous evening and we agreed that this might be an opportunity. We quietly rounded up some of the others: I'd seen Connor Flynn in action, so he was an obvious choice, Tripps is also pretty handy plus he trusted me after I sorted the media during his betting ban, Jack Bishop is a big lad and Shovel McGrath isn't scared of anyone, so that was the team. I insisted there would be no heroics: we were just going to intimidate the guards once they were out of the vehicle and before they had chance to pick up their weapons. The plan was to take their rifles, tie them up with some gaffer tape I'd found in the hotel workshop and leave Tyrone to watch them while the five of us took the gatehouse by surprise. Then a few of us would borrow their

van and go and find out what the hell was going on.

We got in position out of sight in the service area and waited. When the gates swung

open at just before eight o'clock the van that entered was twice the size of the one the

previous night. I just had time to signal to the guys to abort before the doors opened and ten

uniformed soldiers carrying their weapons emerged. We held our breath in the shadows as

they disappeared into the gloom towards the gatehouse. I was thinking fast. It seemed

unlikely they'd increased the number of guards because of the threat to the players, so I had

to assume they must know about the plan to mount a rescue. We decided not to re-join the

squad and instead, we used the lull to blend back into the hotel grounds trying to stay

undetected as long as possible.

The night shift relieved the guards on the gate and set up their base in the gatehouse. There was room for four in the control room, but in the event, they left only two to man the barrier while the other eight headed for the hotel. The six footballers watched as the barrier was opened to let the van through. Then Tyrone spoke up.

'What the fuck's going on, Alec. I thought we were dealing with four security guards not a small army.'

'Yeh, me too, mate,' Alec replied. 'Look, I don't know how else to put this, but I think we've been kidnapped.'

The players opened their mouths to protest but he shushed them with a gesture and carried on.

'I've been thinking something weird's going on ever since we got here. I mean, this hotel, no other guests, no phones and now reinforced guards. I've managed to make contact with the outside world and I'm pretty confident the cavalry's on its way. But they're going to be a few hours so that means we're going to have to stall until then.'

Connor Flynn was the first one to get the message. 'They're going to know exactly how many of us are supposed to be here so that gives us only a few minutes to try and even up the numbers.' He gestured towards the gatehouse. 'I say we take these two out and nick their guns. At least when they send out a search party we're armed, and we've got two less to deal with.'

Alec had to agree with the logic and they decided to go for route one. He approached the gatehouse window.

'Evening lads,' he said to the guards, who recognised him from the evening before. 'Could one of you give me a hand?'

A young boy with a straggly beard put his weapon aside and followed Alec into the shadow beyond the reach of the security lights. Tyrone and Jack Bishop grabbed him on either side while Connor gaffer taped his wrists and ankles. They relieved him of his pistol and the hunting knife on his belt. Then the three of them manhandled him to the service area, securing him in the gardener's hut. Back at the gatehouse it wasn't long before the second guard emerged. He was carrying his weapon and moving much more cautiously. He followed the direction of his colleague into the shadows where he too was quickly disarmed. While Connor secured the tape around his wrists and ankles, Alec helped himself to the remaining weapons and a radio handset from the gatehouse. They reconvened at the service area where he took charge.

'Nice job, lads,' he said. 'Two down; eight to go. Right, it's just after nine and the guys I met earlier won't be back again for at least a couple of hours. As Con says, the guards are going to know we're missing, and I imagine they'll be out looking for us. I think it's time we made ourselves useful.'

It was a spur of the moment decision and one I think about every single day, but I honestly don't believe it made the ultimate situation any worse. We divided up the weapons between us with me and Tyrone taking assault rifles and a spare magazine. Connor and Tripps could shoot so I gave them and Bishop a handgun each and Shovel got a knife. Our objective was to reduce the number of guards that our rescuers had to deal with without attracting attention. We did a quick tour of the laundry room, the larder and the cold store looking for a secure place we could lure them to.

At first things went well. We stuck to the shadows and went round to the far side of the main building. All the lights were on in the dining room, and we could see the gunmen, still carrying their weapons, in with the squad. There was no doubt any more about what was going on: we were looking at a hostage scene. One of the men who acted like the leader was speaking while others worked in pairs to secure the exits. Another one was looking at some paperwork and we watched him do a visual count of the numbers in the group. He spotted the discrepancy straight away and I saw him whisper in the ear of the guy at the front. He paused momentarily to take in the information then he picked up his radio set. The voice that came through in my pocket was a short burst of Arabic. When he received no reply he repeated the same phrase then, after a pause, he switched to English.

'This is Captain Ahmed Sheik. I am here with my men to secure this hotel for your safety and protection. Please give yourselves up by walking with your hands in the air to the hotel reception. I guarantee you will not be harmed.'

He warned us that we were risking our lives and those of our teammates if we didn't do as he asked. As he was talking, I watched him gesture to four of his men to get out into the grounds which was our cue to take up positions.

Me, Connor and Jack went to the laundry area where we hid opposite the open door. The guards took their time searching the grounds, so it was twenty minutes before they reached us. We could see two of them casually enter the courtyard outside the laundry and check out the doorway. When we were certain they weren't being followed, Jack jumped them with a linen trolley, pinning them to the wall, giving me a Connor the chance to grab their weapons. Jack held them while we tied them up and locked them inside the laundry room. With another two out of the way we were left with the four men in the dining room and two more in the grounds for team Tyrone to deal with. Unfortunately, he wasn't quite so lucky.

Bad luck or everything turns to shit: sometimes it's hard to tell the difference. Tyrone Pelforth and Shovel McGrath took up positions in a courtyard outside the kitchen delivery door with Ronan Tripps inside. Unfortunately, when the two Saudis appeared, they triggered a security light which lit up the entire scene giving away the footballer's positions. Both sides seemed as shocked as the other as they found themselves suddenly face to face. In the split-second standoff that followed, two things happened: the thumb of one of the guards moved instinctively to his safety catch tripping his rifle into fire mode. And Shovel twitched. Tyrone was aware of both and tried to react, but he was too late. McGrath launched himself across the two-metre divide between him and guards. As he did, his opponent fired a single close range shot into the player's stomach, rocking him back on his heels. As the echo of the shot died, away McGrath collapsed onto the ground his body oozing a slick of dark, shiny blood.

Tyrone was the first to speak. 'I need to help him,' he said, gesturing to Shovel as slowly and calmly as he could.

He moved his arms apart holding the rifle unthreateningly in one hand and gently placing it on the ground. He eased it out of reach with his foot before inching forward and lowering himself to a crouch to tend to the injured player. His eyes never left the shooter who looked like he couldn't decide whether to fire again or run away. In the end, he raised his

rifle stock and made to club it in Tyrone's face. The player had a ponderous reputation on the

pitch, but his reactions this time were anything but. He caught the rifle and pulled it hard

towards him, catching the Saudi off balance. As the soldier stumbled, Tyrone whipped

forward with a powerful head butt hitting him squarely in the face. His nose exploded filling

his face with blood. In the confusion that followed there was a crack of pistol shots before the

security light went off. Sensing his opportunity, Tyrone tightened his grip on the rifle and ran

for the exit, the sound of footsteps just behind him. He tripped the light again as he reached

the edge of the courtyard and threw himself into a bush by the side of the path. Only then did

he glimpse Tripps following his lead and the pair ended up struggling almost comically in the

undergrowth. Looking back towards the kitchen, they could see both Arabs were down lying

in a crumpled heap near McGrath's lifeless body.

'Nice work, mate,' said Tyrone, 'It was kill or be killed, and you probably just saved

our lives.

Tripps nodded slowly, a stunned look on his face. He was finding it hard to take in the

facts that Shovel McGrath was dead, and he'd just killed two men.

Tyrone gave him as long as he could but knew they had to move. 'We've gotta' go,

mate,' he said. 'The sound of gunshots is going to bring everyone running in this direction.

We need to grab those bastards' weapons and get out of here.'

'What about Shovel?' Tripps asked, still confused. 'We can't just leave him.'

'We don't have a choice,' Tyrone said, softly. They'll have heard the shots and if we

stay, we'll be picked up for sure. We'll come back for him when it's safe.'

When we heard the shots Me, Connor and Bishop were tucked in behind the changing

rooms near the swimming pool on the other side of the hotel. We had a good view of the dining room so we could see the Saudi leader's reaction. He picked up his radio and rapid-fire Arabic was soon going off in my pocket. There was no response from any of his crew. I was cheering inside as he repeated the message. Then he switched to English again.

'This is Captain Ahmed Sheik. I am giving you a final opportunity. Walk towards the hotel reception with your hands up and you will not be harmed. If you do not give yourselves up my men will start killing hostages.'

That was the word he used: 'hostages'. I watched his face as he spoke. Then he put the radio set down and looked around the room. All I could see was indecision. He lifted a hand towards two of his men as if to send them out to look for us. Then he appeared to change his mind. His position was not helped by the reaction of the England squad. On hearing the suggestion that hostages would be killed, they were predictably aggressive. As a team they started advancing threateningly towards the guards, gesturing as if daring them to fire the machine guns they were holding. Captain Sheik looked increasingly out of his depth: his orders, wherever they came from, clearly did not include executing prisoners. The situation was tense and getting worse. He pulled out his handgun and fired into the ceiling which stopped the English advance momentarily, but they were soon in the faces of their captors again sensing they had the momentum. It was left to Helen Bell to step forward and try to diffuse a volatile situation. From her body language and hand gestures it was clear she was asking for everyone to calm down.

Out in the grounds Tyrone and Tripps found another lookout position and stayed put until they were completely satisfied that the Arab army wasn't about to descend. Then they emerged gingerly to take stock of where they were. By this point, they were loaded up with three assault rifles and three pistols between them which made it hard to move around undetected. Tyrone suggested they head towards the beach and look for somewhere to stash some of the guns. It was a decision with fatal consequences.

They picked a spot behind the treeline a few metres from the hotel's flagpole and dropped their spare cache into a bush before moving along the beach. Seconds later they emerged by the swimming pool where they nearly tripped over Alec, Connor and Bishop.

'Where's the Shovel?' Alec whispered.

Tyrone shook his head. 'He didn't make it,' he said, simply. 'He brought a shovel to a gunfight, made a run at the guards and they pretty much blew him apart.'

They were all silent, taking in the seriousness of the situation, until Alec said, 'We'll go back for him when we're done. What happened to the guards?'

Tyrone shrugged. 'They were fucking amateurs, man. Last time we saw them, they were in a crumpled heap on the floor. We didn't check their pulses, but there was no life in their eyes: I'd say they're not getting up again.'

'That's one thing I suppose. The big picture is we've reduced the number of guards from ten to the four you can see through that window. After a bit of a standoff, they seem to have settled down but they're not going risk losing any more men. So that leaves us free to go where we want. We'll find out in a few minutes whether help's on the way then our job is make sure they know where to find us. The only fly in the ointment, judging by what we've seen tonight, is I think Captain Ahab in there is expecting something. He and his boys are twitchy and unpredictable so we're going to have keep an eye on them. Tyrone, you stay here with Tripps and keep watch. The rest of us will try and connect with Full English and then we'll see if this thing's on or whether we need a change of plan.

In the air high above the Persian Gulf a dozen parachutes were drifting silently towards the inky black water. On the end of them were eight SBS and SAS soldiers, three high-speed RIB boats and enough weaponry to get the job done. Once they hit the water, the men were quickly reunited with their inflatables. They recovered their weapons and sank the platforms the hardware had been mounted on. They were soon skimming across the water towards the Saudi coast. Meanwhile on the ground, Michaela and Full English were making their way, lights out, across the sand dunes. Progress was slow and it was well after eleven by the time they were on the beach. Michaela hadn't shared her plan with them but insisted throughout the journey that they were to drop her and leave immediately. She jumped out of the jeep with one last barked command at them to get going and ran off into the darkness.

Photographer Grill, or Grill the Snapper to give him his full title, had been given his nickname when someone asked him his favourite way of cooking fish. It was a typical smart journalist's question, but the name stuck. Egg, the journalist on the other hand, claimed he had a masters in embryology. But as a pair, Full English fancied themselves as war reporters. An exchange of glances early in the drive from Dammam confirmed neither had any intention of leaving. As Michaela disappeared into the night, they simply turned the car around, drove behind a dune and parked up. The lighting would be a challenge for Grill's cameras, but he got himself into position just outside the hotel garden fence. He had a view across the beach where he set about recording Egg's first piece to camera. Sadly for the duo, their footage was not destined to become their breakthrough moment, but it did make a valuable contribution to the inquiry that followed the night's events.

I left Tyrone and the others watching the dining room while I took Connor to the beach to connect with Full English. We heard their car rather than saw it as they were running without lights but on the beach, they were silhouetted by the refinery behind them. We watched as a single figure jumped out and ran towards us while the jeep turned and drove away. The figure stuck to the shadows, so it was not until she was almost on top of us that I recognised Michaela. There was a lot to catch up on, but this wasn't the time. She said that British Special Forces were on their way and would land on the beach around one. It

was left to us to work out a plan to guide them in.

With just over an hour to wait, I got Michaela a gun then took her and Connor to find

a hotel room directly overlooking the beach. We got as many lights together as we could and

hoped they would be visible enough through the window to indicate our position. When we

went back to check on Tyrone everything seemed calm enough. Now that the threats had

stopped, most of the players were sitting at tables, their heads resting on their arms. The

guards obviously knew their position was vulnerable, so they had rigged what looked like

explosives to the main doors. They were positioned at the back of the room with the England

squad acting as human shields in front of them. They wouldn't be able to stay like that for

ever, but as I looked on, they seemed ready for an imminent attack.

Whilst we were moving around the grounds, we checked on the Saudis we had

captured earlier. I was confident the laundry room was secure but opened it just in case. Sure

enough, two uniformed men were inside asleep on a pile of bedding. They barely stirred as

the door opened. We approached the gardener's workshop cautiously and with good reason.

The two guards had clearly managed to free themselves from the gaffer tape and had beaten

the flimsy padlock securing the door. They had no weapons but the presence of two hostiles

in the grounds was an unwelcome distraction. We went back to warn Tyrone and the rest to

be on the alert.

An hour later there was still no sign of the two marauding Saudis. Alec kept the group

of six together in one place rotating two lookouts whilst the others dozed. As the clock edged

towards one a.m. he took a final look at the dining room and roused the team.

'Connor, go through the back entrance of the hotel and up to the room we were in

earlier. At one o'clock exactly I want you to flash the lights in there as hard as you can for at least ten minutes. Then you can come down and join the rest of us on the beach. I'll get forward to meet whatever's coming while you four split up and try and deal with those stray guards. Get yourselves into a safe position where you can see what's happening but not where you're in danger of being picked off. We don't think they're armed but we can't be sure.'

'Yeh, about that,' said Tyrone. 'We couldn't carry all the guns we took so we stashed some near the flagpole. They weren't obvious, but I suppose someone could have found them.'

'Shit. Ok, so they're out there and possibly armed. There's nowhere to go outside the grounds and they've been way too quiet, so we have to work on the basis that they're planning to make a nuisance of themselves. Move with extreme caution and remember, if the shooting starts it's going to be impossible to tell who's friend or foe. If in doubt just keep your head down. Right Con, off you go. The rest of us are going to hang back as late as possible. When I move forward I need you to cover me.

The presence of two armed enemy soldiers, however poorly trained, evened up the odds, and not in a good way. Alec and his team twitched nervously in the shadows, but they didn't have long to wait. The faint buzz of outboard motors was audible almost as soon as they left the pool. Above them Connor was signalling wildly and the buzz got rapidly louder as the source came straight towards them. Alec waited until it was possible to make out three distinct boats. He nudged his mates and ran by the shortest possible route reaching cover unscathed.

The RIBs hit the beach at high speed with their motors being hauled out of the water at the last minute. One soldier from each boat, equipped with night vision goggles, jumped forward and took up a firing position.

'Possible armed hostiles,' Alec yelled.

He had barely got the words out before they there was a burst of automatic weapon fire and bullets ripped through the air in their direction. One of the rescue party went down while the others returned fire. The shooting stopped as soon as it started and the fallen man's crew pulled him back onto the boat. As they did, there was another single shot with a distinctive metallic clunk to it and Connor's voice could be heard yelling, 'I fucking got 'im. 'ave that, you bastard.'

Alec looked out from behind his rock to see a face he recognised speaking with a familiar Scottish accent.

'Fuckin' magic. It had to be youse lot, didn't it?'

'Sergeant Geddes. It's great to see you.'

Chapter 27

'Right, sitrep. Let's get this done.'

In action, SAS Sergeant Geddes was even more imposing than when they had met on the lad's day out in Hereford. Alec tried to give him what he needed.

'There are six of us, Michaela who's ex-Police and some of the boys you met before. There are four armed men in a room with thirty-seven of the England camp: players, coaches and admin. They've been in there seven hours. There's one more somewhere in the grounds and probably armed. On their side, it's four killed and two captured. They're locked in laundry room. One of ours is down.'

He looked up for confirmation he was on the right lines.

Geddes wasn't in the mood for small talk. 'Come on laddie: weapons, ammunition, comms, threat assessment.'

'Err, right. Each of the guards has an assault rifle and a handgun, ammunition levels unknown. No external comms but we could try to make walkie talkie contact,' he said, holding out the handset.'

'We're not here for a fucking chat. Threat assessment?'

'They threatened to kill hostages earlier but there's been no sign they're willing to follow through. It looks like they've booby-trapped the main door to the dining room but there's a rear door which is accessible via the kitchen. They have positioned themselves at the back of the room with the players and staff in front of them as a shield.'

'Any other staff or personnel of any kind?'

'No.'

'Right, let's get up close for a proper look.' He stood up and addressed his unit. 'Mike, Alan, Taff, you stay here with Andy. The rest of you, we're following this lad here.'

The dining room was subtly different from when they last looked. The doors still appeared wired up to explosives, the squad were still at their tables but now they were alert and pensive. Behind them the Saudis were nowhere to be seen. Geddes got on the radio.

'Four tangos on the loose and may be heading your way.'

'Roger that,' came the reply.

'Right, Alec, pass me that walkie talkie. Have you got a name for the fuckwit in charge of this shower o' shite?'

Alec told him, and he picked up the yellow plastic handset in disgust.

'Captain Sheik. My name is Gavin and I'm a sergeant with British Special Forces. I'm here with my unit to extract the British nationals that you are holding and bring them home by any means necessary. We want to do that as quickly and safely as possible, so I'm going to offer you two choices. You can stand aside and put your weapons down and watch us leave, or we will hunt you down and kill you, and then we'll be on our way. The choice is yours. Me and my men are better trained and better equipped and if you do not stand down, we will kill you. If you want to live, I need you out in the open with your weapons on the ground and your hands in the air. If you do as I ask, you have my personal guarantee that no one will be harmed. You have two minutes. If I don't see you out in the open with your weapons on the ground and your hands in the air, then we will be coming for you.'

His radio crackled into life. 'Movement on the beach. Four tangos moving into the lights hands up.'

'Roger that. Do not shoot unless threatened. Repeat do not shoot unless threatened. Hold at your location. We're on our way.'

Geddes left two men back to watch the dining room. The rest pushed forward towards the beach where they disarmed the four Saudis. They searched them for any remote detonation devices and sat them down in a tight group. He posted two men to keep watch then hustled back to the hostages, shouting at them through the windows.

'Good evening, I'm with the British Army. We're here to get you home. Now, is everyone ok?'

There was nodding and a cheer from inside the room.

'Right, just sit tight while we get you out of there.'

He pointed to the exit into the kitchen. 'Two of my men will be coming through that door any second so don't be alarmed. Now, can anyone tell me about the double doors here?'

'Six of us are tied to a trip switch,' came a voice from within. 'If we move, the doors blow.'

Geddes acknowledged the information and radioed his men for an explosives expert and some cutting gear. They worked efficiently moving the bulk of the squad out through the kitchens and onto the beach while making the remainder safe. Two of the unit carried McGrath's body and within minutes the entire party was mustered by the RIBs.

'Right, listen up everyone. We have three inflatables to take you to rendezvous with HMS Montrose anchored about twenty-five klicks offshore. From there you'll get checked over then taken to a port in Bahrain where you'll soon be on a plane home. However, there's only room for fourteen on each inflatable so one of them is going to do two trips. Each boat has two crew so that means a maximum of twelve of you with each one. Andy needs medical attention so he's going with the forward party. We don't want to be moving your player's body when we're shorthanded, so he'll be on the first boat too. That leaves thirty-four of you to go now and the rest to wait here. Kevin here is going to sort you into groups. Munday, Dagg, Flynn and Pelforth I'd be grateful if you'd stay behind and I need another five volunteers.'

Minutes later the RIBs were loaded up and buzzing out to sea towards the Navy frigate. On the beach one of the special forces crew had already broken out a small gas cooker to get a brew on before Geddes took charge again.

'With the load they're carrying they'll need to keep their speed down, so I estimate we're here until at least zero-three-hundred hours. Danny why don't you take Alec here and see what you can rustle up for us from the kitchen.'

At the apparent end to hostilities and the appearance of food, two figures, one carrying a camera, were seen walking along the beach with their hands up. One of the soldiers trained his rifle sites on them but Michaela intervened.

'It's ok, I know these guys. They're the journalists who got me here. Looks like they chose to ignore my instructions but they're ok to have something to eat, aren't they?'

Geddes looked suspicious. 'Fuckin' journalists? Have youse been out there the entire time?'

The pair nodded that they had.

'Alright, I'll do you a deal. You give me the memory cards out of all your cameras and recording equipment and you can eat.'

Egg started to protest. 'You've no right to take our work. We weren't doing anything wrong…'

'No laddie, you didn't let me finish. Your choice is you give me the memory cards and you get to eat, or I take them and you don't. Which is it to be?'

Defeated, Grill flicked open his camera and handed over an SD card, glaring at Michaela who shrugged, helplessly.

A few minutes later she was sitting beside Alec as they finished off plates of turkey ham, rice and salad. 'Why did you come?' he asked. 'We had it covered.'

'I didn't know that, did I. For all I knew, you were being held at gunpoint and the lads would never have found you.'

'Well, I'm glad you did. It's good to see you, although right now Dubai sounds like it would have been the better choice.'

He yawned and Geddes caught his eye.

'Welcome to the wonderful world of the SAS,' he said. 'We're either bored shitless or scared shitless. Aye, aye, they must have made better time than I thought. Right lads, prepare to move out.'

None of the rest of the group had noticed anything, but half a minute later the familiar drone of the RIB could be heard clearly. Crew and players alike got up stiffly from the ground and started to get ready while Geddes went over to the Saudis.

'Captain Ahab? Thanks for your cooperation. If we meet again in a thousand years, it will be a thousand years too soon.'

As he spoke, he saw movement out of the corner of his eye as a figure ran along the beach. He yelled at his men and drew his handgun dropping to the floor in a crouch. He loosed off a double tap and the figure stumbled but kept running spraying bullets in all directions from his automatic weapon. Soon the rest of the unit were raining down fire but he made it a few more metres, dragging himself across the sand then exploded in a huge fireball. In the light of the flames Alec could see Michaela, her face contorted with pain. He lifeblood was gushing from a vicious gunshot to the neck. He pulled her to him and put pressure on the wound calling out to Geddes for help, but it was hopeless. She died in his arms moments later.

Part 3

Chapter 28 May 2022

Into your hands, Father of mercies, we commend our brother, Lachlan, in the sure and certain hope that he will rise with Christ on the last day. Merciful Lord, turn toward us and listen to our prayers: open the gates of paradise to your servant and help us who remain to comfort one another with assurances of faith, until we all meet in Christ and are with you and with our brother for ever.

'Amen!'

Most of those present hadn't known Shovel McGrath by any other name. Hearing the priest call him Lachlan just added to the strangeness of the occasion. Father Michael was holding back the tears and only his sense of responsibility to the family was keeping him going. He had, he told the congregation, Christened the player himself twenty-seven years ago, and it was here at the Sacred Heart church, where he was first introduced to players from the team he would go on to join: his beloved Aston Villa.

The club was well represented with players and management determined to be there for one of their own despite their obvious pain. They stood next to members of the England squad who had been alongside Shovel in Saudi. The church was packed with family and friends from his school sports teacher to his first girlfriend. They were all part of a community he whose memory's he would always be in his prime. Outside, a dozen film crews and hordes of press were recording the occasion with one eye on the church door, ready to follow the player's cortège through streets lined with locals to Villa Park stadium.

The death of a senior member of the England football team in such violent circumstances made the headlines, but McGrath wasn't the only one to suffer loss that night. This was Simon Cauldwell's fourth such service in a week and Alec's second.

He had been dreading Michaela's funeral. Her death was so sudden and pointless that closure was the last thing he was ready for. Aside from his own feelings of rage and grief, he hadn't wanted to face her parents who he was certain would blame him. In the event they surprised him.

'It was the happiest we've seen her since her accident,' Michaela's mother said. 'The therapy helped, but I know the two of you moving in together gave her the confidence to feel that life was finally moving forward again.'

Her dad was in pain, but he recognised that he wasn't the only one hurting. 'She loved you, Alec and she was a very good judge of character. I never had to give any of her boyfriends the third degree because they had to be pretty special for her to bring them home. I'm so sorry for your loss.'

Their kindness was almost harder to deal with than a slap in the in face. 'I just wish I could have kept her safe,' he said, simply.

Cauldwell had ghosted in at the back of the small Kent church and melted away at the end of the service. But Alec stayed on, determined to do right by Michaela's parents. The wake was a sombre affair with guests struggling to understand how someone they knew could have died so young and far from home. Michaela's parents made a huge effort to speak with everyone and Alec followed their lead. He could recognise Michaela in both of them and saw for the first time the strength and courage of the partners that had given life to the woman he loved.

'You'll always be welcome, Alec,' said her mum, when the last of their guests had gone, 'and I hope we'll be able to talk to you from time to time as we all come to terms with losing Michaela.'

Her father looked suddenly resolved. 'There was something we wanted to talk to you about. She had close to ten million pounds in her bank account and we don't know of anything in her career or any business interests that would explain how it got there. I'm sure you must know about it. Can you at least put our minds at rest that she wasn't doing something illegal.'

'Your daughter was the straightest person I ever knew and there were many times when she kept me honest too. I'm sure she was a brilliant police officer and she stayed incorruptible to the end. The money was hers: she earned it and paid a heavy price for it. Now it's right that it comes to you. I hope you'll find a way of using it to keep her memory alive.'

For sergeant Gavin Geddes, Birmingham was his third visit to church that week and he was furious. As hard as it was to bury two of his men, telling Andy Stevenson that the bullet he took on that Saudi beach had ended his career was ten-times worse. Members of the Regiment know the risks when they join, but all of them would agree that being paralysed was way worse than dying. Geddes stood at the back alongside Alec and Simon Cauldwell, the three of them looking on stone-faced and dry-eyed as the family filed past. They were almost the last to leave as the Sacred Heart emptied out onto a beautiful May morning. Instead of joining the procession they diverted to a nearby bar of the same name. On a matchday this working men's club would be buzzing. Today it felt sullen and cold despite the warmth of early summer outside. A few regulars brooded silently over their pints, not lifting their heads to acknowledge the newcomers.

Alec was the first to speak. 'Thanks for coming, Gavin and you too, Simon. I know the family won't realise who you are, but it means a lot to me. We've been through a lot together.'

'Well, you can fuckin' leave me out of your adventures from now on.'

Geddes spat the words out and Alec's instinct for self-preservation kicked in. He went to buy the drinks. Three pints in, Geddes was starting to cool down.

'I don't blame you, son, and I'm glad we got most of youse home. I just don't know how the fuck you ended up there in the first place.'

Alec started to answer, but Cauldwell jumped in. 'The inquiry starts tomorrow, so I hope you'll get your answer, Gav.'

The veteran soldier stared into his beer and Alec took his queue. 'Yeh, about that; have you guys been called to appear?'

'I'll be keeping in the background,' said Simon. Officially, I didn't have anything to do with the operation, although Michaela may have told you differently.'

'She didn't know who else to call,' said Alec, quietly. 'I'm with you Gavin. I warned Damien Scott that the tour of Saudi was a bad idea.'

Cauldwell looked concerned. 'I would advise you to keep that piece of information very much to yourself. If it turns out you knew something that you didn't pass on, they'll feed you through the mincer. Believe me, no good can come from you or the inquiry pointing fingers at the Secretary of State.'

'I know, the party line will be dutifully followed: the tour was a triumph hijacked by unknown hostiles for reasons I can't speculate on.'

'What was that you were saying about answers?' said Geddes. 'Sounds like it'll be the usual fuckin' whitewash, and my men's' families will never know why they died.'

The inquiry was every bit as brutal as Cauldwell had suggested. A panel of six suits and spooks were installed in the windowless basement of an office building south of Vauxhall Bridge. Alec sweated through three hours of aggressive questioning relaying as much as he could remember of events in Saudi. He had been worried that their brush with the Riyadh Mutawa would be exposed, but the panel had bigger concerns. Instead, they spent the time going over every minute of the tour from the moment they reached Dammam. Numbers and descriptions of hotel staff, uniforms and vehicle registration numbers of the guards. Nothing was too insignificant. Halfway through, he was starting to believe the failure of the tour and the deaths of those involved were all his fault. He was genuinely surprised when the chair wrapped up and told him he was free to go.

When he emerged he was wrung out like a damp cheesecloth and smelt like one too. He retrieved his mobile and stepped outside into the shadow of Vauxhall Cross in search of coffee. As soon as he turned it on, his phone pinged half a dozen times from the same unrecognised number.

Need to meet with you urgently

Call this number the instant you receive this message

Speak with nobody about the messages

Imperative we meet soonest

Plane waiting to bring you to Switzerland

Tell nobody of your movements

Alec put two and two together and made a rapid calculation that the pressure had been ramped up further on the Old Man. He extracted Cauldwell from the inquiry room and took him into his confidence.

'I haven't given you details of what Michaela and I were working on, but now feels like a good time to bring you into the loop. Among other things, we've been digging into

FIFA for months, ever since Madrid, in fact. We've gone through the Council members, the Bid Evaluation task force and of course the members themselves. I'll give you the long story some other time. But for now, all you need to know is we had strong suspicions that someone was putting pressure on FIFA. There was the shooting of course, but also their bank accounts were targeted and even the FIFA video game was hit. We never managed to pin down exactly where the attacks were coming from, but everything pointed to the Middle East. With what we know about the Wembley bombing, we suspect that Sheikh Abdullah was behind it.'

'Ok, it's possible, I guess, but why do I need to know this now?'

Alec showed him the text messages. 'These are from the FIFA President. He's in trouble and it could be our way in. Plus I think it has something to do with the World Cup.'

Cauldwell made a calculation of his own. 'Let's call him,' he said.

Rather than use Alec's phone Cauldwell gave him access to a secure line. As predicted, it was the Old Man who picked up. He sounded shaken.

'Get to Northolt airport. There is a plane on standby for you under the name of GoAhead Sport and Media. A car will be waiting when you reach Zurich. I will see you in two hours.'

'I'm not going to be much use to you on my own; I need to bring a friend of mine; a trusted colleague.'

There was a pause before the Old Man assented. 'Keep the circle tight,' he said, hanging up immediately.

'If he's got any, sense that number won't work again,' Cauldwell said, as the taxi he'd flagged down took off west towards the airport.

'He's not being that careful. GoAhead is the same company he used to do those dodgy media rights deals a few years back.'

On the plane, Cauldwell got the longer version of Alec and Michaela's investigation into FIFA.

'Obviously this is mainly Michaela's work, right?' he suggested.

Alec gazed through the plane's portholes over Mont Blanc and the Swiss Alps. 'Let's just say, you'd have to work bloody hard to take her place as my partner.'

'Too soon?'

'Course it's too soon. It's always going to be too bloody soon. I don't know what I'm going to do, Simon. You must have lost friends and colleagues. How do you just move on?'

'Rushbourne's asked me to look out for you,' he deflected. 'We can't have you going off on another alcobender. I know Michaela got you back on the straight and narrow after Wembley and, without stating the obvious, my role's going to be different. But, you know, I'm here. Now, why do you think this has something to do with the World Cup?'

Instead of the usual route to FIFA HQ, the blacked-out S-class Mercedes followed the afternoon traffic into the city, parking outside a downtown office. The driver made no move to get out and instead pressed a speed-dial number on the car's display. He had a brief conversation in German before pulling away again and turning into a side street. A couple of turns later, he drew up at a small hotel indicating to his passengers that their host was inside.

The Old Man had half hidden himself behind a pillar in reception, but he was on his feet as soon as his guests had cleared the revolving door. He looked old and seemed to have shrunk since Alec had seen him last, but his manner was still vigorous. Having made sure he had their attention, he walked quickly towards the hotel's interior and into a small conference room. There was coffee in a jug and cups on the table, but no pleasantries were exchanged. Only when they were safely installed with the door closed did he start to speak.

'Thank you for coming at such short notice.' He swallowed hard then continued. 'I need your help. My granddaughter, Alexa, has been taken from her boarding school in Saint Gallen. The school called my son in law this morning to say she didn't come to breakfast. When they checked her room, they found only a letter addressed to me.'

He handed over a sheet of paper on which was typed a single sentence.

The girl loses a finger every 24 hours until you give me what I want.

'I can't go to the police,' he went on, 'there's no one in FIFA I can turn to, you're the only one I could think of who might be able to help.'

Questions formed immediately on Cauldwell's lips, but Alec jumped in.

'There's nothing we can do: you have to give him what he wants. Can you do that?'

Tears formed in the Old Man's rheumy eyes. He nodded his head slowly, a defeated look on his face. 'I thought there might be something, but you're right and I should have known. I'm sorry to bring you here for no reason.'

'Do you want to tell me what he's asking for?'

'It's Qatar,' he started, hesitantly. 'Sheikh Abdullah wants the semi-finals to be between Belarus and Ukraine, Turkey and Germany.'

Alec was exasperated 'What? All of this is about match fixing?'

Cauldwell wasn't so sure. 'It sounds more like a recipe for riots.'

'He also wants the games to be played simultaneously at the two stadiums closest to each other in Doha, and he wants the security contract for the World Cup. You were right before when you said FIFA was under attack. This has been the story for months. He will stop at nothing to get what he wants.'

The room was quiet while everyone worked through the implications of what they had been told.

It was Cauldwell who spoke first. 'So, we have all the ingredients for mass civil unrest and one man has the power to control it. I'd say our shady Sheikh is planning a coup. We'd need to put our analysts on it to work out the possible outcomes, but I don't think we can knowingly allow the World Cup to be used in this way. You can't agree to his demands.'

Alec was indignant. 'I know what Michaela would say if she was here. She'd say "Don't be ridiculous. A girl's life is in danger. You'll have to save the world another day."'

He turned towards the Old Man. 'What do you need to show him? Now, in the next few hours, that would mean Alexa is released unharmed?'

'On the scheduling of matches and fixing of the teams to play, I can't give him anything. I don't know if he knows what he's asking, but to guarantee those semi-finals would mean corrupting the whole tournament. Even if I could do that, Belarus has never qualified, Turkey is also unlikely to make the finals and, given the situation, Ukraine just can't field a team. The draw is next week and it's going to be televised live. You've seen how it works: the balls are drawn randomly, so I couldn't fix it even if I wanted to.'

'Ok, but if it's just crowd trouble that he's looking for, that shouldn't be hard to engineer. Most crowds are volatile and football crowds more than most. All he would have to do is get the alcohol restrictions lifted. What about the security contract?'

The Old Man looked uncomfortable. 'The contract was awarded more than two years ago after an international tender. I can't reopen it without a reason.'

'There must be a whole load of reasons for revisiting it. What about corruption? Isn't there a FIFA employee that you can put in the frame for taking a bung from the winning company?'

'FIFA contracts are complicated and arrangements with third parties are not uncommon...'

'What I'm hearing is you've already had the fucking money,' Alec interrupted. 'Well, you'll just fucking well have to give it back, or watch your granddaughter arrive in the post one finger at a time.'

The Old Man recoiled sharply at the suggestion. 'What I was going to say is that this is not our biggest problem.'

The visitors looked at him intently.

'The contract has been awarded to a local Qatari company so accusing them of corruption would be politically impossible, especially as it is owned by a senior member of the Royal Family and not Sheikh Abdullah's branch of it.'

Alec slumped into his seat, picked up his coffee cup and swirled the thick black liquid around in it.

'Simon? Anything we can do?'

'What are you suggesting?'

'I don't know. We're here, there's probably only a couple of guys holding the girl...'

'Don't even go there. We don't have any idea where to look or what we're up against. And even if we did, I'm a member of the UK security services with absolutely no licence to operate in support of a Swiss citizen in their home country. You were right at the start: there's nothing we can do.'

'Ok, ok, I'm just thinking aloud. So, what he's asked for is impossible, yes? I mean, you can't give it to give him and neither can anyone else.'

The Old Man nodded.

Cauldwell took his cue. 'I think I can see where Alec's going here. Assuming he's not completely insane, you should be able to reason with him, persuade him to accept something else which gets him to the same place via a slightly different route. His alternative is to start cutting a teenaged girl's fingers off and there aren't many people who enjoy doing that. Can you think of something you can deliver?'

'You're right,' said Alec, more confident now. 'Unless it's Japan against… I don't know, Belgium, you can be pretty sure the crowd is a tinderbox waiting to be ignited. Arranging for a supply of cheap alcohol and some heavy-handed kettling would get everyone primed for trouble. And as for the security contract, what if it isn't *the* security contract, just *a* security contract. You'd have to finesse it somehow with the existing contract holder, but maybe some of the teams have raised concerns that the size and experience of the local security might not be enough especially in light of the global situation – something vague like that. They would continue to do all the public stuff, you know, no loss of face, but behind the scenes there would be a special layer of security for teams, VIPs, sponsors and broadcasters.'

Simon glared and shook his head. 'I didn't mean we go that far. As I've already said, we can't knowingly allow the World Cup to be used to stage a coup in a sovereign country, and we certainly can't collude in making it happen. Aiding and abetting isn't just for bank robbers, you know.'

Alec's devious mind was already ahead of him. 'We're just talking about buying time today. Pull out the existing security contract, change some of the details and give him that. Make his some promises about crowds and hopefully you get Alexa back. Then you've got three months to sort out the consequences.'

The other two men went quiet as they worked through the consequences. Then Alec cleared his throat. 'Erm, leaving aside the *what*, I'd like to bring up the question of *why*. I mean, as Simon says, we're colluding with you in a plan which could see us accused of stirring up a war in a sovereign country. What's in it for us?'

The Old Man smiled broadly for the first time since they arrived. 'This is the easy part,' he said. 'You want the World Cup in 2030; I have control over the bidding process. As the American's say, *do the math*.'

'We've just talked about you making some empty promises to a crazed killer holding a bolt cutter to your granddaughter's fingers, so you'll forgive me for being a bit sceptical.'

The Old Man opened his hands, lifted his shoulders and put on his most winning smile. 'I guess you'll just have to trust me.'

'Yeh, you see that's where I have a problem. Then again, we now know about your soft spot for Alexa and where we can find her, so I guess we have some leverage.'

The Old Man's smiled hardened. 'After my years in sports politics I have learned to become quite a judge of character. I don't think Alexa is in any danger from you, Alec so, as I say, you'll just have to trust me.'

The atmosphere in the room went down 10 degrees when Sheikh Abdullah's voice came on the speaker phone.

'What do you have for me?'

'Your Excellency, you must understand there are limits to my power to control the things you asked for,' The Old Man wheedled.

'Then your granddaughter's fate is your responsibility.'

'I really don't think you want to hurt her. Why add kidnap and torture to your crimes?'

'What happens to her is a matter of indifference to me. As for my crimes, you let me worry about those. You just have to decide if this is the moment when you give me what I need, because when the girl runs out of fingers, I'm coming after you.'

Alec was busy scribbling notes and holding them up in front of the FIFA boss who hesitated and then picked up the negotiation again.

'Let us take a step back. I am sure you have no allegiance to Belarus, Germany Ukraine or Turkey playing in the semi-finals. I think you really just want a volatile crowd, am I right?'

There was no response but something in the silence suggested the Qatari was listening.

'And I think it's the same way with the security contract. Are you not just looking for an excuse to put your men on the streets?'

Dead air filled the room.

'In which case,' the Old Man ploughed on, 'perhaps what we should be talking about are ways we can help each other.'

'Get to the point. I'm not sure how you expect me to help you.'

'My interests are the interests of football but let us aah… cut to the chase. On the second point, you know, I'm sure, that a contract for security was signed a long time ago with a company owned by your brother, Sheikh Jassim. It would therefore be disrespectful in the extreme, not to say illegal, for me to try to reopen a tender.'

There was a deep sigh on the line.

'But, but… what I can do is consider whether our usual crowd security arrangements are sufficient. There is a lot to be concerned about in the world today. We could reasonably argue that it is appropriate to bring in some outside support, with a very specific remit, to supplement the excellent work already going on.'

The Old Man's face was as twisty as his words and would have been amusing had the stakes not been so high.

'And on the first point?'

The FIFA man breathed and started to ease into his role as international diplomat.

'You are a man of the world, Sheikh Abdullah, and you have seen that not all football fans are as restrained and dignified as your fellow countrymen. Consider what took place in London at the Euros. Many people were shocked that the stiff upper lip of the English proved so ready to turn into a snarl. But, for myself, this was not a surprise. You want to know the truth? I take no pleasure in saying it, but football fans the world over are like a box of cheap fireworks: one stray spark and boom! This spark can easily be delivered with a few elements over which I have control. If it's a baying mob you need, Your Excellency, a baying mob you shall have. I will see to it that the timing, the location and, yes, even the identity of the teams which progress to the semi-final are guaranteed to build the tension. Then, into the mix I will throw my sparks and voila! Now, shall we turn to the release of my granddaughter?'

'You assume two things,' came the voice over the airwaves. 'First, that you have guessed my intentions correctly and, second, that I trust that your words will be turned into actions. On both points, you are wrong. But I will tell you what I will do. You can come and get your granddaughter. After all, three months is a long time to hold her, and I have no doubt that she will prove useful leverage as we get closer to the World Cup. I just want two things; a draft contract and a press release to the effect that you have awarded it. You have seven hours before the first 24 are up. If I have these two before then she may even keep all her fingers.'

The room swung into action as the line was cut. Alec found his media skills employed drafting an announcement for the world's press. Written in the driest terms it would hardly cause a storm, but it did give Sheikh Abdullah a guarantee of sorts that a contract would be agreed. Within the hour, the 10-line release had appeared on Reuters and the Press Association's sports wire. The contract itself was a bigger task to deliver, but FIFA's lawyers were used to the Old Man's way of doing busines. They did a quick cut and paste job on the main security contract, fudged the deliverables and removed any reference to payment on either side. The bones of a deal were printed, signed and scanned before the end of the business day. No one questioned the Old Man when he instructed the lawyer to email it to Qatar without reference to anyone else on the Council. In some matters, at least, he still held sway. All they received by way of reply was an address in a town a couple of kilometres up the valley from St Gallen.

They agreed that Cauldwell would pick up the girl and return her to school, hopefully no worse for her experience. The Old Man's driver was summoned, and they were soon speeding on the one-hour trip eastwards.

Privacy glass ensured the Mercedes' passenger was not able to be identified, but the car itself stood out like a Panzer even in the affluent streets of Switzerland. Cauldwell asked to circle the address several times before parking up a few metres away. He left the driver with strict instructions whilst he went into the property. He had to assume he had drawn the attention of the occupants but, in the event, Alexa was alone and apparently unconcerned. With airpods in her ears and head buried in her phone, an eyeroll was the only giveaway that she registered him at all. She was no more communicative on the short drive back to school. Her reluctant portrayal of the two men she had spent the past twenty hours with could have described practically any Caucasian males between the ages of twenty and fifty.

Left alone with the Old Man, Alec managed to extract a similar promise to the Qatari that the Team GB bid would receive his support. The guarantee, such as it was, was in the form of an interview but with three great soundbites: that the UK was his preferred candidate for the 2030 World Cup; that he felt FIFA had the power to bring healing after the terrible atrocity surrounding the Euro finals: and, critically, that China was not allowed to bid and he couldn't imagine any circumstances which would change that situation. It wasn't much, but it was the best Alec was going to get. He would place the story in the British media and that of all the bidding countries although he wasn't naïve enough to imagine the Old Man would stick to his word. He could be just as encouraging to any of the other bidders before Alec was on the plane back to London.

Chapter 29

'I'm thinking of starting a magazine,' Alec said. 'In fact, I'm kicking myself that I didn't think of it before. After all, the media is one of my biggest strengths and there's no better way to guarantee the message than by owning the pages it will appear in.'

Seated at the breakfast bar in St Katherine docks, Mikey Reid looked sceptically over the top of his coffee. He'd become a permanent fixture in the penthouse since Chenille had kicked him out and Alec was glad of the company. He wasn't at all sure the player was moving the needle on their plan to win the FIFA World Cup but at least he had given up the James Bond references.

'A Magazine? Knock yourself out, mate, but the pictures are going have to be good to get FIFA Council members reading it. What are you thinking: private jet porn, luxury yacht porn and property porn with bit of porn thrown in?'

'I'd struggle to find a printer to deliver the kind of stuff some of those bastards are in to. Anyway, I'm not thinking about the actual FIFA members. There's one group we haven't thought about yet: their wives. They have way more influence than anyone gives them credit for, and I think we could get some useful support that way. I'm thinking of calling it *Football Widow*. What do you think?'

'I can see where you're coming from but it's kinda' dark. It's a shame *Ballon d'Or* is already taken 'cos that would've been a great title'

'That's not a bad shout, but if we can't call it the golden ball, what about *Le Jeu d'Or,* the golden game? And we can have features on lifestyle and fashion and especially what to do in Qatar during the World Cup. Then we throw in something about human right abuses in China and how the shopping's really shit and they tell their hubbies for vote for us.'

'Obviously I'm never gonna read it but, yeh, why not? Doesn't it cost a fortune to launch a magazine, though?'

'Obviously, yes, if you do it properly. What I'm talking about is a really targeted publication with a few carefully chosen readers who will get their copies personally. We'd only need to print a couple of hundred.'

'Who's going to write it? With all the other stuff we've got going on, you're not going to have time to do it.'

'I don't know. Hugo's doing the financial stuff, we've got the Full English digging up dirt on the bidders and council members, the influencers are spreading fake news in rival bidding countries and the lawyers are poised with the McMafia orders. That leaves me twiddling my thumbs: I reckon I could be doing more.'

'You're forgetting that what you know about rich middle-aged women wouldn't make a column let alone a magazine. Number of wives I've had, I'd be better than you and I can't even write.'

'I'm not thinking of doing any actual writing. I was chatting to the fashion editor at *The Guardian* last week. She's just had her column replaced by that blonde airhead out of Made in Chelsea so I reckon she'd be up for producing the words. I'd just be behind the scenes, overseeing production and everything. Anyway, I'm still thinking about it.'

'Good for you. I'm off to play golf with Stevie and Tyrone. D'you wanna come?'

'I thought you had work to do for your coaching badges. Anyway, I'd love to but I've been summoned by the Team GB bid committee. Somebody there thinks the tide is turning and they want to talk to me again.'

For no good reason that Alec could figure out, the mood of the bid committee was buoyant. He looked around the room at warm handshakes and smiling faces and wondered where the positivity had come from. From his experience, if there was ever something about sport that didn't make sense, the answer was always money, and he wasn't wrong this time either.

Sports Minister Damien Scott brought the meeting to order. 'Good morning, everyone. I'd like to start with what for most of you won't be news at all. In fact, it's probably the most widely trailed announcement since Prince Andrew's announcement that the sad loss of his passport meant he was unavailable to attend a US court.' There was full-throated laughter all round. 'I refer, of course, to Mike Deighton's incredibly generous offer of an extra million pounds of funding which, it is no exaggeration to say, will go a very long way to securing our prize.'

'I had a bit of a windrush on the bitcoin, didn't I?' Deighton explained. 'I don't understand all this cryptobollocks. But I'll tell you something: that's the most money anyone's made lying in bed since Monica Lewinski.'

PR man, Malcolm Tonghe shuddered. 'I do hope the stains come out of the sheets.'

'Don't you worry about that, Malcolm. I've got enough money to buy John Lewis and Marks and Spencer if I need new ones, so I'm not going to be tossed up any time soon.'

He grinned lasciviously at TV presenter Gabby Gallagher. Damien Scott took advantage of a moment's pause to grab the agenda back. 'The other piece of news which you may not know is that Keith thinks Spain-Portugal are about to withdraw.'

'That's right, Damien,' said Sir Keith Hale, sole British representative at FIFA. 'We knew their bid was on the rocks, but my spies in the camp tell me their chairman is about to step down and take their biggest backer with him. That leaves GB-2030 as unopposed European bidder and should mean we pick up the support of UEFA and our fellow Europeans. With Azeris pulling out a few weeks ago and Alec's latest promise from the President about the Chinese not being allowed to bid, I'd say we're in poll position.'

Alec said nothing, but took quiet satisfaction from the knowledge that his threat to go public with the salacious private life of SpaPo's chairman had worked. The Spanish football administrator had little choice but to hang up his boots. What was it about these characters that they had to go to such extremes to get their kicks? Azerbaijan hadn't been a surprise to him either although Hugo Ashburton had been lucky to intercept a major transfer of funds from the Cayman Islands to the bid's bank account. Putting him and his tame hacker on thirty percent of any money they were able to steal was a powerful motivation. And it still left Alec with enough to engineer a spike in the value of bitcoin. That, and Elon Musk's Twitter login.

'Yes, from the competition perspective, it's almost like someone is giving us a helping hand,' said Damien Scott, his eyes fixed on the meeting's visitor. 'How are things looking from where you sit, Alec?'

'I wouldn't trust the Old Man on China. Their support for Russia would make them a pariah in any other situation but he's as likely to argue that he's the one keeping the dialogue going in the civilised world.'

'The President doesn't rule by fiat, Alec,' Hale interjected. 'There are thirty-seven of us on the Council and I think we can rely on the Europeans and members from the English-speaking countries.'

'By my reckoning that makes twelve,' said Scott, 'and, looking down the list, at least half of the rest have geopolitical reasons to swing behind China. So, the maths isn't in our favour assuming there's a Chinese bid. Any sense of how the other bids and doing, Alec?'

'I agree pretty much with Sir Keith. Morocco hasn't made any impression and the Latin American bid seems too divided to be taken seriously.'

'So, 50:50 between us and the Chinese then,' Deighton said. 'We'd have taken odds like that when we started. It isn't train surgery, is it? We just need to put our boulders to the wheel for one last push.'

Alec nodded along with the rest, content to leave them feeling they had a chance. Privately, he still had doubts: there were some on the council with an *anyone but the Brits* attitude and a lot more waverers who would need to be dragged kicking and screaming into the GB-2030 camp. He had a few tricks still to play but was sure he'd need each one and more if they were to pull off a win.

Twenty-four hours later he was sitting in the St Katharine Docks Café with Ashley Freeman, freshly appointed editor of *Le Jeu D'Or*.

'Delighted to have you on the team, Ashley. The key thing is that we hit the ground running with this thing. There's no time for focus groups or editorial angst: we just agree the synopsis and get it done so you've got complete editorial freedom. You can make up whatever you want, from whoever you want and no one's ever going to call you on it.'

'Ooh, talk dirty to me,' she breathed. 'This feels exquisitely naughty. I'm used to dragging the stories in. Who knew I could have saved myself all the hard work and just made them up?

The way her micro skirt rode up as she crossed and uncrossed her legs gave Alec the impression their definitions of hard work might be rather different. However, he had no doubt she was the person for the job. He was about to suggest lunch when his phone rang, bringing him up short.

'I'd better take this,' he said, 'I'll send you over a one-pager later confirming terms and dates for the next three months and let's get together again when you've had chance to put a plan together. It's great to have you on board.'

He watched in appreciation as the journalist wiggled her way across the café. Then he swiped right to accept the call.

'Kevin Mooney, how's it going?'

'I'm grand, Alec lad. I trust the life of a football spy is treating you well. I wondered if you could clear something up for me.'

'Go on, mate. I'll do what I can.'

Mooney's final season had ended in glorious mediocrity and Alec braced himself to be pitched with some sort of money-making scheme. What the northern Irishman actually said to say turned out to be worse.

'So, I was just looking at the odds of GB-2030 winning the rights to host the World Cup. I've fancied getting a wee bet on for a while, and I noticed a very strange thing. When I looked yesterday, we were odds-on favourites; now we're out to 6:1. So I'm thinking either I've finally got a value bet to get behind or there's something going on that I don't know. And I figure there's no better person to ask than the inside man himself. So what is it, Al? Should I be getting a bet on or not?'

As the footballer was talking, Alec googled FIFA news on his laptop and immediately saw what had brought about the abrupt change in the bid's chances. PA Sport was the first, but the list of international media running the story was growing as he watched. Contrary to his most recent comments, the FIFA President had been in advanced discussions with the

Chinese. They had persuaded him to allow their bid to proceed to the final stages 'as a learning experience'.

'They have no expectation that their bid will be successful or even that it would be put forward to the FIFA Congress,' he was quoted as saying. 'As you know, under FIFA rules they are not allowed to bid unless Congress passes and extraordinary amendment. But we cannot let this deter a genuine and honest bidder from gaining as much as they can from the process. As a result, I have encouraged them to remain in the competition and offered the assistance of my Secretary General, Guillermo Salz, to be their guide.'

Alec raised a private eyebrow at the news of Salz's arrest was proving no barrier to holding his FIFA position, then said: 'I think I might know what's happened to shift the odds: the Old Man's keeping the Chinese in the competition. That may be just his way of keeping some competitive element to the bid, but GB-2030 will still be pushing ahead. Whether that makes it a value bet is your call.'

'That's bollocks, Alec, you mealy-mouthed fucker. Is the bid going to win or not?'

'All I can say is if the Chinese were to be allowed to bid unopposed, then 6:1 against probably flatters our chances. However, there's are always stuff going on behind the scenes that even the bookies don't know about. If I was a betting man, I'd say evens was about right.'

'You're a cunning bastard, so you are. What's going on then?'

Alec muttered something about working his contacts and ended the call as soon as he could. In truth, the possibility of an officially sanctioned Chinese bid put a huge spanner in his works. He was going to need time to work out what if anything they could do to throw the juggernaut off course. Back in the apartment he decided to call a team meeting.

Three days later Alec was in an anonymous out-of-town hotel pouring the coffees and making the introductions. First to join him was a thin man with a high-domed head, his remaining hair matching his suit and muted tie. Gray to the point of invisibility, Paul Parsons was known universally as 'the rottweiler'. Juniors at the mid-sized City law firm where he was a partner tended to assume the nickname was a joke, a play on his mild demeanour. By the time his opponents discovered his teeth sunk deep into the most sensitive parts of their business it was too late. Hugo Ashburton's room-filling bonhomie got progressively louder as he walked from reception to the conference room. He was accompanied by a pale, furtive individual of indeterminate gender who he introduced as Trix, the hacker. Even louder was the noise of the Lamborghini which Stevie Mac insisted on leaving as close to the entrance as possible. Judging by their clothes, Mikey Reid and Tyrone Pelforth had come fresh from the golf course. Kevin Mooney emerged from an Uber Prius to complete the line-up of former footballers. Next to arrive was the photographer-journalist duo, Full English, both dressed in black. The feminine curves and blonde hair of *Le Jeu D'Or* editor, Ashley Freeman turned everyone's head, so no one saw Simon Cauldwell arrive. They were just aware that his seat was occupied. Last to arrive, inevitably, were the influencers.

Alec kicked off proceedings.

'We'll skip the formalities. You've got names on the seating plan and you all know why we're here. Up 'till now, me and Michaela have called the shots and you guys have responded brilliantly. We've had some successes, particularly engineering the exit of Spain-Portugal – well done to the Full English for that one; the financial collapse of Azerbaijan's bid – Hugo, Trix you got lucky but spectacular work; the bitcoin bump which combined with a bit of social media pressure from our influencers injected some much-needed funds into GB-2030 and I know Paul has some long but deep hooks into the assets of several FIFA Council members.

Unfortunately, the game just changed. Michaela's gone and I'm on my own. As if that wasn't bad enough, the Old Man's announcement that China is going to be allowed to bid means the kind of rapid reaction tactics we've been using are not going to work. So, we're up against much tougher opposition and time is running out. If we have to get support from outside this room, that's ok, but we need to leave this meeting with a plan so that from here on we focus only on execution. I've asked our embedded intelligence agent to set the scene so we get a better idea of what we're up against.'

The eyes of everyone around the table had been fixed on Alec but now they turned to Simon Cauldwell. He nodded to Alec and addressed his audience.

'The first thing to say is that the Chinese are probably not listening to this meeting, but don't expect that to last. They are going to be looking in exhaustive detail at everything that's happened so far during the bidding process: they're going to find out why the Spanish chair quit, they're going to discover Paul's legal hooks and they're going to work out how Azerbaijan lost its money. They are going to put all the pieces of the jigsaw together and pretty soon they'll work out that there is a shadow operation behind the GB bid. And, when they do, they're going to come out fighting. Alec talked about execution, and I would only add that it's about personal, individual execution. When this meeting ends, we won't meet again unless Alec decides to throw a party after the FIFA vote. In the meantime, whatever we decide, whatever you commit to, the success of the entire project depends on you delivering your part.'

Cauldwell had the room's attention. Hugo looked particularly uncomfortable at the thought that some Chinese spooks might be rummaging through his dirty digital laundry. He never did have the stomach for things to get messy. The others around the table sat forward in their chairs and waited for Cauldwell's analysis.

'I'm going to split my comments into two parts: defensive and offensive,' he continued. 'Whatever you think you know about the Chinese, they are not all powerful outside their own country, but we have to assume they will discover the tactics you've tried so far. Those gaps will be plugged this week if they're not already, so we're going to be looking for new ideas, I'm afraid.

'On the Chinese side, they're going to go on the offensive and that means two things. GB-2030 will be in their sites. They'll rake up anything personal they can and a raid on the bank accounts isn't out of the question either, if they can engineer one. Alec has already warned them what's coming but we can expect some changes in the official bid team as the heat gets turned up. The Chinese don't really have the legal route open to them, but they will be using all available means to coerce FIFA Council members into supporting their bid. They've got form for kidnap, blackmail, threatening family members and freezing assets at home but, as you've proved, it's only a small step from there to an international operation. Whatever leverage you think we've got over Council members at the moment, you can expect the other side to apply an equal amount of pressure.

'Second, that means they're coming after you. Beijing will leave no stone unturned in the hunt for anyone using covert measures to support the British bid. They may be surprised at first that we would do anything like this, but they won't stay on the back foot for long. So, proceed with extreme caution. There must be no further communication between this group. We've set up an encrypted Whatsapp channel for you all but it's one-to-one only with an anonymous mailbox so no traceability. As I've already said, once we leave here, you're on your own. Any questions?'

'You said kidnap, blackmail, threatening family members and something to do with money,' said one of the influencers. 'I mean, I'm all about living my best life and giving my fans what they want. I'm getting the strong feeling that my work here is done.'

'Point taken,' said Alec, 'but let's not get ahead of ourselves. You're here because you've got something to offer. Between us, we're going to come up with a plan, then we'll decide, as a group, who gets to put it into action. Ok?'

There was a shrug from the end of the table and no one else spoke. Alec took that as tacit approval to move ahead. Seven long hours later, the plan had taken shape.

Chapter 30

The Chinese embassy in London had grown used to a small crowd of protestors outside its doors. The Ambassador had called in a favour from the Metropolitan Police Chief who had agreed to move the ragtag bunch across the street, but it seemed only to make them more persistent. Had this been Nanjing or Wuhan, they would have been removed in seconds, only reappearing when they had renounced their protest years later. But this was London and every morning the same faces erected their photo wall of Uighur Muslims they claimed had been detained or disappeared, and the chanting began. Now they were back again on this normal Thursday morning in September. The protest had become such a familiar backdrop to life at the embassy that it took a few minutes to register that there was something different about today. Instead of the usual half dozen, there were forty, then sixty and then a hundred demonstrators. As the crowd swelled to 500, a TV film crew showed up. By the time the Ambassador had called his police contact there were over a thousand people spilling across Portland Place. The police were quickly on the scene, but all they could do was contain the situation and try and keep the traffic flowing in and out of London's West End.

The evening news bulletins led with the story and outraged protestors were determined to take full advantage of the oxygen of publicity. Interviewers on the spot struggled to make much sense of the situation. It appeared the demo centred around a Premier League footballer, Li Fangzou, a reserve team player at one of the London clubs. The claim was he had been forcibly taken back to China for "re-education". The crowd were scant on details but determined not to allow one of their own (albeit adopted) players to suffer such an indignity. Religious leaders were wheeled into studios where they took the opportunity to denounce Chinese treatment of its Muslim minority. At Friday prayers around the world, the usual calls for death were directed at China rather than America and five-star red flags were burnt instead of the regular stars and stripes.

The Chinese Ambassador to London was quick to communicate with other embassies around the world. All reported the same thing: a non-existent footballer, large crowds and worldwide Muslim protests against China. He called a press conference and issued a statement to the effect that the story was completely false, but the media knew a useful villain when they saw one and they didn't back down. The BBC decided not to continue showing coverage of the protests, but Stevie Mac's appearance as a pundit on Match of the Day did the job for them. He took the opportunity to repeat the claims and call for the Premier League's take-the-knee campaign to focus on the Uighurs. The newspapers doubled down on the story. They knew it was fake news but there were equally sure that to admit they'd fallen for it would make them look gullible. Anyway, they figured the Chinese were known to be persecuting minorities so deserved everything they got.

In another coffee shop in a different part of London, Ashley Freeman was reviewing proofs of the first edition of *Le Jeu d'Or* with satisfaction. The designer she had hired had done a fantastic job. The top feature was dedicated to the winter holiday plans of Cristiano Ronaldo's wife complete with arty photos of the Caribbean clubs and leading restaurants she was likely to be seen at. The meat of the magazine was an exposé of life as the wife of a football administrator entitled *Because You're Worth It*. The survival guide featured top tips for the tagalong spouse revolving around shopping, beauty spas and 5-star hotels. These were topics Freeman was determined to become expert in with Alec's generosity. She had decided to ignore the Uighur protests completely but expressed excitement about the World Cup being in a Muslim country in her editorial. She judged that a veiled reference to the need for future hosts to welcome all cultures and creeds was enough to make the point. The "interview" with Michelle Obama talking about her work with poor children was particularly pleasing. Putting words into the mouth the former First Lady felt thrillingly illicit, but she told herself it was better copy than Obama's PRs would have written. And it did save a huge amount of time. She felt that the wives of rich and powerful men would like to feel they were in touch with the poor even if getting down and dirty was the last thing on their minds. She With her new powers, she made Michelle extend a personal invitation to attend a women's empowerment conference in Doha during the World Cup. Freeman wasn't sure what this was going to involve but it was Alec's idea. And if there was the possibility of an all-expenses-paid luxury trip to Qatar, she wasn't going to turn it down.

The designer had found some ads online for a range of super high-end jewellery and couture brands ensuring the whole publication ached with empty desire. It was full of needy aspiration to a lifestyle that was conspicuously bling. Most fashionistas would be reaching for the sick bag before they could hiss *déclassé, darling*. Perfect. She checked the pages again making sure there was nothing to lead back to anyone connected with the shadow bid, gave the green light to the printer and emailed her first invoice to Alec.

Across town, Alec picked up his phone and called Simon Cauldwell. The response he received took him by surprise.

'How many in the group have you called from this phone since the meeting?'

'Ermm, not sure. A few, I suppose.'

'I need the list. They're in danger. Alec, I can't believe that you, of all people, would be the weak link. Let me spell this out for you. Somewhere out there in the hacking division of the People's Army is a highly accomplished Chinese operative who is trying to break into your phone as we speak. If you've ever sent or received a TikTok message or clicked on the wrong phishing link, they own your phone. And once they open the door, they'll download all your contacts, every message and details of every call you've made.'

'Ok, I get it. They're looking to connect the dots and I'm the only one with a connection to everyone else. I'll switch to burners from now on, but how do you think they've got on to me so quickly?'

'They may not have done, but that's got to be our working assumption. That fake news is a big red flag that will convince them they're being played. They're going to send someone down every rabbit hole until they find out who's responsible. This phone stays turned off in a draw until this is all over. Now, we weren't supposed to be communicating, so I assume this is important.'

'Well, yes. You've seen my team is doing its bit. Our latest bit of media manipulation must have sown doubts in the minds of Muslin council members when it comes to China. So, we're making progress, but I wanted to know what's happening at your end with Sheikh Abdullah. This was all about an alignment of objectives, remember. I don't want mine to be lost in some sort of realpolitik.'

'I put an analyst on it when we got back from Zurich. Her assessment is that he will try and use the World Cup to push his own agenda. Ordinarily we would assume Qatari domestic politics, but the Wembley bomb and connection to Chechnya suggests he has bigger ambitions. If he's capable of an atrocity like that, a domestic coup could be the least of it. If he sees himself as a modern-day Ataturk he could try to use Qatari wealth and power to establish a new Caliphate.'

Alec thought for a moment. 'That sounds like it's so bad it's good. I mean if it was just local politics, no one's going to want to get involved. But if it involves the entire Muslim world and threatens to light a fire from Agadir to Islamabad, then that's a reason to mobilise, right?'

'Up to a point, and the diplomats are back channelling hard. The problem is it takes us into UN Security Council territory. Even if we could get enough support for a resolution, which we wouldn't, where would that get us? We're never going to get legal cover for pre-emptive action in Qatar against one of its own royals. The best we can hope for is that we happen to be in the right place at the right time with enough manpower to kill the Sheikh's plan at birth if not conception.'

'That sounds unlikely. I mean what are the chances, because I'm beginning to see my part of this bargain going up in smoke.'

'Nigel's talk of stars aligning was always at the improbable end of optimistic but there are things we are looking at. The World Cup means a large number of people moving around which can provide cover for all sorts, so don't give up hope.'

'You need to bring me in on the plan though. Working around a football tournament isn't your everyday theatre of operations and you're going find it a lot easier with football guys involved.'

'Ermm, right,' Cauldwell responded, sceptically.' 'Well, we're still talking, aren't we?'

Cauldwell's warning over continued use of his mobile phone presented Alec with a dilemma: he needed to call Switzerland, but the Old Man would only take his call if he recognised the number. In the end it wasn't really a choice. The FIFA President sounded much chippier than the last time they had spoken.

'Mr. Munday, I hadn't expected to hear from you quite so quickly. What did you think of my idea? It's genius, don't you think?'

The question floored Alec, momentarily, but he did some quick mental calculations and revised his agenda.

'I haven't got all the details in front of me. Do you want to run me through how you see it?'

'It's not a hard concept, Alec. China hosts in 2030 and the UK becomes the first nation to stage the newly formed *biennale* in 2032. And the best part of all? It's going to be sixty-six years after 1966 and I'm sure I don't need to remind you of the significance of that date to England.'

'And idea this has already been communicated with the GB-2030 bid team?'

'Guillermo just ended his call with Sir Keith Hale, your council member. He seemed very pleased with the suggestion, and I assumed he had shared the good news with you.'

'I'm sure he has spoken with the Chairman of the committee, but I guess I'm not always the first to hear everything.'

Alec's brain was whirring. GB-2030 was being rumped and dumped in favour of the Chinese. Of course, Hale was happy: he got a win without having to land a punch. The Old Man also got one of the biggest football nations swinging behind his idea of a World Cup in 2032. But staging the most unpopular tournament in all of sport was a long way from British ambitions to restoring soft power.

'When would the decision be taken? We've worked hard to get into poll position and we're not about to give that up on the basis of a promise from you.'

'This has already been considered. We have learned from experience that awarding two cycles at the same time is never a good idea. Sir Keith agreed that we would need to have a basic bid process but GB66 would be guaranteed to make the final vote.'

'I'm not sure Sir Keith represents the feeling of the bid on this one,' he said. 'And I have to tell you that I won't be recommending your proposal.'

He could hear the smile in the Old Man's voice.

'Disunity in the bidding team never works out well, Alec. Think about it, you're guaranteed to have the World Cup in the UK and two years will be over before you know it. My advice to you is to use your voice to unify the bid behind this auspicious date. This is your chance to make history.'

Alec red flashed the footballers on his team. The move amounted to no more than an encrypted Whatsapp invite to play golf the next day, but those who received it knew what it meant. The back nine at The Grove was the ideal place to avoid being overheard. He gave Simon Cauldwell the heads up via a newly acquired burner phone and was assured that the message would go upstairs and back down again before the footballers teed off. The instruction, when it came, wasn't as unequivocal as he'd hoped. Prime Minister Donald 'Ducky' Ellington was disappointed, obviously, but as long as a decision to bring the World Cup to the UK was taken before his re-election campaign started the following spring then it was job done as far as he was concerned. By all means try and stick to the original plan but under no circumstances should they jeopardise a win for the sake of scoring points over FIFA or the Chinese.

The reaction from the golfers was predictable with Stevie Mac the most outraged.

'The Old Man's taking the piss, isn't he? No one wants the World Cup every two years. We'd be the most hated country in Europe if we hosted the first one.'

Tyrone and Mikey were just as adamant that being the first to support the plan would be a disaster.

'The fuckin' two-year thing is all about money and the big European leagues are dead against it,' said Mikey. 'We'd have the Germans, the French, the Spanish; everyone would fuckin' hate us.'

'True story, bro', and doesn't Ellington realise he's going to lose the vote of every football fan in the country?' Tyrone added.

Only Kevin Mooney was unconvinced.

'I reckon he's worked out there's a decent chance he'll win either way,' he said. 'I mean, he can be the Prime Minister that buries the embarrassment of 2010. And if it really blows up in his face, he just has to blame football's greed. And he'll still get the bounce when fans get their heads around the fact that we're going to be hosting the World Cup. For FIFA it's a winner too. China gets 2030 with our blessing and the Old Man divides the European bloc vote. I'd say he's playing a blinder.'

His remarks took the wind out of the group's sails. Much as they hated to admit it, Mooney was right. A boycott would never hold out against the tsunami of a home World Cup. Some people would try and take a stand, but in the end, they'd go with the flow.

'What are our choices?' Tyrone asked.

'It's all in the timing of the decision,' Alec said. They're talking about a separate bid process for 2032 which I'm thinking has got to take at least a year to organise making it after the UK election. That's no good to Ellington. He wants the World Cup to boost his chance of getting re-elected.'

'So, we've got a choice,' said Mooney. 'If you reckon you've got leverage with the FIFA Council you can push for an earlier decision and get the British government to swing behind 2032. Or we squeeze them the to reject the Old Man's *biennale*, hold out for 2030 and take our chances.'

'I agree,' said Stevie. 'Which one do you think we should go for?'

'If it was down to the five of us, which one would we chose?'

'That's easy,' said Mikey. 'We'd say fuck FIFA and fuck the Chinese and go all out for the 'W' in 2030.'

Chapter 31 December 2022

The last time they visited Qatar, Alec had dismissed Michaela's bad feelings about the place: this time, he needed no persuading. This time it was like a nightmare. He arrived twenty-four hours after a violent haboob had hit, dumping thousands of tons of sand onto the city. The air was thick with dust and the sun appeared only as a silvery disk. What light penetrated was unnatural, like an eclipse. He had expected Doha to be dwarfed by the outsized World Cup but what he actually saw was much weirder. As his car cruised in from the airport, a series of ever more-outlandish vehicles loomed Mad Max-style out of the gloom. Huge, overinflated tyres supported black steel exoskeletons. On top men in black uniforms manned gun turrets or carried automatic weapons. These fearsome attack vehicles were joined by troop carriers, squat amour-plated trucks also in black with coaxial machine guns above bullbarred snouts. As if these weren't enough, vast black lorries – part earth movers, part tow trucks – lumbered along spewing out clouds of diesel fumes. Their remorseless caterpillar treads threatened to destroy anything that got in their way. The futuristic combat rigs all sported the same Islamic symbol: a drawn sword underneath an ornate swirl of Arabic writing picked out in silver against the black.

Alec had never been to a World Cup, but he was pretty sure this none had ever involved paramilitary forces on the streets. He asked the driver for an explanation but the only reply he got was: 'Special World Cup security, sir.'

The Old Man had clearly kept his promise, which was a first. The outrageous assault vehicles roared along the Corniche, the city's seafront promenade, turning it into a shore-lined Fury Road. The troop carriers were stationed down every side street each containing more men in black tactical combat gear. They directed small gangs of migrant workers protected from the dust only by cotton boiler suits, their faces shielded by ragged keffiyehs. They were the only people on the streets.

Alec had been watching the group stage of the competition grinding on from the comfort of his sofa. The only thing he had found odd was that the event had really failed to catch fire. Normally effusive broadcasters were dipping into their barrel of superlatives and coming up empty. Now he could see why. The media were clearly under a strict embargo not to report on the security operation. But no amount of censorship could stop the oppressive atmosphere of the streets translating onto the pitches and into the studios. The lack of spectacle was not helped by the lowest number of goals of any tournament since the 1930s. The bigger teams showed a distinct lack of endeavour, happy to play the percentages and do just enough to qualify for the knockout stage. The most colourful part of the show so far was the rainbow flag-waving gay rights parade that had become a permanent fixture outside the Corniche's fan park. Then, just as the competition was threatening to take off, the sandstorm hit turning Doha's stadiums into dust bowls and bringing a temporary halt to play.

The clean-up was still going three days later, but the tournament's medical director had pronounced the air clear enough to play in, so at least the games were back on. Alec had paid a small fortune for a basic room at the Cigale but spent most of his time in the lobby of the Mandarin Oriental. Inside it was almost possible to forget the taste of sand except for the heavy thrum of the aircon struggling against the clogging dust. True to form, FIFA had commandeered the best hotel in town for its use which made reception a melting pot of officials, lobbyists, bid representatives and press. It was several minutes before Alec located the other members of his on-the-ground influencing operation, Tyrone Pelforth and Kevin Mooney. He had congratulated himself when he heard that the pair were going to be in town – Tyrone as an FA ambassador and Kevin boosting the home nations quota as a TV pundit – but several days in, things were not going well. Ahead of the Congress, Council members had a full diary of meetings, but during every break the trio attempted to take one or two aside and impress upon them the wisdom of voting for GB-2030. The early encounters were like the opening rounds of a boxing match: each side sizing up the other, neither prepared to reveal too much. As the knockout stages of the competition gathered pace, Alec decided it was time to ramp up the pressure. He as good as told one that the legal case for unexplained wealth could be made to disappear, another that details of a messy scandal could be kept out of the press and another that he would get exclusive access to lucrative ticket and travel deals. In each case he received a lukewarm reassurance of support.

'We know the UK bid is very strong and it is definitely among the most attractive that we have to consider,' they told him. 'Do trust that we will make the best decision for the future of the sport.'

Alec was reminded of the advice he received from a veteran lobbyist: 'The only voter you can be sure is telling the truth is the one who says he won't vote for you.'

'I don't get it,' he vented to Tyrone once the Council was back in session. 'We've worked our arses off to get what should be real arm-twisting leverage, turning over rocks to find money and sleaze, but it's like they don't care at all. I've gone way past being subtle: my threats are direct and we know they're damaging. Still I'm getting the same glib PR bollocks. What is going on?'

In the end, it was Kevin who found out the answer. At the next break he eavesdropped on several Council member's conversations and reported back.

'We're wasting our fuckin' time,' he said, with characteristic bluntness. 'You may think you've got their balls in a blender, but the Old Man's just pulled the plug out. The ballot's going to be public all right, but he's not going to reveal any individual member's votes. And the devious bastard's going to insist all hostile actions and threats are dropped in exchange for supporting the GB bid for 2032. So I'm afraid Alec, lad, they're all going to follow the silk road to China.

Alec felt suddenly tired. The guys were good, but there were times when he really missed Michaela. 'Ok, I think it's time to talk to Ashley and roll out plan B,' he said.

The *Jeu d'Or* editor had been busy. She'd just gone through the proofs of the final edition which would be delivered to FIFA members and their wives the following evening. It included a scurrilous leader from Full English on the chance of a new global pandemic emerging from China. Kim Kardashian had apparently joined the list of guest contributors with a byline on the hidden shopping opportunities in London's pop-up boutiques. Now Ashley Freeman was holding court in the Presidential suite at the W Hotel at a special invitation-only gathering of FIFA Council wives. Following an exclusive after-hours retail experience at the luxury Villaggio mall, she had laid on an exhibition of diamond jewellery and a private fashion show. At Alec's request, she had teased the possibility of a FIFA wives conference assuring her by now adoring acolytes that Melania Trump herself was going to be gracing them with her presence. She had started by dropping Michelle Obama's name but got a much more positive reaction when she mentioned the woman tethered to Donald's gilded cage. Maybe they sympathised.

As Alec arrived, Freeman was taking delivery of a full rail of ballgowns to be modelled later that evening. The couture, selected from Europe's leading fashion houses, was their reward for enduring FIFA's traditional World Cup after party. After all, she persuaded them, their husbands would get the credit from having a beautiful woman on their arms, so it was only fair that they should pay for the privilege. The dresses were being shown off by stick-thin models, but there was a team of seamstresses standing ready to shorten and widen for their intended owners once they had signed over north of $30,000 for the privilege.

'You look like you're in your element,' said Alec, thumbing through the fabrics. 'I know nothing about fashion, but this lot must be worth a fortune.

'They're insured for half a million dollars, darling, so I hope your hands are clean. Our FIFA wives are spending money like water and everyone's falling over themselves to be part of the show. When this is all over, I think I may have found my calling. I could certainly get used to the lifestyle.'

'Well, the road ahead may just be about to get a bit bumpy: it's the semi-finals tomorrow and the first day of the Congress and we're no further forward. I need you to switch to with plan B.'

'Oh fuck,' Freeman said, languidly. 'I knew it was too good to last. I take it we haven't by some miracle secured Ivana's presence?'

"fraid not.'

'So, just what do you think I'm going to do with my ladies? They really don't have any interest in a conference, you know? I've secured a guest appearance from the Emir's second wife who well understands the perils of the kept woman, but it's hardly box office.'

'What can I say? There's that comedienne you found who should move things along smoothly. They'll start with a coach tour of Doha's landmarks then have some coffee. All you have to do after that is keep them in the room until 12.30, when the Congress is in session. We'll do the rest.'

The next morning the football widows in their luxury coach were the first to leave the hotel. Determined to make an impression on Ivana, the ladies had outdone each other with their fashion choices. Ashley was there to greet them, complementing each one on a Channel handbag, a Moschino belt or, in one case, a terrifyingly tight, electric blue Dior dress. Alec was watching in the shadows with Tyrone and Kevin as they tottered and wobbled towards the bus.

'Mutton dressed up as lamb,' Kevin muttered, screwing up his eyes. 'That's Demi Rose in twenty years, so it is.'

'That, mate is one of the most influential FIFA wives. She's married to the CONCACAF President, so don't you go upsetting her.'

With their wives off the scene, the Congress visibly relaxed. Council members started to mingle with ordinary delegates in the knowledge that it could never hurt to build their bases. After fifteen minutes they were steered towards their limousines while the rest took their places alongside the media on a designated minibus or coach. Watching from the wings were several bottle-blonde girls in short skirts and high heels. It wasn't Dubai, but the World Cup had attracted an influx of pneumatic Russian hookers keen to release the tensions of a busy football executive.

This morning they weren't eyeing up potential punters. Their instincts were honed to spot danger and, they saw what rest of the crowd did not. Alec followed their line of sight. He didn't see it at first, but then it hit him. The road outside was empty. No monster trucks, no gun-toting intimidation, no black uniforms checking every vehicle. With his focus on the Congress, he'd forgotten that tonight was the night of the semi-finals. He thought back to Sheik Abdullah's demands over the airwaves to Switzerland: two matches to be played simultaneously. Now that moment had almost arrived and it was surely no coincidence that the mood on the streets was eerily quiet. He chose to keep his thoughts to himself. He and the lads with him had a day's work ahead but he secretly hoped that Simon Cauldwell was somewhere out there with a plan.

The venue for the 72nd FIFA Congress was the Doha International Conference Centre whose main claim to fame was as home to the world's only spiral escalator. That and its size: the scrum that had cluttered up the Mandarin Oriental's lobby would soon be almost lost in the DICC's vastness. The limos disgorged their passengers who greeted each other like old friends. It was as if the twenty-minute journey had induced temporary amnesia and they had completely forgotten they'd just had breakfast together. The Congress was diverse in that the 211 middle aged and elderly men were of all races, colours and creeds. Those from the Middle East sported gleaming white robes and several African and South Pacific members wore their national dress, but the vast bulk had opted for suits in colours as muted as their conversations. The only exceptions to the male and stale rule were a handful of famous footballing faces, time travellers from the modern game.

They all made their way through the lines of media and lobbyists, up the sweeping staircase and into the congress hall. A few minutes later, screens relaying the action to the assembled ranks outside flickered into life. Most had now taken their seats and the top table positions were being slowly filled. Only once everyone was in place did the Secretary General stand and start the applause which echoed around the hall for a full seven minutes as the President made his usual theatrical entrance. He paused on the threshold, smiling a half smile and shaking his head as the ovation rang out. He lifted a deferential hand then moved into the room shaking hands, squeezing shoulders, singling out members in the crowd for a special wave and, all the while basking in the adulation. He completed almost a full circle of the room before finally mounting the podium, taking his seat and indicating to Guillermo Salz to bring the meeting to order.

Members of the press pack had placed bets on the timing of his entrance. A journalist from Das Bild in Germany took the sweepstake with a winning guess of seven minutes and thirteen seconds. Veteran FIFA watchers rolled their eyes, but even the most jaded were secretly impressed by the sight of a master empresario at the height of his powers. Outside, the city might be burning, but in here the air was rarefied as Salz's voice came over the speaker and the Congress was finally in session.

Most of those downstairs found their way to a coffee station to load up with enough caffeine and cheap calories to see them through the morning. Alec checked his watch but otherwise kept his focus on the screen. On the basis that there was no reason to change a wining formular, the format of the session was identical to that of the Council. A pre-selected Council member stood to champion a motion then a second and third stood to offer variations on the same theme. The President listened attentively appearing, at least, to give each speaker his full consideration. Occasionally he would ask a question of clarification if he felt a point had not been sufficiently emphasised. When the speakers had concluded, he summarised, giving his own spin and highlighting any benefits he felt would particularly appeal to his audience. He then invited members to pick up the polling device in their seats and express their views. In every case, the motion was passed with an on-screen graphic showing almost unanimous support. The early items were procedural and went through without controversy, before the Congress turned its attention to a proposal to allow China to bid for the World Cup in 2030. The Old Man himself introduced the idea with apparent reluctance. It was an 'unusual' suggestion, he said, and one which 'needed to be weighed carefully' with 'no unseemly rush to judgement.' He apologised to Congress for asking them to consider such a momentous decision at short notice but nevertheless, 'this was the moment for such an idea to be considered.'

The Malaysian head of the Asian Football Confederation was the pre-arranged champion for the motion, but his endorsement had barely got out of second gear before the Old Man slapped him down. Congress, he declared, should hear from someone less closely associated with Chinese interests. The Malay looked wounded and confused but deferred graciously. The member for Uruguay was just about to take to his feet in support when his phone buzzed and he glanced at the message. At the same time, several others in the room did the same. Alec watched intently as looks of concern and alarm spread across their faces and they showed the messages to their neighbours. The top table looked on bemused until one of their number also received a message and his phone was passed along to the Presidential chair.

'My friends,' he began, 'I have been made aware of a disturbing development. I notice that some of you may also have received similar news and I will ask my secretary to take a moment to verify that the messages do indeed refer to the same thing.'

Alec watched the Old Man's face as Salz moved among the delegates. It was an expressionless mask but his eyes flickered constantly in rapid calculation. In the end Alec new the game was up before his secretary reported back. The Old Man rose to his feet judging that one of his legendary scene-chewing speeches was what he felt the occasion required.

'My friends,' he said, his hands spread wide. 'Members of the FIFA family; my family. It is as I feared: our beloved FIFA is under attack. The latest cowardly attempt to disrupt the proper functioning of our organisation is directed not at us, the Congress who know what it is to suffer. No, it is directed against our wives who, according to the information we have just received, are being held against their will pending the outcome of this vote. If we decide that China should not be allowed to bid then, we are told, our wives will be released unharmed and probably unaware of the danger they have been in. And if we vote in favour of one of our constitutional members being allowed to compete, then what? The result is not specified, but the threat is implicit. I say that we cannot allow ourselves to be bullied in this way. I move that we vote immediately on the motion before us and simultaneously send a message to these desperate cowards that they will never win.'

The vote was called, and members picked up their remote voting devices. The bar graph climbed more slowly than before but gathered momentum and, in the end, the result of the vote was as decisive as those before it. Alec was crestfallen. It was a reckless throw of the dice and the Old Man had seen through it. He had called Alec's bluff knowing he would never do anything to harm a group of defenceless women. Guillermo Salz announced a break in proceedings to allow those concerned to check on their spouses and the Congress trooped down to a shocked lobby. Journalists crowded around members who had received a message and within minutes, the story had spread around the world. Salz himself prowled through the lobby looking for one man. He approached Alec, Kevin and Tyrone, his eyes blazing and demanded that they follow him.

Being summoned to a meeting with the President was an uncomfortable experience at the best of times. Today Alec felt like he was being asked to sit on a corkscrew and spin. He registered the others, but the Old Man's anger was directed at Alec alone.

'Mr. Munday, you have proved yourself to be at the heart of trouble wherever it appears, and today is no exception. This latest stunt leads me to conclude just one thing: there will never be a UK host of a FIFA World Cup while I am President. You have an expression, '*over my dead body*' and that is what comes to my mind now. I tell you something, it gives me no pleasure, but you have brought this on yourself. Despite what your media constantly reports, I have always tried to be fair to all the bidders for FIFA events. We need them as much as they desire us, and the GB-2030 bid was given every chance in this competition. Now though, you have crossed a line from which there is no return and you have shamed yourself and this process.'

Alec was not normally ill tempered, but he flipped from browbeaten to belligerent in as much time as it took the Old Man to take his next breath.

'Don't talk to me about shame,' he spat. 'You have no shame. You sit there like some medieval despot presiding over the most corrupt organisation in sport. The only reason we're here in Qatar is because you sold the World Cup down the river, and where has it got you? A total clusterfuck of a tournament with no goals, no fans, protestors on every corner and armed thugs on the streets about to stage a coup. Everyone in the game – the players, the broadcasters, the sponsors, and the fans – they're just roadkill on your insatiable drive to line your pockets and those of that appalling cabal you call the FIFA Council. Let me remind you that *you* called *me* when your granddaughter was in danger, that we shook hands on a deal which *you* have reneged on, so *you* are the one who should be ashamed. Your so-called process is so warped that any nation not prepared to shovel huge piles of cash into your vaults has to resort to the dark arts just to get a seat at the table. So, yes we got up to some tricks but you made the rules of this god-forsaken game. It is you that should feel shame and have the world see your grasping venality for what it is.'

The Old Man raised his hand to interrupt but Alec was in full flow.

'Do you know what is happening outside as we speak? One of your *honourable* fucking members is plotting to overthrow his own government and the hosts of this competition. You and I both know that you made all this possible and put the lives of hundreds of football fans at risk. Do you know what? I have wasted too much time on this discredited shitshow as it is. I'm going out to try and prevent a bloodbath. So, screw you and screw your fucking bid. Whoever is stupid enough to trust their country to your cancerous cronies deserves everything they get.

Chapter 32

It was just a few hours until the semi-finals but outside the congress centre the streets were almost deserted. Lurid signs welcoming visitors to the World Cup hung limply from every lamppost, but it seemed the world had already gone home. The wind had finally subsided leaving a thick coating of greige dust on every surface. On the horizon, the skyscrapers of the distant downtown rose like muted spectres out of the haze of the eternal city.

Alec stood with Kevin and Tyrone, silent and still seething, then they all three burst out laughing.

'As rants go, that was one of your best,' Kevin said admiringly. '*Cancerous cronies*, that was a good one. You've a way with words, so you do.'

Alec had to admit he was quite proud of himself and some of his harsher descriptions of FIFA would no doubt make it into his *Guardian* column at some point. Storming out of the meeting had given him some satisfaction, but he was under no illusions about the chances of Team GB winning the right to host the 2030 World Cup: a big fat zero. He called Freeman.

'It's all over,' he told her. 'You'd better let the ladies go.'

'Let them go, darling? They have no idea they're not free to leave whenever they want. Obviously, we had to be able to deny any real attempt at kidnap and extortion, so we ran a little exercise about treachery. I asked them to imagine they had been taken prisoner and to text their husbands with the news. So far half of them haven't had a reply; the rest received a cursory word or two then their gallant spouses apparently went back to their meeting. It's hard to know whether they've gone down or up in the women's estimation, although I suspect they were already at quite a low ebb.'

'An exercise in treachery? Sounds like the latest volume in the history of FIFA. So how are you going to keep them entertained?'

'Obviously la Trump won't be joining us, which caused some grumbling, but I started serving the drinks early and now they're all in a beauty workshop. They'll be fine until we run out of makeup or trowels to apply it with.'

'Ooh, put those claws away. Just make sure they all go away with the latest issue of *Jeu d'Or* and you work here is officially done. Thanks for everything, Ashley.'

'It was a pleasure, darling, and if there's ever some made up journalism or luxury sampling to be done, I do hope you'll keep me in mind. By the way, my flight back's not for a couple of days so I might just keep the charade going for a little bit longer, if it's ok with you. Harvey Nicks Doha couldn't do a private opening for us until tomorrow and the manager has literally promised to fill my tote bag with the wealth of the forty thieves if I take my ladies to his store.'

'Knock yourself out, and if you're still around once the vote is announced, you can come to the wake for the Team GB bid.'

Alec hung up, confident there would be no further blowback from their stunt. Commandeering one of the FIFA shuttle buses, he, Kevin and Tyrone headed towards the high-rise centre of the city along tumbleweed roads. Where earlier, black-uniformed crews backed up by preposterous combat vehicles were manning checkpoints and watchtowers, now the barriers were propped open and the watchers had been relieved of their posts. The only sign of life was the occasional security vehicle parked up in a sideroad. No one was out on the sidewalks and any cars steered clear of the areas around the city centre and World Cup sites. Alec was reminded of reports of wildlife finding safe ground ahead of a tsunami or earthquake. He wasn't superstitious, but he had to wonder whether the locals had a premonition of what was coming.

The Qatari organisers had built two giant fanparks which were the smiling face of the World Cup for the outside world. They had taken advantage of the unique winter schedule to ship in fences and catering trucks that had spent the summer at Europe's biggest music festivals. Everything was dressed in World Cup branding and the lighting was spectacular. No one would ever suspect they'd come straight from Tommorowland or Glastonbury. Alcohol was served as usual at Doha's international hotels but, in deference to FIFA, the parks had been given special liquor licences making them the two venues in town where beer was available for less than $20 a glass. The minibus cruised past the Aspire fanzone, a vast pop-up village in the shadow of the Khalifa International Stadium. The illuminated park could cater for over 40,000 people and the bars were already doing a brisk trade ahead of the first of the evening's semi-finals. Outside, Gay Pride protesters had just emerged from the shadows to get the parade started again. Foreign fans, many of whom were staying in tented "glamp sites" in the desert, streamed in large numbers towards the area. Their enthusiasm to come out onto the street was in stark contrast to the locals who, if they left their apartments at all, made quick local trips before scurrying like desert rats back to safety. Following their instructions, the TV cameramen kept their lenses trained on the visitors enjoying a drink and the thump of the music, seemingly oblivious to the dystopian nightmare being unveiled behind them. Their masters ensured there was no way viewers around the world would get anything but a positive impression. The driver ferried them along the Corniche towards the second fanzone while the lads changed clothes in the back. By the time they were dropped off near to the Lusail Stadium they looked like any other football supporters taking their place in the wide, snaking queue into the park.

Inside, the layout had been designed to mirror a music festival with a main stage sporting a huge screen and booming speaker system. There were over thirty bars and the smell of fast-food outlets filled the evening air. Organisers had tried to create different viewing experiences even going so far as to bring in rows of terraces to make visitors feel at home. It was a good effort but probably lost on most fans who were just looking for some reasonably-priced lubrication ahead of the game.

Despite a crowd already thousands strong, Cauldwell was easy to spot lurking in the shade of a vinyl awning decorated with sponsors' logos. As Alec approached, he could see a group of around thirty men in various tactical outfits drinking coffee in the tent behind them.

He nodded an acknowledgement to Cauldwell. 'Friends of yours?'

'Hopefully more useful, given the circumstances. All the competing countries send a few gendarmes or whatever to help police their fans. We managed to persuade several of them that a contingent of their elite forces would be a better option, and now seems as good a time as any to get acquainted.'

'When the Sheikh spoke to the Old Man in Switzerland he was focused on the semi-finals so, unless anything's changed, tonight's the night, right?'

Cauldwell nodded. 'That's what we're planning for and everything on the street says we're right. We haven't pinpointed where that army of his is camped, but they're out there ready to make their move.'

'And you think this is the place they'll do it. Will you be able to intervene if it comes to it?'

'We can certainly make a nuisance of ourselves until reinforcements arrive.'

'What do you think is going to happen?'

'It's hard to be sure, but if you study the insurgent's playbook, they follow pretty much the same basic plot: control the military and storm the president's residence. The semi-finals give them the best opportunity to do that. The Khalifa Stadium and Aspire Fanzone are close to the main offices of Qatar's Ministry of Defence and we are just down the road from the Emir's palace. If I'm right, they're going to move on both tonight.'

Alec was shocked. 'What, you think they are going to use fans to storm the buildings?'

'Not as such. I'm guessing they'll try to create a human stampede and use hot pursuit as cover to do it themselves. It's what I would do if I was going to stage a coup with limited numbers.'

'Hot pursuit? Is that where I can chase a burglar into my neighbour's garden?'

'Same basic principle, and in the heat of an apparent riot threatening damage to sensitive property, no one's going to argue with them.'

'But that puts fans in direct line of fire. Hundreds could be shot or crushed.'

Alec looked at the enthusiastic crowds thronging the bars, none of them aware how perilous their position could be. He thought back to the telephone conversation in the backroom of a Swiss hotel. The Qatari pretender had got pretty much everything he asked for: the security contract, the alcohol and two semi-finals on the same evening. The only thing that hadn't materialised was the exact teams competing, but looking at the sea of people in front of him, Alec knew it wouldn't matter. When it came to it, crowd trouble or panic were guaranteed if they came under attack.

'I wonder if the Old Man even put up a struggle,' he said.

'Let's assume not,' said Cauldwell. 'We had our chance, but realistically anyone with the Sheikh's power, money and determination was never going to give up. If it hadn't been threats to kill the Old Man's granddaughter, he'd have found another way.'

The days were short in the Middle East at this time of year and the sky was a rapidly darkening gradient of burnt orange to black. Arc lights were positioned around the perimeter and suspended from strategically positioned gantries to light up the fanpark like a studio. That made the area outside dark and ominous and completely impenetrable to any wayward cameras even though the sun had barely set.

'What are we going to do?'

'We'll do what we can. On the basis that the men in black shirts aren't expecting a fightback, we'll slow them down and try to keep them away from the Palace until local troops arrive. The Americans have a large base up north and have sent a welcoming committee of their own to the Defence Ministry. We've got the start of an improvised plan here, but that's as much as I can say.'

Alec watched with Kevin and Tyrone as the park continued to fill up. Half an hour later, it was almost full, and the traveling supporters were clustered in large groups around the various bars.

'They've done a grand job here, don't you think?' Kevin said. 'With the price of a beer at our hotel, I've half a mind to go and join in myself.'

'It's tempting,' Tyrone agreed, 'but however cheap the beer is, I don't fancy being in that crowd if an attack comes.'

Alec was looking around him. 'Have you noticed the cameras have all gone? I wonder if they've been tipped off.'

'Nah, you know what those Steadicam guys are like,' said Tyrone. 'Remember when Mason got his double leg brake last year? We had to physically stop them filming him writhing around on the floor. If they thought something was going down, they'd be here to shoot it.'

'They've probably just been moved into the stadium with two games going on at once,' Kevin agreed.

'Seems a shame though. I mean, we want the world to see what's going on. Perhaps we should get our phones out. You could do a commentary as well, Kev. This is your chance to put that media training into practice.'

The Irishman pulled out his iPhone and turned the camera on himself.

Good evening, my name's Kevin Mooney and I'm with FA ambassador Tyrone Pelforth and football's answer to Johnny English, Alec Munday. You join us live from the Lusail Fanzone in Doha where the crowds are expectant ahead of tonight's World Cup semi-finals. This is one of only two places in town where you can get a drink for less than ten dollars, so it's perhaps no surprise that both sides are out in numbers.

Mooney's media career was in its infancy, but he got into his stride and became more serious as he did so.

So far, the mood is buoyant but there are rumours flying around this evening that someone is determined to spoil the party. For days now we've witnessed the sight of paramilitary forces on the streets of this city. Today has been different. It has been eerily quiet and the concern among insiders is that those forces have chosen tonight, the busiest of the World Cup so far, to launch an all-out offensive against the regime here.

As he spoke, Cauldwell tensed beside him. He gestured at a bank of headlights that had suddenly appeared, stretching along the length the fence perimeter fence.

'Looks like we've got company.'

Poking his head under the canopy, Cauldwell called out: 'Showtime lads.'

It was all encouragement the unit behind him needed. They grabbed body armour and assault rifles, checked their side arms and were soon lost in the gloom.

Outside Mooney had flipped his selfie lens around and focused on the crowd and the row of lights behind them.

This is the scene here in the fanpark where all the signs are that those rumours could be true. Look beyond the crowd and the big screens, and you'll see a row of lights in the distance moving towards us. You probably can't hear their engines over the top of the entertainment, but we're seeing upwards of, I'd say, thirty large vehicles approaching the western edge of the park. They're coming closer. And now they've completely disappeared. I can't be certain, but I'd say that means those vehicles are now parked up just behind the temporary fence surrounding the park. What their intentions are is anyone's guess, but for now all we can do is wait to find out.

Kevin was so focused on the action at that end of the park that he was taken off guard when what sounded like a demolition site erupted behind them. He spun around and picked up the commentary again.

I've just heard what sounds like earthworks from just behind us at the Eastern edge of the park by the entrance gates. Some fans are looking alarmed: they're starting to get wind of something going on. But what they don't know is that the attack seems like it's coming from both sides. And, oh, my God, now we get to see what that noise was about as the gates have just been ripped off their moorings by a pair of enormous tow trucks. They're the kind of things you'd use if a bus or a lorry has broken down. Now they've attached their hooks to the gates and dragged them away like they were made of tinfoil. And they're coming back for more, hooking up to the fences either side and ripping a great big hole in the perimeter. They seem determined to take down as much of the fence as possible. The fans are cheering, maybe they didn't have tickets, and now they're streaming in towards the bars. The tow trucks have dragged the fences away down the road and left them and that seems to be their work done. They've unhooked and driven off but that noise you can hear is from the other end of the park where the military trucks have just broken through. They're tearing through the fencing as if it was made of paper. They've scythed through the main stage and the bars and now they're driving at high speed straight at the fans. They're firing automatic weapons into the air from the trucks and, oh, God, this is awful. Some of the fans are literally being crushed under the wheels of the convoy. The rest of the crowd has worked out something's wrong and now the entire mass of people are panicking and surging in an attempt to try and escape. There are helicopters above us circling with their spotlights flashing over us and driving towards the entrance. Maybe now we see why the fences were dragged away.

'Time to go,' Alec yelled, dragging Kevin by the arm and running at high speed out of the park. The three sprinted onto the Corniche and along the road.

'This is going to be a massacre. Where the fuck's Cauldwell?'

His question was answered a hundred yards later as they found themselves facing a barrier made from white 4x4s parked side on across the road. Cauldwell stepped out from behind the lead car and yelled at them to join him. Once they had reached the relative safety of the Landcruisers, Kevin took a moment to get his breath back then started filming again.

We've come out of the fanpark and onto the Corniche, Doha's coast road, where we're positioned between the crowd and the Emir's palace a couple of hundred yards behind me. Now that they've got the crowd on the move, the terrorists seem to have slowed down but are still driving them relentlessly in our direction. The gap they made in the fence suggests their orders probably don't involve mass slaughter, but those screams you can hear are enough to know that the men driving those vehicles have got blood on their hands tonight.

Kevin let the camera keep recording while he took a moment to get his bearings and guess at Cauldwell's plan. He picked up the commentary again a few seconds later.

Over to my left is the entrance to the Souk Waqif, the city's open-air market and the men I'm with are hoping to persuade the fans to move in that direction. The market is a maze of narrow streets and the assault vehicles won't be able to follow them in there. I'm not showing you the men's faces as they need to keep their identities secret, but if they can pull it off, many lives will be saved.

He carried on filming as the fans who were ahead of the crowd came running along the seafront road. They were looking desperately for a way out, but their attackers had picked the spot well. With the sea on one side and a blind wall on the other, the only option was forward. The screaming tide of humanity continued to flow with no regard for any among them who couldn't keep pace. It was a tough watch, but in the followspot lights of the helicopters, Kevin filmed those who fell and were trampled. He felt their relatives were going to want to know how they died.

As the confused and disorientated crowd got nearer, half of the special forces unit moved to the front of the barricade of cars. They yelled and waved and occasionally fired into the air to turn the tide off course and in to the Souk Waqif. In normal times, the bazaar's stalls of exotic animals and birds, silks and spices, restaurants and shisha bars would be packed with traders and their customers. For now, it was mercifully empty and thousands of fans were able to lose themselves in the relative safety of its narrow arches and high-walled squares. As they streamed into the market, the crowd behind them started to get the message. The 4x4s peeled off taking up positions alongside and behind them in an attempt to form a protective shield in front of the advancing vehicles of Sheikh Abdullah's forces. Given a new target, the military convoy tried brute force to brush the Landcruisers out of the way. Cauldwell's men jumped from their cars seconds before they were rammed by the onrushing forces who were blown backwards by high explosives. The barricade had been boobytrapped.

The torn and twisted combat trucks blocked the way for those behind them, bringing the attack to a temporary standstill. Fans continued to pour forward using the lull to escape their pursuers. The sound of rockets and the dull crump of explosives drowned out all other noises as the militants were reduced to firing mortars and relying on air support to try and clear a path. It took three RPGs, but in the end, they opened up enough of a route through the tangled wreckage to advance two abreast. Cauldwell's men were there to meet them with another two 4x4s and there was a momentary standoff as the two sides based each other. Knowing what was coming, the military convoy tried to divert. At the same time they unleashed a stream of cannon fire in all directions. The Landcruisers recognised the signs of panic and drove straight at their target, bailing out only seconds before the collision. With their options narrowing along with the road, Sheikh Abdullah's men had no option it but to abandon their vehicles and take their chances on foot.

On the ground they were tactically weak and poorly equipped against the sharply honed skills of Europe's elite soldiers. In the lights of the remaining vehicles the men in black uniforms were easy targets and rapidly picked off. Once they started taking casualties, their discipline collapsed and soon it was every man for himself. They ran back the way they had come looking for a way out or somewhere to melt away. Cauldwell's men continued to target those they could see but they were happy to let the rest escape. It wasn't their job to bring the defeated insurgents to justice. The wail of sirens in the distance indicated that the promised reinforcements were on their way. Cauldwell's men would stay in position only long enough to ensure the insurgents were not in a position to regroup then it was their turn to melt back into anonymity.

Alec watched, mesmerised, from behind one of the 4x4s. Even from the safety of his vantage point, his senses were completely overwhelmed. The scene playing out in front of him was confused and he could only look on as ricocheting bullets claimed their victims. His head jerked this way and that as attack vehicles exploded in flames or helicopters rained down fire onto the road below. Crowds still surged towards him and he watched helplessly as they were blown off their feet by the blast of high explosives. Suddenly that vision fell away as his eye was drawn to something at the back of the action. An armour-plated Bentley was crouched, lights off, behind the melee. Now its headlights blazed but, rather than move

forward, it reversed rapidly, spun and quit the scene at high speed.

Chapter 33

Alec grabbed Kevin and Tyrone.

'Come on, there's something we need to do.'

He fumbled under the dash of one of the remaining 4x4s, found the key and kicked

the car into life. He threw it into gear as the boys swung themselves into the passenger seats.

Seconds later the battlefield was just an orange glow in their rear-view mirror. Alec drove

along the city's seafront, past the serene grandeur of the Emir's Palace, scanning each

intersection. Doha's central tourist area is a series of concentric circles and he soon picked up

the Bentley as it cruised through the city a couple of blocks further out. Without any attempt

at evasive action, the lone vehicle executed a wide right turn across four lanes of traffic

joining the city's main arterial road heading southwest.

'Do you want to tell us what's going on?' Tyrone asked.

Alec just gripped the wheel and nodded muttering: 'Go on, you bastard.' He turned

sharply to follow then floored the gas pedal reducing the gap between the vehicles. As they

passed the city limits the traffic thinned and he gained ground further. When the streetlights

ran out, they were alone on the road just yards behind the luxury car and driving at high

speed into the dark of the desert night.

'Who do you think is in there?' Tyrone tried again.

'If I'm right, it's Sheikh Abullah. He's worked out the game's up and he's trying to get out of the country. This road runs the sixty miles to the Saudi border. I reckon that's where he's headed.'

'It's certainly the kind of car that fucker would drive,' Kevin agreed. 'And you think we can take him on?'

'Well, we're going to try. Cauldwell seemed to have his hands full, and we can't just let him get away.'

'So, what's the plan?'

'I haven't really got that far, have I? Tyrone do you want to check in the back there to see if we've got any weapons.'

'Nothing,' he said, moments later, 'except what looks like high explosives and I can't see any detonators.'

'Shit.'

'Alec you're gonna have to come up with something soon, so you are. At this rate we'll be at the border in half an hour.'

Alec glanced down at the speedometer which was showing close to 110 miles an hour. Kevin had a point.

'I saw this thing on TV once,' said Tyrone. 'There was a properly long car chase along a dark road and they were just going faster and faster.'

'Mate, this isn't helping.'

'Yeh, but in the end how they did it was the cops backed off and turned out their lights then followed at a distance. The guy thinks he's in the clear, so he stops panicking and slows down. Then they built up a proper speed and accelerated past him and once they drew level, they forced him off the road.'

'Yeh, you see that's the bit where we're going to struggle,' said Kevin, 'especially with Alec at the wheel. That's not the Sheikh's driving is it? He'll have someone who's a trained driver and at least one armed bodyguard with him. If we did force them off the road then we'd be in real trouble.'

'You may as well back off anyway,' said Tyrone. 'We're not getting anywhere like this.'

Alec was about to do as he was asked when the brake lights of the Bentley blazed ahead of them. It swung sharply right off the blacktop and onto the dunes. Alec slowed to a stop and watched as the Sheikh's car churned through the sand.

'What do you think we should do?

'You've got to follow it, haven't you?' said Kevin. 'No rush, though. We've got the perfect motor for desert terrain, and that Bentley's so heavy I reckon he'll soon be stuck up to his axles. So, take your time, follow along and we'll try and think of a plan for what we do when we catch the fucker.'

They kept a couple of hundred yards back, but the luxury marque was easy to spot as it picked out a path between the undulations. After a couple of slow miles, a change in the angle of its lights showed that the car was climbing. Alec hung back and watched it surge up a huge dune with apparent ease.

'It doesn't seem to be struggling,' he said. 'So, I suppose we'll just have to go after them.'

He selected low gear ratio, picked out sand mode on the gearbox then took a deep breath. He started up the slope gingerly but soon lost traction even in the 4x4.

'You've got to get on the power a bit more than that,' said Tyrone. 'Do you want me to have a go?'

'No. I've got this,' Alec said, as the engine roared.

The 4x4 responded, sliding its way uphill as traction was transferred between the wheels. Alec concentrated hard on keeping them in a straight line until Kevin piped up from beside him.

'Err, I hate to say this, lads, but they've disappeared.'

They all looked into the darkness ahead of them and saw nothing but stars.

'They must have got to the top of the hill and taken off down the other side,' Tyrone said. 'Just keep the power on but be prepared to brake when you reach the top.'

The kept climbing and Alec started to relax as he got more used to the surface slipping beneath them. He was just starting to enjoy himself when the sand ran out.

'Fuck! Hold on,' he said, as he slammed on the anchors. The car slewed to one side but came to a stop perched as a precarious angle. They looked around in every direction but everywhere was black.

Tyrone took the lead. 'We need to get out, work out where that Bentley is and check the slope ahead of us. We can't just plough ahead; we could be driving off a cliff.'

Alec put the selector into park and engaged the handbrake. He turned the engine off then the three of them stepped out onto the sand. They moved around the vehicle straining their eyes as they tried to make out anything in the inky blackness. The temperature of the air outside the car had dropped and the tick of the cooling engine was the only sound disturbing the desert silence.

'Where the fuck is he?' came a strong Northern Irish accent out of the gloom.

'Dunno, mate,' replied Tyrone, 'but I don't like the look of this slope. It's properly steep that side. I don't know how that car could have made it down.'

Alec opened his mouth to speak but was drowned out by the sudden bellow of a six-litre engine. The scene was flooded with light as the Bentley lurched out of the darkness and drove straight at them. The three players scattered as it slammed heavily into the 4x4 and kept pushing until it was over the lip of the dune. Its work done, the Bentley reversed and swung in a 180-degree arc then ploughed off the way it came.

'We are properly fucked,' came Kevin's harsh diction, when it was quiet again.

Tyrone wasn't convinced. 'Not necessarily. Shine your camera torches down there and let's see what we've got.'

He half slid, half clambered down the sandy slope in the dim light and found the Landcruiser lying with two of its wheels off the ground at the bottom. He climbed in through the passenger door, slid across and tried the ignition. Remarkably, the car started, and he was soon churning through the sand. Tyrone had clearly taken on board more of the track day lessons than Alec and he zigzagged his way across the side of the hill and back to the top. He picked up the others and was soon racing back towards the road his passengers struggling to keep in their seats.

'We've got to make up some time on the sand, where we've got the advantage,' he said, by way of an apology. 'If they're too far ahead by the time we reach the road, we'll never catch up.'

The Bentley was indeed making heavy going of the sand and it wasn't long before they were closing in on its taillights. They were barely 150 yards behind when it bumped back onto the road and roared off again into the night. Tyrone was soon bouncing the Landcruiser onto the tarmac behind them. He turned off all their lights but kept them in touch with the target. The Sheikh's car was running at full speed and Tyrone could only watch as it accelerated away from them. It built up a considerable lead before slowing dramatically. It was almost stationary as Tyrone pulled closer and flicked on the Toyota's lights. He slowed to a crawl keeping fifty yards between them and the Qataris.

'I think they might have done some damage when they rammed us back there,' said Tyrone. 'By the sound of that engine they're not going to be going too much further.'

'How far are we to the border?' Kevin asked.

'We've maybe done thirty miles, so halfway by my reckoning. What's the plan Alec?'

'Ok, I've been thinking about the explosives in the back. When we reach them, I think we drive into the driver's door putting him out of action. Then we put a burning rag in the tank of this car, leg it and wait for the whole lot to explode.'

Kevin was dismissive. 'That's the biggest fucking pile of shite I've heard you come out with, so it is. Cars don't burn from a rag in the tank and even if they did, the explosives need a detonator to set them off. He'll have a bodyguard in the front passenger seat and another with him in the back, so all your plan would do is invite them to get out and kill us then steal our car to get to the border. No, Alec, you'll have to do better than that.'

'Ok, so what's your plan, then?'

'I don't have one, but then I wasn't the one that dragged us all off into the desert. I'll tell you what though, we're going to have to come up with something soon as Tyrone's about to run into them.'

It was true. The Bentley had stopped and three men with handguns had taken up positions beside it. Tyrone pulled up around fifty yards away, then started revving the engine.

'I reckon I can clip one of them and hit the corner of the Bentley and spin it around and knock out the others. Hold on.'

'No,' yelled Alec and Kevin, simultaneously. Then Alec's phone rang. It was Simon Cauldwell.

'Alec, if you're where I think you are you're about to be totally the wrong place at a completely disastrous time.'

'What?'

'Stop the car! Get out. And run like fuck.'

Cauldwell's voice was loud enough for Tyrone to get the message. He hit the brakes and the Toyota nosedived towards the road as it screeched to a halt. The three occupants threw open the doors and scrambled out. They sprinted back along the road then off into the dunes by its flank and didn't stop running until they were over a hundred yards away. Only when they were sheltered behind a dome of rough sand did they pause to look back. When they did, they saw the rear lighting cluster of the Bentley receding slowly as it tried to limp away from the scene. The only thing Alec saw was desperate, futile hope. Hope was the last thing Sheikh Abdullah would ever give up: hope that he would get away with his crimes, hope that he would bring off his master plan, maybe even hope that the world would see the wisdom of the sacrifices made for the greater good. In the end, though he was doomed by hope, and it was hope that killed him.

Milliseconds later events moved into reverse. The sky was lit up by a blinding phosphorus flash followed by a hissing crack as the sound of two hellfire missiles chased the warheads themselves. Almost instantaneously the ground shook with the force of both vehicles being vapourised and they were pinned down by falling debris. Finally, when the roar of the explosions had died away, the thudding blades of two Apache helicopter gunships, the source of the rockets, penetrated the ringing ears of the onlookers.

Chapter 34

Qatar is a Disneyfied country where the incursions of an ever-encroaching desert are repelled by the will of the magic kingdom. So, it was no surprise that, by sunup the next morning, there was barely a trace of the pitched battles of the night before. The crushed bodies of fallen fans had been spirited away to be dealt with discreetly by Doha's various foreign embassies. The shells of burnt-out vehicles had been dragged away and the paramilitaries who had wreaked such devastation were nowhere to be seen. They had been replaced by an army of migrant labourers who were working with brooms to remove the dark scorch marks on the corniche. Within hours, the wreckage of the Lusail fanpark had been consigned to a hanger beyond the reach of prying cameras. The city had once again succumbed to the ruling elite's pathological desire to present only its gilded face to the world. In a country where the media is the servant of the Emir and his minions, none of the newspapers carried the story and there was no footage on either local or international networks. Even those who had seen the action with their own eyes were left wondering whether they had dreamt the entire thing. The only hint at the events of the evening before was a short release from the Qatari Ministry of Information.

His Royal Highness, Prince Sheikh Abdullah bin Saud bin Muhammad bin Ali bin Jassim Al Thani was killed last night in a freak accident on the Salwa Road. There will be a day of mourning tomorrow.

Alec opened his eyes and looked across at the woman-shaped bump in the bed beside him where a still-sleeping Ashley Freeman was breathing steadily. The fuzzy details of the previous evening started to come back to him.

FIFA's media machine was wilfully oblivious to events outside the stadium. It had valuable television obligations to meet and insisted the two semi-finals should go ahead regardless of the carnage on the streets. Doha felt utterly surreal when Alec, Kevin and Tyrone got back to the city. The clean-up crew were already in full swing taking advantage of the distraction provided by the football. The trio, stilled dazed, decided there was nothing else for it but to head for the bar of the W Hotel where they found Ashley already installed. The beer helped to numb the whiplash they felt from being ripped from peace to war and back again.

By the time matches were over, their brains had started to process the events of the evening and their legs had started to follow instructions. Kevin left to meet up with some of his broadcast colleagues and Tyrone was back on duty for the FA, leaving Alec and Ashley alone. It was her suggestion to go up to his room for some no-strings company '*while we still remember how to do it'*. Now she was coming to with a satisfied smile still on her face.

'Did we…?' he started.

'Oh, don't even go there, darling,' she said, propping herself up sexily on one elbow. You were just as keen as me, so don't try and pretend I took advantage of your drunken state.'

'Fair enough, and I remember enough to know that it was fun. Would you like some coffee?'

He got out of bed and fired up the in-room machine.

'It's weird, you know. I've spent almost every day of the past eighteen months thinking about the Sheikh. I've fantasised about how it would feel to know that he was dead, how I might finally be able to look the relatives of the Wembley bombing in the eye and tell them I'd got even on their behalf. But this morning I don't feel anything at all, just a great big anti-climax. When I was playing football, we'd get to a big game, a final, and we'd push so hard for the win that when the final whistle went there would be total euphoria, everyone going crazy. Then the next day I'd wake up feeling completely flat, not miserable exactly, just with a totally low vibe. It was like the world should have changed, but somehow it hadn't. That's what today feels like. I've been fixated on that bastard for so long that I really I should feel something different now that he's gone. I should be punching the air, but all I feel is just a bit empty.'

She hadn't expected a philosophical discussion. 'You'll get over it,' she said. 'I know something that will make you feel better, and it's not coffee.'

She pulled the sheets back, daring him to turn her down. An hour later his phone pinged with a message from Nigel Rushbourne: *Congratulations. You did a good thing and many lives will be saved because of you. The Qataris won't ever say so publicly, but behind the scenes they are delighted. Well done.*

Alec read the message twice then showed it to Ashley. 'I wonder whether getting rid of the Sheikh was his objective all along. I mean, it was a long shot, but it turns out it was easier than winning the World Cup.'

'How's that going, by the way?'

'The vote's later this afternoon. Qatar may be in mourning but that's not going to stop FIFA going about its business.'

'Are you going to the congress hall?'

'I'll get down there for the announcement but there's not really much point spending the day there. What do you fancy doing? I've done enough 4x4 desert driving to see me through this life and the next, but we could charter a yacht for the day, get the boys together, pack a picnic together and tour some of the islands.'

'Don't bother for me. I've got lunch with my ladies then we're being chaperoned around Harvey Nicks. I'll see you later, though.'

The crush at the Doha International Conference Centre was the biggest of the week, boosted by the presence of the bid teams and their entourages. News had filtered through during the course of the day that Morocco had withdrawn from the competition. No one was sure whether their bid had ever been serious, and perhaps they had been surprised to get as far as they had. After the previous day's vote the Chinese were odds-on favourites. With the dogged GB bid still with a point to prove, the North African journeymen judged they had got as much positive press from the process as they were going to. Their exit left a dozen of their continental cousins with votes going begging. The bookies, along with most commentators, were reading the geopolitical tealeaves and coming up with only one outcome.

Being pictured shaking hands with the Old Man is as welcome an addition to a world leader's photo album as shots with Jeffrey Epstein or Vladimir Putin. As a result, most heads of state find excuses not to attend these occasions in person. Having not left China for over two years, President Xi was not about to choose the FIFA Congress for his first foreign outing. Instead, he chose quantity over familiarity sending at least a dozen identikit mandarins in poorly cut suits in his place. The crusty Zheng Zhi, captain of the Chinese national football team and the country's only true great of the game, was hard at work pressing the flesh with FIFA Council members. Alongside him there was a clutch of apparent celebrities surrounded by a gaggle of fangirls and boys. Not known outside their native China, the stars could have been lookalikes for all anyone could tell, and the incessant shrieking from the groupies was jarring. However, with a cast of at least two hundred, the Asian bid could not be faulted for effort.

On the British side, Donald 'Ducky' Ellington had found himself unavoidably detained by matters of State, so declined to make the trip. Damien Scott had been reshuffled and the PM judged that his new Secretary of State for Media and Sport would leave a trail of destruction behind her, so handed the job to a junior minister. The young man, one of the newly elected MPs from the north of England, stood gawping at the chandeliers like a teenager on his first day at sixth form college. Trying manfully to save the day were Saint Marcus of Manchester and the Croydon de Bruyne himself who were being shepherded around by the FA's PR girl, Samantha and a posse of FA ambassadors. Meanwhile, a red-faced Malcolm Tonghe was having a stand-up row with FIFA Secretary General, Guillermo Salz. In his hand he held a flimsy document and was stabbing insistently at key passages within it.

Alec had heard a rumour doing the rounds of the press pack that files had been slipped under hotel room doors of sleeping Congress members last night. GB-2030 stood accused of extortion and fraud, which was fair enough. What was out of order was CCTV footage catching young members of the Chinese bid team in the act of corrupting the voting process. Tonghe waved the paper in the Swiss administrator's face while Alec watched. He knew the reality was, if anything, far more shocking than anything the Chinese had concocted.

The rival bidders disappeared into the hall for their final preparations, Tonghe still berating the FIFA man. Alec turned his attention to life in the lobby where it was like a royal stag do. The delegates, knowing there was a chance they would appear on television sets around the world, were dressed to impress. Previously dowdy members from the northern hemisphere were now sporting garish ties to match their federation lapel pins. But it was those from the global south who really lent some colour to proceedings. Locals from around the Middle East had been wearing robes throughout the congress but today their plain white keffiyeh had been replaced by red checks. Joining them were shalwar kameez, angarkha and dhoti-sporting members from the Indian subcontinent and even a full colonel's uniform from the Malaysian representative. There were some weird and wonderful costumes from the Oceanian federations, but it was the Africans who really hit the heights. Their brightly batiked robes and intricately embroidered dashiki tunics were set off by matching kente kufi caps and more than a few wooden spears or shields. As ever, the gathering was predominantly male and the whiff of testosterone caught in Alec's nostrils. The ritual glad handing had been amped up as delegates around the lobby risked spilling their coffee to clasp each other in the customary FIFA man hugs.

Some of the more experienced reporters managed to take a delegate or two aside to assess the mood of the room. They knew they were in for a long morning and were desperate for whatever titbits they could use to pad and fill for the live news shows back home. Peppered throughout the crowd were a few famous footballing faces adding sporting glamour to the occasion. They took their places at strategic points in the main hall as the FIFA Congress was declared formally back in session.

As the crowds cleared, Alec saw Nigel Rushbourne striding towards them, an ever-hopeful look on his face.

'Alec, so good to see you,' he said, grasping his and shaking it warmly. 'How do you rate our chances?'

Alec looked at him, glumly. 'The vote yesterday allowing the Chinese to bid was the big one and there's not really anything we can do about it.'

'Any chinks in their armour?'

'Oh, plenty.' Alec looked around to make sure they weren't being overhead and lowered his voice. 'Half of the suits on the Chinese bid team send their children to English boarding schools despite their official salaries being only around $1200 per month. We found interests in casinos in Macau, luxury yachts in Cannes and beachfront properties in Barbados. We even put together a news report in Chinese to discredit them, but that's only news in China and state media killed the story even before it was picked up on the socials. We could go public in the western press, but it would really be for spite rather than to achieve what we set out to. If Michaela were here, she would no doubt have some ideas but, honestly, I think we'll be lucky to get the World Cup in 2032 now.'

'Well, as Marvin Lee Aday would say: Two Out of Three Ain't Bad.'

Alec looked baffled. 'Who?'

'Meat Loaf, 1977,' came the reply, although Alec, shaking his head, was no more enlightened.

'Never mind,' he said. 'Two out of three? The Sheikh, the World Cup: what's the third thing?'

'The third thing?' said the spook, with a twisted smile. 'Where do you want me to start? We'll certainly get a big dividend from our Qatari friends for our part in sorting out their little local difficulty. As we speak, they are helping Simon and his team unpick Sheikh Abdullah's network. That represents a quantum leap forward for our anti-terror efforts which would otherwise have taken years to achieve. Then there's the boost to the Union that a combined UK bid made it to the finish line without falling apart. Win or lose, Damien Scott tells me the PM is delighted.'

Alec shook his head feeling, not for the first time, that he had been played. As they spoke, the video screen flickered into life and the room was filled with the Old Man's voice telling a silent and attentive Congress in serious tones what they and the rest of the world already knew: their final order of business was the election of a host for the 2030 World Cup. As he droned on, the banqueting staff cleared the coffee cups and replaced trays of pastries with glasses, wine and punchbowls full of ice and bottles of beer. This was all the invitation the assembled hacks needed and they all but ran to grab a drink.

Each of the bidders had fifteen minutes to make their case after which there were questions from the floor. The press pack, most of whom could recite the salient points of each potential host in their sleep, kept their attention firmly focused on the bar, wandering back to the screen only when the Old Man stood up sombrely to give his summing up.

'My friends, on your behalf I would like to express my gratitude to both the bid teams here today and to all of those who have been a part of this process. We hope it has been an instructive one and that you will carry forward any lessons learned for future competitions.'

Then he addressed the delegates, his eyes singling out chosen faces in the crowd. 'The Council presents you with a very happy dilemma,' he intoned. 'Each of the countries represented here today would host an exemplary FIFA World Cup. Their organising capabilities are both proven to be of the highest standard and we have only to look at the recent winter Olympics and last year's Euros to see what kind of hosts they would be.'

This barbed comment cut several ways at once. The reminder of the Wembley Stadium debacle was calculated to cast shade on Team GB-2030, but Beijing's games with its fake snow and hazmat suits was widely viewed as lacklustre and oppressive even without the politics that lay behind them. The Presidential gaze alighted on the bid teams. His face radiated the closest impression he could give of genuine appreciation. He looked around the room, judging the effect his words were having.

'In their own ways, both bids have presented an inspirational vision for our competition in 2030, but, as you are all aware, we have a duty, not just to our international competitions, but to the future of our universal game of football. Before you make your choice, I should like to highlight a couple of the points from each bid that I encourage you to give particular weight to in your considerations. Taking our old friends from Great Britain, we know they have a proud footballing heritage and would no doubt roll out the welcome mat for the... *homecoming* of a sport they had a hand in creating. The English have an expression: *'Home is where the heart is'*. So, I ask you, where is your heart in this matter? Now we turn to consider our new friends from China. We have yet to get to know them well, but already we see their willingness to learn about our beautiful game. The Chinese also have a saying: *'Give a man a bowl of rice and you feed him for a day; teach him how to grow his own rice and you feed him for life.'* So, your choice is between a country which is already rich in football traditions or one which, one way or another, will be the future for our sport. Will we settle for the undoubted comforts of home, or will we step forward into the world as teachers? In short, is football coming home or is it reaching out? Make your choice and make it well. The voting is now open.'

The camera panned around the room and Malcolm Tonghe's stony face briefly filled the screen. The display then split between the faces in the room and the electronic scoreboard where two coloured bars had started off on their journey from left to right.

Rushbourne couldn't resist a comment. 'With friends like that, who needs enemies?'

Alec just nodded, watching the screen where the moving colour blocks were gathering speed. The Chinese were already well ahead but then the momentum shifted. GB-2030 gained on their opponents and soon the two bars were impossible to separate. The camera returned to the top table where the President watched the screen, a barely disguised look of alarm clear in his eyes. As the seconds ticked by, the Chinese total stalled while Team GB's tally continued its steady progress across the screen. There were gasps around the room and spontaneous clapping from the Brits. The Old Man couldn't contain himself. He stood in his chair, glowering at the assembled delegates, then he appeared to stumble forward. His hand clutched his chest and the colour drained from his face. Guillermo Salz grabbed the President's shoulders and eased him back into his seat while the room looked on in horror, some pressing repeatedly on their remote voting devices.

The scoreboard registered that 211 votes had been cast and the result was unequivocal. Salz murmured something to his boss who acknowledged only in twitching spasms beside him. Salz took control smoothly but decisively. He pulled the microphone towards him and stood up while everyone in the room held their breath.

'The votes have been counted,' he said, 'and I declare that the host of the 2030 World Cup will be Great Britain.'

The British contingent hadn't dared to believe the result, but with the announcement, they let out a huge cheer and punched the air. As one, the Chinese delegation stood up and stormed out of the room.

Chapter 35

There were two attempted coups in Qatar that week, the first unsuccessful, the second less so. Paramedics called to the DICC suspected an aneurism and the Old Man was heavily sedated before being rushed to the country's world class Aspetar hospital. Barely had the ambulance pulled away than Guillermo Salz took his opportunity. He proposed an emergency motion and bounced Congress into appointing him acting President. There were loud protests at the speed of his move, but Salz argued that the organisation needed a unifying leader during what remained of the World Cup. He would, he assured them, be a safe pair of hands at a time of crisis, an interim leader only for as long as it took for the President recover.

The Old Man's promise that a British World Cup would take place *over his dead body* was not kept but he would never return to full strength.

Before the evening was out, Salz's first act of what would be a short Presidential term was to instruct the FIFA IT department back in Switzerland to wipe his email account. He figured this would make it all but impossible to link him personally to involvement in corruption. Unfortunately for him, he failed to consider that there are at least two parties to every email. Swiss investigators would spend the next two years painstakingly piecing together the mosaic of correspondence from the outside until they built a case against him. Given his boss's refusal to engage with digital communications, it was Salz with his fingerprints on every significant piece of correspondence. It struck many outsiders as a miscarriage of justice, but, while the old Man lived out a peaceful retirement in a mansion beside Lake Geneva, Salz was thrown under the bus by an organisation which never considered him one of their own.

Meanwhile, back in Doha the Chinese had been so confident of victory that they had booked out the Museum of Islamic Art for a lavish party. Finding themselves with an unexpected vacancy, the venue offered the space to the British at a knock-down price which they were only too happy to pay. The room had been wired up with a video link to Beijing and this was hastily rerouted to London to allow Don Ellington to join them, an England shirt stretched over his collar and tie.

'Congratulations everyone for the exceptional job you've done,' he boomed. 'I always had complete confidence that GB-2030 would win. I only wish I was there in person to share in the celebrations with you. I think I speak for football fans up and down the land when I say, the nation owes you a debt of gratitude. The best bid won the day, and we can all look forward to a British World Cup which will be as big and successful a sporting event as any we've ever staged. Well done to all of you and enjoy your evening.'

Malcolm Tonghe seemed to have pre-empted the Prime Minister's advice to enjoy himself. He and Mike Deighton weaved their way unsteadily towards Alec who was standing with Nigel Rushbourne.

'How does it feel to be wrong, Alec?' he asked 'We did it. We fucking did it, and no thanks to you.'

'Yes, you professor of doom,' slurred Deighton. 'It turns out it isn't rocket fuel, we just needed to run the best bid.'

'What can I say, gentlemen?' said Alec. 'You played a blinder and I've never been happier to have called it wrong. What do you think was the turning point, Malc? After all the Chinese seemed to have all the aces what with spreading football to 1.3 billion people and, no doubt, swelling FIFA's coffers too.'

'It's like the cream rising to the top, Alec,' he preened. 'In the end, quality shines through. The Chinese will have their turn, but I think FIFA could just see that we wanted it more.'

Alec almost choked on his beer and even Deighton looked sceptical.

'Well, as I say, well done again, mate. Great job.'

Alec shook their hands warmly and watched as the pair toddled off to harangue some members of the British media.

'Admirable restraint, dear boy,' said Rushbourne. 'I warned you you'd get no thanks for your efforts but that took true self control. I must say, I was surprised at the announcement myself. I rather took it from your comments that the Chinese had it in the bag and was braced to offer commiserations. I can't imagine it was one last diplomatic heave so what did you actually do to secure the win?'

Alec nodded towards Mikey Reid, Kevin Mooney and Stevie Mac who had just glided past the museum's security.

'Footballers can get in anywhere, particularly during a World Cup. If they turn up to a game, they'll get VIP seats, if they present themselves in front of a TV camera, they'll automatically be given airtime and there's no security guard in the world who's going to turn away such recognizable faces to a meeting of footballers. My friends hid in plain sight at the heart of the FIFA Congress. I just made sure they had the tools to interfere with the remote voting system. The manufacturers claim it's guaranteed tamper proof, but it turned out that wasn't quite true. If you are within the operating field of the system, all you actually need to do is overwhelm the airwaves with a portable radio transmitter operating on the same frequency as the handsets. All it took was a few tweaks from our remote tech team to win the day.'

Alec wasn't about to reveal the role that Hugo Ashburton and his sidekick Trix had played. Their hack, engineered from a meeting room above the congress hall, had identified the radio frequency despite it changing before every vote. They had then unleashed the zombie handsets carried by the footballers within the room, overturning enough of the Chinese tally to register a win for GB-2030. All within seconds of the vote being called.

Rushbourne nodded in genuine appreciation. 'When we met for the first time, I said we would do three things to win: we'd have the strongest technical bid, we'd win hearts and minds with our ground game, and we'd cheat. I had no idea I was talking to some of the best schemers in the business. I'm sorry beyond words that Michaela is not here to share this moment with us but I'm sure she played her part, even today. Anyway, it looks like discretion is the better part of valour. Your friends are approaching, and I'd rather avoid any questions. Well done, Alec: no doubt we'll meet again.'

Mikey, Kevin and Stevie Mac had helped themselves to bottles of beer and joined Alec, handing over small electronic devices as they did. Ashley Freeman came over too and Alec clinked his bottle with theirs.

'Great job lads,' he said, stashing the remotes in his jacket. 'And you Ashley, of course.'

Stevie was still buzzing. 'I can't believe it fuckin' worked, mate. Did you see the Old Man's face? I never thought I'd be glad to see someone collapse but that was priceless.'

'He'd have fallen on his arse if you're man hadn't been there to catch him,' Kevin chipped in. 'And now youse lot have got the World Cup, so you have.'

'You'll get some games, won't you?'

'Oh, I don't care either way, me. I had ten grand on GB-2030 at 15:1 so it's win-win all ends up.'

'Drinks are on you tonight then, Kev.' said Mikey.

'You're joking, right? Prices in this town? If you want some craic tonight, you can pay for it yourself.'

'How's it going Alec, mate?' asked Stevie, taking him to one side, genuine concern in his eyes. 'We've been worried about you, you know, after what happened to Michaela. But there's been no time to say anything. What are you gonna do now?'

'I haven't stopped to think about it, to be honest. I do know I'm going to miss her but part of me isn't surprised we didn't end up making a life together. I always thought I was punching. I mean she was beautiful and funny and so much smarter than me at everything.'

Ashley caught wind of the conversation and draped herself around Alec. 'Are you talking about me, darling?'

Alec squirmed, and even Stevie Mac looking embarrassed. 'I tell you who is punching,' he said trying to change the subject, 'and that's Tyrone, hanging out with all those supermodels.'

'I'm not punching,' said Tyrone, who had appeared at the edge of the group with Simon Cauldwell. 'I've never laid a finger on them.'

'Punching, you know? As in punching above your weight. We're not talking domestics, man.'

'I know what it means,' said Tyrone, more slowly this time.

Cauldwell flicked out a little finger and it brushed the player's hand. Maybe it was a prompt, but Alec caught the gesture.

'You two? No, Fucking, Way! I mean, I'm not surprised you're gay, Ty. We've always known, to be honest. But how long have you two been... you know?

'Since Wembley. What can I say?'

Kevin Mooney was standing on the sidelines looking bored. He took another couple of swigs of his beer then couldn't stand it anymore.

'Look, when you lot have stopped with all the fuckin' Love Island bollocks. I just wanted to say, here's to us. Saving the world and winning the World Cup in the same week has got to be worth a toast.'

They all clinked glasses and welcomed a booming Hugo Ashburton and his sidekick to the party. Mooney wasn't quite done, however.

'And, you know, when this is over, after the finals, when we're back home. Well, if we're all at a loose end, I've got a wee bit of a scheme going that I think you'll be interested in.'

Also by Phil Savage

If you have enjoyed Back Stronger you're going to love the first book in the Alec Munday Series, Kick Back

Kick Back introduces Alec as he moves from football into the dark and dangerous world of match fixing. This page turner goes into the homes and lives of top footballers visiting the world's most glamourous hangouts and some of its murkiest criminal hideaways.

Plus, you are personally invited to download your FREE Alec Munday novella, Give Back. This story of footballers-turned philanthropists starts, implausibly enough, with a tweed tracksuit. Get your copy today from www.philsavage.org

Printed in Great Britain
by Amazon

82645526R00205